Aurelian

by William Wa

NOTICE.

This book--a sequel to Zenobia--published nearly ten years ago under the name of 'Probus,' was soon republished, in several places abroad, under that of 'Aurelian.' So far from complaining of the innovation, I could not but regard it as a piece of good fortune, as I had myself long thought the present a more appropriate title than the one originally chosen. Add to this, that the publisher of the work, on lately proposing a new edition, urgently advised the adoption of the foreign name, and I have thought myself sufficiently warranted in an alteration which circumstances seemed almost to require, or, at least, to excuse.

W. W.

* * * * *

AURELIAN.

The record which follows, is by the hand of me, NICOMACHUS, once the happy servant of the great Queen of Palmyra, than whom the world never saw a queen more illustrious, or a woman adorned with brighter virtues. But my design is not to write her eulogy, or to recite the wonderful story of her life. That task requires a stronger and a more impartial hand than mine. The life of Zenobia by Nicomachus, would be the portrait of a mother and a divinity, drawn by the pen of a child and a worshipper.

My object is a humbler, but perhaps also a more useful one. It is to collect and arrange, in their proper order, such of the letters of the most noble LUCIUS MANLIUS PISO, as shall throw most light upon his character and times, supplying all defects of incident, and filling up all chasms that may occur, out of the knowledge which more exactly than any one else, I have been able to gather concerning all that relates to the distinguished family of the Pisos, after its connection with the more distinguished one still, of the Queen of Palmyra.

It is in this manner that I propose to amuse the few remaining days of a green old age, not without hope both to amuse and benefit others also. This is a labor, as those will discover who read, not unsuitable to one who stands trembling on the verge of life, and whom a single rude blast may in a moment consign to the embraces of the universal mother. I will not deny that my chief satisfaction springs from the fact, that in collecting these letters, and binding them together by a connecting narrative, I am engaged in the honorable task of tracing out some of the steps by which the new religion has risen to its present height of power. For whether true or false, neither friend nor foe, neither philosopher nor fool, can refuse to admit the regenerating and genial influences of its so wide reception upon the Roman character and manners. If not the gift of the gods, it is every way worthy a divine origin; and I cannot but feel myself to be worthily occupied in recording the deeds, the virtues, and the sufferings, of those who put their faith in it, and, in times of danger and oppression, stood forth to defend it. Age is slow of belief. The thoughts then cling with a violent pertinacity to the fictions of its youth, once held to be the most sacred realities. But for this I should, I believe, myself long ago have been a Christian. I daily pray to the Supreme Power that my stubborn nature may yet so far yield, that I may be able, with a free and full assent, to call myself a follower of Christ. A Greek by birth, a Palmyrene by choice and adoption, a Roman by necessity--and these are all honorable names--I would yet rather be a Christian than either. Strange that, with so strong desires after a greater good, I should remain fixed where I have ever been! Stranger still, seeing I have moved so long in the same sphere with the excellent Piso, the divine Julia--that emanation of God--and the god-like Probus! But there is no riddle so hard for man to read as himself. I sometimes feel most inclined toward the dark fatalism of the stoics, since it places all things beyond the region of conjecture or doubt.

Yet if I may not be a Christian myself--I do not, however, cease both to hope and pray--I am happy in this, that I am permitted by the Divine Providence to behold, in these the last days of life, the quiet supremacy of a faith which has already added so much to the common happiness, and promises so much more. Having stood in the midst, and looked upon the horrors of two persecutions of the Christians--the first by Aurelian and the last by Diocletian--which last seemed at one moment as if it would accomplish its work, and blot out the very name of Christian--I have no language in which to express the satisfaction with which I sit down beneath the peaceful shadows of a Christian throne, and behold the general security and exulting freedom enjoyed by the many millions throughout the vast empire of the great Constantine. Now, everywhere around, the Christians are seen, undeterred by any apprehension of violence, with busy hands reerecting the demolished temples of their pure and spiritual faith; yet not unmindful, in the mean time, of the labor yet to be done, to draw away the remaining multitudes of idolaters from the superstitions which, while they infatuate, degrade and brutalize them. With the zeal of the early apostles of this religion, they are applying themselves, with untiring diligence, to soften and subdue the stony heart of hoary Paganism, receiving but too often, as their only return, curses and threats--now happily vain--and retiring from the assault, leading in glad triumph captive multitudes. Often, as I sit at my window, overlooking, from the southern slope of the Quirinal, the magnificent Temple of the Sun, the proudest monument of Aurelian's reign, do I pause to observe the labors of the artificers who, just as it were beneath the shadow of its columns, are placing the last stones upon the dome of a Christian church. Into that church the worshippers shall enter unmolested; mingling peacefully, as they go and return, with the crowds that throng the more gorgeous temple of the idolaters. Side by side, undisturbed and free, do the Pagans and Christians, Greeks, Jews, and Egyptians, now observe the rites, and offer the worship, of their varying faiths. This happiness we owe to the wise and merciful laws of the great Constantine. So was it, long since, in Palmyra, under the benevolent rule of Zenobia. May the time never come, when Christians shall do otherwise than now; when, remembering the wrongs they have received, they shall retaliate torture and death upon the blind adherents of the ancient superstition!

These letters of Piso to Fausta the daughter of Gracchus, now follow.

LETTER I.

FROM PISO TO FAUSTA.

I am not surprised, Fausta, that you complain of my silence. It were strange indeed if you did not. But as for most of our misdeeds we have excuses ready at hand, so have I for this. First of all, I was not ignorant, that, however I might fail you, from your other greater friend you would experience no such neglect; but on the contrary would be supplied with sufficient fulness and regularity, with all that could be worth knowing, concerning either our public or private affairs. For her sake, too, I was not unwilling, that at first the burden of this correspondence, if I may so term it, should rest where it has, since it has afforded, I am persuaded, a pleasure, and provided an occupation that could have been found nowhere else. Just as a flood of tears brings relief to a bosom laboring under a heavy sorrow, so has this pouring out of herself to you in frequent letters, served to withdraw the mind of the Queen from recollections, which, dwelt upon as they were at first, would soon have ended that life in which all ours seem bound up.

Then again, if you accept the validity of this excuse, I have another, which, as a woman, you will at once allow the force of. You will not deem it a better one than the other, but doubtless as good. It is this: that for a long time I have been engaged in taking possession of my new dwelling upon the Coelian, not far from that of Portia. Of this you may have heard, in the letters which have reached you; but that will not prevent me from describing to you, with more exactness than any other can have done it, the home of your old and fast friend, Lucius Manlius Piso; for I think it adds greatly to the pleasure with which we think of an absent friend, to be able to see, as in a picture, the form and material and position of the house he inhabits, and even the very aspect and furniture of the room in which he is accustomed to pass the most of his time. This to me is a satisfaction greater than you can well conceive, when, in my ruminating hours, which are many, I return to Palmyra, and place myself in the circle with Gracchus, Calpurnius, and yourself. Your palace having now been restored to its former condition, I know where to find you at the morning, noon, and evening hour; the only change you have made in the former arrangements being this: that whereas when I was your guest, your private apartments occupied the eastern wing of the palace, they are now in the western, once mine, which I used then to maintain were the most agreeable and noble of all. The prospects which its windows afford of the temple, and the distant palace of the queen, and of the evening glories of the setting sun, are more than enough to establish its claims to an undoubted superiority; and if to these be added the circumstance, that for so long a time the Roman Piso was their occupant, the case is made out beyond all peradventure.

But I am describing your palace rather than my own. You must remember my paternal seat on the southern declivity of the hill, overlooking the course of the Tiber as it winds away to the sea. Mine is not far from it, but on the northern side of the hill, and thereby possessing a situation more favorable to comfort, during the heats of summer--I loving the city, as you well know, better if anything during the summer than the winter months. Standing upon almost the highest point of the hill, it commands a wide and beautiful prospect, especially toward the north and east, the eye shooting over the whole expanse of city and suburbs, and then resting upon the purple outline of the distant mountains. Directly before me are the magnificent structures which crown the Esquiline, conspicuous among which, and indeed eminent over all, are the Baths of Titus. Then, as you will conjecture, the eye takes in the Palatine and Capitol hills, catching, just beyond the last, the swelling dome of the Pantheon, which seems rather to rise out of, and crown, the Flavian Amphitheatre, than its own massy walls. Then, far in the horizon, we just discern the distant summits of the Appenines, broken by Soracte and the nearer hills.

The principal apartments are on the northern side of the palace, opening upon a portico of Corinthian columns, running its entire length and which would not disgrace Palmyra itself. At the eastern extremity, are the rooms common to the family; in the centre, a spacious hall, in the adorning of which, by every form of art, I have exhausted my knowledge and taste in such things; and at the western extremity, my library, where at this moment I sit, and where I have gathered around me all in letters and art that I most esteem. This room I have decorated for myself and Julia--not for others. Whatever has most endeared itself to our imaginations, our minds, or our hearts, has here its home. The books that have most instructed or amused; the statuary that most raises and delights us; the pictures on which we most love to dwell; the antiquities that possess most curiosity or value, are here arranged, and in an order that would satisfy, I believe, even your fastidious taste.

I will not weary you with any more minute account of my new dwelling, leaving that duty to the readier pen of Julia. Yet I cannot relieve you till I have spoken of two of the statues which occupy the most conspicuous niche in the library. You will expect me to name Socrates and Plato, or Numa and Seneca-- these are all there, but it is not of either of them that I would speak. They are the venerable founders of the Jewish and Christian religions, MOSES and CHRIST. These statues, of the purest marble, stand side by side, at one extremity of the apartment; and immediately before them, and within the wondrous sphere of their influences stands the table at which I write, and where I pursue my inquiries in philosophy and religion. You smile at my enthusiasm, Fausta, and wonder when I shall return to the calm sobriety of my ancient faith. In this wonder there are a thousand errors--but of these hereafter. I was to tell you of these sculptures. Of the statue of Moses, I possess no historical account, and know not what its claim may be to truth. I can only say, it is a figure truly grand, and almost terrific. It is of a size larger than life, and expresses no sentiment so perfectly as authority--the authority of a rigorous and austere ruler--both in the attitude of the body and the features of the countenance. The head is slightly raised and drawn back, as if listening, awe-struck, to a communication from the God who commissioned him, while his left hand supports a volume, and his right grasps a stylus, with which, when the voice has ceased, to record the communicated truth. Place in his hands the thunderbolt, and at his feet the eagle, and the same form would serve for Jupiter the Thunderer, except only that to the countenance of the Jewish prophet there has been imparted a rapt and inspired look, wholly beyond any that even Phidias could have fixed upon the face of Jove. He who wrought this head must have believed in the sublimities of the religion whose chief minister he has made so to speak them forth, in the countenance and in the form; and yet who has ever heard of a Jew sculptor?

The statue of Christ is of a very different character; as different as the Christian faith is from that of the Jewish, notwithstanding they are still by many confounded. I cannot pretend to describe to you the holy beauty that as it were constitutes this perfect work of art. If you ask what authority tradition has invested it with, I can only say that I do not know. All I can affirm with certainty, is this, that it once stood in the palace of Alexander Severus, in company with the images of other deified men and gods, whom he chiefly reverenced. When that excellent prince had fallen under the blows of assassins, his successor and murderer, Maximin, having little knowledge or taste for what was found in the palace of Alexander, those treasures were sold, and the statue of Christ came into the hands of a distinguished and wealthy Christian of that day, who, perishing in the persecution of Decius, his descendants became impoverished, and were compelled to part with even this sacred relic of their former greatness. From them I purchased it; and often are they to be seen, whenever for such an object they can steal away from necessary cares, standing before it and renewing, as it would seem, their vows of obedience, in the presence of the founder of their faith. The room is free to their approach, whenever they are thus impelled.

The expression of this statue, I have said, is wholly different from that of the

Hebrew. His is one of authority and of sternness; this of gentleness and love. Christ is represented, like the Moses, in a sitting posture, with a countenance, not like his raised to Heaven, but bent with looks somewhat sad and yet full of benevolence, as if upon persons standing before him. Fraternity, I think, is the idea you associate with it most readily. I should never suppose him to be a judge or censor, or arbitrary master, but rather an elder brother; elder in the sense of wiser, holier, purer; whose look is not one of reproach that others are not as himself, but of pity and desire; and whose hand would rather be stretched forth to lift up the fallen than to smite the offender. To complete this expression, and inspire the beholder with perfect confidence, the left hand rests upon a little child, who stands with familiar reverence at his knee, and looking up into his face seems to say, 'No evil can come to me here.'

Opposite this, and at the other extremity of the apartment, hangs a picture of Christ, representing him in very exact accordance with the traditional accounts of his features and form, a description of which exists, and is held by most authentic, in a letter of Publius Lentulus, a Roman of the same period. Between this and the statue there is a close resemblance, or as close as we usually see between two heads of Caesar, or of Cicero. Marble, however, is the only material that suits the character and office of Jesus of Nazareth. Color, and its minute effects, seem in some sort to degrade the subject. I retain the picture because of its supposed truth.

Portia, as you will believe, is full of wonder and sorrow at these things. Soon after my library had received its last additions, my mother came to see what she had already heard of so much. As she entered the apartment, I was sitting in my accustomed seat, with Julia at my side, and both of us gazing in admiration at the figures I have just described. We were both too much engrossed to notice the entrance of Portia, our first warning of her presence being her hand laid upon my head. We rose and placed her between us.

'My son,' said she, looking intently as she spoke upon the statues before us, 'what strange looking figures are these? That upon my left might serve for Jupiter, but for the roll and the stylus. And why place you beings of character so opposite, as these appear to have been, side by side? This other upon my right--ah, how beautiful it is! What mildness in those eyes, and what a divine repose over the form, which no event, not the downfall of a kingdom nor its loss, would seem capable to disturb. Is it the peace loving Numa?'

'Not so,' said Julia; 'there stands Numa, leaning on the sacred shield, from the centre of which beams the countenance of the divine Egeria.'

'Yes, I see it,' replied Portia; and rising from her seat, she stood gazing round the apartment, examining its various appointments. When her eye had sought out the several objects, and dwelt upon them a moment, she said, in tones somewhat reproachful, as much so as it is in her nature to assume:

'Where, Lucius, are the gods of Rome? Do those who have, through so many ages, watched over our country, and guarded our house, deserve no honor at your hands? Does not gratitude require at least that their images should be here, so that, whether you yourself worship them or not, their presence may inspire others with reverence? But alas for the times! Piety seems dead; or, with the faith that inspires it, it lives, but in a few, who will soon disappear, and religion with them. Whose forms are these, Lucius? concerning one I can now easily surmise--but the other, this stern and terrific man, who is he?'

'That,' I replied, 'is Moses, the founder of Judaism.'

'Immortal gods!' exclaimed Portia, 'the statue of a Jew in the halls of the Pisos! Well may it be that Rome approaches her decline, when her elder sons turn against her.'

'Nay, my mother, I am not a Jew.'

'I would thou wert, rather than be what I suppose thou art, a Christian. The Jew, Lucius, can boast of antiquity, at least, in behalf of his religion. But the faith which you would profess and extend, is but of yesterday. Would the gods ever leave mankind without religion? Is it only to-day that they reveal the truth? Have they left us for these many ages to grope along in error? Never, Lucius, can I believe it. It is enough for me that the religion of Rome is old as Rome, to endear it to my heart, and commend it to my understanding. It is not for the first time, to-day, that the gods have spoken.'

'But, my dear mother,' I rejoined, 'if age makes truth, there are older religions than this of Rome. Judaism itself is older, by many centuries. But it is not because a religion is new or old, that I would receive or reject it.' The only question is, does it satisfy my heart and mind, and is it true? The faith which you engrafted upon my infant mind, fails to meet the wants of my nature, and upon looking for its foundations, I find them not.'

'Is thy nature different from mine, Lucius? Surely, thou art my own child! It has satisfied me and my nature. I ask for nothing else, or better.'

'There are some natures, mother, by the gods so furnished and filled with all good desires and affections, that their religion is born with them and is in them. It matters little under what outward form and administration of truth they dwell; no system could injure them--none would greatly benefit. They are of the family of God, by birth, and are never disinherited.'

'Yes, Portia,' said Julia, 'natural and divine instincts make you what others can become only through the powerful operation of some principle out of, and superior to, anything they find within. For me, I know not what I should have been, without the help which Christianity has afforded. I might have been virtuous, but I could not have been happy. You surely rejoice, when the weak find that in any religion or philosophy which gives them strength. Look, Portia, at that serene and benignant countenance, and can you believe that any truth ever came from its lips, but such as must be most comforting and exalting to those who receive it?'

'It would seem so indeed, my child,' replied Portia, musingly, 'and I would not deprive any of the comforts or strength which any principle may impart. But I cannot cease to think it dangerous to the state, when the faith of the founders of Rome is abandoned by those who fill its highest places. You who abound in leisure and learning, may satisfy yourselves with a new philosophy; but what shall these nice refinements profit the common herd? How shall they see them to be true, or comprehend them? The Romans have ever been a religious people; and although under the empire the purity of ancient manners is lost, let it not be said that the Pisos were among those who struck the last and hardest blows at the still stout root of the tree that bore them.'

'Nothing can be more plain or intelligible,' I replied, 'than the principles of the Christian religion; and wherever it has been preached with simplicity and power, even the common people have readily and gratefully adopted it. I certainly cannot but desire that it may prevail. If any thing is to do it, I believe this is the power that is to restore, and in a still nobler form, the ancient manners of which you speak. It is from Christianity that in my heart I believe the youthful blood is to come, that being poured into the veins of this dying state, shall reproduce the very vigor and freshness of its early age. Rome, my mother, is now but a lifeless trunk--a dead and loathsome corpse--a new and warmer current must be infused, or it will soon crumble into dust.'

'I grieve, Lucius, to see you lost to the good cause of your country, and to the altars of her gods; for who can love his country, and deny the gods who made and preserve it? But then who am I to condemn? When I see the gods to hurl thunderbolts upon those who flout them, it will be time enough for us mortals to assume the robes of judgment. I will hope that farther thought will reclaim you from your truant wanderings.'

Do not imagine, Fausta, that conversations like this have the least effect to chill the warm affections of Portia towards us both. Nature has placed within her bosom a central heat, that not only preserves her own warmth, but diffuses itself upon all who approach her, and changes their affections into a likeness of her own. We speak of our differing faiths, but love none the less. When she had paused a moment after uttering the last words, she again turned her eye upon the statue of Christ, and, captivated by its wondrous power, she dwelt upon it in a manner that showed her sensibilities to be greatly moved. At length she suddenly started, saying:

'If truth and beauty were the same thing, one need but to look upon this and be a believer. But as in the human form and face, beauty is often but a lie, covering over a worse deformity than any that ever disfigures the body, so it may be here. I cannot but admire and love the beauty; it will be wise, I suppose, not to look farther, lest the dream be dissolved.'

'Be not afraid of that, dearest mother; I can warrant you against disappointment. If in that marble you have the form of the outward beauty, here, in this roll, you will find the inward moral beauty of which it is the shrine.'

'Nay, nay, Lucius, I look no farther or deeper. I have seen too much already.'

With these words, she arose, and we accompanied her to the portico, where we walked, and sat, and talked of you, and Calpurnius, and Gracchus.

Thus you perceive I have told you first of what chiefly interests myself: now let me turn to what at this moment more than everything else fills all heads in Rome--and that is Livia. She is the object of universal attention, the centre of all honor. It is indescribable, the sensation her beauty, and now added to that, her magnificence, have made and still make in Rome. Her imperial bearing would satisfy even you; and the splendor of her state exceeds all that has been known before. This you may be surprised to hear, knowing what the principles of Aurelian have been in such things; how strict he has been himself in a more than republican simplicity, and how severe upon the extravagances and luxuries of others, in the laws he has enacted. You must remember his prohibition of the use of cloth of gold and of silk, among other things--foolish laws to be suddenly promulged among so vain and corrupt a population as this of Rome. They have been the ridicule and scorn of rich and poor alike; of the rich, because they are so easily violated in private, or evaded by the substitution of one article for another; of the poor, because, being slaves in spirit, they take a slave's pride in the trappings and state of their masters; they love not only to feel but to see their superiority. But since the eastern expedition, the reduction of Palmyra, and the introduction from abroad of the vast flood of foreign luxuries which has inundated Rome and Italy itself the principles and the habits of the Emperor have undergone a mighty revolution. Now, the richness and costliness of his dress, the splendor of his equipage, the gorgeousness of his furniture, cannot be made to come up to the height of his extravagant desires. The silk which he once denied to the former Empress for a dress, now, variously embroidered, and of every dye, either hangs in ample folds upon the walls, or canopies the royal bed, or lends its beauty to the cushioned seats which everywhere, in every form of luxurious ease, invite to repose. Gold, too, once prohibited, but now wrought into every kind of cloth, or solid in shape of dish, or vase, or cup, or spread in sheets over the very walls and ceilings of the palace, has rendered the traditions of Nero's house of gold no longer fabulous. The customs of the eastern monarchs have also elevated or perverted the ambition of Aurelian, and one after another are taking place of former usages. He is every day more difficult of access, and surrounds himself, his palaces, and apartments, by guards and officers of state. In all this, as you will readily believe, Livia is his willing companion, or rather, I should perhaps say, his prompting and ruling genius. As without the world at her feet, it would be impossible for her insane pride to be fully satisfied, so in all that is now done, the Emperor still lags behind her will. But beautifully, it can be denied by none, does she become her greatness, and gives more lustre than she receives, to all around her. Gold is doubly gold in her presence; and even the diamond sparkles with a new brilliancy on her brow or sandal.

Livia is, of all women I have ever seen or known; made for a Roman empress. I used to think so when in Palmyra, and I saw her, so often as I did, assuming the port and air of imaginary sovereignty. And now that I behold her filling the very place for which by nature she is most perfectly fitted, I cannot but confess that she surpasses all I had imagined, in the genius she displays for her great sphere, both as wife of Aurelian, and sovereign of Rome. Her intellect shows itself stronger than I had believed it to be, and secures for her the homage of a class who could not be subdued by her magnificence, extraordinary as it is. They are captivated by the brilliancy of her wit, set off by her unequalled beauty, and, for a woman, by her rare attainments, and hover around her as some superior being. Then for the mass of our rich and noble, her ostentatious state and imperial presence are all that they can appreciate, all they ask for, and more than enough to enslave them, not only to her reasonable will, but to all her most tyrannical and whimsical caprices. She understands already perfectly the people she is among; and through her quick sagacity, has already risen to a power greater than woman ever before held in Rome.

We see her often--often as ever--and when we see her, enjoy her as well. For with all her ambition of petty rule and imposing state, she possesses and retains a goodness of heart, that endears her to all, in spite of her follies. Julia is still her beloved Julia, and I her good friend Lucius; but it is to Zenobia that she attaches herself most closely; and from her she draws most largely of the kind of inspiration which she covets. It is to her, too, I believe, that we may trace much of the admirable wisdom--for such it must be allowed to be--with which Livia adorns the throne of the world.

Her residence, when Aurelian is absent from the city, is near us in the palace upon the Palatine; but when he is here, it is more remote, in the enchanted gardens of Sallust. This spot, first ennobled by the presence of the great historian, to whose hand and eye of taste the chief beauties of the scene are to be traced, then afterward selected by Vespasian as an imperial villa, is now lately become the chosen retreat of Aurelian. It has indeed lost a part of its charms since it has been embraced, by the extension of the new walls, within the limits of the city; but enough remain to justify abundantly the preference of a line of emperors. It is there that we see Livia most as we have been used to do, and where are forcibly brought to our minds the hours passed by us so instructively in the gardens of Zenobia. Often Aurelian is of our company, and throws the light of his strong intellect upon whatever subject it is we discuss. He cannot, however, on such occasions, thoroughly tame to the tone of gentle society, his imperious and almost rude nature. The peasant of Pannonia will sometimes break through, and usurp the place of emperor; but it is only for a moment; for it is pleasing to note how the presence of Livia quickly restores him to himself; when, with more grace than one would look for, he acknowledges his fault, ascribing it sportively to the fogs of the German marshes. It amuses us to observe the power which the polished manners and courtly ways of Livia exercise over Aurelian, whose ambition seems now as violently bent upon subduing the world by the displays of taste, grace, and magnificence, as it once was to do it--and is still indeed--by force of arms. Having astonished mankind in one way, he would astonish them again in quite another; and to this later task his whole nature is consecrated with as entire a devotion as ever it was to the other. Livia is in all these things his model and guide; and never did soldier learn to catch, from the least motion or sign of the general, his will, than does he, to the same end, study the countenance and the voice of the Empress. Yet is there, as you will believe knowing the character of Aurelian as well as you do, nothing mean nor servile in this. He is ever himself, and beneath this transparent surface, artificially assumed, you behold, feature for feature, the lineaments of the fierce soldier glaring forth in all their native wildness and ferocity. Yet we are happy that there exists any charm potent enough to calm, but for hours or days, a nature so stern and cruel as to cause perpetual fears for the violences in which at any moment it may break out. The late slaughter in the very streets of Rome, when the Coelian ran with the blood of fifteen thousand Romans, butchered within sight of their own homes, with the succeeding executions, naturally fill us with apprehensions for the future. We call him generous, and magnanimous, and so he is, compared with former tyrants who have polluted the throne--Tiberius, Commodus, or Maximin; but what title has he to that praise, when tried by the standard which our own reason supplies of those great virtues? I confess it was not always so. His severity was formerly ever on the side of justice; it was indignation at crime or baseness which sometimes brought upon him the charge of cruelty--never the wanton infliction of suffering and death. But it certainly is not so now. A slight cause now rouses his sleeping passions to a sudden fury, often fatal to the first object that comes in his way. But enough of this.

Do not forget to tell me again of the Old Hermit of the mountains, and that you have visited him--if indeed he be yet among the living.

Even with your lively imagination, Fausta, you can hardly form an idea of the sensation which my open assertion of Christian principles and assumption of the Christian name has made in Rome. I intended when I sat down to speak only of this, but see how I have been led away! My letters will be for the most part confined, I fear, to the subjects which engross both myself and Julia most--such as relate to the condition and prospects of the new religion, and to the part which we take in the revolution which is going on. Not that I shall be speechless upon other and inferior topics, but that upon this of Christianity I shall be garrulous and overflowing. I believe that in doing this, I shall consult your preferences as well as my own. I know you to be desirous of principles better than any which as yet you have been able to discover, and that you will gladly learn whatever I may have it in my power to teach you from this quarter. But all the teaching I shall attempt will be to narrate events as they occur, and state facts as they arise, and leave them to make what impression they may.

When I just spoke of the sensation which my adoption of the Christian system had caused in Rome, I did not mean to convey any idea like this, that it has been rare for the intelligent and cultivated to attach themselves to this despised religion. On the contrary, it would be true were I to say, that they who accept Christianity, are distinguished for their intelligence; that estimated as a class, they rank far above the lowest. It is not the dregs of a people who become reformers of philosophy or religion; who grow dissatisfied with ancient opinions upon exalted subjects, and search about for better, and adopt them. The processes involved in this change, in their very nature, require intelligence, and imply a character of more than common elevation. It is neither the lowest nor the highest who commence, and at first carry on, a work like this; but those who fill the intermediate spaces. The lowest are dead as brute matter to such interests; the highest--the rich, the fashionable, the noble, from opposite causes just as dead; or if they are alive at all, it is with the rage of denunciation and opposition. They are supporters of the decent usages sanctioned by antiquity, and consecrated by the veneration of a long line of the great and noble. Whether they themselves believe in the system which they uphold or not, they are equally tenacious of it. They would preserve and perpetuate it, because it has satisfied, at any rate bound and overawed, the multitude for ages: and the experiment of alteration or substitution is too dangerous to be tried. Most indeed reason not, nor philosophize at all, in the matter. The instinct that makes them Romans in their worship of the power and greatness of Rome, and attachment to her civil forms, makes them Romans in their religion, and will summon them, if need be, to die for the one and the other.

Religion and philosophy have accordingly nothing to hope from this quarter. It is those whom we may term the substantial middle classes, who, being least hindered by prejudices and pride of order, on the one hand, and incapacitated by ignorance on the other, have ever been the earliest and best friends of progress in any science. Here you find the retired scholar, the thoughtful and independent farmer, the skilful mechanic, the enlightened merchant, the curious traveller, the inquisitive philosopher--all fitted, beyond those of either extreme, for exercising a sound judgment upon such questions, and all more interested in them. It is out of these that Christianity has made its converts. They are accordingly worthy of universal respect. I have examined with diligence, and can say that there live not in Rome a purer and more noble company than the Christians. When I say however that it is out of these whom I have just specified, that Christianity has made its converts, I do not mean to say out of them exclusively. Some have joined them in the present age, as well as in every age past, from the most elevated in rank and power. If in Nero's palace, and among his chief ministers, there were Christians, if Domitilla, Domitian's niece, was a Christian, if the emperor Philip was a Christian, so now a few of the same rank may be counted, who openly, and more who secretly, profess this religion. But they are very few. So that you will not wonder that when the head of the ancient and honorable house of the Pisos, the friend of Aurelian, and allied to the royal family of Palmyra, declared himself to be of this persuasion, no little commotion was observable in Rome--not so much among the Christians as among the patricians, among the nobility, in the court and palace of Aurelian. The love of many has grown cold, and the outward tokens of respect are withheld. Brows darkened by the malignant passions of the bigot are bent upon me as I pass along the streets, and inquiries, full of scornful irony, are made after the welfare of my new friends. The Emperor changes not his carriage toward me, nor, I believe, his feelings. I think he is too tolerant of opinion, too much a man of the world, to desire to curb and restrain the liberty of his friends in the quarter of philosophy and religion. I know indeed on the other hand, that he is religious in his way, to the extreme of superstition, but I have observed no tokens as yet of any purpose or wish to interfere with the belief or worship of others. He seems like one who, if he may indulge his own feelings in his own way, is not unwilling to concede to others the same freedom.

* * * * *

As I was writing these last sentences, I became conscious of a voice muttering in low tones, as if discoursing with itself, and upon no very agreeable theme. I heeded it not at first, but wrote on. At length it ran thus, and I was compelled to give ear:

Patience, patience--greatest of virtues, yet hardest of practice! To wait indeed for a kingdom were something, though it were upon a bed of thorns; to suffer for the honor of truth, were more; more in itself, and more in its rewards. But patience, when a fly stings, or a fool speaks, or worse, when time is wasted and lost, is--the virtue in this case mayhap is greater after all-- but it is harder, I say, of practice--that is what I say--yet, for that very reason, greater! By Hercules! I believe it is so. So that while I wait here, my virtue of patience is greater than that of these accursed Jews. Patience then, I say, patience!'

'What in the name of all antiquity,' I exclaimed, turning round as the voice ceased, 'is this flood of philosophy for? Wherein have I offended?'

'Offended!' cried the other; 'Nay, noble master, not offended. According to my conclusion, I owe thee thanks; for while I have stood waiting to catch thy eye and ear, my virtue has shot up like a wild vine. The soul has grown. I ought therefore rather to crave forgiveness of thee, for breaking up a study which was so profound, and doubtless so agreeable too.'

'Agreeable you will certainly grant it, when I tell you I was writing to your ancient friend and pupil, the daughter of Gracchus.'

'Ah, the blessings of all the gods upon her. My dreams are still of her. I loved her, Piso, as I never loved beside, either form, shadow, or substance. I used to think that I loved her as a parent loves his child--a brother his sister; but it was more than that. Aristotle is not so dear to me as she. Bear witness these tears! I would now, bent as I am, travel the Syrian deserts to see her; especially if I might hear from her mouth a chapter of the great philosopher. Never did Greek, always music, seem so like somewhat more divinely harmonious than anything of earth, as when it came through her lips. Yet, by Hercules! she played me many a mad prank! 'Twould have been better for her and for letters, had I chastised her more, and loved her less. Condescend, noble Piso, to name me to her, and entreat her not to fall away from her Greek. That will be a consolation under all losses, and all sorrows.'

'I will not fail to do so. And now in what is my opinion wanted?'

'It is simply in the matter of these volumes, where thou wilt have them bestowed. The cases here, by their superior adorning, seem designed for the great master of all, and his disciples; and it is here I would fain order them. Would it so please thee?'

'No, Solon, not here. That is designed for a very different Master and his disciples.'

Solon looked at me as if unwilling to credit his ears, hoping that something would be added more honorable to the affronted philosopher and myself. But nothing coming, he said:

'I penetrate--I apprehend. This, the very centre and post of honor, thou reservest for the atheistical Jews. The gods help us! I doubt I should straight resign my office. Well, well; let us hope that the increase of years will bring an increase of wisdom. We cannot look for fruit on a sapling. Youth seeks novelty. But the gods be thanked! Youth lasts not long, but is a fault daily corrected; else the world were at a bad pass. Rome is not fallen, nor the fame of the Stagyrite hurt for this. But 'tis grievous to behold!'

So murmuring, as he retreated to the farther part of the library, with his bundle of rolls under his arm, he again busied himself in the labors of his office.

I see, Fausta, the delight that sparkles in your eye and breaks over your countenance, as you learn that Solon, the incomparable Solon, is one of my household. No one whom I could think of, appeared so well suited to my wants as librarian, as Solon, and I can by no means convey to you an idea of the satisfaction with which he hailed my offer; and abandoning the rod and the brass tablets, betook himself to a labor which would yield him so much more leisure for the perusal of his favorite authors, and the pursuit of his favorite studies. He is already deep in the question, 'whether the walls of Troy were accommodated with thirty-three or thirty-nine gates,' and also in this, 'what was the method of construction adopted in the case of the wooden horse, and what was its capacity?' Of his progress in these matters, I will duly inform you.

But I weary your patience. Farewell.

* * * * *

Piso, alluding in this letter to the slaughter on the Coelian Hill, which happened not long before it was written, I will add here that whatever color it may have pleased Aurelian to give to that affair--as if it were occasioned by a dishonest debasement of the coin by the directors of the mint--there is now no doubt, on the part of any who are familiar with the history of that period, that the difficulty originated in a much deeper and more formidable cause, well known to Aurelian himself, but not spoken of by him, in alluding to the event. It is certain, then, that the civil war which then befel, for such it was, was in truth the breaking out of a conspiracy on the part of the nobles to displace Aurelian--'a German peasant,' as they scornfully designated him--and set one of their own order upon the throne. They had already bought over the chief manager of the public mint--a slave and favorite of Aurelian--and had engaged him in creating, to serve the purposes which they had in view, an immense issue of spurious coin. This they had used too liberally, in effecting some of the preliminary objects of their movement. It was suspected, tried, proved to be false, and traced to its authors. Before they were fully prepared, the conspirators were obliged to take to their arms, as the only way in which to save themselves from the executioner. The contest was one of the bloodiest ever known within the walls of the city. It was Aurelian, with a few legions of his army, and the people--always of his part--against the wealth and the power of the nobility, and their paid adherents. In one day, and in one battle, as it may be termed, fifteen thousand soldiers and citizens were slain in the streets of the capital. Truly does Piso say, the streets of the Coelian ran blood. I happily was within the walls of the queen's palace at Tibur; but well do I remember the horror of the time--especially the days succeeding the battle, when the vengeance of the enraged conqueror fell upon the noblest families of Rome, and the axe of the executioner was blunted and broken with the savage work which it did.

No one has written of Aurelian and his reign, who has not applauded him for the defence which he made of his throne and crown, when traitorously assailed within the very walls of the capital; but all unite also in condemning that fierce spirit of revenge, which, after the contest was over and his power secure, by confiscation, banishment, torture and death, involved in ruin so many whom a different treatment would have converted into friends. But Aurelian was by nature a tyrant; it was accident whenever he was otherwise. If affairs moved on smoothly, he was the just or magnanimous prince; if disturbed and perplexed, and his will crossed, he was the imperious and vindictive tyrant.

LETTER II.

FROM PISO TO FAUSTA.

You need not, dear Fausta, concern yourself on our behalf. I cannot think that your apprehensions will be realized. Rome never was more calm than now, nor apparently has there ever a better temper possessed its people. The number of those who are sufficiently enlightened to know that the mind ought not to be in bondage to man, but be held answerable to God alone for its thoughts and opinions, is becoming too great for the violences and cruelties of former ages to be again put in practice against us. And Aurelian, although stern in his nature, and superstitious beyond others, will not, I am persuaded, lend himself either to priests or people to annoy us. If no principle of humanity prevented him, nor generosity of sentiment, he would be restrained, I think, by his attachments to so many who bear the hated name.

And this opinion I maintain, notwithstanding a recent act on the part of the Emperor, which some construe into the expression of unfavorable sentiments toward us. I allude to the appointment of Fronto, Nigridius Fronto, to be chief priest of the temple of the Sun, which has these several years been building, and is now just completed. This man signalized himself, both under Decius and Valerian, for his bitter hatred of the Christians, and his untiring zeal in the work of their destruction. The tales which are told of his ferocious barbarity, would be incredible, did we not know so well what the hard Roman heart is capable of. It is reported of him, that he informed against his own sisters, who had embraced the Christian faith, was with those who hunted them with blood-hounds from their place of concealment, and stood by, a witness and an executioner, while they were torn limb from limb, and devoured. I doubt not the truth of the story. And from that day to this, has he made it his sole office to see that all the laws that bear hard upon the sect, and deprive them of privileges and immunities, are not permitted to become a dead letter. It is this man, drunk with blood, whom Aurelian has put in chief authority in his new temple, and made him, in effect, the head of religion in the city. He is however not only this. He possesses other traits, which with reason might commend him to the regard of the Emperor. He is an accomplished man, of an ancient family, and withal no mean scholar. He is a Roman, who for Rome's honor or greatness, as he would on the one hand sacrifice father, mother, daughter, so would he also himself. And Rome, he believes, lives but in her religion; it is the life-blood of the state. It is these traits, I doubt not, that have recommended him to Aurelian, rather than the others. He is a person eminently fitted for the post to which he is exalted; and you well know that it is the circumstance of fitness, Aurelian alone considers, in appointing his own or the servants of the state. Probus thinks differently. And although he sees no cause to apprehend immediate violence, confesses his fears for the future. He places less reliance than I do upon the generosity or friendship of Aurelian. It is his conviction that superstition is the reigning power of his nature, and will sooner or later assert its supremacy. It may be so. Probus is an acute observer, and occupies a position more favorable to impartial estimates, and the formation of a dispassionate judgment, than I.

This reminds me that you asked for news of Probus, my 'Christian pedagogue,' as you are wont to name him. He is here, adorning, by a life of severe simplicity and divine benevolence, the doctrine he has espoused. He is a frequent inmate of our house, and Julia, not less than myself, ever greets him with affectionate reverence, as both friend and instructor. He holds the chief place in the hearts of the Roman Christians; for even those of the sect who differ from him in doctrine and in life, cannot but acknowledge that never an apostle presented to the love and imitation of his followers an example of rarer virtue. Yet he is not, in the outward rank which he holds, at the head of the Christian body. Their chiefs are, as you know, the bishops, and Felix is Bishop of Rome, a man every way inferior to Probus. But he has the good or ill fortune to represent more popular opinions, in matters both of doctrine and practice than the other, and of course easily rides into the posts of trust and honor. Ho represents those among the Christians--for, alas! there are such among them--who, in seeking the elevation and extension of Christianity, do not hesitate to accommodate both doctrine and manner to the prejudices and tastes of both Pagan and Jew. They seek converts, not by raising them to the height of Christian principle and virtue, but by lowering these to the level of their grosser conceptions. Thus it is easy to see that in the hands of such professors, the Christian doctrine is undergoing a rapid process of deterioration. Probus, and those who are on his part, see this, are alarmed, and oppose it; but numbers are against them, and consequently power and authority. Already, strange as it may seem, when you compare such things with the institution of Christianity, as effected by its founder, do the bishops, both in Rome and in the provinces, begin to assume the state and bearing of nobility. Such is the number and wealth of the Christian community, that the treasuries of the churches are full; and from this source the pride and ambition of their rulers are luxuriously fed. If, as you walk through the street which crosses from the Quirinal to the Arch of Titus, lined with private dwellings of unusual magnificence, you ask whose is that with a portico, that for beauty and costliness rather exceeds the rest, you are told, 'That is the dwelling of Felix, the Bishop of Rome;' and if it chance to be a Christian who answers the question, it is done with ill-suppressed pride or shame, according to the party to which he belongs. This Felix is the very man, through the easiness of his dispositions, and his proneness to all the arts of self-indulgence, and the imposing graciousness of his carriage, to keep the favor of the people, and at the same time sink them, without suspicion on their part, lower and lower toward the sensual superstitions, from which, through so much suffering and by so many labors, they have but just escaped, and accomplish an adulterous and fatal union between Christianity and Paganism; by which indeed Paganism may be to some extent purified and exalted, but Christianity defiled and depressed. For Christianity, in its essence, is that which beckons and urges onward, not to excellence only, but to perfection. Of course its march is always in advance of the present. By such union with Paganism then, or Judaism, its essential characteristic will disappear; Christianity will, in effect, perish. You may suppose, accordingly, that Probus, and others who with him rate Christianity so differently, look on with anxiety upon this downward tendency, and with mingled sorrow and indignation upon those who aid it--oftentimes actuated, as is notorious, by most corrupt motives.

* * * * *

I am just returned from the shop of the learned Publius, where I met Probus, and others of many ways of thinking. You will gather from what occurred, better than from anything else I could say, what occupies the thoughts of our citizens, and how they stand affected.

I called to Milo to accompany me, and to take with him a basket in which to bring back books, which it was my intention to purchase.

'I trust, noble master,' said he, 'that I am to bear back no more Christian books.'

'Why so?'

'Because the priests say that they have magical powers over all who read them, or so much as handle them; that a curse sticks wherever they are or have been. I have heard of those who have withered away to a mere wisp; of others who have suddenly caught on fire, and vanished in flame and smoke; and of others, whose blood has stood still, frozen, or run out from all parts of the body, changed to the very color of your shoe, at their bare touch. Who should doubt that it is so, when the very boys in the streets have it, and it is taught in the temples? I would rather Solon, noble master, went in my stead. Mayhap his learning would protect him.'

I, laughing, bade him come on. 'You are not withered away yet, Milo, nor has your blood run out; yet you have borne many a package of these horrible books. Surely the gods befriend you.'

'I were else long since with the Scipios.' After a pause of some length, he added, as he reluctantly, and with features of increased paleness, followed in my steps:

'I would, my master, that you might be wrought with to leave these ways. I sleep not for thinking of your danger. Never, when it was my sad mischance to depart from the deserted palace of the great Gallienus, did I look to know one to esteem like him. But it is the truth when I affirm, that I place Piso before Gallienus, and the lady Julia before the lady Salonina. Shall I tell you a secret?'

'I will hear it, if it is not to be kept.'

'It is for you to do with it as shall please you. I am the bosom friend, you may know, of Curio, the favorite slave of Fronto--'

'Must I not publish it?'

'Nay, that is not the matter, though it is somewhat to boast of. There is not Curio's fellow in all Rome. But that may pass. Curio then, as I was with him at the new temple, while he was busied in some of the last offices before the dedication, among other things, said: 'Is not thy master Piso of these Christians?' 'Yes,' said I, 'he is; and were they all such as he, there could be no truth in what is said of them.' 'Ah!' he replied, 'there are few among the accursed tribe like him. He has but just joined them; that's the reason he is better than the rest. Wait awhile, and see what he will become. They are all alike in the end, cursers, and despisers, and disbelievers, of the blessed gods. But lions have teeth, tigers have claws, knives cut, fire burns, water drowns.' There he stopped. 'That's wise,' I said, 'who could have known it?' 'Think you,' he rejoined, 'Piso knows it? If not, let him ask Fronto. Let me advise thee,' he added, in a whisper, though in all the temple there were none beside us, 'let me advise thee, as thy friend, to avoid dangerous company. Look to thyself; the Christians are not safe.' 'How say you,' I replied, 'not safe? What and whom are they to fear? Gallienus vexed them not. Is Aurelian----' 'Say no more,' he replied, interrupting me, 'and name not what I have dropped, for your life. Fronto's ears are more than the eyes of Argus, and his wrath more deadly than the grave.'

'Just as he ended these words, a strong beam of red light shot up from the altar, and threw a horrid glare over the whole dark interior. I confess I cried out with affright. Curio started at first, but quickly recovered, saying that it was but the sudden flaming up of the fire that had been burning on the altar, but which shortly before he had quenched. 'It is,' said he, 'an omen of the flames that are to be kindled throughout Rome.' This was Curio's communication. Is it not a secret worth knowing?'

'It tells nothing, Milo, but of the boiling over of the wrath of the malignant Fronto, which is always boiling over. Doubtless I should fare ill, were his power equal to his will to harm us. But Aurelian is above him.'

'That is true; and Aurelian, it is plain, is little like Fronto.'

'Very little.'

'But still I would that, like Gallienus, thou couldst only believe in the gods. The Christians, so it is reported, worship and believe in but a man,--a Jew,--who was crucified as a criminal, with thieves and murderers.' He turned upon me a countenance full of unaffected horror.

'Well, Milo, at another time I will tell you what the truth about it is. Here we are now, at the shop of Publius.'

The shop of Publius is remarkable for its extent and magnificence, if such a word may be applied to a place of traffic. Here resort all the idlers of learning and of leisure, to turn over the books, hear the news, discuss the times, and trifle with the learned bibliopole. As I entered, he saluted me in his customary manner, and bade me 'welcome to his poor apartments, which for a long time,' he said, 'I had not honored with my presence.'

I replied that two things had kept me away: the civil broils in which the city had just been involved, and the care of ordering the appointments of a new dwelling. I had come now to commence some considerable purchases for my vacant shelves, if it might so happen that the books I wanted were to be found in his rooms.

'There is not,' he replied, 'a literature, a science, a philosophy, an art, or a religion, whose principal authors are not to be found upon the walls of Publius. My agents are in every corner of the empire, of the east and west, searching out the curious and the rare, the useful and the necessary, to swell the catalogue of my intellectual riches. I believe it is established, that in no time before me, as nowhere now, has there been heard of a private collection like this for value and for number.'

'I do not doubt what you say, Publius. This is a grand display. Your ranges of rooms show like those of the Ulpian. Yet you do not quite equal, I suppose, Trajan's for number?'

'Truly not. But time may bring it to pass. What shall I show you? It pleases me to give my time to you. I am not slow to guess what it is you now, noble Piso, chiefly covet. And I think, if you will follow me to the proper apartment, I can set before you the very things you are in search of. Here upon these shelves are the Christian writers. Just let me offer you this copy of Hegesippus, one of your oldest historians, if I err not. And here are some beautifully executed copies, I have just ordered to be made, of the Apologies of Justin and Tertullian. Here, again, are Marcion and Valentinus; but perhaps they are not in esteem with you. If I have heard aright, you will prefer these tracts of Paul, or Artemon. But hold, here is a catalogue. Be pleased to inspect it.'

As I looked over the catalogue, I expressed my satisfaction that a person of his repute was willing to keep on sale works so generally condemned, and excluded from the shops of most of his craft.

'I aim, my dear friend--most worthy Piso--to steer a midway course among contending factions. I am myself a worshipper of the gods of my fathers. But I am content that others should do as they please in the matter, I am not, however, so much a worshipper--in your ear--as a bookseller. That is my calling. The Christians are become a most respectable people. They are not to be overlooked. They are, in my judgment, the most intelligent part of our community. Wasting none of their time at the baths and theatres, they have more time for books. And then their numbers too! They are not fewer than seventy thousand!--known and counted. But the number, between ourselves, Piso of those who secretly favor or receive this doctrine, is equal to the other! My books go to houses, ay, and to palaces, people dream not of.'

'I think your statements a little broad,' said a smooth, silvery voice, close at our ears. We started, and beheld the Prefect Varus standing at our side. Publius was for a moment a little disconcerted; but quickly recovered, saying in his easy way, 'A fair morning to you! I knew not that it behooved me to be upon my oath, being in the presence of the Governor of Rome. I repeat, noble Varus, but what I hear. I give what I say as the current rumor. That is all--that is all. Things may not be so, or they may; it is not for me to say. I wish well to all; that is my creed.'

'In the public enumerations of the citizens,' replied the Prefect, inclining with civility to Publius, 'the Christians have reached at no time fifty thousand. As for the conjecture touching the number of those who secretly embrace this injurious superstition, I hold it utterly baseless. It may serve a dying cause to repeat such statements, but they accord not with obvious fact.'

'Suspect me not, Varus,' hastily rejoined the agitated Publius, 'of setting forth such statements with the purpose to advance the cause of the Christians. I take no part in this matter. Thou knowest that I am a Roman of the old stamp. Not a Roman in my street is more diligently attentive to the services of the temple than I. I simply say again, what I hear as news of my customers. The story which one rehearses, I retail to another.'

'I thank the gods it is so,' replied the man of power.

'During these few words, I had stood partly concealed by a slender marble pillar. I now turned, and the usual greetings passed with the Prefect.

'Ah! Piso! I knew not with certainty my hearer. Perhaps from you'--smiling as he spoke--'we may learn the truth. Rome speaks loudly of your late desertion of the religion and worship of your fathers, and union with the Galileans. I should say, I hoped the report ill founded, had I not heard it from quarters too authentic to permit a doubt.'

'You have heard rightly, Varus,' I rejoined. 'After searching through all antiquity after truth, I congratulate myself upon having at last discovered it, and where I least expected, in a Jew. And the good which I have found for myself, I am glad to know is enjoyed by so many more of my fellow-citizens. I should not hesitate to confirm the statement made by Publius, from whatever authority he may have derived it, rather than that which has been made by yourself. I have bestowed attention not only upon the arguments which support Christianity, but upon the actual condition of the Christian community, here and throughout the empire. It is prosperous at this hour, beyond all former example. If Pliny could complain, even in his day, of the desertion of the temples of the gods, what may we now suppose to be the relative numbers of the two great parties? Only, Varus, allow the rescript of Gallienus to continue in force, which merely releases us from oppressions, and we shall see in what a fair trial of strength between the two religions will issue.'

'That dull profligate and parricide,' replied Varus, 'not content with killing himself with his vices, and his father by connivance, must needs destroy his country by his fatuity. I confess, that till that order be repealed, the superstition will spread.'

'But it only places us upon equal ground.'

'It is precisely there where we never should be placed. Should the conspirator be put upon the ground of a citizen? Were the late rebels of the mint to be relieved from all oppression, that they might safely intrigue and conspire for the throne?'

'Christianity has nothing to do with the empire,' I answered, 'as such. It is a question of moral, philosophical, religious truth. Is truth to be exalted or suppressed by edicts?'

'The religion of the state,' replied Varus, 'is a part of the state; and he who assails it, strikes at the dearest life of the state, and--forgive me--is to be dealt with--ought to be dealt with--as a traitor.'

'I trust,' I replied, 'that that time will never again come, but that reason and justice will continue to bear sway. And it is both reasonable and just, that persons who yield to none in love of country, and whose principles of conduct are such as must make good subjects everywhere, because they first make good men, should be protected in the enjoyment of rights and privileges common to all others.'

'If the Christians,' he rejoined, 'are virtuous men, it is better for the state than if they were Christians and corrupt men. But still that would make no change in my judgment of their offence. They deny the gods who preside over this nation, and have brought it up to its present height of power and fame. Their crime were less, I repeat, to deny the authority of Aurelian. This religion of the Galileans is a sore, eating into the vitals of an ancient and vigorous constitution, and must be cut away. The knife of the surgeon is what the evil cries out for and must have--else come universal rottenness and death. I mourn that from the ranks of the very fathers of the state, they have received an accession like this of the house of Piso.'

'I shall think my time and talent well employed,' I replied, 'in doing what I may to set the question of Christianity in its true light before the city. It is this very institution, Varus, which it needs to preserve it. Christianize Rome, and you impart the very principle of endurance, of immortality. Under its present corruptions, it cannot but sink. Is it possible that a community of men can long hold together as vicious as this of Rome?--whose people are either disbelievers of all divine existences, or else ground to the earth by the most degrading superstitions? A nation, either on the one hand governed by superstition, or, on the other, atheistical, contains within itself the disease which sooner or later will destroy it. You yourself, it is notorious, have never been within the walls of a temple, nor are Lares or Penates to be found within your doors.'

'I deny it not,' rejoined the Prefect. 'Most who rise to any intelligence, must renounce, if they ever harbored it, all faith in the absurdities and nonsense of the Roman religion. But what then? These very absurdities, as we deem them, are holy truth to the multitude, and do more than all bolts, bars, axes, and gibbets, to keep them in subjection. The intelligent are good citizens by reflection; the multitude, through instincts of birth, and the power of superstition. My idea is, as you perceive, Piso, but one. Religion is the state, and for reasons of state must be preserved in the very form in which it has so long upheld the empire.'

'An idea more degrading than yours, to our species,' I replied, 'can hardly be conceived. I cannot but look upon man as something more than a part of the state. He is, first of all, a man, and is to be cared for as such. To legislate for the state, to the ruin of the man, is to pamper the body, and kill the soul. It is to invert the true process. The individual is more than the abstraction which we term the state. If governments cannot exist, nor empires hold their sway, but by the destruction of the human being, why let them fall. The lesser must yield to the greater. As a Christian, my concern is for man as man. This is the essence of the religion of Christ. It is philanthropy. It sees in every human soul a being of more value than empires, and its purpose is, by furnishing it with truths and motives, equal to its wants, to exalt it, purify it, and perfect it. If, in achieving this work, existing religions or governments are necessarily overturned or annihilated, Christianity cares not, so long as man is the gainer. And is it not certain, that no government could really be injured, although it might apparently, and for a season, by its subjects being raised in all intelligence and all virtue? My work therefore, Varus, will be to sow truth in the heart of the people, which shall make that heart fertile and productive. I do not believe that in doing this Rome will suffer injury, but on the contrary receive benefit. Its religion, or rather its degrading superstitions, may fall, but a principle of almighty energy and divine purity will insensibly be substituted in their room. I labor for man--not for the state.'

'And never, accordingly, most noble Piso, did man, in so unequivocal words, denounce himself traitor.'

'Patriot! friend! benefactor! rather;' cried a voice at my side, which I instantly recognized as that of Probus. Several beside himself had drawn near, listening with interest to what was going on.

'That only shows, my good friend,' said Varus, in his same smiling way, and which seems the very contradiction of all that is harsh and cruel, 'how differently we estimate things. Your palate esteems that to be wholesome and nutritious food, which mine rejects as ashes to the taste, and poison to the blood. I behold Rome torn and bleeding, prostrate and dying, by reason of innovations upon faith and manners, which to you appear the very means of growth, strength, and life. How shall we resolve the doubt--how reconcile the contradiction? Who shall prescribe for the patient? I am happy in the belief, that the Roman people have long since decided for themselves, and confirm their decision every day as it passes, by new acts and declarations.'

'If you mean,' said Probus, 'to say that numbers and the general voice are still against the Christians, I grant it so. But I am happy too in my belief, that the scale is trembling on the beam. There are more and better than you wot of, who hail with eager minds and glad hearts, the truths which it is our glory, as servants of Christ, to propound. Within many a palace upon the seven hills, do prayers go up in his name; and what is more, thousands upon thousands of the humbler ranks, of those who but yesterday were without honor in their own eyes, or others'--without faith--at war with themselves and the world--fit tools for and foe of the state to work with--are to-day reverers of themselves, worshippers of God, lovers of mankind, patriots who love their country better than ever before, because they now behold in every citizen not only a citizen, but a brother and an immortal. The doctrine of Christianity, as a lover of man, so commends itself, Varus, to the hearts of the people, that in a few more years of prosperity, and the face of the Roman world will glow with a new beauty; love and humanity will shine forth in all its features.

'That is very pretty,' said Varus, his lip slightly curling, as he spoke, but retaining his courteous bearing, 'yet methinks, seeing this doctrine is so bewitching, and is withal a heaven-inspired wisdom, the God working behind it and urging it on, it moves onward with a pace something of the slowest. Within a few of three hundred years has it appealed to the human race, and appealed in vain. The feeblest and the worst of mankind have had power almost to annihilate it, and more than once has it seemed scarce to retain its life. Would it have been so, had it been in reality what you claim for it, of divine birth? Would the gods suffer their schemes for man's good to be so thwarted, and driven aside by man? What was this boasted faith doing during the long and peaceful reigns of Hadrian, and the first Antonine? The sword of persecution was then sheathed, or if it fell at all, it was but on a few. So too under Vespasian, Titus, Nerva, Commodus, Severus, Heliogabalus, the Philips, Gallienus, and Claudius?'

'That is well said,' a Roman voice added, of one standing by the side of Varus, 'and is a general wonder.'

'I marvel it should be a wonder,' rejoined Probus. 'Can you pour into a full measure? Must it not be first emptied? Who, Varus, let him try as he may, could plant the doctrine of Christ in thy heart? Could I do it, think you?--or Piso?'

'I trow not.'

'And why, I pray you?'

'It is not hard to guess.'

'Is it not because you are already full of contrary notions, to which you cling tenaciously, and from which, perhaps, no human force could drag you? But yours is a type of every other Roman mind to which Christianity has been offered. If you receive it not at once, should others? Suppose the soul to be full of sincere convictions as to the popular faith, can the gospel easily enter there? Suppose it skeptical, as to all spiritual truth; can it enter there? Suppose it polluted by vice can it easily enter there? Suppose it like the soul of Fronto,----'

'Hush! hush!' said several voices. Probus heeded them not.

'Suppose it like the soul of Pronto, could it enter there? See you not then, by knowing your own hearts, what time it must demand for a new, and specially a strict doctrine, to make its way into the minds of men? 'Tis not easier to bore a rock with one's finger, than to penetrate a heart hardened by sin or swelled with prejudice and pride. And if we say, Varus, this was a work for the God to do--that he who originated the faith should propagate it--I answer, that would not be like the other dealings of the divine power. He furnishes you with earth and seed, but he ploughs not for you, nor plants, nor reaps. He gives you reason, but he pours not knowledge into your mind. So he offers truth; but that is all. He compels no assent; he forces no belief. All is voluntary and free. How then can the march of truth be otherwise than slow? Truth, being the greatest thing below, resembles in its port the motion of the stars, which are the greatest things above. But like theirs, if slow, it is ever sure and onward.'

'The stars set in night.'

'But they rise again. Truth is eclipsed often, and it sets for a night; but never is turned aside from its eternal path.'

'Never, Publius,' said the Prefect, adjusting his gown, and with the act filling the air with perfume 'never did I think to find myself within a Christian church.

Your shop possesses many virtues. It is a place to be instructed in.' Then turning to Probus, he soothingly and in persuasive tones, added, 'Be advised now, good friend, and leave off thy office of teacher. Rome can well spare thee. Take the judgment of others; we need not thy doctrine. Let that alone which is well established and secure. Spare these institutions, venerable through a thousand years. Leave changes to the gods.'

Probus was about to reply, when we were strangely interrupted. While we had been conversing, there stood before me, in the midst of the floor of the apartment, a man, whose figure, face, and demeanor were such that I hardly could withdraw my eye from him. He was tall and gaunt, beyond all I ever saw, and erect as a Priorian in the ranks. His face was strongly Roman, thin and bony, with sunken cheeks, a brown and wrinkled skin--not through age, but exposure--and eyes more wild and fiery than ever glared in the head of Hun or hyena. He seemed a living fire-brand of death and ruin. As we talked, he stood there motionless, sometimes casting glances at our group, but more frequently fixing them upon a roll which he held in his hands.

As Varus uttered the last words, this man suddenly left his post, and reaching us with two or three strides, shook his long finger at Varus, saying, at the same time,

'Hold, blasphemer!'

The Prefect started as if struck, and gazing a moment with unfeigned amazement at the figure, then immediately burst into a laugh, crying out,

'Ha! ha! Who in the name of Hecate have we here? Ha! ha!--he seems just escaped from the Vivaria.'

'Thy laugh,' said the figure, 'is the music of a sick and dying soul. It is a rebel's insult against the majesty of Heaven; ay, laugh on! That is what the devils do; it is the merriment of hell. What time they burn not, they laugh. But enough. Hold now thy scoffing, Prefect Varus, for, high as thou art, I fear thee not: no! not wert thou twice Aurelian, instead of Varus. I have somewhat for thee. Wilt hear it?'

'With delight, Bubo. Say on.'

'It was thy word just now, 'Rome needs not this doctrine,' was it not?'

'If I said it not, it is a good saying, and I will father it.'

"Rome needs not this doctrine; she is well enough; let her alone!' These were thy words. Need not, Varus, the streets of Rome a cleansing river to purify them? Dost thou think them well enough, till all the fountains have been let loose to purge them? Is Tarquin's sewer a place to dwell in? Could all the waters of Rome sweeten it? The people of Rome are fouler than her highways. The sewers are sweeter than the very worshippers of our temples. Thou knowest somewhat of this. Wast ever present at the rites of Bacchus?--or those of the Cyprian goddess? Nay, blush not yet. Didst ever hear of the gladiator Pollex?--of the woman Cina?--of the boy Lius, and the fair girl Fannia--proffered and sold by the parents, Pollex and Cina, to the loose pleasures of Gallienus? Now I give thee leave to blush! Is it nought that the one half of Rome is sunk in a sensuality, a beastly drunkenness and lust, fouler than that of old, which, in Judea, called down the fiery vengeance of the insulted heavens? Thou knowest well, both from early experience and because of thy office, what the purlieus of the theatres are, and places worse than those, and which to name were an offence. But to you they need not be named. Is all this, Varus, well enough? Is this that venerable order thou wouldst not have disturbed? Is that to be charged as impiety and atheism, which aims to change and reform it? Are they conspirators, and rebels, and traitors, whose sole office and labor is to mend these degenerate morals, to heal these corrupting sores, to pour a better life into the rotting carcass of this guilty city? Is it for our pastime, or our profit, that we go about this always dangerous work? Is it a pleasure to hear the gibes, jests, and jeers of the streets and the places of public resort? Will you not believe that it is for some great end that we do and bear as thou seest--even the redemption, and purifying, and saving of Rome? I love Rome, even as a mother, and for her am ready to die. I have bled for her freely in battle, in Gaul, upon the Danube, in Asia, and in Egypt. I am willing to bleed for her at home, even unto death, if that blood might, through the blessing of God, be a stream to cleanse her putrifying members. But O, holy Jesus! why waste I words upon one whose heart is harder than the nether millstone! Thou preachedst not to Pilate, nor didst thou work thy wonders for Herod. Varus, beware!'

And with these words, uttered with a wild and threatening air, he abruptly turned away, and was lost in the crowds of the street.

While he raved, the Prefect maintained the same unruffled demeanor as before. His customary smile played around his mouth, a smile like no other I ever saw. To a casual observer, it would seem like every other smile, but to one who watches him, it is evident that it denotes no hilarity of heart, for the eyes accompany it not with a corresponding expression, but on the contrary, look forth from their beautiful cavities with glances that speak of anything rather than of peace and good-will. So soon as the strange being who had been declaiming had disappeared, the Prefect, turning to me, as he drew up his gown around him, said,

'I give you joy, Piso, of your coadjutor. A few more of the same fashion, and Rome is safe.' And saluting us with urbanity, he sallied from the shop.

I had been too much amazed, myself, during this scene, to do anything else than stand still, and listen, and observe. As for Probus, I saw him to be greatly moved, and give signs of even deep distress. He evidently knew who the person was--as I saw him make more than one ineffectual effort to arrest him in his harangue--and as evidently held him in respect, seeing he abstained from all interruption of a speech that he felt to be provoking wantonly the passions of the Prefect, and of many who stood around, from whom, so soon as the man of authority had withdrawn, angry words broke forth abundantly.

'Well did the noble Prefect say, that that wild animal had come forth like a half-famished tiger from the Vivaria,' said one.

'It is singular,' observed another, 'that a man who pretends to reform the state, should think to do it by first putting it into a rage with him, and all he utters.'

'Especially singular,' added a third, 'that the advocate of a religion that, as I hear, condemns violence, and consists in the strictness with which the passions are governed, should suppose that he was doing any other work than entering a breach in his own citadel, by such ferocity. But it is quite possible his wits are touched.'

'No, I presume not,' said the first; 'this is a kind of zeal which, if I have observed aright, the Christians hold in esteem.'

As these separated to distant parts of the shop, I said to Probus, who seemed heavily oppressed by what had occurred, 'What deon dwells in that body that has just departed?'

'Well do you say deon. The better mind of that man seems oft-times seized upon by some foul spirit, and bound--which then acts and speaks in its room. But do you not know him?'

'No, truly; he is a stranger to me, as he appears to be to all.'

'Nevertheless, you have been in his company. You forget not the Mediterranean voyage?'

'By no means. I enjoyed it highly, and recall it ever with delight.'

'Do you not remember, at the time I narrated to you the brief story of my life, that, as I ended, a rough voice from among the soldiers exclaimed, 'Where now are the gods of Rome?' This is that man, the soldier Macer; then bound with fellow soldiers to the service in Africa, now a Christian preacher.'

'I see it now. That man impressed me then with his thin form and all-devouring eyes. But the African climate, and the gash across his left cheek, and which seems to have slightly disturbed the eye upon that side, have made him a different being, and almost a terrific one. Is he sound and sane?'

'Perfectly so,' replied Probus, 'unless we may say that souls earnestly devoted and zealous, are mad. There is not a more righteous soul in Rome. His conscience is bare, and shrinking like a fresh wound. His breast is warm and fond as a woman's--his penitence for the wild errors of his pagan youth, a consuming fire, which, while it redoubles his ardor in doing what he may in the cause of truth, rages in secret, and, if the sword or the cross claim him not, will bring him to the grave. He is utterly incapable of fear. All the racks and dungeons of Rome, with their tormentors, could not terrify him.'

'You now interest me in him. I must see and know him. It might be of service to him and to all, Probus, methinks, if he could be brought to associate with those whose juster notions might influence his, and modify them to the rule of truth.'

'I fear not. What he sees, he sees clearly and strongly, and by itself. He understands nothing of one truth bearing upon another, and adding to it, or taking from it. Truth is truth with him--and as his own mind perceives it--not another's. His conscience will allow him in no accommodations to other men's opinions or wishes; with him, right is right, wrong is wrong. He is impatient under an argument as a war-horse under the rein after the trumpet sounds. It is unavoidable therefore but he should possess great power among the Christians of Rome. His are the bold and decisive qualities that strike the common mind. There is glory and applause in following and enduring under such a leader. Many are fain to believe him divinely illuminated and impelled, to unite the characters of teacher and prophet; and from knowing that he is so regarded by others, Macer has come almost to believe it himself. He is tending more and more to construe every impulse of his own mind into a divine suggestion, and I believe honestly experiences difficulty in discriminating between them. Still, I do not deny that it would be of advantage for him more and more to come in contact with sober and enlightened minds. I shall take pleasure, at some fitting moment, to accompany you to his humble dwelling; the rather as I would show you also his wife and children, all of whom are like himself Christians.'

'I shall not forget the promise.'

Whereupon we separated.

I then searched for Publius, and making my purchases, returned home, Milo following with the books.

As Milo relieved himself of his burden, discharging it upon the floor of the library, I overheard him to say,

'Lie there, accursed rolls! May the flames consume you, ere you are again upon my shoulders! For none but Piso would I have done what I have. Let me to the temple and expiate.'

'What words are these?' cried Solon, emerging suddenly at the sound from a recess. 'Who dares to heap curses upon books, which are the soul embalmed and made imperishable? What have we here? Aha! a new treasure for these vacant shelves, and most trimly ordered.'

'These, venerable Greek,' exclaimed Milo, waving him away, 'are books of magic! oriental magic! Have a care! A touch may be fatal! Our noble master affects the Egyptians.'

'Magic!' exclaimed Solon, with supreme contempt; 'art thou so idiotic as to put credence in such fancies? Away!--hinder me not!' And saying so, he eagerly grasped a volume, and unrolling it, to the beginning of the work, dropped it suddenly, as if bitten by a serpent.

'Ha!' cried Milo, 'said I not so? Art thou so idiotic, learned Solon, as to believe in such fancies? How is it with thee? Is thy blood hot or cold?--thy teeth loose or fast?--thy arm withered or swollen?'

Solon stood surveying the pile, with a look partly of anger, partly of sorrow.

'Neither, fool!' he replied. 'These possess not the power nor worth fabled of magic. They are books of dreams, visions, reveries, which are to the mind what fogs would be for food, and air for drink, innutritive and vain. Papias!--Irenes!--Hegesippus!--Polycarp!--Origen!--whose names are these, and to whom familiar? Some are Greek, some are Latin, but not a name famous in the world meets my eye. But we will order them on their shelves, and trust that time, which accomplishes all things, will restore reason to Piso. Milo, essay thy strength--my limbs are feeble--and lift these upon yonder marble; so may age deal gently with thee.'

'Not for their weight in wisdom, Solon, would I again touch them. I have borne them hither, and if the priests speak truly, my life is worth not an obolus. I were mad to tempt my fate farther.'

'Avaunt thee, then, for a fool and a slave, as thou art!'

'Nay now, master Solon, thy own wisdom forsakes thee. Philosophers, they say, are ever possessors of themselves, though for the rest they be beggars.'

'Beggar! sayest thou? Avaunt! I say, or Papias shall teach thee'--and he would have launched the roll at the head of Milo, but that, with quick instincts, he shot from the apartment, and left the pedagogue to do his own bidding.

So, Fausta, you see that Solon is still the irritable old man he was, and Milo the fool he was. Think not me worse than either, for hoping so to entertain you. I know that in your solitude and grief, even such pictures may be welcome.

When I related to Julia the scene and the conversation at the shop of Publius, she listened not without agitation, and expresses her fears lest such extravagances, repeated and become common, should inflame the minds both of the people and their rulers against the Christians. Though I agree with her in lamenting the excess of zeal displayed by many of the Christians, and their needless assaults upon the characters and faith of their opposers, I cannot apprehend serious consequences from them, because the instances of it are so few and rare, and are palpable exceptions to the general character which I believe the whole city would unite in ascribing to this people. Their mildness and pacific temper are perhaps the very traits by which they are most distinguished, with which they are indeed continually reproached. Yet individual acts are often the remote causes of vast universal evil--of bloodshed, war, and revolution. Macer alone is enough to set on fire a city, a continent, a world.

I rejoice, I cannot tell you how sincerely, in all your progress. I do not doubt in the ultimate return of the city to its former populousness and wealth, at least. Aurelian has done well for you at last. His disbursements for the Temple of the Sun alone are vast, and must be more than equal to its perfect restoration. Yet his overthrown column you will scarce be tempted to rebuild. Forget not to assure Gracchus and Calpurnius of my affection. Farewell.

LETTER III.

FROM PISO TO FAUSTA.

You are right, Fausta, in your unfavorable judgment of the Roman populace.

The Romans are not a people one would select to whom to propose a religion like this of Christianity. All causes seem to combine to injure and corrupt them. They are too rich. The wealth of subject kingdoms and provinces finds its way to Rome; and not only in the form of tribute to the treasury of the empire, but in that of the private fortunes amassed by such as have held offices in them for a few years, and who then return to the capital to dissipate in extravagance and luxuries, unknown to other parts of the world, the riches wrung by violence, injustice, and avarice from the wretched inhabitants whom fortune had delivered into their power. Yes, the wealth of Rome is accumulated in such masses, not through the channels of industry or commerce; it arrives in bales and ship-loads, drained from foreign lands by the hand of extortion. The palaces are not to be numbered, built and adorned in a manner surpassing those of the monarchs of other nations, which are the private residences of those, or of the descendants of those who for a few years have presided over some distant province, but in that brief time, Verres-like, have used their opportunities so well as to return home oppressed with a wealth which life proves not long enough to spend, notwithstanding the aid of dissolute and spendthrift sons. Here have we a single source of evil equal to the ruin of any people. The morals of no community could be protected against such odds. It is a mountain torrent tearing its way through the fields of the husbandman, whose trees and plants possess no strength of branch or root to resist the inundation.

Then in addition to all this, there are the largesses of the Emperor, not only to his armies, but to all the citizens of Rome; which are now so much a matter of expectation, that rebellions I believe would ensue were they not bestowed. Aurelian, before his expedition to Asia, promised to every citizen a couple of crowns--he has redeemed the promise by the distribution, not of money but of bread, two loaves to each, with the figure of a crown stamped upon them. Besides this, there has been an allowance of meat and pork--so much to all the lower orders. He even contemplated the addition of wine to the list, but was hindered by the judicious suggestion of his friend and general, Mucapor, that if he provided wine and pork, he would next be obliged to furnish them fowls also, or public tumults might break out. This recalled him to his senses. Still however only in part, for the other grants have not been withdrawn. In this manner is this whole population supported in idleness. Labor is confined to the slaves. The poor feed upon the bounties of the Emperor, and the wealth so abundantly lavished by senators, nobles, and the retired proconsuls.

Their sole employment is, to wait upon the pleasure of their many masters, serve them as they are ready enough to do, in the toils and preparations of luxury, and what time they are not thus occupied, pass the remainder of their hours at the theatres, at the circuses, at games of a thousand kinds, or in noisy groups at the corners of the streets and in the market-places.

It is become a state necessity to provide amusements for the populace in order to be safe against their violence. The theatres, the baths, with their ample provisions for passing away time in some indolent amusement or active game, are always open and always crowded. Public or funeral games are also in progress without intermission in different parts of the capital. Those instituted in honor of the gods, and which make a part of the very religion of the people are seldom suspended for even a day. At one temple or another, in this grove or that, within or without the walls, are these lovers of pleasure entertained by shows, processions, music, and sacrifices. And as if these were not enough, or when they perchance fail for a moment, and the sovereign people are listless and dull, the Flavian is thrown open by the imperial command, the Vivaria vomit forth their maddened and howling tenants either to destroy each other, or dye the dust of the arena with the blood of gladiators, criminals, or captives. These are the great days of the Roman people; these their favorite pleasures. The cry through the streets in the morning of even women and boys, 'Fifty captives to-day for the lions in the Flavian,' together with the more solemn announcement of the same by the public heralds, and by painted bills at the corners of the streets, and on the public baths, is sure to throw the city into a fever of excitement, and rivet by a new bond the affections of this blood-thirsty people to their indulgent Emperor.

Hardly has the floor of the amphitheatre been renewed since the cessation of the triumphal games of Aurelian, before it is again to be soaked with blood in honor of Apollo, whose magnificent temple is within a few days to be dedicated.

Never before I believe was there a city whose inhabitants so many and so powerful causes conspired to corrupt and morally destroy. Were I to give you a picture of the vices of Rome, it would be too dark and foul a one for your eye to read, but not darker nor fouler than you will suppose it must necessarily be to agree with what I have already said. Where there is so little industry and so much pleasure, the vices will flourish and shoot up to their most gigantic growth. Not in the days of Nero were they more luxuriant than now. Aurelian, in the first year of his reign, laid upon them a severe but useful restraint, and they were checked for a time. But since he has himself departed from the simplicity and rigor of that early day, and actually or virtually repealed the laws which then were promulgated for the reformation of the city in its manners, the people have also relapsed, and the ancient excesses are renewed.

This certainly is not a people who, in its whole mass, will be eager to receive the truths of a religion like this of Christianity. It will be repulsive to them. You are right in believing that among the greater part it will find no favor. But all are not such as I have described. There are others different in all respects, who stand waiting the appearance of some principles of philosophy or religion which shall be powerful enough to redeem their country from idolatry and moral death as well as raise themselves from darkness to light. Some of this sort are to be found among the nobles and senators themselves,--a few among the very dregs of the people, but most among those who, securing for themselves competence and independence by their own labor in some of the useful arts, and growing thoughtful and intelligent with their labor, understand in some degree, which others do not, what life is for and what they are for, and hail with joy truths which commend themselves to both their reason and their affections. It is out of these, the very best blood of Rome, that our Christians are made. They are, in intelligence and virtue, the very bone and muscle of the capital, and of our two millions constitute no mean proportion,--large enough to rule and control the whole, should they ever choose to put forth their power. It is among these that the Christian preachers aim to spread their doctrines, and when they shall all, or in their greater part, be converted, as, judging of the future by the past and present, will happen in no long time, Rome will be safe and the empire safe. For it needs, I am persuaded, for Rome to be as pure as she is great, to be eternal in her dominion, and then the civilizer and saviour of the whole world. O, glorious age!--not remote--when truth shall wield the sceptre in Caesar's seat, and subject nations of the earth no longer come up to Rome to behold and copy her vices, but to hear the law and be imbued with the doctrine of Christ, so bearing back to the remotest province precious seed, there to be planted, and spring up and bear fruit, filling the earth with beauty and fragrance.

* * * * *

These things, Fausta, in answer to the questions at the close of your letter, which betray just such an interest in the subject which engrosses me, as it gives me pleasure to witness.

I have before mentioned the completion of Aurelian's Temple of the Sun and the proposed dedication. This august ceremony is appointed for tomorrow, and this evening we are bidden to the gardens of Sallust, where is to be all the rank and beauty of Rome. O that thou, Fausta, couldst be there!

* * * * *

I have been, I have seen, I have supped, I have returned; and again seated at my table beneath the protecting arm of my chosen divinity, I take my pen, and, by a few magic flourishes and marks, cause you, a thousand leagues away, to see and hear what I have seen and heard.

Accompanied by Portia and Julia, I was within the palace of the Emperor early enough to enjoy the company of Aurelian and Livia before the rest of the world was there. We were carried to the more private apartments of the Empress, where it is her custom to receive those whose friendship she values most highly. They are in that part of the palace which has undergone no alterations since it was the residence of the great historian, but shines in all the lustre of a taste and an art that adorned a more accomplished age than our own. Especially, it seems to me, in the graceful disposition of the interiors of their palaces, and the combined richness and appropriateness of the art lavished upon them, did the genius of the days of Hadrian and Vespasian surpass the present. Not that I defend all that that genius adopted and immortalized. It was not seldom licentious and gross in its conceptions, however unrivalled in the art and science by which they were made to glow upon the walls, or actually speak and move in marble or brass. In the favorite apartment of Livia, into which we were now admitted, perfect in its forms and proportions, the walls and ceilings are covered with the story of Leda, wrought with an effect of drawing and color, of which the present times afford no example. The well-known Greek, Polymnestes, was the artist. And this room in all its embellishments is chaste and cold compared with others, whose subjects were furnished to the painter by the profligate master himself.

The room of Leda, as it is termed, is--but how beautiful it is I cannot tell. Words paint poorly to the eye. Believe it not less beautiful, nor less exquisitely adorned with all that woman loves most, hangings, carpets and couches, than any in the palace of Gracchus or Zenobia. It was here we found Aurelian and Livia, and his niece Aurelia. The Emperor, habited in silken robes richly wrought with gold, the inseparable sword at his side, from which, at the expense of whatever incongruity, he never parts--advanced to the door to receive us, saying,

'I am happy that the mildness of this autumn day permits this pleasure, to see the mother of the Pisos beneath my roof. It is rare nowadays that Rome sees her abroad.'

'Save to the palace of Aurelian,' replied my mother, I now, as is well known, never move beyond the precincts of my own dwelling. Since the captivity and death of your former companion in arms, my great husband, Cneius Piso, the widow's hearth has been my hall of state, these widow's weeds my only robes. But it must be more than private grief, and more than the storms of autumn or of winter, that would keep me back when it is Aurelian who bids to the feast.'

'We owe you many thanks,' replied the Emperor. 'Would that the loyalty of the parents were inherited by the children;' casting towards me, as he saluted me at the same time, a look which seemed to say that he was partly serious, if partly in jest. After mutual inquiries and salutations, we were soon seated upon couches beneath a blaze of light which, from the centre of the apartment, darted its brightness, as it had been the sun itself, to every part of the room.

'It is no light sorrow to a mother's heart,' said Portia, 'to know that her two sons, and her only sons, are, one the open enemy of his country, the other--what shall I term you, Lucius?--an innovator upon her ancient institutions; and while he believes and calls himself--sincerely, I doubt not--the friend of his country, is in truth, as every good Roman would say--not an enemy, my son, I cannot use that word, but as it were--an unconscious injurer. Would that the conqueror of the world had power to conquer this boy's will!'

'Aurelian, my mother,' I replied, 'did he possess the power, would hesitate to use it in such a cause. But it is easy to see that it would demand infinitely more power to change one honest mind than to subdue even the world by the sword.'

Aurelian for a brief moment looked as if he had received a personal affront.

'How say you,' said he, 'demands it more power to change one mind than conquer a world? Methinks it might be done with something less. My soldiers often maintain with violence a certain opinion; but I find it not difficult to cause them to let it go, and take mine in its place. The arguments I use never fail.'

'That may be,' I replied, 'in matters of little moment. Even in these however, is it not plain, Aurelian, that you cause them not to let go their opinion, but merely to suppress it, or affect to change it? Your power may compel them either to silence, or to an assertion of the very contrary of what they but just before had declared as their belief, but it cannot alter their minds. That is to be done by reason only, not by force.'

'By reason first,' answered the emperor; 'but if that fail, then by force. The ignorant, and the presumptuous, and the mischievous, must be dealt with as we deal with children. If we argue with them, it is a favor. It is our right, as it is better, to command and compel.'

'Only establish it that such and such are ignorant, and erroneous, and presumptuous, and I allow that it would be right to silence them. But that is the very difficulty in the case. How are we to know that they, who think differently from ourselves, are ignorant or erroneous? Surely the fact of the difference is not satisfactory proof.'

'They,' rejoined Aurelian, 'who depart from a certain standard in art are said to err. The thing in this case is of no consequence to any, therefore no punishment ensues. So there is a standard of religion in the State, and they who depart from it may be said to err. But, as religion is essential to the State, they who err should be brought back, by whatever application of force, and compelled to conform to the standard.'

'In what sense,' said Portia, 'can common and ignorant people be regarded as fit judges of what constitutes, or does not constitute, a true religion? It is a subject level scarce to philosophers. If, indeed, the gods should vouchsafe to descend to earth and converse with men, and in that manner teach some new truth, then any one, possessed of eyes and ears, might receive it, and retain it without presumption. Nay, he could not but do so; but not otherwise.'

'Now have you stated,' said I, 'that which constitutes the precise case of Christianity. They who received Christianity in the first instance, did it not by balancing against each other such refined arguments as philosophers use. They were simply judges of matters of fact--of what their eyes beheld, and their ears heard. God did vouchsafe to descend to earth, and, by his messenger, converse with men, and teach new truth. All that men had then to do was this, to see whether the evidence was sufficient that it was a God speaking; and that being made plain, to listen and record. And at this day, all that is to be done is to inquire whether the record be true. If the record be a well-authenticated one of what the mouth of God spoke, it is then adopted as the code of religious truth. As for what the word contains--it requires no acute intellect to judge concerning it--a child may understand it all.'

'Truly,' replied Portia, 'this agrees but ill with what I have heard and believed concerning Christianity. It has ever been set forth as a thing full of darkness and mystery, which it requires the most vigorous powers to penetrate and comprehend.'

'So has it ever been presented to me,' added the Emperor. 'I have conceived it to be but some new form of Plato's dreams, neither more clear in itself, nor promising to be of more use to mankind. So, if I err not, the learned Porphyrius has stated it.'

'A good fact,' here interposed Julia, 'is worth more in this argument than the learning of the most learned. Is it not sufficient proof, Aurelian, that Christianity is somewhat sufficiently plain and easy, that women are able to receive it so readily? Take me as an unanswerable argument on the side of Piso.'

'The women of Palmyra,' replied the Emperor, 'as I have good reason to know, are more than the men of other climes. She who reads Plato and the last essays of Plotinus, of a morning, seated idly beneath the shadow of some spreading beech, just as a Roman girl would the last child's story of Spurius about father Tiber and the Milvian Bridge, is not to be received in this question as but a woman, with a woman's powers of judgment. When the women of Rome receive their faith as easily as you do, then may it be held as an argument for its simplicity. But let us now break off the thread of this discourse, too severe for the occasion, and mingle with our other friends, who by this must be arrived.'

So, with these words, we left the apartment where we had been sitting, the Emperor having upon one side Portia, and on the other Livia, and moved toward the great central rooms of the palace, where guests are entertained, and the imperial banquets held.

The company was not numerous; it was rather remarkable for its selectness. Among others not less distinguished, there were the venerable Tacitus, the consul Capitolinus, Marcellinus the senator, the prefect Varus, the priest Fronto, the generals Probus and Mucapor, and a few others of the military favorites of Aurelian.

Of the conversation at supper, I remember little or nothing, only that it was free and light, each seeming to enjoy himself and the companion who reclined next to him. Aurelian, with a condescending grace, which no one knows how better to assume than he, urged the wine upon his friends, as they appeared occasionally to forget it, offering frequently some new and unheard of kind, brought from Asia, Greece, or Africa, and which he would exalt to the skies for its flavor. More than once did he, as he is wont to do in his sportive mood, deceive us; for, calling upon us to fill our goblets with what he described as a liquor surpassing all of Italy, and which might serve for Hebe to pour out for the gods, and requiring us to drink it off in honor of Bacchus, Pan, or Ceres, we found, upon lifting our cups to drain them, that they had been charged with some colored and perfumed medicament more sour or bitter than the worst compound of the apothecary, or than massican overheated in the vats. These sallies, coming from the master of the world, were sure to be well received; his satellites, of whom not a few, even on this occasion, were near him, being ready to die with excess of laughter,--the attendant slaves catching the jest, and enjoying it with noisy vociferation. I laughed with the rest, for it seems wise to propitiate, by any act not absolutely base, one, whose ambitious and cruel nature, unless soothed and appeased by such offerings, is so prone to reveal itself in deeds of darkness.

When the feast was nearly ended, and the attending slaves were employed in loading it for the last time with fruits, olives, and confections, a troop of eunuchs, richly habited, entered the apartment to the sound of flutes and horns, bearing upon a platter of gold an immense bowl or vase of the same material, filled to the brim with wine, which they placed in the centre of the table, and then, at the command of the Emperor, with a ladle of the same precious material and ornamented with gems, served out the wine to the company. At first, as the glittering pageant advanced, astonishment kept us mute, and caused us involuntarily to rise from our couches to watch the ceremony of introducing it, and fixing it in its appointed place. For never before, in Rome, had there been seen, I am sure, a golden vessel of such size, or wrought with art so marvellous. The language of wonder and pleasure was heard, on every side, from every mouth. Even Livia and Julia, who in Palmyra had been used to the goblets and wine-cups of the Eastern Demetrius, showed amazement, not less than the others, at a magnificence and a beauty that surpassed all experience, and all conception. Just above where the bowl was placed, hung the principal light, by which the table and the apartment were illuminated, which, falling in floods upon the wrought or polished metal and the thickly strewed diamonds, caused it to blaze with a splendor which the eyes could hardly bear, and, till accustomed to it, prevented us from minutely examining the sculpture, that, with lavish profusion and consummate art, glowed and burned upon the pedestal, the swelling sides, the rim and handles of the vase, and covered the broad and golden plain upon which it stood. I, happily, was near it, being seated opposite Aurelian, and on the inner side of the table, which, as the custom now is, was of the form of a bent bow, so that I could study at my leisure the histories and fables that were wrought over its whole surface. Julia and Livia, being also near it on the other side of the table, were in the same manner wholly absorbed in the same agreeable task.

Livia, being quite carried out of herself by this sudden and unexpected splendor--having evidently no knowledge of its approach--like a girl as she still is, in her natural, unpremeditated movements, rose from her couch and eagerly bent forward toward the vase, the better to scan its beauties, saying, as she did so,

'The Emperor must himself stand answerable for all breaches of order under circumstances like these. Good friends, let all, who will, freely approach, and, leaving for a moment that of Bacchus, drink at the fountain of Beauty.' Whereupon all, who were so disposed, gathered round the centre of the table.

'This,' said Varus, 'both for size, and the perfect art lavished upon it, surpasses the glories fabled of the buckler of Minerva, whose fame has reached us.'

'You say right; it does so,' said the Emperor 'That dish of Vitellius was inferior in workmanship, as it was less in weight and size than this, which, before you all I here name "THE CUP OF LIVIA." Let us fill again from it, and drink to the Empress of the world.'

All sprang in eager haste to comply with a command that carried with it its own enforcement.

'Whatever,' continued the Emperor, when our cups had been drained, 'may have been the condition of art in other branches of it, in the time of that Emperor, there was no one then whose power over the metals, or whose knowledge of forms, was comparable with that of our own Demetrius; for this, be it known, is the sole work of the Roman--and yet, to speak more truly, it must be said the Greek--Demetrius, aided by his brother from the East, who is now with him. Let the music cease; we need that disturbance no more; and call in the brothers Demetrius. These are men who honor any age, and any presence.'

The brothers soon entered; and never were princes or ambassadors greeted with higher honor. All seemed to contend which should say the most flattering and agreeable thing. 'Slaves,' cried the Emperor, 'a couch and cups for the Demetrii.'

The brothers received all this courtesy with the native ease and dignity which ever accompany true genius. There was no offensive boldness, or presuming vanity, but neither was there any shrinking cowardice nor timidity. They felt that they were men, not less distinguished by the gods, than many or most of those, in whose presence they were, and they were sufficient to themselves. The Roman Demetrius resembles much his brother of Palmyra, but, in both form and countenance, possesses beauty of a higher order. His look is contemplative and inward; his countenance pale and yet dark; his features regular and exactly shaped, like a Greek statue; his hair short and black; his dress, as was that of him of Palmyra, of the richest stuffs, showing that wealth had become their reward as well as fame.

'Let us,' cried the Emperor, 'in full cups, drawn from the Livian fount, do honor to ourselves, and the arts, by drinking to the health of Demetrius of Palmyra, and Demetrius of Rome.' Every cup was filled, and drained. 'We owe you thanks,' then added Aurelian, 'that you have completed this great work at the time promised; though I fear it has been to your own cost, for the paleness of your cheeks speaks not of health.'

'The work,' replied the Roman Demetrius, 'could not have been completed but for the timely and effectual aid of my Eastern brother, to whose learned hand, quicker in its execution than my own, you are indebted for the greater part of the sculptures, upon both the bowl and dish.'

'It is true, noble Emperor,' said the impetuous brother, 'my hand is the quicker of the two, and in some parts of this work, especially in whatever pertains to the East, and to the forms of building or of vegetation, or costume seen chiefly or only there, my knowledge was perhaps more exact and minute than his; but, let it be received, that the head that could design these forms and conceive and arrange these histories, and these graceful ornaments--to my mind more fruitful of genius than all else--observe you them? have you scanned them all?--belongs to no other than Demetrius of Rome. In my whole hand, there resides not the skill that is lodged in one of his fingers;--nor, in my whole head, the power that lies behind one of his eyes.'

The enthusiasm of the Eastern brother called up a smile upon the faces of all, and a blush upon the white cheek of the Roman.

'My brother is younger than I,' he said, 'and his blood runs quicker. All that he says, though it be a picture of the truest heart ever lodged in man, is yet to be taken with abatement. But for him, this work would have been far below its present merit. Let me ask you especially to mark the broad border, where is set forth the late triumph, and ambassadors, captives, and animals of all parts of the earth, especially of the East, are seen in their appropriate forms and habits. That is all from the chisel of my brother. Behold here'--and rising he approached the vase, and vast as it was, by a touch, so was it constructed, turned it round--'behold here, where is figured the Great Queen of--'; in the enthusiasm of art, he had forgotten for a moment to whom he was speaking; for at that instant his eye fell upon the countenance of Julia, who stood near him,--while hers at the same moment caught the regal form of Zenobia, bent beneath the weight of her golden chains--and which he saw cast down by an uncontrollable grief. He paused, confused and grieved--saying, as he turned back the vase, 'Ah me! cruel and indiscreet! Pardon me, noble ladies! and yet I deserve it not.'

'Go on, go on, Demetrius,' said Julia, assuming a cheerful air. 'You offend me not. The course of Empire must have its way; individuals are but emmets in the path. I am now used to this, believe me. It is for you rather, and the rest, to forgive in me a sudden weakness.'

Demetrius, thus commanded, resumed, and then with minuteness, with much learning and eloquence, discoursed successively upon the histories, or emblematic devices, of this the chief work of his hands. All were sorry when he ceased.

'To what you have overlooked,' said Aurelian, as he paused, 'must I call you back, seeing it is that part of the work which I most esteem, and in which at this moment I and all, I trust, are most interested--the sculptures upon the platter; which represent the new temple and ceremonies of the dedication, which to-morrow we celebrate.'

'Of this,' replied Demetrius, 'I said less, because perhaps the work is inferior, having been committed, our time being short, to the hands of a pupil--a pupil, however, I beg to say, who, if the Divine Providence spare him, will one day, and that not a remote one, cast a shadow upon his teachers.'

'That will he,' said the brother; 'Flaccus is full of the truest inspiration.'

'But to the dedication--the dedication,' interrupted the hoarse voice of Fronto.

Demetrius started, and shrunk backward a step at that sound, but instantly recovered himself, and read into an intelligible language many of the otherwise obscure and learned details of the work. As he ended, the Emperor said,

'We thank you, Demetrius, for your learned lecture, which has given a new value to your labors. And now, while it is in my mind, let me bespeak, as soon as leisure and inclination shall serve, a silver statue, gilded, of Apollo, for the great altar, which to-morrow will scarce be graced with such a one as will agree with the temple and its other ornaments.'

Demetrius, as this was uttered, again started, and his countenance became of a deadly paleness. He hesitated a moment, as if studying how to order his words so as to express least offensively an offensive truth. On the instant, I suspected what the truth was; but I was wholly unprepared for it. I had received no intimation of such a thing.

'Great Emperor,' he began, 'I am sorry to say--and yet not sorry--that I cannot now, as once, labor for the decoration of the temples and their worship. I am--'

'Ye gods of Rome!--' cried Fronto.

'Peace,' said the Emperor; 'let him be heard. How say you?'

'I am now a Christian; and I hold it not lawful to bestow my power and skill in the workmanship of gods, in whom I believe not, and thus become the instrument of an erroneous faith in others.'

This was uttered firmly, but with modesty. The countenance of the Emperor was overclouded for a moment. But it partially cleared up again, as he said, 'I lay not, Demetrius, the least constraint upon you. The four years that I have held this power in Rome have been years of freedom to my people in this respect. Whether I have done well in that, for our city and the empire, many would doubt. I almost doubt myself.'

'That would they, by Hercules,' said the soft voice of Varus just at my ear, and intended chiefly for me.

'My brother,' said Demetrius, 'will be happy to execute for the Emperor, the work which he has been pleased to ask of me. He remains steadfast in the faith in which he was reared; the popular faith of Athens.'

'Apollo,' said Demetrius of Palmyra 'is my especial favorite among all the gods, and of him have I wrought more statues in silver, gold, or ivory, or of these variously and curiously combined, than of all the others. If I should be honored in this labor, I should request to be permitted to adopt the marble image, now standing in the baths of Caracalla, and once, it is said, the chief wonder of Otho's palace of wonders, as a model after which, with some deviations, to mould it. I think I could make that, that should satisfy Aurelian and Rome.'

'Do it, do it,' said the Emperor,' and let it be seen, that the worshipper of his country's gods is not behind him, who denies them, in his power to do them honor.'

'I shall not sleep,' said the artist, 'till I have made a model, in wax at least, of what at this moment presents itself to my imagination.' Saying which, with little ceremony--as if the Empire depended upon his reaching, on the instant, his chalk and wax, and to the infinite amusement of the company--he rose and darted from the apartment, the slaves making way, as for a missile that it might be dangerous to obstruct.

'But in what way,' said Aurelian, turning to the elder Demetrius, 'have you been wrought upon to abandon the time-honored religion of Rome? Methinks, the whole world is becoming of this persuasion.'

'If I may speak freely--'

'With utmost freedom,' said Aurelian.

'I may then say, that ever since the power to reflect upon matters so deep and high had been mine, I had first doubted the truth of the popular religion, and then soon rejected it, as what brought to me neither comfort nor hope, and was also burdened with things essentially incredible and monstrous. For many years, many weary years--for the mind demands something positive in this quarter, it cannot remain in suspense, and vacant--I was without belief. Why it was so long, before I turned to the Christians, I know not; unless, because of the reports which were so common to their disadvantage, and the danger which has so often attended a profession of their faith. At length, in a fortunate hour, there fell into my hands the sacred books of the Christians; and I needed little besides to show me, that theirs is a true and almighty faith, and that all that is current in the city to its dishonor is false and calumnious. I am now happy, not only as an artist and a Roman, but as a man and an immortal.'

'You speak earnestly,' said Aurelian.

'I feel so,' replied Demetrius; a generous glow lighting up his pale countenance.

'Would,' rejoined the Emperor, 'that some of the zeal of these Christians might be infused into the sluggish spirits of our own people. The ancient faith suffers through neglect, and the prevailing impiety of those who are its disciples.'

'May it not rather be,' said Fronto, 'that the ancient religion of the State, having so long been neglected by those who are its appointed guardians, to the extent that even Judaism, and now Christianity--which are but disguised forms of Atheism--have been allowed to insinuate, and intrench themselves in the Empire; the gods, now in anger, turn away from us, who have been so unfaithful to ourselves; and thus this plausible impiety is permitted to commit its havocs. I believe the gods are ever faithful to the faithful.'

'What good citizen, too,' added Varus, 'but must lament to witness the undermining, and supplanting of those venerable forms, under which this universal empire has grown to its present height of power? He is scarcely a Roman who denies the gods of Rome, however observant he may be of her laws and other institutions. Religion is her greatest law.'

'These are hard questions,' said the Emperor. 'For, know you not, that some of our noblest, and fairest, and most beloved, have written themselves followers of this Gallilean God? How can we deal sharply with a people, at whose head stands the chief of the noble house of the Pisos, and a princess of the blood of Palmyra?'

Although Aurelian uttered these words in a manner almost sportive to the careless ear, yet I confess myself to have noticed at the moment, an expression of the countenance, and a tone in the voice, which gave me uneasiness. I was about to speak, when the venerable Tacitus addressed the Emperor, and said,

'I can never think it wise to interfere with violence, in the matter of men's worship. It is impossible, I believe, to compel mankind to receive any one institution of religion, because different tribes of men, different by nature and by education, will and do demand, not the same, but different forms of belief and worship. Why should they be alike in this, while they separate so widely in other matters? and can it be a more hopeful enterprise to oblige them to submit to the same rules in their religion, than it would be to compel them to feed on the same food, and use the same forms of language or dress? I know that former emperors have thought and acted differently. They have deemed it a possible thing to restore the ancient unity of worship, by punishing with severity, by destroying the lives even, of such as should dare to think for themselves. But their conduct is not to be defended, either as right in itself or best for the state. It has not been just or wise, as policy. For is it not evident, how oppression of those who believe themselves to be possessed of truth important to mankind, serves but to bind them the more closely to their opinions? Are they, for a little suffering, to show themselves such cowards as to desert their own convictions, and prove false to the interests of multitudes? Rather, say they, let us rejoice, in such a cause, to bear reproach. This is the language of our nature. Nay, such persons come to prize suffering, to make it a matter of pride and boasting. Their rank among themselves is, by and by, determined by the readiness with which they offer themselves as sacrifices for truth and God. Are such persons to be deterred by threats, or the actual infliction of punishment?'

'The error has been,' here said the evil-boding Fronto, 'that the infliction of punishment went not to the extent that is indispensable to the success of such a work. The noble Piso will excuse me; we are but dealing with abstractions. Oppress those who are in error, only to a certain point, not extreme, and it is most true they cling the closer to their error. We see this in the punishment of children. Their obstinacy and pride are increased, by a suffering which is slight, and which seems to say to the parent, 'He is too timid, weak, or loving, to inflict more.' So too with our slaves. Whose slaves ever rose a second time against the master's authority, whose first offence, however slight, was met, not by words or lashes, but by racks and the cross?'

'Nay, good Fronto, hold; your zeal for the gods bears you away beyond the bounds of courtesy.'

'Forgive me then, great sovereign, and you who are here--if you may; but neither time nor place shall deter me, a minister of the great god of light, from asserting the principles upon which his worship rests, and, as I deem, the Empire itself. Under Decius, had true Romans sat on the tribunals; had no hearts, too soft for such offices, turned traitors to the head; had no accursed spirit of avarice received the bribes which procured security, to individuals, families, and communities; had there been no commutations of punishment, then--'

'Peace, I say, Fronto; thou marrest the spirit of the hour. How came we thus again to this point? Such questions are for the Council-room or the Senate. Yet, truth to say, so stirred seems the mind of this whole people in the matter, that, in battle, one may as well escape from the din of clashing arms, or the groans of the dying, as, in Rome, avoid this argument. Nay, by my sword, not a voice can I hear, either applauding, disputing, or condemning, since I have set on foot this new war in the East. Once, the city would have rung with acclamations, that an army was gathering for such an enterprise. Now, it seems quite forgotten that Valerian once fell, or that, late though it be, he ought to be avenged. This Jewish and Christian argument fills all heads, and clamors on every tongue. Come, let us shake off this deon in a new cup, and drink deep to the revenge of Valerian.'

'And of the gods,' ejaculated Fronto, as he lifted the goblet to his lips.

'There again?' quickly and sharply demanded Aurelian, bending his dark brows upon the offender.

'Doubtless,' said Portia, 'he means well, though over zealous, and rash in speech. His heart, I am sure, seconds not the cruel language of his tongue. So at least I will believe; and, in the meantime, hope, that the zeal he has displayed for the ancient religion of our country, may not be without its use upon some present, who, with what I trust will prove a brief truancy, have wandered from their household gods, and the temples of their fathers.'

'May the gods grant it,' added Livia; 'and restore the harmony, which should reign in our families, and in the capital. Life is over brief to be passed in quarrel. Now let us abandon our cups. Sir Christian Piso! lead me to the gardens, and let the others follow as they may our good example.'

The gardens we found, as we passed from the palace, to be most brilliantly illuminated with lamps of every form and hue. We seemed suddenly to have passed to another world, so dream-like was the effect of the multitudinous lights as they fell with white, red, lurid, or golden glare, upon bush or tree, grotto, statue, or marble fountain.

'Forget here, Lucius Piso,' said the kind-hearted Livia, 'what you have just heard from the lips of that harsh bigot, the savage Fronto. Who could have looked for such madness! Not again, if I possess the power men say I do, shall he sit at the table of Aurelian. Poor Julia too! But see! she walks with Tacitus. Wisdom and mercy are married in him, and both will shed comfort on her.'

'I cannot but lament,' I replied, 'that a creature like Fronto should have won his way so far into the confidence of Aurelian. But I fear him not; and do not believe that he will have power to urge the Emperor to the adoption of measures, to which his own wisdom and native feelings must stand opposed. The rage of such men as Fronto, and the silent pity and scorn of men immeasurably his superiors, we have now learned to bear without complaint, though not without some inward suffering. To be shut out from the hearts of so many, who once ran to meet us on our approach; nor only that, but to be held by them as impious and atheistical, monsters whom the earth is sick of, and whom the gods are besought to destroy--this is a part of our burden which we feel to be heaviest. Heaven preserve to us the smiles, and the love of Livia.'

'Doubt not that they will ever be yours. But I trust that sentiments, like those of Tacitus, will bear sway in the councils of Aurelian, and that the present calm will not be disturbed.'

Thus conversing, we wandered on, beguiled by such talk, and the attractive splendors of the garden, till we found ourselves separated, apparently by some distance, from our other friends; none passed us, and none met us. We had reached a remote and solitary spot, where fewer lamps had been hung, and the light was faint and unequal. Not sorry to be thus alone, we seated ourselves on the low pedestal of a group of statuary--once the favorite resort of the fair and false Terentia--whose forms could scarcely be defined, and which was enveloped, at a few paces distant, with shrubs and flowers, forming a thin wall of partition between us and another walk, corresponding to the one we were in, but winding away in a different direction. We had sat not long, either silent or conversing, ere our attention was caught by the sound of approaching voices, apparently in earnest discourse. A moment, and we knew them to be those of Fronto, and Aurelian.

'By the gods, his life shall answer it,' said Aurelian with vehemence, but with suppressed tones; 'who but he was to observe the omens? Was I to know, that to-day is the Ides, and to-morrow the day after? The rites must be postponed.'

'It were better not, in my judgment,' said Fronto, 'all the other signs are favorable. Never, Papirius assured me, did the sacred chickens seize so eagerly the crumbs. Many times, as he closely watched, did he observe them--which is rare--drop them from their mouths overfilled. The times he has exactly recorded. A rite like this put off, when all Rome is in expectation, would, in the opinion of all the world, be of a more unfavorable interpretation, than if more than the day were against us.'

'You counsel well. Let it go on.'

'But to ensure a fortunate event, and propitiate the gods, I would early, and before the august ceremonies, offer the most costly and acceptable sacrifice.'

'That were well also. In the prisons there are captives of Germany, of Gaul, of Egypt, and Palmyra. Take what and as many as you will. If we ever make sure of the favor of the gods, it is when we offer freely that which we hold at the highest price.'

'I would rather they were Christians,' urged Fronto.

'That cannot be,' said Aurelian. 'I question if there be a Christian within the prison walls; and, were there hundreds, it is not a criminal I would bring to the altar, I would as soon offer a diseased or ill-shaped bull.'

'But it were an easy matter to seize such as we might want. Not, O Aurelian, till this accursed race is exterminated, will the heavens smile as formerly upon our country. Why are the altars thus forsaken? Why are the temples no longer thronged as once? Why do the great, and the rich, and the learned, silently withhold their aid, or openly scoff and jeer? Why are our sanctuaries crowded only by the scum and refuse of the city?'

'I know not. Question me not thus.'

'Is not the reason palpable and gross to the dullest mind? Is it not because of the daily growth of this blaspheming and atheistical crew, who, by horrid arts seduce the young, the timid, and above all the women, who ever draw the world with them, to join them in their unhallowed orgies, thus stripping the temples of their worshippers, and dragging the gods themselves from their seats? Think you the gods look on with pleasure while their altars and temples are profaned or abandoned, and a religion, that denies them, rears itself upon their ruins?'

'I know not. Say no more.'

'Is it possible, religion or the state should prosper, while he, who is not only Vicegerent of the gods, Universal Monarch, but what is more, their sworn Pontifex Maximus, connives at the existence and dissemination of the most dangerous opinions--'

'Thou liest.'

'Harboring even beneath the imperial roof, and feasting at the imperial table, the very heads and chief ministers of this black mischief--'

'Hold, I say. I swear by all the gods, known and unknown, that another word, and thy head shall answer it. Is my soul that of a lamb, that I need this stirring up to deeds of blood? Am I so lame and backward, when the gods are to be defended, that I am to be thus charged? Let the lion sleep when he will; chafed too much, and he may spring and slay at random. I love not the Christians, nor any who flout the gods and their worship--that thou knowest well. But I love Piso, Aurelia, and the divine Julia--that thou knowest as well. Now no more.'

'For my life,' said Fronto, 'I hold it cheap, if I may but be faithful to my office and the gods.'

'I believe it, Fronto. The gods will reward thee. Let us on.'

In the earnestness of their talk they had paused, and stood just before us, being separated but by a thin screen of shrubs. We continued rooted to our seats while this conversation went on, held there both by the impossibility of withdrawing without observation, and by a desire to hear--I confess it--what was thus in a manner forced upon me, and concerned so nearly, not only myself, but thousands of my fellow-Christians.

When they were hidden from us by the winding of the path, we rose and turned toward the palace.

'That savage!' said Livia. 'How strange, that Aurelian, who knows so well how to subdue the world, should have so little power to shake off this reptile.'

'There is power enough,' I replied; 'but alas! I fear the will is wanting. Superstition is as deep a principle in the breast of Aurelian as ambition and of that, Fronto is the most fitting high-priest. Aurelian places him at the head of religion in the state for those very qualities, whose fierce expression has now made us tremble. Let us hope that the Emperor will remain where he now is, in a position from which it seems Fronto is unable to dislodge him, and all will go well.'

We soon reached the palace, where, joining Julia and Portia, our chariot soon bore us to the Coelian Hill. Farewell.

LETTER IV.

FROM PISO TO FAUSTA.

I promised you, Fausta, before the news should reach you in any other way, to relate the occurrences and describe the ceremonies of the day appointed for the dedication of the new Temple of the Sun. The day has now passed, not without incidents of even painful interest to ourselves and therefore to you, and I sit down to fulfil my engagements.

Vast preparations had been making for the occasion, for many days or even months preceding, and the day arose upon a city full of expectation of the shows, ceremonies, and games, that were to reward their long and patient waiting. For the season of the year the day was hot, unnaturally so; and the sky filled with those massive clouds, piled like mountains of snow one upon another, which, while they both please the eye by their forms, and veil the fierce splendors of the sun, as they now and then sail across his face, at the same time portend wind and storm. All Rome was early astir. It was ushered in by the criers traversing the streets, and proclaiming the rites and spectacles of the day, what they were, and where to be witnessed, followed by troops of boys, imitating, in their grotesque way, the pompous declarations of the men of authority, not unfrequently drawing down upon their heads the curses and the batons of the insulted dignitaries. A troop of this sort passed the windows of the room in which Julia and I were sitting at our morning meal. As the crier ended his proclamation, and the shouts of the applauding urchins died away, Milo, who is our attendant in preference to any and all others, observed,

'That the fellow of a crier deserved to have his head beat about with his own rod, for coming round with his news not till after the greatest show of the day was over.'

'What mean you?' I asked. 'Explain.'

'What should I mean,' he replied, 'but the morning sacrifice at the temple.'

'And what so wonderful,' said Julia, 'in a morning sacrifice? The temples are open every morning, are they not?'

'Yes, truly are they,' rejoined Milo; 'but not for so great a purpose, nor witnessed by so great crowds. Curio wished me to have been there, and says nothing could have been more propitious. They died as the gods love to have them.'

'Was there no bellowing nor struggling, then?' said Julia.

'Neither, Curio assures me; but they met the knife of the priest as they would the sword of an enemy on the field of battle.'

'How say you?' said Julia, quickly, turning pale; 'do I hear aright, Milo, or are you mocking? God forbid that you should speak of a human sacrifice.'

'It is even so, mistress. And why should it not be so? If the favor of the gods, upon whom we all depend, as the priests tell us, is to be purchased so well in no other way, what is the life of one man, or of many, in such a cause? The great Gallienus, when his life had been less ordered than usual after the rules of temperance and religion, used to make amends by a few captives slain to Jupiter; to which, doubtless, may be ascribed his prosperous reign. But, as I was saying, there was, so Curio informed me at the market not long afterwards, a sacrifice, on the private altar of the temple, of ten captives. Their blood flowed just as the great god of the temple showed himself in the horizon. It would have done you good, Curio said, to see with what a hearty and dexterous zeal Fronto struck the knife into their hearts--for to no inferior minister would he delegate the sacred office.'

'Lucius,' cried Julia, 'I thought that such offerings were now no more. Is it so, that superstition yet delights itself in the blood of murdered men?'

'It is just so,' I was obliged to reply. 'With a people naturally more gentle and humane than we of Rome this custom would long ago have fallen into disuse. They would have easily found a way, as all people do, to conform their religious doctrine and offerings to their feelings and instincts. But the Romans, by nature and long training, lovers of blood, their country built upon the ruins of others, and cemented with blood--the taste for it is not easily eradicated.

There are temples where human sacrifices have never ceased. Laws have restrained their frequency--have forbidden them, under heaviest penalties, unless permitted by the state--but these laws ever have been, and are now evaded; and it is the settled purpose of Fronto, and others of his stamp, to restore to them their lost honors, and make them again, as they used to be, the chief rite in the worship of the gods. I am not sorry, Julia, that your doubts, though so painfully, have yet been so effectually, removed.'

Julia had for some time blamed, as over-ardent, the zeal of the Christians. She had thought that the evil of the existing superstitions was over-estimated, and that it were wiser to pursue a course of more moderation; that a system that nourished such virtues as she found in Portia, in Tacitus, and others like them, could not be so corrupting in its power as the Christians were in the habit of representing it; that if we could succeed in substituting Christianity quietly, without alienating the affections, or shocking too violently the prejudices, of the believers in the prevailing superstitions, our gain would be double. To this mode of arguing I knew she was impelled, by her love and almost reverence for Portia; and how could I blame it, springing from such a cause? I had, almost criminally, allowed her to blind herself in a way she never would have done, had her strong mind acted, as on other subjects, untrammelled and free. I was not sorry that Milo had brought before her mind a fact which, however revolting in its horror to such a nature as hers, could not but heal while it wounded.

'Milo,' said Julia, as I ended, 'say now that you have been jesting; that this is a piece of wit with which you would begin in a suitable way an extraordinary day; this is one of your Gallienus fictions.'

'Before the gods,' replied Milo, 'I have told you the naked truth. But not the whole; for Curio left me not till he had shown how each had died. Of the ten, but three, he averred, resisted, or died unwillingly. The three were Germans from beyond the Danube--brothers, he said, who had long lain in prison till their bones were ready to start through the skin. Yet were they not ready to die. It seemed as if there were something they longed--more even than for life or freedom--to say; but they might as well have been dumb and tongueless, for none understood their barbarous jargon. When they found that their words were in vain, they wrung their hands in their wo, and cried out aloud in their agony. Then, however, at the stern voice of Fronto, warning them of the hour, they ceased--embraced each other, and received the fatal blow; the others signified their pleasure at dying so, rather than to be thrown to wild beasts, or left to die by slow degrees within their dungeon's walls. Two rejoiced that it was their fate to pour out their blood upon the altar of a god, and knelt devoutly before the uplifted knife of Fronto. Never, said Curio, was there a more fortunate offering. Aurelian heard the report of it with lively joy, and said that 'now all would go well.' Curio is a good friend of mine; will it please you to hear these things from his own lips?'

'No,' said Julia; 'I would hear no more. I have heard more than enough. How needful, Lucius, if these things are so, that our Christian zeal abate not! I see that this stern and bloody faith requires that they who would deal with it must carry their lives in their hand, ready to part with nothing so easily, if by so doing they can hew away one of the branches, or tear up one of the roots of this ancient and pernicious error. I blame not Probus longer--no, nor the wild rage of Macer.'

'Two, lady, of the captives were of Palmyra; the Queen's name and yours were last upon their lips.'

'Great God! how retribution like a dark pursuing shadow hangs upon the steps of guilt! Even here it seeks us. Alas, my mother! Heaven grant that these things fall not upon your ears!'

Julia was greatly moved, and sat a long time silent, her face buried in her hands, and weeping. I motioned to Milo to withdraw and say no more. Upon Julia, although so innocent of all wrong--guiltless as an infant of the blame, whatever it may be, which the world fixes upon Zenobia--yet upon her, as heavily as upon her great mother, fall the sorrows, which, sooner or later, overtake those, who, for any purpose, in whatever degree selfish, have involved their fellow-creatures in useless suffering. Being part of the royal house, Julia feels that she must bear her portion of its burdens. Time alone can cure this grief.

But you are waiting, with a woman's impatient curiosity, to hear of the dedication.

At the appointed hour, we were at the palace of Aurelian on the Palatine, where a procession pompous as art, and rank, and numbers could make it, was formed, to move thence by a winding and distant way to the temple near the foot of the Quirinal. Julia repaired with Portia to a place of observation near the temple--I to the palace, to join the company of the Emperor. Of the gorgeous magnificence of the procession I shall tell you nothing. It was in extent, and variety of pomp and costliness of decoration, a copy of that of the late triumph; and went even beyond the captivating splendor of the example. Roman music--which is not that of Palmyra--lent such charms as it could to our passage through the streets to the temple, from a thousand performers.

As we drew near to the lofty fabric, I thought that no scene of such various beauty and magnificence had ever met my eye. The temple itself is a work of unrivalled art. In size it surpasses any other building of the same kind in Rome, and for excellence of workmanship and purity of design, although it may fall below the standard of Hadrian's age, yet, for a certain air of grandeur, and luxuriance of invention in its details, and lavish profusion of embellishment in gold and silver, no temple, nor other edifice, of any preceding age, ever perhaps resembled it. Its order is the Corinthian, of the Roman form, and the entire building is surrounded by its graceful columns, each composed of a single piece of marble. Upon the front, is wrought Apollo surrounded by the Hours. The western extremity is approached by a flight of steps, of the same breadth as the temple itself. At the eastern, there extends beyond the walls, to a distance equal to the length of the building, a marble platform, upon which stands the altar of sacrifice, which is ascended by various flights of steps, some little more than a gently rising plain, up which the beasts are led that are destined to the altar.

When this vast extent of wall and column, of the most dazzling brightness, came into view, everywhere covered, together with the surrounding temples, palaces, and theatres, with a dense mass of human beings, of all climes and regions, dressed out in their richest attire--music from innumerable instruments filling the heavens with harmony--shouts of the proud and excited populace, every few moments, and from different points, as Aurelian advanced, shaking the air with their thrilling din--added to, still further, by the neighing of horses, and the frequent blasts of the trumpet--the whole made more solemnly imposing by the vast masses of clouds which swept over the sky, now suddenly unveiling, and again eclipsing, the sun, the great god of this idolatry, and from which few could withdraw their gaze;--when, at once, this all broke upon my eye and ear, I was like a child who, before, had never seen aught but his own village, and his own rural temple, in the effect wrought upon me, and the passiveness with which I abandoned myself to the sway of the senses. Not one there, was more ravished than I was, by the outward circumstance and show. I thought of Rome's thousand years, of her power, her greatness, and universal empire, and, for a moment, my step was not less proud than that of Aurelian.

But, after that moment, when the senses had had their fill, when the eye had seen the glory, and the ear had fed upon the harmony and the praise, then I thought and felt very differently. Sorrow and compassion for these gay multitudes were at my heart; prophetic forebodings of disaster, danger, and ruin to those, to whose sacred cause I had linked myself, made my tongue to falter in its speech, and my limbs to tremble. I thought that the superstition, that was upheld by the wealth and the power, whose manifestations were before me, had its roots in the very centre of the earth--far too deep down for a few like myself ever to reach them. I was like one, whose last hope of life and escape is suddenly struck away.

I was aroused from these meditations, by our arrival at the eastern front of the temple. Between the two central columns, on a throne of gold and ivory, sat the Emperor of the world, surrounded by the senate, the colleges of augurs and haruspices, and by the priests of the various temples of the capital, all in their peculiar costume. Then, Fronto, the priest of the temple, standing at the altar, glittering in his white and golden robes like a messenger of light--when the crier had proclaimed that the hour of worship and sacrifice had come, and had commanded silence to be observed--bared his head, and, lifting his face up toward the sun, offered, in clear and sounding tones, the prayer of dedication. As he came toward the close of his prayer, he, as is so usual, with loud and almost frantic cries, and importunate repetition, called upon all the gods to hear him, and then, with appropriate names and praises, invoked the Father of gods and men to be present.

Just as he had thus solemnly invoked Jupiter by name, and was about to call upon the other gods in the same manner, the clouds, which had been deepening and darkening, suddenly obscured the sun; a distant peal of thunder rolled along the heavens; and, at the same moment, from out the dark recesses of the temple, a voice of preternatural power came forth, proclaiming, so that the whole multitude heard the words,--'God is but one; the King eternal, immortal, invisible.'

It is impossible to describe the horror that seized those multitudes. Many cried out with fear, and each seemed to shrink behind the other. Paleness sat upon every face. The priest paused as if struck by a power from above. Even the brazen Fronto was appalled. Aurelian leaped from his seat, and by his countenance, white and awe-struck, showed that to him it came as a voice from the gods. He spoke not; but stood gazing at the dark entrance into the temple, from which the sound had come. Fronto hastily approached him, and whispering but one word as it were into his ear, the Emperor started; the spell that bound him was dissolved; and, recovering himself--making indeed as though a very different feeling had possessed him--cried out in fierce tones to his guards,

'Search the temple; some miscreant, hid away among the columns, profanes thus the worship and the place. Seize him, and drag him forth to instant death.'

The guards of the Emperor, and the servants of the temple, rushed in at that bidding, and searched in every part the interior of the building. They soon emerged, saying that the search was fruitless. The temple, in all its aisles and apartments, was empty.

The ceremonies, quiet being again restored, then went on. Twelve bulls, of purest white and of perfect forms, their horns bound about with fillets, were now led by the servants of the temple up the marble steps to the front of the altar, where stood the cultrarii and haruspices, ready to slay them and examine their entrails. The omens,--as gathered by the eyes of all from the fierce strugglings and bellowings of the animals, as they were led toward the place of sacrifice, some even escaping from the hands of those who had the management of them, and from the violent and convulsive throes of others as the blow fell upon their heads, or the knife severed their throats,--were of the darkest character, and brought a deep gloom upon the brow of the Emperor. The report of the haruspices, upon examination of the entrails, was little calculated to remove that gloom. It was for the most part unfavorable. Especially appalling was the sight of a heart, so lean and withered, that it scarce seemed possible that it should ever have formed a part of a living animal. But more harrowing than all, was the voice of Fronto, who, prying with the haruspices into the smoking carcass of one of the slaughtered bulls, suddenly cried out with horror, that 'no heart was to be found.'

The Emperor, hardly to be restrained by those near him from some expression of anger, ordered a more diligent search to be made.

'It is not in nature that such a thing should be,' he said. 'Men are, in truth, sometimes without hearts; but brutes, as I think, never.'

The report was however confidently confirmed. Fronto himself approached, and said that his eye had from the first been upon the beast, and the exact truth had been stated.

The carcasses, such parts as were for the flames, were then laid upon the vast altar, and the flames of the sacrifice ascended.

The heavens were again obscured by thick clouds, which, accumulating into heavy volumes, began now, nearer and nearer, to shoot forth lightning, and roll their thunders. The priest commenced the last office, prayer to the god to whom the new temple had been thus solemnly consecrated. He again bowed his head, and again lifted up his voice. But no sooner had he invoked the god of the temple and besought his ear, than again, from its dark interior, the same awful sounds issued forth, this time saying, 'Thy gods, O Rome, are false and lying gods. God is but one.'

Aurelian, pale, as it seemed to me; with superstitious fear, again strove to shake it off, giving it artfully and with violence the appearance of offended dignity. His voice was a shriek rather than a human utterance, as he cried out,

'This is but a Christian device; search the temple till the accursed Nazarene be found, and hew him piecemeal--' More he would have said, but, at the instant, a bolt of lightning shot from the heavens, and, lighting upon a large sycamore which shaded a part of the temple court, clove it in twain. The swollen cloud, at the same moment, burst, and a deluge of rain poured upon the city, the temple, the gazing multitude, and the just kindled altars. The sacred fires went out in hissing and darkness; a tempest of wind whirled the limbs of the slaughtered victims into the air, and abroad over the neighboring streets. All was confusion, uproar, terror, and dismay. The crowds sought safety in the houses of the nearest inhabitants, in the porches, and in the palaces. Aurelian and the senators and those nearest him, fled to the interior of the temple. The heavens blazed with the quick flashing of the lightning, and the temple itself seemed to rock beneath the voice of the thunder. I never knew in Rome so terrific a tempest. The stoutest trembled, for life hung by a thread. Great numbers, it has now been found, in every part of the capital, fell a prey to the fiery bolts. The capital itself was struck, and the brass statue of Vespasian in the forum thrown down and partly melted. The Tiber in a few hours overran its banks, and laid much of the city on its borders under water.

But, ere long, the storm was over. The retreating clouds, but still sullenly muttering in the distance as they rolled away, were again lighted up by the sun, who again shone forth in his splendor. The scattered limbs of the victims were collected and again laid upon the altar. Dry wood being brought, the flames quickly shot upward and consumed to the last joint and bone the sacred offerings. Fronto once more stood before the altar, and now uninterrupted performed the last office of the ceremony. Then, around the tables spread within the temple to the honor of the gods, feasting upon the luxuries contributed by every quarter of the earth, and filling high with wine, the adverse omens of the day were by most forgotten. But not by Aurelian. No smile was seen to light up his dark countenance. The jests of Varus and the wisdom of Porphyrius alike failed to reach him. Wrapped in his own thoughts, he brooded gloomily over what had happened, and strove to read the interpretation of portents so unusual and alarming.

I went not in to the feast, but returned home reflecting as I went upon the events I had witnessed. I knew not what to think. That in times past, long after the departure from the earth of Jesus and his immediate followers, the Deity had interposed in seasons of peculiar perplexity to the church, and, in a way to be observed, had manifested his power, I did not doubt. But for a long time such revelations had wholly ceased. And I could not see any such features in the present juncture, as would, to speak as a man, justify and vindicate a departure from the ordinary methods of the Divine Providence. But then, on the other hand, I could not otherwise account for the voice, nor discover any way in which, had one been so disposed, he could so successfully and securely have accomplished his work. Revolving these things, and perplexed by doubts, I reached the Coelian--when, as I entered my dwelling, I found, to my great satisfaction, Probus seated with Julia, who at an early period, foreseeing the tempest, had with Portia withdrawn to the security of her own roof.

'I am glad you are come at length,' said Julia as I entered; 'our friend has scarce spoken. I should think, did I not know the contrary, that he had suddenly abandoned the service of truth and become a disciple of Novatus. He hath done little but groan and sigh.'

'Surely,' I replied, 'the occasion warrants both sighs and groans. But when came you from the temple?'

'On the appearance of the storm, just as Fronto approached the altar the first time. The signs were not to be mistaken, by any who were not so much engrossed by the scene as to be insensible to all else, that a tempest was in the sky, and would soon break upon the crowds in a deluge of rain and hail--as has happened. So that warning Portia of the danger, we early retreated--she with reluctance; but for myself, I was glad to be driven away from a scene that brought so vividly before me the events of the early morning.'

'I am glad it was so,' I replied; 'you would have been more severely tried, had you remained.' And I then gave an account of the occurrences of the day.

'I know not what to make of it,' she said as I ended 'Probus, teach us what to think. I am bewildered and amazed.'

'Lady,' said Probus, 'the Christian service is a hard one.'

'I have not found it so, thus far; but, on the other hand, a light and easy one.'

'But the way is not ever so smooth, and the path, once entered upon, there is no retreat.'

'No roughness nor peril, Probus, be they what they may, can ever shake me. It is for eternity I have embraced this faith, not for time--for my soul, not for my body.'

'God be thanked that it is so. But the evils and sorrows that time has in store, and which afflict the body, are not slight. And sometimes they burst forth from the overburdened clouds in terrific violence, and poor human strength sinks and trembles, as to-day before the conflict of the elements.'

'They would find me strong in spirit and purpose, I am sure, Probus, however my woman's frame of flesh might yield. No fear can change my mind, nor tear me from the hopes which through Christ I cherish more, a thousand fold, than this life of an hour.'

'Why, why is it so ordained in the Providence of God,' said Probus, 'that truth must needs be watered with tears and blood, ere it will grow and bear fruit? When, as now, the sky is dark and threatening, and the mind is thronged with fearful anticipations of the sorrows that await those who hold this faith, how can I, with a human heart within me, labor to convert the unbelieving? The words falter upon my tongue. I turn from the young inquirer, and with some poor reason put him off to another season. When I preach, it is with a coldness that must repel, and it is that which I almost desire to be the effect. My prayers never reach heaven, nor the consciences of those who hear. Probus, they say, is growing worldly. His heart burns no longer within him. His zeal is cold. We must look to Macer. I fear, lady, that the reproaches are well deserved. Not that I am growing worldly or cold, but that my human affections lead me away from duty, and make me a traitor to truth, and my master.'

'O no, Probus,' said Julia; 'these are charges foolish and false. There is not a Christian in Rome but would say so. We all rest upon you.'

'Then upon what a broken reed! I am glad it was not I who made you a Christian.'

'Do you grieve to have been a benefactor?'

'Almost, when I see the evils which are to overwhelm the believer. I look round upon my little flock of hearers, and I seem to see them led as lambs to the slaughter--poor, defenceless creatures, set upon by worse than lions and wolves. And you, lady of Piso, how can I sincerely rejoice that you have added your great name to our humble roll, when I think of what may await you. Is that form to be dragged with violence amid the hootings of the populace to the tribunal of the beast Varus? Are those limbs for the rack or the fire?'

'I trust in God they are not, Probus. But if they are needed, they are little to give for that which has made me so rich, and given wings to the soul. I can spare the body, now that the soul can live without it.'

'There spoke the universal Christian! What but truth could so change our poor human nature into somewhat quite divine and godlike! Think not I shrink myself at the prospect of obstruction and assault. I am a man loose upon the world, weaned by suffering and misfortune from earth, and ready at any hour to depart from it. You know my early story. But I in vain seek to steel myself to the pains of others. From what I have said, I fear lest you should think me over-apprehensive. I wish it were so. But all seems at this moment to be against us.'

'More then,' said Julia, 'must have come to your ears than to ours. When last we sat with the Emperor at his table, he seemed well inclined. And when urged by Fronto, rebuked him even with violence.'

'Yes, it was so.'

'Is it then from the scenes of to-day at the temple that you draw fresh omens of misfortune? I have asked you what we should think of them.'

'I almost tremble to say. I stood, Piso, not far from you, upon the lower flight of steps, where I think you observed me.'

'I did. And at the sound of that voice from the temple, methought your face was paler than Aurelian's. Why was that?'

'Because, Piso, I knew the voice.'

'Knew it! What mean you?'

'Repeat it not--let it sink into your ear, and there abide. It was Macer's.'

'Macer's? Surely you jest.'

'Alas! I wish it were a jest. But his tones were no more to be mistaken than were the thunder's.'

'This, should it be known, would, it is plain to see, greatly exasperate Aurelian. It would be more than enough for Fronto to work his worst ends with. His suspicions at once fell upon the Christians.'

'That,' said Probus, 'was, I am confident, an artifice. The countenance, struck with superstitious horror, is not to be read amiss. Seen, though but for a moment, and the signature is upon it, one and unequivocal. But with quick instinct the wily priest saw his advantage, seized it, and, whether believing or not himself, succeeded in poisoning the mind of Aurelian and that of the multitude. So great was the commotion among the populace, that, but for the tempest, I believe scarce would the legions of the Emperor have saved us from slaughter upon the spot. Honest, misguided Macer--little dost thou know how deep a wound thou hast struck into the very dearest life of the truth, for which thou wouldst yet at any moment thyself freely suffer and die!'

'What,' said Julia, 'could have moved him to such madness?'

'With him,' replied Probus, 'it was a deed of piety and genuine zeal for God; he saw it in the light of an act god-like, and god-directed. Could you read his heart, you would find it calm and serene, in the consciousness of a great duty greatly performed. It is very possible he may have felt himself to be but an instrument in the hand of a higher power, to whom he gives all the glory and the praise. There are many like him, lady, both among Christians and Pagans. The sybils impose not so much upon others as upon themselves. They who give forth the responses of the oracle, oft-times believe that they are in very truth full of the god, and speak not their own thoughts, but the inspirations of him whose priests they are. To themselves more than to others are they impostors. The conceit of the peculiar favor of God, or of the gods in return for extraordinary devotion, is a weakness that besets our nature wherever it is found. An apostle perhaps never believed in his inspiration more firmly than at times does Macer, and others among us like him. But this inward solitary persuasion we know is nothing, however it may carry away captive the undiscriminating multitude.'

'Hence, Probus, then, I suppose, the need of some outward act of an extraordinary nature to show the inspiration real.'

'Yes,' he replied. 'No assertion of divine impulses or revelations can avail to persuade us of their reality, except supported and confirmed by miracle. That, and that only, proves the present God. Christ would have died without followers had he exhibited to the world only his character and his truth, even though he had claimed, and claimed truly, a descent from and communion with the Deity. Men would have said, 'This is an old and common story. We see every day and everywhere those who affect divine aid. No act is so easy as to deceive one's self. If you propose a spiritual moral system and claim for it a divine authority, show your authority by a divine work, a work impossible to man, and we will then admit your claims. But your own inward convictions alone, sincere as they may be, and possibly founded in truth, pass with us for nothing. Raise one that was dead to life, and we will believe you when you reveal to us the spiritual world and the life to come.'

'I think,' said Julia, 'such would be the process in my own mind. There seems the same natural and necessary connection here between spiritual truths and outward acts, as between the forms of letters or the sound of words, and ideas. We receive the most subtle of Plato's reasonings through words--those miracles of material help--which address themselves to the eye or ear. So we receive the truths of Jesus through the eye witnessing his works, or the ear hearing the voice from Heaven.--But we wander from Macer, in whom, from what you have told us, and Piso has known, we both feel deeply interested. Can he not be drawn away from those fancies which possess him? 'Tis a pity we should lose so strong an advocate, to some minds so resistless, nor only that, but suffer injury from his extravagance.'

'It is our purpose,' I replied, 'to visit him to try what effect earnest remonstrance and appeal may have. Soon as I shall return from my promised and now necessary visit to Marcus and Lucilia, I shall not fail, Probus, to request you to accompany me to his dwelling.'

'Does he dwell far from us?' asked Julia.

'His house, if house it may be called,' replied Probus, 'is in a narrow street, which runs just behind the shop of Demetrius, midway between the Capitol and the Quirinal. It is easily found by first passing the shop and then descending quick to the left--the street Janus, our friend Isaac's street, turning off at the same point to the right. At Macer's, should your feet ever be drawn that way, you would see how and in what crowded space the poor live in Rome.'

'Has he then a family, as your words seem to imply?'

'He has; and one more lovely dwells not within the walls of Rome. In his wife and elder children, as I have informed Piso, we shall find warm and eloquent advocates on our side. They tremble for their husband and father, whom they reverence and love, knowing his impetuosity, his fearlessness and his zeal. Many an assault has he already brought upon himself, and is destined, I fear, to draw down many more and heavier.'

'Heaven shield them all from harm,' said Julia. 'Are they known to Demetrius? His is a benevolent heart, and he would rejoice to do them a service. No one is better known too or respected than the Roman Demetrius: his name merely would be a protection.'

'It was from Macer,' replied Probus, 'that Demetrius first heard the truth which now holds him captive. Their near neighborhood brought them often together. Demetrius was impressed by the ardor and evident sincerity so visible in the conversation and manners of Macer; and Macer was drawn toward Demetrius by the cast of melancholy--that sober, thoughtful air--that separates him so from his mercurial brother, and indeed from all. He wished he were a Christian. And by happy accidents being thrown together--or rather drawn by some secret bond of attraction--he in no long time had the happiness to see him one. From the hand of Felix he received the waters of baptism.'

'What you have said, Probus, gives me great pleasure. I am not only now sure that Macer and his little tribe have a friend at hand, but the knowledge that such a mind as that of Demetrius has been wrought upon by Macer, has served to raise him in my esteem and respect. He can be no common man, and surely no madman.'

'The world ever loves to charge those as mad,' said Probus, 'who, in devotion to a great cause, exceed its cold standard of moderation. Singular, that excess virtue should incur this reproach, while excess in vice is held but as a weakness of our nature!'

We were here interrupted by Milo, who came to conduct us to the supper room; and there our friendly talk was prolonged far into the night.

When I next write, I shall have somewhat to say of Marcus, Lucilia, and the little Gallus. How noble and generous in the Queen, her magnificent gift! When summer comes round again, I shall not fail, together with Julia, to see you there. How many recollections will come thronging upon me when I shall again find myself in the court of the Elephant, sitting where I once sat so often and listened to the voice of Longinus. May you see there many happy years. Farewell.

* * * * *

Nothing could exceed the sensation caused in Rome by the voice heard at the dedication, and among the adherents of the popular faith, by the unlucky omens of the day and of the sacrifice. My office at that time called me often to the capital, and to the palace of Aurelian, and threw me frequently into his company and that of Livia. My presence was little heeded by the Emperor, who, of a bold and manly temper, spoke out with little reserve, and with no disguise or fear, whatever sentiments possessed him. From such opportunities, and from communications of Menestheus, the secretary of Aurelian, little took place at the palace which came not to my knowledge. The morning succeeding the dedication I had come to the city bringing a packet from the Queen to the Empress Livia. While I waited in the common reception room of the palace, I took from a case standing there, a volume and read. As I read, I presently was aroused by the sound of Aurelian's voice. It was as if engaged in earnest conversation. He soon entered the apartment accompanied by the priest of the new temple.

'There is something,' he said as he drew near, 'in this combination of unlucky signs that might appal a stouter spirit than mine. This too, after a munificence toward not one only but all the temples, never I am sure surpassed. Every god has been propitiated by gifts and appropriate rites. How can all this be interpreted other than most darkly--other than as a general hostility--and a discouragement from an enterprise upon which I would found my glory. This has come most unlooked for. I confess myself perplexed. I have openly proclaimed my purpose--the word has gone abroad and travelled by this to the court of Persia itself, that with all Rome at my back I am once more to tempt the deserts of the East.'

He here suddenly paused, being reminded by Fronto of my presence.

'Ah, it matters not;' he said; 'this is but Nichomachus, the good servant of the Queen of Palmyra. I hope,' he said, turning to me, 'that the Queen is well, and the young Faustula?'

'They are well,' I replied.

'How agree with her these cooler airs of the west? These are not the breezes of Arabia, that come to-day from the mountains.'

'She heeds them little,' I replied, 'her thoughts are engrossed by heavier cares.'

'They must be fewer now than ever.'

'They are fewer, but they are heavier and weigh upon her life more than the whole East once did. The remembrance of a single great disaster weighs as a heavier burden than the successful management of an empire.'

'True, Nichomachus, that is over true.' Then, without further regarding me, he went on with his conversation with Fronto.

'I cannot,' he said, 'now go back; and to go forward may be persumptuous.'

'I cannot but believe, great Emperor,' said Fronto, 'that I have it in my power to resolve your doubts, and set your mind at ease.'

'Rest not then,' said Aurelian with impatience--'but say on.'

'You sought the gods and read the omens with but one prayer and thought. And you have construed them as all bearing upon one point and having one significancy--because you have looked in no other direction. I believe they bear upon a different point, and that when you look behind and before, you will be of the same judgment.'

'Whither tends all this?'

'To this--that the omens of the day bear not upon your eastern expedition, but upon the new religion! You are warned as the great high priest, by these signs in heaven and on earth--not against this projected expedition, which is an act of piety,--but against this accursed superstition, which is working its way into the empire, and threatening the extermination and overthrow of the very altars on which you laid your costly offerings. What concern can the divinities feel in the array of an army, destined to whatever service, compared with that which must agitate their sacred breasts as they behold their altars cast down or forsaken, their names profaned, their very being denied, their worshippers drawn from them to the secret midnight orgies of a tribe of Atheists, whose aim is anarchy in the state and in religion; owning neither king on earth nor king in heaven--every man to be his own priest--every man his own master! Is not this the likeliest reading of the omens?'

'I confess, Fronto,' the Emperor replied, the cloud upon his brow clearing away as he spoke, 'that what you say possesses likelihood. I believe I have interpreted according to my fears. It is as you say--the East only has been in my thoughts. It cannot in reason be thought to be this enterprize, which, as you have said, is an act of piety--all Rome would judge it so--against which the heavens have thus arrayed themselves. Fronto! Fronto! I am another man! Slave,' cried he aloud to one of the menials as he passed, 'let Mucapor be instantly summoned. Let there be no delay. Now can my affairs be set on with something more of speed. When the gods smile, mountains sink to mole-hills. A divine energy runs in the current of the blood and lends more than mortal force to the arm and the will.'

As he spoke, never did so malignant a joy light up the human countenance as was to be seen in the face of Fronto.

'And what then,' he hastily put in as the Emperor paused, 'what shall be done with these profane wretches?'

'The Christians! They must be seen to. I will consider. Now, Fronto, shall I fill to the brim the cup of human glory. Now shall Rome by me vindicate her lost honor and wipe off the foulest stain that since the time of Romulus has darkened her annals.'

'You will do yourself and the empire,' rejoined the priest, 'immortal honor. If danger ever threatened the very existence of the state it is now from the secret machinations of this god-denying tribe.'

'I spake of the East and of Valerian, Fronto. Syria is now Rome's. Palmyra, that mushroom of a day, is level with the ground. Her life is out. She will be hereafter known but by the fame of her past greatness, of her matchless Queen, and the glory of the victories that crowned the arms of Aurelian. What now remains but Persia?'

'The Christians,' said the priest, shortly and bitterly.

'You are right, Fronto; the omens are not to be read otherwise. It is against them they point. It shall be maturely weighed what shall be done. When Persia is swept from the field, and Ctesiphon lies as low as Palmyra, then will I restore the honor of the gods, and let who will dare to worship other than as I shall ordain! Whoever worships them not, or other than them, shall die.'

'In that spoke the chief minister of religion--the representative of the gods. The piety of Aurelian is in the mouths of men not less than his glory. The city resounds with the praise of him who has enriched the temples, erected new ones, made ample provision for the priesthood, and fed the poor. This is the best greatness. Posterity will rather honor and remember him who saved them their faith, than him who gained a Persian victory. The victory for Religion too is to be had without cost, without a step taken from the palace gate or from the side of her who is alike Aurelian's and the empire's boast.'

'Nay, nay, Fronto, you are over-zealous. This eastern purpose admits not of delay. Hormisdas is new in his power. The people are restless and divided. The present is the moment of success. It cannot bear delay. To-morrow, could it be so, would I start for Thrace. The heavens are propitious. They frown no longer.'

'The likeliest way, methinks,' replied the priest, 'to insure success and the continued favor of the gods in that which they do not forbid, were first to fulfil their commands in what they have enjoined.'

'That, Fronto, cannot be denied. It is of weight. But where, of two commands, both seem alike urgent, and both cannot be done at once, whether we will or not, we must choose, and in choosing we may err.'

'To an impartial, pious mind, O Emperor, the god of thy worship never shone more clear in the heavens than shines his will in the terrific signs of yesterday. Forgive thy servant, but drawn as thou art by the image of fresh laurels of victory to be bound about thy brow, of the rich spoils of Persia, of its mighty monarch at thy chariot wheels, and the long line of a new triumph sweeping through the gates and the great heart of the capital,--and thou art blind to the will of the gods, though writ in the dread convulsions of the elements and the unerring language of the slaughtered victims.'

'Both may be done--both, Fronto. I blame not your zeal. Your freedom pleases me. Religion is thus, I know, in good hands. But both I say may be done. The care of the empire in this its other part may be left to thee and Varus, with full powers to see that the state, in the matter of its faith, receives no harm. Your knowledge in this, if not your zeal, is more than mine. While I meet the enemies of Rome abroad, you shall be my other self, and gain other victories at home.'

'Little, I fear, Aurelian, could be done even by me and Varus leagued, with full delegated powers, opposed as we should be by Tacitus and the senate and the best half of Rome. None, but an arm omnipotent as thine, can crush this mischief. I see thou knowest not how deep it has struck, nor how wide it has spread. The very foundations of the throne and the empire are undermined. The poison of Christian atheism has infected the whole mind of the people, not only throughout Rome, but Italy, Gaul, Africa, and Asia. And for this we have to thank whom? Whom but ourselves? Ever since Hadrian-- otherwise a patriot king--built his imageless temples, in imitation of this barren and lifeless worship; ever since the weak Alexander and his superstitious mother filled the imperial palace with their statues of Christ, with preachers and teachers of his religion; ever since the Philips openly and without shame professed his faith; ever, I say, since these great examples have been before the world, has the ancient religion declined its head, and the new stalked proudly by. Let not Aurelian's name be added to this fatal list. Let him first secure the honor of the gods--then, and not till then, seek his own.'

'You urge with warmth, Fronto, and with reason too. Your words are not wasted; they have fallen where they shall be deeply pondered. In the meantime I will wait for the judgment of the augurs and haruspices; and as the colleges report, will hold myself bound so to act.'

So they conversed, and then passed on. I was at that time but little conversant with the religious condition of the empire. I knew but little of the character of the prevailing faith and the Pagan priesthood; and I knew less of the new religion as it was termed. But the instincts of my heart were from the gods, and they were all for humanity. I loved man, whoever he was, and of whatever name or faith; and I sickened at cruelties perpetrated against him, both in war, and by the bloody spirit of superstition. I burned with indignation therefore as I listened to the cold-blooded arguings of the bigoted priest, and wept to see how artfully he could warp aside the better nature of Aurelian, and pour his own venom into veins, that had else run with human blood, at least not with the poisoned current of tigers, wolves, and serpents, of every name and nature most vile. My hope was that, away from his prompter, the first purpose of Aurelian would return and have its way.

LETTER V.

FROM PISO TO FAUSTA.

I am now returned from my long intended visit to the villa of Marcus, and have much to say concerning it.

But, first of all, rejoice with me in a fresh demonstration of good will, on the part of Aurelian towards Zenobia. And what think you it is? Nothing less than this, that Vabalathus has been made, by Aurelian and the senate, king of Armenia! The kingdom is not large, but large enough for him at his present age--if he shall show himself competent, additions doubtless will be made.

Our only regret is, that the Queen loses thus his presence with her at Tibur. He had become to his mother all that a son should be. Not that in respect to native force he could ever make good the loss of Julia, or even of Livia, but, that in all the many offices which an affectionate child would render to a parent in the changed circumstances of Zenobia, he has proved to be a solace and a support.

The second day from the dedication, passing through the Porta Asinaria with Milo at my side, I took the road that winds along the hither bank of the Tiber, and leads most pleasantly, if not most directly, to the seat of my friends--and you are well aware how willingly I sacrifice a little time on the way, if by doing so I can more than make up the loss by obtaining brighter glimpses of earth and sky. Had I not found Christianity, Fausta, this would have been my religion. I should have forsaken the philosophers, and gone forth into the fields, among the eternal hills, upon the banks of the river, or the margin of the ever-flowing ocean, and in the lessons there silently read to me, I should, I think, have arrived at some very firm and comfortable faith in God and immortality. And I am especially happy in this, that nature in no way loses its interest or value, because I now draw truth from a more certain source. I take the same pleasure as before, in observing and contemplating her various forms, and the clearer light of Christianity brings to view a thousand beauties, to which before I was insensible. Just as in reading a difficult author, although you may have reached his sense in some good degree, unaided, yet a judicious commentator points out excellences, and unfolds truths, which you had either wholly overlooked, or but imperfectly comprehended.

All without the city walls, as within, bore witness to the graciousness of the Emperor in the prolonged holiday he had granted the people. It was as if the Saturnalia had arrived. Industry, such as there ever is, was suspended; all were sitting idle, or thronging some game, or gathering in noisy groups about some mountebank. As we advanced farther, and came just beyond the great road leading to Tibur, we passed the school of the celebrated gladiator Sosia, at the door of which there had just arrived from the amphitheatre, a cart bearing home the bodies of such as had been slain the preceding day, presenting a disgusting spectacle of wounds, bruises, and flowing blood.

'There was brave fighting yesterday,' said Milo; these are but a few out of all that fell. The first day's sport was an hundred of the trained gladiators, most of them from the school of Sosia, set against a hundred picked captives of all nations. Not less than a half of each number got it. These fellows look as if they had done their best. You've fought your last battle, old boys--unless you have a bout with Charon, who will be loath, I warrant you beforehand, to ferry over such a slashed and swollen company. Now ought you in charity,' he continued, addressing a half-naked savage, who was helping to drag the bodies from the cart, 'to have these trunks well washed ere you bury them, or pitch them into the Tiber, else they will never get over the Styx--not forgetting too the ferriage--' what more folly he would have uttered, I know not, for the wretch to whom he spoke suddenly seized the lash of the driver of the cart, and laid it over Milo's shoulders, saying, as he did it,

'Off, fool, or my fist shall do for you what it did for one of these.'

The bystanders, at this, set up a hoarse shouting, one of them exclaiming, so that I could hear him--

'There goes the Christian Piso, we or the lions will have a turn at him yet. These are the fellows that spoil our trade.'

'If report goes true, they won't spoil it long,' replied another.

No rank and no power is secure against the affronts of this lawless tribe; they are a sort of licensed brawlers, their brutal and inhuman trade rendering them insensible to all fear from any quarter. Death is to them but as a scratch on the finger--they care not for it, when nor how it comes. The slightest cause--a passing word--a look--a motion--is enough to inflame their ferocious passions, and bring on quarrel and murder. Riot and death are daily occurrences in the neighborhood of these schools of trained assassins. Milo knew their character well enough, but he deemed himself to be uttering somewhat that should amuse rather than enrage, and was mortified rather than terrified, I believe, at the sudden application of the lash. The unfeigned surprise he manifested, together with the quick leap which his horse made, who partook of the blow, was irresistibly ludicrous. He was nearly thrown off backwards in the speed of the animal's flight along the road. It was some time before I overtook him.

'Intermeddling,' I said to Milo, as I came up with him, 'is a dangerous vice.

How feel your shoulders?'

'I shall remember that one-eyed butcher, and if there be virtue in hisses or in thumbs, he shall rue the hour he laid a lash on Gallienus, poor fellow! Whose horsemanship is equal to such an onset? I'll haunt the theatre till my chance come.'

'Well, well, let us forget this. How went the games yesterday?'

'Never, as I hear,' he said, 'and as I remember, were they more liberal, or more magnificent. Larger, or more beautiful, or finer beasts, neither Asia nor Africa ever sent over. They fought as if they had been trained to it, like these scholars of Sosia, and in most cases they bore away the palm from them. How many of Sosia's men exactly fell, it is not known, but not fewer than threescore men were either torn in pieces, or rescued too much lacerated to fight more.'

'What captives were sacrificed?'

'I did not learn of what nation they were, nor how many. All I know, is what I witnessed toward the end of the sport. Never before did I behold such a form, nor such feats of strength! He was another Hercules. It was rumored he was from the forests of Germany. If you will believe it, which I scarce can, though I saw it, he fought successively with six of Sosia's best men, and one after another laid them all sprawling. A seventh was then set upon him, he having no time to breathe, or even drink. Many however cried out against this. But Romans, you know, like not to have their fun spoiled, so the seventh was not taken off. As every one foresaw, this was too much by just one for the hero; but he fought desperately, and it is believed Sosia's man got pushes he will never recover from. He was soon however on his knees, and then on his back, the sword of his antagonist at his throat, he lying like a gasping fish at his mercy--who waited the pleasure of the spectators a moment, before he struck. Then was there a great shouting all over the theatre in his behalf, besides making the sign to spare him. But just at the moment, as for him ill fortune would have it, some poltroon cried out with a voice that went all over the theatre, 'The dog is a Christian!' Whereupon, like lightning, every thumb went up, and down plunged the sword into his neck. So, master, thou seest what I tell thee every day, there is small virtue in being a Christian. It is every way dangerous. If a thief run through the streets the cry is, a Christian! a Christian! If a man is murdered, they who did it accuse some neighboring Christian, and he dies for it. If a Christian fall into the Tiber, men look on as on a drowning-dog. If he slip or fall in a crowd, they will help to trample him to death. If he is sick or poor, none but his own tribe will help him. A slave has a better chance. Even the Jew despises him, and spits upon his gown as he passes. What but the love of contempt and death can make one a Christian, 'tis hard to see. Had that captive been other than a Christian, he would not have fallen as he did.'

'Very likely. But the Christians, you know, frequent not the amphitheatre. Had they been there in their just proportion to the rest, the voice would at least have been a divided one.'

'Nay, as for that.' he rejoined, 'there were some stout voices raised in his behalf to the last, but too few to be regarded. But even in the streets, where all sorts are found, there is none to take the Christian's part--unless it be that old gashed soldier of the fifth legion, who stalks through the streets as though all Rome were his. By the gods, I believe he would beard Aurelian himself! He will stand at a corner, in some public place, and preach to the crowds, and give never an inch for all their curses and noise. They fear him too much, I believe, to attack him with aught but words. And I wonder not at it. A few days since, a large dog was in wicked wantonness, as I must allow, set upon a poor Christian boy. Macer, so he is called about the city, at the moment came up. Never tiger seized his prey as he seized that dog, and first dashing out his brains upon the pavement, pursued then the pursuers of the boy, and beat them to jelly with the carcase of the beast, and then walked away unmolested, leading the child to his home.'

'Men reverence courage, Milo, everywhere and in all.'

'That do they. It was so with me once, when Gallienus--'

'Gallop, Milo, to that mile-stone, and report to me how far we have come.'

I still as ever extract much, Fausta, from my faithful if foolish slave.

* * * * *

In due time and without hindrance, or accident, I reached the outer gate of my friend's villa.

The gate was opened by Coelia, whose husband is promoted to the place of porter. Her face shone as she saw me, and she hastened to assure me that all were well at the house, holding up at the same moment a curly-headed boy for me to admire, whom, with a blush and a faltering tongue, she called Lucius. I told her I was pleased with the name, for it was a good one, and he should not suffer for bearing it, if I could help it. Milo thought it unlucky enough that it should be named after a Christian, and I am certain has taken occasion to remonstrate with its mother on the subject; but, as you may suppose, did not succeed in infusing his own terrors.

I was first met by Lucilia, who received me with her usual heartiness. Marcus was out on some remote part of the estate, overseeing his slaves. In a few moments, by the assiduous Lucilia and her attendants, I was brushed and washed and set down to a table--though it was so few hours since I had left Rome--covered with bread, honey, butter and olives, a cold capon with salads, and wine such as the cellars of Marcus alone can furnish. As the only way in which to keep the good opinion of Lucilia is to eat, I ate of all that was on the table, she assuring me that everything was from their own grounds--the butter made by her own hands--and that I might search Rome in vain for better. This I readily admitted. Indeed no butter is like hers--so yellow and so hard--nor bread so light, and so white. Even her honey is more delicious than what I find elsewhere, the bees knowing by instinct who they are working for; and the poultry is fatter and tenderer, the hens being careful never to over-fatigue themselves, and the peacocks and the geese not to exhaust themselves in screaming and cackling. All nature, alive and dead, takes upon itself a trimmer and more perfect seeming within her influences.

I had sat thus gossipping with Lucilia, enjoying the balmy breezes of a warm autumn day, as they drew through the great hall of the house, when, preceded by the bounding Gallus, the master of the house entered in field dress of broad sun-hat, open neck, close coat depending to the knees, and boots that brought home with them the spoils of many a well-ploughed field.

'Well, sir Christian,' he cried, 'I joy to see thee, although thus recreant. But how is it that thou lookest as ever before? Are not these vanities of silk, and gold, and fine clothes, renounced by those of the new religion? Your appearance says nay, and, by Jupiter! wine has been drunk already! Nay, nay, Lucilia, it was hardly a pagan act to tempt our strict friend with that Falernian.'

'Falernian is it?'

'Yes, of the vintage of the fourth of Gallienus. Delicious, was it not? But by and by thou shalt taste something better than that--as much better as that is than anything of the same name thou didst ever raise to thy lips at the table of Aurelian. Piso! never was a face more welcome! Not a soul has looked in upon us for days and days. Not, Lucilia, since the Kalends, when young Flaccus, with a boat-load of roysterers, dropt down the river. But why comes not Julia too? She could not leave the games and theatres, hah?'

'Marcus,' said Lucilia, 'you forget it was the princess who first seduced Lucius. But for that eastern voyage for the Persian Calpurnius, Piso would have been still, I dare say, what his parents made him. Let us not yet however stir this topic; but first of all, Lucius, give us the city news. How went the dedication? we have heard strange tales.'

'How went it by report?' I asked.

'O, it would be long telling,' said Lucilia. 'Only, for one thing, we heard that there was a massacre of the Christians, in which some said hundreds, and some, thousands fell. For a moment, I assure you, we trembled for you. It was quickly contradicted, but the confirmation afforded by your actual presence, of your welfare, is not unwelcome. You must lay a part of the heartiness of our reception, especially the old Falernian, to the account of our relieved fears. But let us hear.'

I then went over the last days in Rome, adding what I had been able to gather from Milo, when it was such that I could trust to it. When I had satisfied their curiosity, and had moreover described to Lucilia the dresses of Livia on so great an occasion, and the fashions which were raging, Marcus proposed that I should accompany him over his farm, and observe his additions and improvements, and the condition of his slaves. I accepted the proposal with pleasure, and we soon set forth on our ramble, accompanied by Gallus, now riding his stick and now gambolling about the lawns and fields with his dog.

I like this retreat of Curtius better almost than any other of the suburban villas of our citizens. There is an air of calm senatorial dignity about it which modern edifices want. It looks as if it had seen more than one generation of patrician inhabitants. There is little unity or order--as those words are commonly understood--observable in the structure of the house, but it presents to the eye an irregular assemblage of forms, the work of different ages, and built according to the taste and skill of distant and changing times. Some portions are new, some old and covered with lichens, mosses, and creeping plants. Here is a portico of the days of Trajan, and there a tower that seems as if it were of the times of the republic. Yet is there a certain harmony and congruity running through the whole, for the material used is everywhere the same--a certain fawn-colored stone drawn from the quarries in the neighborhood; and each successive owner and architect has evidently paid some regard to preceding erections in the design and proportions of the part he has added. In this unity of character, as well as in the separate beauty or greatness of distinct parts, is it made evident that persons of accomplishment and rank have alone possessed it. Of its earlier history all that Curtius has with certainty ascertained is, that it was once the seat of the great Hortensius, before he had, in the growth of his fame and his riches, displayed his luxurious tastes in the wonders of Tusculum, Bauli, or Laurentum. It was the first indication given by him of that love of elegant and lavish wastefulness, that gave him at last as wide a celebrity as his genius. The part which he built is well known, and although of moderate dimensions, yet displays the rudiments of that taste that afterward was satisfied only with more than imperial magnificence. Marcus has satisfied himself as to the very room which he occupied as his study and library, and where he prepared himself for the morning courts; and in the same apartment--hoping as he says to catch something from the genius of the place--does he apply himself to the same professional labors. His name and repute are now second to none in Rome. Yet, young as he is, he begins to weary of the bar, and woo the more quiet pursuits of letters and philosophy. Nay, at the present moment, agriculture claims all his leisure, and steals time that can ill be spared from his clients. Varro and Cato have more of his devotion than statutes and precedents.

In the disposition of the grounds, Marcus has shown that he inherits something of the tastefulness of his remote predecessor; and in the harvest that covers his extensive acres, gives equal evidence that he has studied, not without profit, the labors of those who have written upon husbandry and its connected arts. Varro especially is at his tongue's end.

We soon came to the quarter of the slaves--a village almost of the humble tenements occupied by this miserable class. None but the women, children, sick and aged, were now at home--the young and able-bodied being abroad at work. No new disturbances have broken out, he tells me; the former severity, followed by a well-timed lenity, having subdued or conciliated all. Curtius, although fond of power and of all its ensigns, yet conceals not his hatred of this institution, which has so long obtained in the Roman state, as in all states. He can devise no way of escape from it; but he sees in it the most active and general cause of the corruption of morals which is spread everywhere where it prevails. He cannot suppress his contempt of the delusion or hypocrisy of our ancestors in terming themselves republicans.

'What a monstrous solecism was it,' he broke out with energy, 'in the times preceding the empire, to call that a free country which was built upon the degradation and slavery of half of its population. Rome never was a republic. It was simply a faction of land and slave holders, who blinded and befooled the ignorant populace, by parading before them some of the forms of liberty, but kept the power in their own hands. They were a community of petty kings, which was better in their mind than only one king, as in the time of the Tarquins. It was a republic of kingdoms and of kings, if you will. Now and then, indeed, the people bustled about and shook their chains, as in the times of the institution of the tribune's office, and those of the Gracchi. But they gained nothing. The patricians were still the kings who ruled them. And among no people can there be liberty where slavery exists--liberty, I mean, properly so called. He who holds slaves cannot, in the nature of things, be a republican; but, in the nature of things, he is on the other hand a despot. I am one. And a nation of such individuals is an association of despots for despotic purposes, and nothing else nor better. Liberty in their mouths is a profanation of the sacred name. It signifies nothing but their liberty to reign. I confess, it is to those who happen to be the kings a very agreeable state of things. I enjoy my power and state mightily. But I am not blind to the fact--my own experience teaches it--that it is a state of things corrupt and rotten to the heart--destructive everywhere of the highest form of the human character. It nurses and brings out the animal, represses and embrutes the god that is within us. It makes of man a being of violence, force, passion, and the narrowest selfishness; while reason and humanity, which should distinguish him, are degraded and oppressed. Such men are not the stuff that republics are made of. A republic may endure for a time in spite of them, owing to fortunate circumstances of another kind; but wherever they obtain a preponderance in the state, liberty will expire, or exist only in the insulting forms in which she waved her bloody sceptre during most of our early history. Slavery and despotism are natural allies.'

'I rejoice,' I said, 'to find a change in you, at least in the theory which you adopt.'

'I certainly am changed,' he replied; 'and such as the change may be, is it owing, sir Christian, to thy calm and yet fiery epistles from Palmyra. Small thanks do I owe thee for making me uncomfortable in a position from which I cannot escape. Once proud of my slaves and my power, I am already ashamed of both; but while my principles have altered, my habits and character, which slavery has created and nursed remain beyond any power of man, so far as I can see, to change them. What they are, you well know. So that here, in my middle age, I suffer a retribution, that should have been reserved till I had been dismissed from the dread tribunal of Rhadamanthus.'

'I see not, Curtius, why you should not escape from the position you are in, if you sincerely desire it, which I suppose you do not.'

'That, to be honest--which at least I am--is I believe the case.'

'I do not doubt it, as it is with all who are situated like yourself. Most, however, defend the principle as well as cling to the form of slavery.'

'Nay, that I cannot do. That I never did, since my beard was grown. I fancy myself to have from the gods a good heart. He is essentially of a corrupt heart who will stand for slavery in its principle. He is without anything generous in his nature. Cold selfishness marks and makes him. But supposing I as sincerely desired to escape--as I sincerely do not--what, O most wise mentor, should be the manner?'

'First and at once, to treat them no longer as slaves, but as men.'

'That I am just beginning to do. What else?'

'If you are sincere, as I say, and moreover, if you possess the exalted and generous traits which we patricians ever claim for ourselves, show it them by giving their freedom one by one to those who are now slaves, even though it result in the loss of one half of your fortune. That will be a patrician act. What was begun in crime by others, cannot be perpetuated without equal crime in us. The enfranchised will soon mingle with the people, and, as we see every day, become one with it. This process is going on at this moment in all my estates. Before my will is executed, I shall hope to have disposed in this manner of every slave in my possession.'

'One can hardly look to emulate such virtues as this new-found Christian philosophy seems to have engendered within thy noble bosom, Piso; but the subject must be weighed. There is nothing so agreeable in prospect as to do right; but, like some distant stretches of land and hill, water and wood, the beauty is all gone as it draws near. It is then absolutely a source of pain and disgust. I will write a treatise upon the great theme.'

'If you write, Curtius, I shall despair of any action, all your philanthropy will evaporate in a cloud of words.'

'But that will be the way, I think, to restore my equanimity. I believe I shall feel quite easy after a little declamation. Here, Lucius, regale thyself upon these grapes. These are from the isles of the Grecian Archipelago, and for sweetness are not equalled by any of our own. Gallus, Gallus, go not so near to the edge of the pond; it is deep, as I have warned you. I have lampreys there, Piso, bigger than any that Hortensius ever wept for. Gallus, you dog! away, I say.'

But Gallus heeded not the command of his father. He already was beginning to have a little will of his own. He continued playing upon the margin of the water, throwing in sticks for his dog to bring to him again. Perceiving his danger to be great, I went to him and forcibly drew him away, he and his dog setting up a frightful music of screams and yelping. Marcus was both entertained and amazed at the feat.

'Piso,' he jocosely cried out, 'there is a good deal of the old republican in you. You even treat free men as slaves. That boy--a man in will--never had before such restraint upon his liberty.'

'Liberty with restraint,' I answered, 'operating upon all, and equally upon all, is the true account of a state of freedom. Gallus unrestrained is a slave--a slave of passion and the sport of chance. He is not truly free until he is bound.'

With such talk we amused ourselves as we wandered over the estate, through its more wild and more cultivated parts. Dinner was presently announced, and we hastened to the house.

Lucilia awaited us in a small six-sided cabinet, fitted up purposely for a dining-room for six or eight persons. It was wholly cased with a rich marble of a pale yellow hue, beautifully panelled, having three windows opening upon a long portico with a southern aspect, set out with exotics in fancifully arranged groups. The marble panels of the room were so contrived that, at a touch, they slipped aside and disclosed in rich array, here the choicest wines, there sauces and spices of a thousand sorts, and there again the rarest confections brought from China and the East. Apicius himself could have fancied nothing more perfect--for the least dissatisfaction with the flavor of a dish, or the kind of wine, could be removed by merely reaching out the hand and drawing, from an inexhaustible treasure-house, both wines and condiments, such as scarce Rome itself could equal. This was an apartment contrived and built by Hortensius himself.

The dinner was worthy the room and its builder, the marbles, the prospect, the guest, the host, and the hostess. The aforementioned Apicius would have never once thought of the panelled cupboards. No dish would have admitted of addition or alteration.

When the feasting was over, and with it the lighter conversation, and more disjointed and various, which usually accompanies it, Marcus arose, and withdrawing one of the sliding panels, with much gravity and state, drew forth a glass pitcher of exquisite form filled with wine, saying, as he did so,

'All, Piso, that you have as yet tasted is but as water of the Tiber to this. This is more than nectar. The gods have never been so happy as to have seen the like. I am their envy. It is Falernian, that once saw the wine vaults of Heliogabalus! Not a drop of Chian has ever touched it. It is pure, unadulterate. Taste, and be translated.'

I acknowledged, as I well might, its unequalled flavor.

'This nectarean draught,' he continued, 'I even consider to possess purifying and exalting qualities. He who drinks it is for the time of a higher nature. It is better for the temper than a chapter of Seneca or Epictetus. It brings upon the soul a certain divine calm, favorable beyond any other state to the growth of the virtues. Could it become of universal use, mankind were soon a race of gods. Even Christianity were then made unnecessary--admitting it to be that unrivalled moral engine which you Christians affirm it to be. It is favorable also to dispassionate discussion, Piso, a little of which I would now invite. Know you not, I have scarce seen you since your assumption of your new name and faith? What bad demon possessed you, in evil hour, to throw Rome and your friends into such a ferment?'

'Had you become, Lucius,' said Lucilia, 'a declaiming advocate of Epicurus, or a street-lecturer upon Plato, or turned priest of Apollo's new temple, it would have all been quite tolerable, though amazing--but Christian!'--

'Yes, Lucius, it is too bad,' added Marcus. 'If you were in want of moral strength, you would have done better to have begged some of my Falernian. You should not have been denied.'

'Or,' said Lucilia, 'some of my Smyrna cordial.'

'At least,' continued Marcus, 'you might have come to me for some of my wisdom, which I keep ready, at a moment's warning, in quantities to suit all applicants.'

'Or to me,' said Lucilia, 'for some of my every day good-sense, which, you know, I possess in such abundance, though I have not sat at the feet of philosophers.'

'But seriously, Lucius,' began Marcus in altered mood, 'this is a most extraordinary movement of yours. I should like to be able to interpret it. If you must needs have what you call religion, of which I, for my part, can see no earthly occasion, here were plenty of forms in which to receive it, more ancient and more respectable than this of the Christians.'

'I am almost unwilling to converse on this topic with you, Marcus,' I rejoined, 'for there is nothing in your nature, or rather in your educated nature, to which to appeal with the least hope of any profitable result, either to me, or you. The gods have, as you say, given you a good heart--I may add too, a most noble head; but, yourself and education together, have made you so thoroughly a man of the world, that the interests of any other part of your nature, save those of the intellect and the senses, are to you precisely as if they did not exist.'

'Right, Lucius; therein do I claim honor and distinction. The intangible, the invisible, the vague, the shadowy, I leave to women and priests--concerning myself only with the substantial realities of life. Great Jupiter! what would become of mankind were we all women, and priests? How could the courts go on--senates sit, and deliberate--armies conquer? I think the world would stand still. However, I object not to a popular faith, such as that which now obtains throughout, the Roman world. If mankind, as history seems to prove, must and will have something of the kind, this perhaps is as good as anything else; and, seeing it has once become established and fixed in the way it has, I think it ought no more to be disturbed than men's faith in their political institutions. Our concern should be, merely to regulate it, that it grow not too large, and so overlay and crush the state. Fanatics and bigots must be hewn away. There must be an occasional infusion of doubt and indifference into the mass, to keep it from fermenting. You cannot be offended, Lucius, at the way in which I speak of your new-adopted faith. I think no better of any other. Epicureans, Stoics, Platonists, Jews, Christians, they are all alike to me. I hold them all at arms length. I have listened to them all; and more idle, indigested fancies never did I hear--no, not from the new-fledged advocate playing the rhetorician at his first appearance.'

'I do not wonder, Curtius, that you have turned away dissatisfied with the philosophers. I do not wonder that you reject the popular superstitions. But I do wonder, that you will prejudge any question, or infer the intrinsic incredibility of whatever may take the form of religion, from the intrinsic incredibility of what the world has heretofore possessed. It surely is not a philosophical method.'

'Not in other things, I grant,' replied Marcus; 'but concerning this question of popular superstition, or religion, the only philosophical thing is, to discard the whole subject, as one deserving severe investigation. The follies which the populace have, in all nations, and in all time, adopted, let them be retained, and even defended and supported by the State. They perform a not unimportant office in regulating the conduct, and manners of men--in preserving a certain order in the world. But beyond this, it seems to me, the subject is unworthy the regard of a reflecting person. One world and one life is enough to manage at a time. If there be others, and if there be a God who governs them, it will be time enough to know these things when they are made plain to the senses, as these trees and hills now are, and your well-shaped form. This peering into futurity, in the expectation to arrive at certainty, seems to me much as if one should hope to make out the forms of cities, palaces, and groves, by gazing into the empty air, or on the clouds. Besides, of what use?'

'Of what use indeed?' added Lucilia. 'I want no director or monitor, concerning any duty or act, which it falls to me to perform, other than I find within me. I have no need of a divine messenger, to stand ever at my side, to tell me what I must do, and what I must forbear. I have within me instincts and impulses, which I find amply sufficient. The care and duty of every day is very much alike, and a little experience and observation, added to the inward instinct, makes me quite superior to most difficulties and evils as they arise. The gods, or whatever power gave us our nature, have not left us dependent for these things, either on what is called religion or philosophy.'

'What you say,' I rejoined, 'is partly true. The gods have not left us dependent exclusively, upon either religion, or philosophy. There is a natural religion of the heart and the conscience, which is born with us, grows up with us, and never forsakes us. But then, after all, how defective and incomplete a principle it is. It has chiefly to do, only with our daily conduct; it cannot answer our doubts, or satisfy our most real wants. It differs too with the constitution of the individual. In some, it is a principle of much greater value and efficacy, than in others. Your instincts are clear, and powerful, and direct you aright. But, in another, they are obscure, and weak, and leave the mind in the greatest perplexity. It is by no means all that they want. Then, are not the prevalent superstitions most injurious in their influences upon the common mind? Can you doubt, whether more of good or evil, is derived to the soul, from the ideas it entertains of the character, and providence of the gods? Can you be insensible to the horrible enormities, and nameless vices, which make a part, even of what is called religion? And is there no need--if men will have religion in some form--that they should receive it in a better one? Can you not conceive of such views of God and his worship, of duty, virtue, and immortality being presented, that they shall strike the mind as reasonable in themselves, and of beneficial instead of hurtful power, upon being adopted? Can you not imagine your own mind, and the minds of people generally, to be so devoted to a high and sublime conception of the Divinity, and of futurity, as to be absolutely incapable of an act, that should displease him, or forfeit the hope of immortality?'

'Hardly,' said Marcus and Lucilia.

'Well, suppose it were so. Or rather, if you cannot imagine such a state of things, multitudes can. You are not a fair specimen of our kind, but only of a comparatively small class. Generally--so I have found it--the mind is seeking about for something better than what any human system has as yet proposed, and is confident of nothing more than of this, that men may be put in possession of truths, that shall carry them on as far beyond what their natural instincts now can do, as these instincts carry them on beyond any point to which the brutes ever arrive. This, certainly, was my own conviction, before I met with Christianity. Now, Marcus and Lucilia, what is this Christianity, but a revelation from Heaven, whose aim is to give to you, and to all, such conceptions of God, and futurity, as I have just spoken of?'--I then, finding that I had obtained a hearing, went into an account of the religion of Christ, as I had received it from the books themselves, and which to you I need not repeat. They listened with considerable patience--though I was careful not to use many words--but without any expression of countenance, or manner, that indicated any very favorable change in their opinions or feelings. As I ended, Marcus said,

'I shall always think better of this religion, Lucius, that you have adopted it, though I cannot say that your adopting it, will raise my judgment of you. I do not at present see upon what grounds it stands so firm, or divine, that a citizen is defensible in abandoning for it, an ostensible reception of, and faith in, the existing forms of the State. However, I incline to allow freedom in these matters to scholars and speculative minds. Let them work out and enjoy their own fancies--they are a restless, discontented, ambitious herd, and should, for the sake of their genius, be humored in the particular pursuits where they have placed their happiness. But, when they leave their proper vocation, and turn propagators and reformers, and aim at the subversion of things now firmly established and prosperous, then--although I myself should never meddle in such matters--it is scarcely a question whether the power of the State should interpose, and lay upon them the necessary restraints. Upon the whole, Lucius Piso, I think, that I, and Lucilia, had better turn preachers, and exhort you to return to the faith, or no-faith, which you have abandoned. Leave such things to take care of themselves. What have you gained but making yourself an object of popular aversion or distrust? You have abandoned the community of the polite, the refined, the sober, where by nature you belong, and have associated yourself with a vulgar crew, of-- forgive my freedom, I speak the common judgment, that you may know what it is--of ignorant fanatics or crafty knaves, who care for you no further, than as by your great name, they may stand a little higher in the world. I protest, before Jupiter, that to save others like you from such loss, I feel tempted to hunt over the statute books for some law, now obsolete and forgotten, but not legally dead, that may be brought to bear upon this mischief, and give it another Decian blight, which, if it do not kill, may yet check, and obstruct its growth.'

I replied, 'that from him I could apprehend, he well knew, no such deed of folly or guilt--however likely it was that others might, do it, and glory in their shame; that his nature would save him from such a deed, though his principles might not.' I told him, moreover, 'that I did not despair of his looking upon Christianity with a favorable judgment in good time. He had been willing to hear; and there was that secret charm in the truths and doctrines of Christ's religion, and especially in his character, that, however rudely set forth, the mind could scarcely resist it; against its will, it would, oftentimes, find itself subdued and changed. The seeds I have now dropt upon your hearts, I trust, will some day spring up, and bear such fruit as you yourselves will rejoice in.'

'So,' said Marcus, 'may the wheat spilled into the Tiber, or sown among rocks, or eaten by the birds.'

'And that may be, though not to-day or to-morrow,' I replied. 'The seed of things essential to man's life, as of wheat, is not easily killed. It may be buried for years and years, yet, turned up at length, to the sun, and its life sprouts upward in leaf, and stem, and fruit. Borne down by the waters of the Tiber, and apparently lost, it may be cast up upon the shores of Egypt, or Britain, and fulfil its destiny. The seed of truth is longer-lived still--by reason that what it bears is more essential than wheat, or other grain, to man's best life.'

'Well, well,' said Marcus, 'let us charge our goblets with the bottom of this Falernian, and forgetting whether there be such an entity as truth or not, drink to the health of the princess Julia.'

'That comes nearer our hearts,' said Lucilia, 'than anything that has been spoken for the last hour. When you return, Lucius, Laco must follow you with a mule-load of some of my homely products'---- She was about to add more, when we were all alike startled and alarmed by cries, seemingly of deep distress, and rapidly approaching. We sprang from our seats, when the door of the room was violently flung open, and a slave rushed in, crying out,

'Oh, sir! Gallus--Gallus'--

'What is it? What is it?'--cried Marcus and Lucilia. 'Speak quick--has he fallen--'

'Yes, alas! the pond--the fish-pond--run--fly--'

Distractedly we hurried to the spot already surrounded by a crowd of slaves. 'Who had been with him? Where had he fallen? How did it happen?' were questions hastily asked, but which no one could answer. It was a miserable scene of agony, confusion, and despair--Marcus ordering his slaves to dive into the pond, then uttering curses upon them, and commanding those to whom Gallus was usually entrusted, to the rack. No one could swim, no one could dive. It was long since I had made use of an art which I once possessed, but instantly I cast off my upper garments, and, needing no other direction to the true spot than the barking of the little dog, and his jumping in and out of the water--first learning that the water was deep, and of an even bottom, I threw myself in, and, in a moment, guided by the white dress of the little fellow, I grasped him, and drew him to the surface.

Life was apparently, and probably, to my mind, extinct; but expressing a hope that means might yet be resorted to that should restore him, I bore him in my arms to the house. But it was all in vain. Gallus was dead.

* * * * *

I shall not inflict a new sadness upon you, Fausta, by describing the grief of my friends, or any of the incidents of the days and weeks I now passed with them. They were heavy, and melancholy indeed; for the sorrows, of both Lucilia and Marcus, were excessive and inconsolable. I could do nothing for them, nor say anything to them in the hope to comfort them; yet, while they were thus incapacitated for all action, I could serve them essentially by placing myself at the head of their affairs, and relieving them of common cares and duties, that must otherwise have been neglected, or have proved irksome and oppressive.

The ashes of Gallus, committed to a small marble urn, have been deposited in a tomb in the centre of Lucilia's flower garden, which will soon be embowered by flowers and shrubs, which her hand will delight to train around it.

On the eve of the day when I was to leave them and return to Rome, we sat together in a portico which overlooks the Tiber. Marcus and Lucilia were sad, but, at length, in some sort, calm. The first violence of sorrow had spent itself, and reflection was beginning to succeed.

'I suppose,' said Marcus, 'your rigid faith greatly condemns all this show of suffering, which you have witnessed, Piso, in us, as, if not criminal, at least weak and childish?'

'Not so, by any means,' I rejoined. 'The religion of the Christians, is what one may term a natural religion; it does violence to not one of the good affections and propensities. Coming, as we maintain, from the Creator of our bodies and our minds, it does them no injury, it wars not with any of their natural elements, but most strictly harmonizes with them. It aims to direct, to modify, to heal, to moderate--but never to alter or annihilate. Love of our offspring, is not more according to our nature, than grief for the loss of them. Grief, therefore, is innocent--even as praiseworthy, as love. What trace of human wisdom--much less of divine--would there be in the arrangement, that should first bind us by chains of affection as strong as adamant to a child, or a parent, or a friend, and then treat the sorrow as criminal that wept, with whatever violence, as it saw the links broken and scattered, never again to be joined together?'

'That certainly is a proof that some just ideas are to be found in your opinions,' replied my friend. 'By nothing was I ever more irreconcilably offended in the stoical philosophy, than by its harsh violence towards nature under suffering. To be treated by your philosophy with rudeness and contempt, because you yield to emotions which are as natural, and, therefore, in my judgment, as innocent as any, is, as if one were struck with violence by a friend or a parent, to whom you fled for protection or comfort. The doctrines of all the others failed in the same way. Even the Epicureans hold it a weakness, and even a wrong, to grieve, seeing the injury that is thereby done to happiness. Grief must be suppressed, and banished, because it is accompanied by pain. That too, seemed to me a false sentiment; because, although grief is indeed in some sort painful, yet it is not wholly so, but is attended by a kind of pleasure. How plain it is, that I should suffer greatly more, were I forcibly restrained by a foreign power, or my own, from shedding these tears, and uttering these sighs for Gallus, than I do now while I am free to indulge my natural feelings. In truth, it is the only pleasure that grief brings with it--the freedom of indulging it.'

'He,' I said, as Marcus paused, giving way afresh to his sorrow, 'who embraces the Christian doctrine, is never blamed, condemned, or ridiculed by it for the indulgence of the emotions, to which, the loss of those whom we love, gives birth. But then, at the same time, he will probably grieve and suffer much less under such circumstances than you--not, however, because he is forcibly restrained, but because of the influence upon his mind and his heart, of truths and opinions, which, as a Christian, he entertains, and which, without any will or act of his own, work within him and strengthen and console him. The Christian believing, so firmly as he does, for example, in a God, not only on grounds of reason but of express revelation, and that this God is a parent, exercising a providence over his creatures, regardless of none, loving as a parent all, who has created mankind, not for his own amusement or honor, but that life and happiness might be diffused: they who believe thus, must feel very differently under adversity, from those who, like yourself, believe nothing of it at all, and from those who, like the disciples of the Porch and the Academy, believe but an inconsiderable part of it. Suppose, Marcus and Lucilia, your whole population of slaves were, instead of strangers and slaves, your children, toward whom you experienced the same sentiments of deep affection that you did toward Gallus, how would you not consult for their happiness; and how plain it is, that whatever laws you might set over them, they would be laws of love, the end of which, however they might not always recognize it, would be their happiness--happiness through their virtue. This may represent, with sufficient exactness, the light in which Christians regard the Divinity, and the laws of life under which they find themselves. Admitting, therefore, their faith to be well founded, and how manifest is it that they will necessarily suffer less under adversity than you; and not because any violence is done to their nature, but because of the benignant influences of such truths.'

'What you say,' observed Lucilia, 'affects the mind very agreeably; and gives a pleasing idea, both of the wisdom and mercy of the Christian faith. It seems at any rate to be suited to such creatures as we are. What a pity that it is so difficult to discern truth.'

'It is difficult,' I replied; 'the best things are always so: but it is not impossible; what is necessary to our happiness, is never so. A mind of common powers, well disposed, seeking with a real desire to find, will rarely retire from the search wholly unsuccessful. The great essentials to our daily well-being, and the right conduct of life, the Creator has supplied through our instincts. Your natural religion, of which you have spoken, you find sufficient for most of the occurrences which arise, both of doing and bearing. But there are other emergencies for which it is as evidently insufficient. Now, as the Creator has supplied so perfectly in all breasts the natural religion, which is so essential, it is fair to say and believe, that He would not make additional truths, almost equally essential to our happiness, either of impossible attainment, or encompassed by difficulties which could not, with a little diligence and perseverance, be overcome.'

'It would seem so, certainly,' said Marcus; 'but it is so long since I have bestowed any thought upon philosophical inquiries, that to me the labor would be very great, and the difficulties extreme--for, at present, there is scarcely so much as a mere shred or particle of faith, to which as a nucleus other truths may attach themselves. In truth, I never look even to possess any clear faith in a God--it seems to be a subject wholly beyond the scope and grasp of my mind. I cannot entertain the idea of self-existence. I can conceive of God neither as one, nor as divided into parts. Is he infinite and everywhere, himself constituting his universe?--then he is scarcely a God; or, is he a being dwelling apart from his works, and watching their obedience to their imposed laws? In neither of these conceptions can I rest.'

'It is not strange,' I replied; 'nor that, refusing to believe in the fact of a God until you should be able to comprehend him perfectly, you should to this hour be without faith. If I had waited before believing, until I understood, I should at this moment be as faithless as you, or as I was before I received Christianity. Do I comprehend the Deity? Can I describe the mode of his being? Can I tell you in what manner he sprang into existence? And whether he is necessarily everywhere in his works, and as it were constituting them? Or whether he has power to contract himself, and dwell apart from them, their omniscient observer, and omnipotent Lord? I know nothing of all this; the religion which I receive, teaches nothing of all this. Christianity does not demonstrate the being of a God, it simply proclaims it; hardly so much as that indeed. It supposes it, as what was already well known and generally believed. I cannot doubt that it is left thus standing by itself, untaught and unexplained, only because the subject is intrinsically incomprehensible by us. It is a great fact or truth, which all can receive, but which none can explain or prove. If it is not believed, either instinctively, or through the recognition of it, and declaration of it, in some revelation, it cannot be believed at all. It needs the mind of God to comprehend God. The mind of man is no more competent to reach and grasp the theme through reason, than his hands are to mould a sun. All the reasonings, imaginations, guesses, of self-styled philosophers, are here like the prattlings of children. They make you smile, but they do not instruct.'

'I fear,' said Marcus, 'I shall then never believe, for I can believe nothing of which I cannot form a conception.'

'Surely,' I answered, 'our faith is not bounded by our conceptions, or our knowledge, in other things. We build the loftiest palaces and temples upon foundations of stone, though we can form no conception whatever of the nature of a stone. So I think we may found a true and sufficient religion on our belief in the fact of a God, although we can form no conception whatever of his nature and the mode of his existence.'

But I should fatigue you, Fausta, were I to give you more of our conversation. It ran on equally pleasant, I believe, to all of us, to a quite late hour; in which time, almost all that is peculiar to the faith of the Christians came under our review. It was more than midnight when we rose from our seats to retire to our chambers. But before we did that, a common feeling directed our steps to the tomb of Gallus, which was but a few paces from where we had been sitting. There these childless parents again gave way to their grief and was I stone, that I should not weep with them?

When this act of duty and piety had been performed, we sought our pillows. As for me, I could not sleep for thinking of my friends and their now desolate house. For even to me, who was to that child almost a stranger, and had been so little used to his presence, this place is no longer the same: all its brightness, life, and spirit of gladness, are gone. Everything seems changed. From every place and scene something seems to have been subtracted to which they were indebted for whatever it was that made them attractive. If this is so to me, what must it be to Marcus and Lucilia? It is not difficult to see that a sorrow has settled upon their hearts, which no length of time can heal. I suppose if all their estates had been swept away from them in a night, and all their friends, they would not have been so overwhelmed as by this calamity--in such a wonderful manner were they each woven into the child, and all into each other, as one being. They seem no longer to me like the same persons. Not that they are not often calm, and in a manner possessed of themselves; but that even then, when they are most themselves, there has a dulness, a dreamy absence of mind, a fixed sadness, come over them that wholly changes them. Though they sit and converse with you, their true thoughts seem far away. They are kind and courteous as ever, to the common eye, but I can see that all the relish of life and of intercourse is now to them gone. All is flat and insipid. The friend is coldly saluted; the meal left untasted, or partaken in silence and soon abandoned; the affairs of the household left to others, to any who will take charge of them. They tell me that this will always be so; that however they may seem to others, they must ever experience a sense of loss; not any less than they would if a limb had been shorn away. A part of themselves, and of the life of every day and hour, is taken from them.

How strange is all this, even in the light of Christian faith! How inexplicable, we are ready to say, by any reason of ours, the providence of God in taking away the human being in the first blossoming; before the fruit has even shown itself, much less ripened! Yet is not immortality, the hope, the assurance of immortality, a sufficient solution? To me it is. This will not indeed cure our sorrows--they spring from somewhat wholly independent of futurity, of either the hope, or despair of it,--but it vindicates the ways of the Omnipotent, and justifies them to our reason and our affections. Will Marcus and Lucilia ever rejoice in the consolations which flow from this hope? Alas! I fear not. They seem in a manner to be incapable of belief.

In the morning I shall start for Rome. As soon as there, you shall hear from me again. Farewell.

* * * * *

While Piso was absent from Rome on this visit to his friend, it was my fortune to be several times in the city upon necessary affairs of the illustrious Queen, when I was both at the palace of Aurelian and that of Piso. It was at one of these later visits, that it became apparent to me, that the Emperor seriously meditated the imposing of restrictions of some kind upon the Christians; yet no such purpose was generally apprehended by that sect itself, nor by the people at large. The dark and disastrous occurrences on the day of the dedication, were variously interpreted by the people; some believing them to point at the Christians, some at the meditated expedition of the Emperor, some at Aurelian himself. The popular mind was, however, greatly inflamed against the Christians, and every art was resorted to by the priests of the temples, and those who were as bigoted and savage as themselves among the people, to fan to a devouring flame the little fire that began to be kindled. The voice from the temple, however some might with Fronto himself doubt whether it were not from Heaven, was for the most part ascribed to the Christians, although they could give no explanation of the manner in which it had been produced. But, as in the case of Aurelian himself, this was forgotten in the horror occasioned by the more dreadful language of the omens, which, in such black and threatening array, no one remembered ever to have been witnessed before. None thought or talked of anything else. It was the universal theme.

This may be seen in a conversation which I had with a rustic, whom I overtook as I rode toward Rome, seated on his mule, burdened on either side and behind with the multifarious produce of his farm. The fellow, as I drew near to him, seeming of a less churlish disposition than most of those whom one meets upon the road, who will scarcely return a friendly salute, I feared not to accost him. After giving him the customary good wishes, I remarked upon the excellence of the vegetables which he had in his panniers.

'Yes,' he said, 'these lettuces are good, but not what they would have been but for the winds we have had from the mountains. It has sadly nipped them. I hear the Queen pines away just as my plants do. I live at Norentum. I know you, sir, though you cannot know me. You pass by my door on your way to the city. My children often call me from my work to look up, for there goes the secretary of the good Queen on his great horse. There's no such horse as that on the road. Ha, ha, my baskets reach but to your knee! Well, there are differences in animals and in men too. So the gods will it. One rides upon a horse with golden bits, another upon a mule with none at all. Still I say, let the gods be praised.'

'The gods themselves could hardly help such differences,' I said, 'if they made one man of more natural strength, or more natural understanding than another. In that case one would get more than another. And surely you would not have men all run in one mould--all five feet high, all weighing so much, all with one face, and one form, one heart, and one head! The world were then dull enough.'

'You say true,' he replied; 'that is very good. If we were all alike, there would be no such thing as being rich or poor--no such thing as getting or losing. I fear it would be dull enough, as you say. But I did not mean to complain, sir. I believe I am contented with my lot. So long as I can have my little farm, with my garden and barns, my cattle and my poultry, a kind neighbor or so, and my priest and temple, I care for nothing more.'

'You have a temple then at Norentum?'

'Yes, to Jupiter Pluvius. And a better priest has not Rome itself. It is his brother, some officer of the Emperor's, I take these vegetables to. I hope to hear more this morning of what I heard something when I was last at market. And I think I shall, for, as I learn, the city is a good deal stirred since the dedication the other day.' 'I believe it is,' I answered. 'But of what do you look to hear, if I may ask? Is there news from the East?'

'O no, I think not of the East or the South. It was of something to be done about these Christians. Our temple, you must know, is half forsaken and more, of late. I believe that half the people of Norentum, if the truth were known, have turned Christians or Jews. Unless we wake up a little, our worship cannot be supported, and our religion will be gone. And glad am I to hear, through our priest, that even the Emperor is alarmed, and believes something must be done. You know, than he, there is not a more devout man in Rome. So it is said. And one thing that makes me think so, is this. The brother of our priest, where I am going with these vegetables--here is poultry too, look! you never saw fatter, I warrant you--told him that he knew it for certain, that the Emperor meant to make short work with even his own niece--you know who I mean--Aurelia, who has long been suspected to be a Christian. And that's right. If he punishes any, he ought not to spare his own.'

'That I suppose would be right. But why should he punish any? You need not be alarmed or offended; I am no Christian.'

'The gods be praised therefor! I do not pretend to know the whole reason why. But that seems to be the only way of saving the old religion; and I don't know what way you can possibly have of showing that a religion of yesterday is true, if a religion of a thousand years old is to be made out false. If religion is good for anything--and I for one think it is--I think men ought to be compelled to have it and support it, just as they should be to eat wholesome food, rather than poisonous or hurtful. The laws won't permit us to carry certain things to market, nor others in a certain state. If we do, we are fined or imprisoned. Treat a Christian in the same way, say I. Let them just go thoroughly to work, and our temples will soon be filled again.'

'But these Christians,' I observed, 'seem to be a harmless people.'

'But they have no religion, that anybody can call such. They have no gods, nor altars, nor sacrifices; such can never be harmless. To be sure, as to sacrifices, I think there is such a thing as doing too much. I am not for human sacrifices. Nor do I see the need of burning up a dozen fat oxen or heifers, as was done the other day at the Temple of the Sun. We in Norentum burn nothing but the hoofs and some of the entrails, and the rest goes to the priest for his support. As I take it, a sacrifice is just a sign of readiness to do everything and lose everything for the gods. We are not expected to throw either ourselves, or our whole substance upon the altar; making the sign is sufficient. But, as I said, these Christians have no altar and no sacrifice, nor image of god or goddess. They have, at Norentum, an old ruinous building-- once a market--where they meet for worship; but those who have been present say, that nothing is to be seen; and nothing heard but prayers--to what god no one knows--and exhortations of the priests. Some say, that elsewhere they have what they call an altar, and adorn their walls with pictures and statues. However all this may be, there seems to be some charm about them, or their worship, for all the world is running after them. I long for the news I shall get from Varenus Hirtius. If these omens have not set the Emperor at work for us, nothing will. Here we are at the gates, and I turn toward the Claudian market. May the day go happily with you.'

So we parted; and I bent my way toward the gardens of Sallust.

As I moved slowly along through the streets, my heart was filled with pity for this people, the Christians; threatened, as it seemed to me, with a renewal of the calamities that had so many times swept over them before. They had ever impressed me as a simple-minded, virtuous community, of notions too subtle for the world ever to receive, but which, upon themselves, appeared to exert a power altogether beneficial. Many of this faith I had known well, and they were persons to excite my highest admiration for the characters which they bore. Need I name more than the princess Julia, and her husband, the excellent Piso? Others like them, what wonder if inferior! had also, both in Palmyra, and at Tibur and Rome--for they were to be found everywhere--drawn largely both on my respect and my affections. I beheld with sorrow the signs which now seemed to portend suffering and disaster. And my sympathies were the more moved seeing that never before had there been upon the throne a man who, if he were once entered into a war of opposition against them, had power to do them greater harm, or could have proved a more stern and cruel enemy. Not even Nero or Domitian were in their time to be so much dreaded. For if Aurelian should once league him with the state against them, it would not with him be matter of mere cruel sport, but of conscience. It would be for the honor of the gods, the protection of religion, the greatness and glory of the empire, that he would assail and punish them; and the same fierce and bloody spirit that made him of all modern conquerors the bloodiest and fiercest, it was plain would rule him in any encounter with this humble and defenceless tribe. I could only hope that I was deceived, as well as others, in my apprehensions, or, if that were not so, pray that the gods would be pleased to take their great subject to themselves.

Full of such reflections and emotions I arrived at the palace, and was ushered into the presence of Livia. There was with her the melancholy Aurelia--for such she always seems--who appeared to have been engaged in earnest talk with the Empress, if one might judge by tears fast falling from her eyes. The only words which I caught as I entered were these from Aurelia, 'but, dear lady, if Mucapor require it not, why should others think of it so much? Were he fixed, then should I indeed have to ask strength of God for the trial--' then, seeing me, and only receiving my salutations, she withdrew.

Livia, after first inquiring concerning Zenobia and Faustula, returning to what had just engaged her, said,

'I wish, good Nicomachus, that I had your powers of speech, of which, as you can remember, I have been witness in former days--those happy days in Syria--when you used, so successfully, to withstand and subdue my giddy or headstrong mind. Here have I been for weary hours--not weary neither, for their aim has, I am sure, been a worthy one--but, here have I been persuading, with all the reason and eloquence I could bring to bear, this self-willed girl to renounce these fantastic notions she has imbibed from the Christians, and their books, were it only for the sake of domestic peace. Aurelian is growing daily more and more exasperated against this obscure tribe, and drops, oftener than I love to hear them, dark hints of what awaits them, not excepting, he says, any of whatever rank or name. Not that I suppose that either he, or the senate, would proceed further than imprisonments, banishment, suppression of free speech, the destruction of books and churches; so much indeed I understand from him. But even thus far, and we might lose Aurelia--a thing not to be thought of for a moment. He has talked with her himself, reasoned with her, threatened her; but in vain. Now he has imposed the same task upon me--it is equally in vain. I know not what to do.'

'Because,' I replied, 'nothing can be done. Where it is possible to see, you have eyes within you that can penetrate the thickest darkness as well as any. But here you fail; but only where none could succeed. A sincere honest mind, princess, is not to be changed either by persuasion or force. Its belief is not subject to the will. Aurelia, if I have heard aright, is a Christian from conviction. Evidence made her a Christian--stronger evidence on the side of her former faith can alone unmake her.'

'I cannot reason with her to that extent, Nicomachus,' replied the Empress. 'I know not the grounds of the common faith, any more than those of Christianity. I only know that I wish Aurelia was not a Christian. Will you, Nicomachus, reason with her? I remember your logic of old.'

'Alas, princess, I can engage in no such task! Where I have no faith myself, I should in vain attempt to plant it in others. How, either, can I desire that any mind should remain an hour longer oppressed by the childish and abominable superstitions which prevail in Rome? I cannot but congratulate the excellent Aurelia, so far as the question of truth is concerned, that in the place of the infinite stupidities of the common religion, she has received the, at least, pure and reasonable doctrines of the Christians. You cannot surely, princess, desire her re-conversion?'

'Only for her own sake, for the sake of her safety, comfort, happiness.'

'But in her judgment these are best and only secured where she now is. How thinks Mucapor?'

'As I believe,' answered Livia, 'he cares not in the matter, save for her happiness. He will not wish that she should have any faith except such as she herself wishes. I have urged him to use his power to constrain her, but he loves liberty himself too dearly, he says, to put force upon another.'

'That is right and noble,' I said; 'it is what I should have looked for from

Mucapor.'

'In good sooth, Nicomachus, I believe you still take me but for what I was in Palmyra. Who am I?'

'From a princess you have become an Empress, Empress of Rome, that I fully understand, and I trust never to be wanting in the demeanor that best becomes a subject; but you are still Livia, the daughter of Zenobia, and to her I feel I can never fear to speak with sincerity.'

'How omnipotent, Nicomachus, are simplicity and truth! They subdue me when I most would not. They have conquered me in Aurelia and now in you. Well, well, Aurelia then must take the full weight of her uncle's wrath, which is not light.'

At this moment Aurelian himself entered, accompanied by Fronto. Livia, at the same time, arose and withdrew, not caring, I thought, to meet the eyes of that basilisk, who, with the cunning of a priest, she saw to be usurping a power over Aurelian which belonged of right to her. I was about also to withdraw, but the Emperor constraining me, as he often does, I remained, although holding the priest in still greater abhorrence, I believe, than Livia herself.

'While you have been absent from the city, Fronto,' said Aurelian, 'I have revolved the subjects upon which we last conversed, and no longer doubt where lie, for me, both duty, and the truest glory. The judgment of the colleges, lately rendered, agrees both with yours and mine. So that the very finger of the god we worship points the way.'

'I am glad,' replied Fronto, 'for myself, for you, for Rome, and for the world, that truth possesses and is to sway you. It will be a great day for Rome, greater than when your triumphal array swept through the streets with the world at your chariot-wheels, when the enemy that had so long waged successful war within the very gates, shall lie dead as the multitudes of Palmyra.'

'It will, Fronto. But first I have this to say, and, by the gods, I believe it true, that it is the corruptions of our own religion and its ministers, that is the offence that smells to heaven, quite as much as the presumptuous novelties of this of Judea. I perceive you neither assent to this nor like it. But it is true, I am persuaded, as the gods themselves. I have long thought so; and, while with one hand, I aim at the Gallilean atheism, with the other, I shall aim at those who dishonor, by their vices and hypocrisies, the religion they profess to serve.'

Fronto was evidently disturbed. His face grew pale as the frown gathered and darkened on the brow of Aurelian. He answered not, and Aurelian went on.

'Hellenism, Fronto, is disgraced, and its very life threatened by the vices of her chief ministers. The gods forgive me! in that, while I have purged my legions of drunkards and adulterers, I have left them in the temples. Truly did you say, I have had but one thought in my mind, I have looked but to one quarter of the heavens. My eyes are now unsealed, and I see both ways, and every way. How can we look for the favor of the gods, while their houses of worship, I speak it, Fronto, with sorrow and indignation, but with the knowledge too of the truth of what I say, are houses of appointment while the very inner sanctuaries, and the altars themselves, are little better than the common stews, while the priests are the great fathers of iniquity, corrupters of innocence, the seducers of youth, examples themselves, beyond the fear of rivalry, of all the vice they teach! At their tables, too, who so swollen with meats and drink as the priests? Who, but they, are a by-word, throughout the city, for all that is vilest? What word but priest, stands, with all, as an abbreviation and epitome, of whatever pollutes, and defiles the name of man? Porphyrius says 'that since Jesus has been worshipped in Rome no one has found by experience the public assistance of the gods.' I believe it; and Rome will never again experience it till this black atheism is rooted out. But it is as true, I doubt not, that since their ministers have become ministers of demons, and, from teachers of morals, have turned instructers in vice--for this reason too, as well as for the other, the justly offended deities of Rome have hid themselves from their impious worshippers. Here then, Fronto, is a double labor to be undergone, a double duty to be done, not less than some or all of the labors of Hercules. We are set for this work, and, not till I have begun it--if not finished--will I so much as dream of Persia. What say you?'

Fronto looked like one who had kindled a larger flame than he intended, or knew well how to manage.

'The faults of which you speak, great Emperor, it can be denied by none, are found in Rome, and can never be other than displeasing to the gods. But then, I would ask, when was it ever otherwise? In the earlier ages of the republic, I grant, there was a virtue in the people which we see not now. But that grew not out of the purer administration of religion, but was the product of the times in part--times, in comparison with these, of a primeval simplicity. To live well, was easier then. Where no temptation is, virtue is easy, is necessary. But then it ceases to be virtue. It is a quality, not an acquisition--a gift of the gods, an accident, rather than man's meritorious work.'

'That is very true--well.'

'There may be as much real virtue now, as then. May it not be so?'

'Perhaps--it may. What then?'

'Our complaints of the present, should be softened. But, what chiefly I would urge is this, that since those ages of early virtue--after all, perhaps, like all else at the same period, partly fabulous--Rome has been but what it is, adorned by virtues that have claimed the admiration of the world, and polluted by vices that have drawn upon her the reprobation of the good, yet, which are but such as the world shows its surface over, from the farthest India, to the bleak wastes of Britain. It is, Aurelian, a thing neither strange nor new that vices thrive in Rome. And, long since, have there been those, like Nerva and the good Severus, and the late censor Valerian, who have aimed at their correction. These, and others who, before and since, have wrought in the same work, have done well for the empire. Their aim has been a high one, and the favor of the gods has been theirs. Aurelian may do more and better in the same work, seeing his power is greater and his piety more zealous.'

'These are admitted truths, Fronto, save the last; but whither do they tend?'

'To this. Because, Aurelian, vice has been in Rome; because even the priesthood has been corrupt, and the temples themselves the sties you say they now are--for this, have the gods ever withdrawn their protection? Has Rome ever been the less prosperous? What is more, can we conceive that they who made us of their own fiery mould, so prone to violate the bounds of moderation, would, for yielding to such instincts, interpose in wrath, as if that had happened which was not foreseen, and against which, they had made sure provision? Are the heavens to blaze with the fires of the last day, thunders to roll as if earth were shaken to her centre, the entrails of dumb beasts to utter forth terrific prophecy of great and impending wo, because, forsooth, the people of Rome are by no means patterns of purity--because, perchance, within the temples themselves, an immorality may have been purposed, or perpetrated--because, even the priests themselves have not been, or are not, white and spotless as their robes?'

'There seems some reason in what you say.'

'But, great Emperor, take me not as if I would make myself the shield of vice, to hide it from the blow that would extirpate or cure it. I see, and bewail, the corruptions of the age; but, as they seem not fouler than those of ages which are past, especially than those of Nero and of Commodus, I cannot think that it is against these the gods have armed themselves, but, Aurelian, against an evil which has been long growing, and often assailed and checked, but which has now got to such giant size and strength, that except it be absolutely hewn down, and the least roots torn up and burned, both the altars of our gods, and their capital, called Eternal, and the empire itself, now holding the world in its wide-spread, peace-giving arms, are vanished, and anarchy, impiety, atheism, and the rank vices, which in such times would be engendered, will then reign omnipotent, and fill the very compass of the earth, Christ being the universal king! It is against this the heavens have arrayed their power; and to arouse an ungrateful, thoughtless, impious people, with their sleeping king, that they have spoken in thunder.'

'Fronto, I almost believe you right.'

'Had we, Aurelian, but the eyes of moles, when the purposes of the gods are to be deciphered in the character of events, we should long since have seen that the series of disasters which have befallen the empire since the Gallilean atheism has taken root here, have pointed but to that--that they have been a chastisement of our supineness and sloth. When did Rome, almighty Rome, ever before tremble at the name of barbarian, or fly before their arms? While now, is it not much that we are able to keep them from the very walls of the

Capital? They now swarm the German forests in multitudes, which no man can count; their hoarse murmurs can be heard even here, ready, soon as the reins of empire shall fall into the hands of another Gallienus, to pour themselves upon the plains of Italy, changing our fertile lands and gorgeous cities into another Dacia. These things were not so once; and what cause there is in Rome, so deep, and high, and broad, to resolve for us the reason of this averted face of heaven, save that of which I speak, I cannot guess.'

'Nor I,' said Aurelian; 'I confess it. It must be so My work is not three, nor two; but one. I have brought peace to the empire in all its borders. My legions all rest upon their arms. Not a sword, but is in its sheath--there, for the present, let it be glued fast. The season, so propitious for the great work of bringing again the empire into peace and harmony with the angry gods, seems to have been provided by themselves. How think you, Nicomachus?'--turning suddenly to me, as if now, for the first time, aware that I was standing at his side.

I answered, 'that I was slow to receive the judgment of Fronto or of himself in that matter. That I could not believe that the gods, who should be examples of the virtues to mankind, would ever ordain such sufferings for their creatures as must ensue, were the former violences to be renewed against the Christians. So far from thinking them a nuisance in the state, I considered them a benefit.'

'The Greek too,' said Fronto, breaking in, 'is then a Christian.'

'I am not a Christian, priest, nor, as I think, shall ever be one; but, far sooner would I be one, than take my faith from thee, which, however it might guide me well through the wine vaults of the temple, or to the best stalls of the market, or to the selectest retreats of the suburra, would scarce show the way to heaven. I affront but the corruptions of religion, Aurelian. Sincerity I honor everywhere. Hypocrisy nowhere.' I thought Fronto would have torn me with his teeth and nails. His white face grew whiter, but he stood still.

'Say on,' said the Emperor, 'though your bluntness be more even than Roman.'

'I think,' I continued, 'the Christians a benefit to the state, for this reason;

not that their religion is what they pretend, a heaven-descended one, but that, by its greater strictness, it serves to rebuke the common faith and those who hold it, and infuse into it something of its own spirit. All new systems, as I take it, in their first beginning are strict and severe. It is thus by this quality they supersede older and degenerate ones; not because they are truer, but because they are purer. There is a prejudice among men, that the gods, whoever they may be, and whatever they may be, love virtue in men, and for that accept them. When, therefore, a religion fails to recommend and enforce virtue, it fails to meet the judgment of men concerning the true character and office of a religion, and so with the exception of such beasts, and such there always are, who esteem a faith in proportion to its corruptions, they look with favor upon any new one which promises to be what they want. It is for this reason that this religion from Judea has made its way so far and so soon. But, it will, by and by, degenerate from its high estate, just as others have done, and be succeeded by another that shall raise still higher expectations. In the meantime, it serves the state well, both by the virtue which it enjoins upon its own subjects, and the influence it exerts, by indirection, upon those of the prevalent faiths, and upon the general manners and morals.'

'What you say,' observed Aurelian musingly, 'has some show of sense. So much, at least, may be said for this religion.'

'Yet a lie,' said Fronto, 'can be none the less hateful to the gods, because it sometime plays the part of truth. It is a lie still.'

'Hold,' said Aurelian, 'let us hear the Greek. What else?'

'I little thought,' I replied, 'as I rode toward the city this morning, that I should at this hour be standing in the presence of the Emperor of Rome, a defender of the Christians. I am in no manner whatever fitted for the task. My knowledge is nothing; my opinions, therefore, worth but little, grounded as they are upon the loose reports which reach my ear concerning the character and doctrines of this sect, or upon what little observation I have made upon those whom I have known of that persuasion. Still, I honor and esteem them, and such aid as I can bring them in their straits, shall be very gladly theirs. I will, however, add one thing more to what I have said in answer to Fronto, who represents the gods as more concerned to destroy the Christians than to reform the common religion and the public morals. I cannot think that. Am I to believe that the gods, the supreme directors of human affairs, whose aim must be man's highest well-being, regard with more abhorrence an error than a vice?--an error too that acts more beneficently than most truth, and is the very seed of the purest virtues? I can by no means believe it. So that if I were interpreter of the late omens, I should rather see them pointed at the vices which prevail; at the corruptions of the public morals, which are fouler than aught I had so much as dreamed of before I was myself a witness of them, and may well be supposed to startle the gods from their rest, and draw down their hottest thunderbolts. But I will not say more, when there must be so many able to do so much better in behalf of what I must still believe to be a good cause. Let me entreat the Emperor, before he condemns, to hear. There are those in Rome, of warm hearts, sound heads, and honest souls, from whom, if from any on earth, truth may be heard, and who will set in its just light a doctrine too excellent to suffer, as it must, in my hands.'

'They shall be heard, Nicomachus. Not even a Jew or a Christian shall suffer without that grace; though I see not how it can avail.'

'If it should not avail to plant in your mind so good an opinion of their way as exists in mine,' I resumed, 'it might yet to soften it, and dispose it to a more lenient conduct; and so many are the miseries of life in the natural order of events, that the humane heart must desire to diminish, not increase them. Has Aurelian ever heard the name of Probus the Christian?'

The Emperor turned toward Fronto with a look of inquiry.

'Yes,' said the priest, 'you have heard his name. But that of Felix, the bishop of the Christians, as he is called, is more familiar to you.'

'Felix, Felix, that is the name I have heard most, but Probus too, if I err not.'

'He has been named to you, I am certain,' added Fronto. 'He is the real head of the Nazarenes,--the bishop, but a painted one.'

'Probus is he who turned young Piso's head. Is it not so?'

'The very same; and beside his, the lady Julia's.'

'No, that was by another, one Paul of Antioch, also a bishop and a fast friend of the Queen. The Christians themselves have of late set upon him, as they were so many blood-hounds, being bent upon expelling him from Antioch. It is not long since, in accordance with the decree of some assembled bishops there, I issued a rescript dislodging him from his post, and planting in his place one Domnus. If our purposes prosper, the ejected and dishonored priest may find himself at least safer if humbler. Probus,--I shall remember him. The name leads my thoughts to Thrace, where our greater Probus waits for me.'

'From Probus the Christian,' I said, 'you will receive,' whenever you shall admit him to your presence, a true account of the nature of the Christians' faith and of the actual condition of their community--all which, can be had only from a member of it.'

But little more was said, when I departed, and took my way again towards Tibur.

It seemed to me, from the manner of the Emperor more than from what he said, that he was settled and bound up to the bad work of an assault upon the Christians. To what extent it was in his mind to go, I could not judge; for his language was ambiguous, and sometimes contradictory. But that the darkest designs were harbored by him, over which he was brooding with a mind naturally superstitious, but now almost in a state of exasperation, from the late events, was most evident.

LETTER VI.

FROM PISO TO FAUSTA.

Having confined myself, in my last letter, to the affairs of Marcus and Lucilia, I now, Fausta, turn to those which concern us and Rome.

I found, on my return to the city, that the general anxiety concerning the designs of Aurelian had greatly increased. Many rumors were current of dark sayings of his, which, whether founded in truth or not, contributed to alarm even the most hopeful, and raise serious apprehensions for the fate of this much and long-suffering religion. Julia herself partakes--I cannot say of the alarm--but of the anxiety. She has less confidence than I have in the humanity of the Emperor. In the honours heaped upon Zenobia, and the favors shown herself and Vabalathus, she sees, not so much the outpouring of benevolent feeling, as a rather ostentatious display of imperial generosity, and, what is called, Roman magnanimity. For the true character of the man she looks into the graves of Palmyra, upon her smoking ruins, and upon the blood, yet hardly dry, that stains the pavements of the Coelian. Julia may be right, though I am unwilling to believe it. Her judgment is entitled to the more weight in this severe decision, that it is ever inclined to the side of a too favorable opinion of character and motive. You know her nature too well, to believe her capable of exaggerating the faults of even the humblest. Yet, though such are her apprehensions, she manifests the same calm and even carriage as on the approach of more serious troubles in Palmyra. She is full of deepest interest in the affairs of the Christians, and by many families of the poorer sort is resorted to continually for aid, for counsel, or sympathy. Not one in the whole community is a more frequent and devout attendant upon the services of the church; and, I need not add, that I am her constant companion. The performance of this duty gives a value to life in Rome such as it never had before. Every seventh day, as with the Jews, only upon a different day of the week, do the Christians assemble for the purposes of religious worship. And, I can assure you, it is with no trifling accession of strength for patient doing and patient bearing, that we return to our every-day affairs, after having listened to the prayers, the reasonings, or exhortations of Probus.

So great is the difference in my feelings and opinions from what they were before I left Rome for Palmyra, that it is with difficulty I persuade myself that I am the same person. Between Piso the Pyrronist and Piso the Christian, the distance seems immeasurable--yet in how short a time has it been past. I cannot say that I did not enjoy existence and value it in my former state, but I can say that my enjoyment of it is infinitely heightened as a Christian, and the rate at which I value it infinitely raised. Born and nurtured as I was, with Portia for my mother, a palace for my home, Rome for my country and capital, offering all the luxuries of the earth, and affording all the means I could desire for carrying on researches in study of every kind, surrounded by friends of the noblest and best families in the city,--I could not but enjoy life in some very important sense. While mere youth lasted, and my thoughts never wandered beyond the glittering forms of things, no one could be happier or more contented. All was fair and beautiful around me--what could I ask for more? I was satisfied and filled. But, by and by, my dream of life was disturbed--my sleep broken. Natural questions began to propose themselves for my solution, such, I suppose, as, sooner or later, spring up in every bosom. I began to speculate about myself--about the very self that had been so long, so busy, about everything else beside itself. I wished to know something of myself--of my origin, my nature, my present condition, my ultimate fate. It seemed to me I was too rare and curious a piece of work to go to ruin, final and inevitable--perhaps to-morrow--at all events in a very few years. Of futurity I had heard--and of Elysium--just as I had heard of Jupiter, greatest and best, but, with my earliest youth, these things had faded from my mind, or had already taken upon themselves the character of fable. My Virgil, in which I early received my lessons of language, at once divested them of all their air of reality, and left them naked fiction. The other poets, Livy helping them, continued the same work and completed it. But, bent with most serious and earnest desires toward truth on what seemed to me the greatest theme, I could not remain where I was, and turned with highest expectations to the philosophers. I not only read, but I studied and pondered them with diligence, and with as sincere a desire of arriving at truth as ever scholar sat at the feet of his instructer. The result was anything but satisfying, I ended a universal sceptic, so far as human systems of philosophy were concerned, so far as they pretended to solve the enigma of God and man, of life and death; but with a heart, nevertheless, yearning after truth; and even full of faith, if that may be called faith which would instinctively lay hold upon a God and a hope of immortality; and, though beaten back once and again, by every form which the syllogism could assume, still keep its hold.

This was my state, Fausta, when I was found by Christianity. Without faith, and yet with it; doubting, and yet believing; rejecting philosophy, but leaning upon nature; dissatisfied, but hoping. I cannot easily find words to tell you the change which Christian faith has wrought within me. All I can say is this, that I am now a new man; I am made over again; I am born as it were into another world. Where darkness once was, there is now light brighter than the sun. Where doubt was, there is now certainty. I have knowledge and truth, for error and perplexity. The inner world of my mind is resplendent with a day whose luminary will never set. And even the outer world of appearances and forms shines more gloriously, and has an air of reality which before it never had. It used to seem to me like the gorgeous fabric of a dream, and as if, at some unexpected moment, it might melt into air and nothingness, and I, and all men and things, with it; for there appeared to be no purpose in it; it came from nothing, it achieved nothing, and certainly seemed to conduct to nothing. Men, like insects, came and went; were born, and died, and that was all. Nothing was accomplished, nothing perfected. But now, nature seems to me stable, and eternal as God himself. The world being the great birth-place and nursery of these myriads of creatures, made, as I ever conceived, in a divine likeness, after some godlike model,--for what spirit of other spheres can be more beautiful than a perfect man, or a perfect woman--each animated with the principle of immortality--there is a reason for its existence, and its perpetuity, from whose force the mind cannot escape. It is, and it ever will be; and mankind upon it, a continually happier, and more virtuous brotherhood.

Yes, Fausta, to me as a Christian, everything is new everything better; the inward world, the outward world, the present, and the future. Life is a worthier gift, and a richer possession. I am to myself an object of a thousand-fold greater interest; and every other human being, from a poor animal, that was scarce worthy its wretched existence, starts up into a god, for whom the whole earth may, one day, become too narrow a field either to till, or rule. I am, accordingly, ready to labor both for myself and others. I once held myself too cheap to do much even for myself; for others, I would do nothing, except to feed the hunger that directly appealed to me, or relieve the wretchedness that made me equally wretched. Not so now. I myself am a different being, and others are different. I am ready to toil for such beings; to suffer for them. They are too valuable to be neglected, abused, insulted, trodden into the dust. They must be defended and rescued, whenever their fellow-men--wholly ignorant of what they are, and what themselves are about--would oppress them. More than all, do they need truth, effectually to enlighten and redeem them, and truth they must have at whatever cost. Let them only once know what they are, and the world is safe. Christianity tells them this, and Christianity they must have. The State must not stand between man and truth! or, if it do, it must be rebuked by those who have the knowledge and the courage, and made to assume its proper place and office. Knowing what has been done for me by Christian truth, I can never be content until to others the same good is at least offered; and I shall devote what power and means I possess to this task. The prospect now is of opposition and conflict.

But it dismays not me, nor Julia, nor any of this faith who have truly adopted its principles. For, if the mere love of fame, the excitement of a contest, the prospect of pay or plunder, will carry innumerable legions to the battle-field to leave there their bones, how much more shall the belief of a Christian arm him for even worse encounters? It were pitiful indeed, if a possession, as valuable as this of truth, could not inspire a heroism, which the love of fame or of money can.

These things I have said, to put you fully in possession of our present position, plans, and purposes. The fate of Christianity is to us now as absorbing an interest, as once was the fate of Palmyra.

* * * * *

I had been in the city only long enough to give Julia a full account of my melancholy visit in the country, and to write a part of it to you, when I walked forth to observe for myself the signs which the city might offer, either to confirm, or allay, the apprehensions which were begun to be felt.

I took my way over the Palatine, desiring to see the excellent Tacitus, whose house is there. He was absent, being suddenly called to Baiæ. I turned toward the Forum, wishing to perform a commission for Julia at the shop of Civilis--still alive, and still compounding his sweets--which is now about midway between the slope of the hill and the Forum, having been removed from its former place where you knew it, under the eaves of the Temple of Peace. The little man of 'smells' was at his post, more crooked than ever, but none the less exquisitely arrayed; his wig befitting a young Bacchus, rather than a dried shred of a man beyond his seventieth year. All the gems of the east glittered on his thin fingers, and diamonds, that might move the envy of Livia, hung from his ears. The gales of Arabia, burdened with the fragrance of every flower of that sunny clime, seemed concentrated into an atmosphere around him; and, in truth, I suppose a specimen of every pot and phial of his vast shop, might be found upon his person concealed in gold boxes, or hanging in the merest fragments of bottles upon chains of silver or gold, or deposited in folds of his ample robes. He was odor in substantial form. He saluted me with a grace, of which he only in Rome is master, and with a deference that could not have been exceeded had I been Aurelian. I told him that I wished to procure a perfume of Egyptian origin and name, called Cleopatra's tears, which was reputed to convey to the organs of smell, an odor more exquisite than that of the rarest Persian rose, or choicest gums of Arabia. The eyes of Civilis kindled with the fires of twenty--when love's anxious brow is suddenly cleared up by that little, but all comprehensive word, yes--as he answered,

'Noble Piso, I honor you. I never doubted your taste. It is seen in your palace, in your dress, nay, in the very costume of your incomparable slave, who has done me the honor to call here in your service. But now have you given of it the last and highest proof. Never has the wit of man before compounded an essence like that which lies buried in this porphyry vase.'

'You do not mean that I am to take away a vase of that size? I do not purchase essences by the pound!'

Civilis seemed as if he would have fainted, so oppressed was he by this display of ignorance. My character, I found, was annihilated in a moment. When his presence of mind was recovered, he said,

'This vase? Great Jupiter! The price of your palace upon the Coelian would scarce purchase it! Were its contents suddenly let loose, and spilled upon the air, not Rome only, but Italy, would be bathed in the transporting, life-giving fragrance! Now I shall remove the cover, first giving you to know, that within this larger vase there is a number of smallest bottles, some of glass, others of gold, in each of which are contained a few of the tears, and which are warranted to retain their potency, and lend their celestial peculiarity to your clothes or your apartments, without loss or diminution in the least appreciable degree, during the life of the purchaser. Now, if it please you, bend this way, and receive the air which I shall presently set free. How think you, noble Piso? Art not a new man?

'I am new in my knowledge such as it is Civilis. It is certainly agreeable, most agreeable.'

'Agreeable! So is mount Etna a pretty hill! So is Aurelian a fair soldier! so is the sun a good sized brazier! I beseech thee, find another word. Let it not go forth to all Rome, that the most noble Piso deems the tears of Cleopatra agreeable!'

'I can think no otherwise,' I replied. 'It is really agreeable, and reminds me, more than anything else, of the oldest Falernian, just rubbed between the palms of the hand, which you will allow is to compliment it in no moderate measure. But confess now, Civilis, that you have an hundred perfumes more delicious than this.'

'Piso, I may say this,--they have been so.'

'Ah, I understand you; you admit then, that it is the force of fashion that lends this extraordinary odor to the porphyry vase.'

'Truly, noble Piso, it has somewhat to do with it, it must be acknowledged.'

'It would be curious, Civilis, to know what name this bore, and in what case it was bestowed, and at what price sold, before the Empress Livia fancied it. I think it should have been named, 'Livia's smiles.' It would, at any rate, be a good name for it at thy shop in Alexandria.'

'You are facetious, noble Piso. But that last hint is too good to be thrown away. Truly, you are a man of the world, whose distinction I suppose is, that he has eyes in the hind part of his head, as well as before. But what blame can be mine for such dealing? I am driven; I am a slave. It is fashion, that works these wonders, not I. And there is no goddess, Piso, like her. She is the true creator. Upon that which is worthless, can she bestow, in a moment, inestimable value. What is despised to-day, she can exalt to-morrow to the very pinnacle of honor. She is my maker. One day I was poor, the goddess took me by the hand, and smiled upon me, and the next day I was rich. It was the favorite mistress of Maximin, who, one day--her chariot, Piso, so chance would have it, broke down at my door, when she took refuge in my little shop, then at the corner of the street Castor as you turn towards the Tiber--purchasing a particular perfume, of which I had large store, and boasted much to her, gave me such currency among the rich and noble, that, from that hour, my fortune was secure. No one bought a perfume afterwards but of Civilis. Civilis was soon the next person to the Emperor. And, to this hour, has this same goddess befriended me. And many an old jar, packed away in the midst of rubbish in dark recesses now valueless, do I look upon as nevertheless so much gold--its now despised contents one day to disperse themselves upon kings and nobles, in the senate and the theatres. I need not tell you what this diminutive bottle might have been had for, before the Kalends. Yet, by Hercules, should I have sold it even then for less? for should I not have divined its fortune? The wheel is ever turning, turning. But, most excellent Piso, men of the world are ever generous--'

'Fear nothing, Civilis, I will not betray you. I believe you have spoken real truths. Besides, with Livia on your side, and what could all Rome do to hurt you?'

'Most true, most true. But, may I ask--for one thing has made me astonished--how is it that you, being now, as report goes, a Christian, should come to me to purchase essences? When I heard you had so named yourself, I looked to lose your custom forever after.'

'Why should not a Christian man smell of that which is agreeable, as well as another?'

'Ah, that I cannot say. I have heard--I know nothing, Piso, beyond essences and perfumes--but, I have heard, that the Christians forbear such things, calling them vanities; just as they withdraw too, 'tis said, from the theatres and the circuses.'

'They do, indeed, withdraw from the theatres and circuses, Civilis, because the entertainments witnessed there do, as they judge, serve but to make beasts of men; they minister to vice. But in a sweet smell they see no harm, any more than in a silk dress, in well-proportioned buildings, or magnificent porticoes. Why should it be very wrong or very foolish to catch the odors which the divine Providence plants in the rose, and in a thousand flowers and gums as they wander forth upon the air for our delight, and fasten them up in these little bottles? by which means we can breathe them at all times--in winter as well as in summer, in one country, or clime, as in another. Thy shop, Civilis, is but a flower-garden in another form, and under another name.'

'I shall think better of the Christians for this. I hardly believed the report, indeed, for it were most unnatural and strange to find fault with odors such as these. I shall lament the more, that they are to be so dealt with by the Emperor. Hast thou heard what is reported this morning?'

'No; I am but just from home. How does it go?'

'Why, 'tis nothing other nor less than this, that Aurelian, being resolved to change the Christians all back again into what they were, has begun with his niece the princess Aurelia, and, with violence, insists that she shall sacrifice--which she steadfastly refuses to do. Some say, that she has not been seen at the palace for several days, and that she is fast locked up in the great prison on the Tiber.'

'I do not believe a word of it, Civilis. The Emperor has of late used harsh language of the Christians, I know. But for one word he has spoken, the city has coined ten. And, moreover, the words of the priest Fronto are quoted for those of Aurelian. It is well known he is especially fond of Aurelia; and Mucapor, to whom she is betrothed, is his favorite among all his generals, not excepting Probus.'

'Well, well, may it be as you say! I, for my part, should be sorry that any mishap befel those with whom the most noble Piso is connected; especially seeing they do not quarrel, as I was fain to believe, with my calling. Yet, never before, as I think, have I seen a Christian in my shop.'

'They may have been here without your knowing it.'

'Yes, that is true.'

'Besides, the Christians being in the greater proportion of the middle or humbler classes, seek not their goods at places where emperors resort. They go elsewhere.'

Civilis bowed to the floor, as he replied, 'You do me too much honor.'

'The two cases of perfume which I buy,' I then said, 'are to travel into the far East. Please to secure them accordingly.'

'Are they not then for the princess Julia, as I supposed?'

'They are for a friend in Syria. We wish her to know what is going on here in the capital of all the world.'

'By the gods! you have devised well. It is the talk all over Rome. Cleopatra's tears have taken all hearts. Orders from the provinces will soon pour in. They shall follow you well secured, as you say.'

I enjoy a call upon this whole Roman, and yet half Jew, as much as upon the first citizens of the capital. The cup of Aurelian, is no fuller than the cup of Civilis. The perfect bliss that emanates from his countenance, and breathes from his form and gait, is pleasing to behold--upon whatever founded--seeing it is a state that is reached by so few. No addition could be made to the felicity of this fortunate man. He conceives his occupation to be more honorable than the proconsulship of a province, and his name, he pleases himself with believing, is familiar to more ears than any man's, save the Emperor's, and has been known in Rome for a longer period than any other person's living, excepting only the head of the Senate, the venerable Tacitus. This is all legible in the lines about his mouth and eyes.

Leaving the heaven of the happy man, I turned to the Forum of Augustus, to look at a statue of brass, of Aurelian, just placed among the great men of Rome in front of the Temple of Mars, the Avenger. This statue is the work of Periander, who, with that universality of power which marks the Greek, has made his genius as distinguished here for sculpture, as it was in Palmyra for military defence and architecture. Who, for perfection in this art of arts, is to be compared with the Greek? or for any work, of either the head or the hands, that implies the possession of what we mean by genius? The Greeks have not only originated all that we know of great and beautiful in letters, philosophy and the arts, but, what they have originated, they have also perfected. Whatever they have touched, they have finished; at least, so far as art, and the manner of working, is concerned. The depths of all wisdom and philosophy they have not sounded indeed, though they have gone deeper than any, only because they are in their own essence unfathomable. Time, as it flows on, bears us to new regions to be explored, whose riches constantly add new stores to our wisdom, and open new views to science. But in all art they have reached a point beyond which none have since advanced, and beyond which it hardly seems possible to go. A doric column, a doric temple, a corinthian capital, a corinthian temple--these perfectly satisfy and fill the mind; and, for seven hundred years, no change or addition has been made or attempted that has not been felt to be an injury. And I doubt not that seven thousand years hence, if time could but spare it so long, pilgrims would still go in search of the beautiful from the remotest parts of the world, from parts now unknown, to worship before the Parthenon, and, may I not add, the Temple of the Sun in Palmyra!

Periander has gained new honors by this admirable piece of work. I had hardly commenced my examination of it, when a grating voice at my elbow, never, once heard, to be mistaken for any other, croaked out what was meant as a challenge.

'The greatest captain of this or of any age!'

It was Spurius, a man whom no slight can chill nor, even insult, cause to abate the least of his intrusive familiarity--a familiarity which he covets, too, only for the sake of disputation and satire. To me, however, he is never other than a source of amusement. He is a variety of the species I love occasionally to study.

I told him I was observing the workmanship, without thinking of the man represented.

'If you will allow me to say it,' he rejoined, 'a very inferior subject of contemplation. A statue--as I take it, the thing, that is, for which it is made, is commemoration. If one wants to see fine work in marble, there is the cornice for him just overhead: or in brass, let him look at the doors of the new temple, or the last table or couch of Syphax. The proper subject for man is man.'

'Well, Spurius, on your own ground then. In this brass I do not see brass, nor yet Aurelian--'

'What then, in the name of Hecate?'

'Nothing but intellect--the mind, the soul of the greater artist, Periander. That drapery never fell so upon Aurelian; nor was Aurelian's form or bearing ever like this. It is all ennobled, and exalted above pure nature, by the divine power of genius. The true artist, under every form and every line of nature, sees another form and line of more perfect grace and beauty, which he chooses instead, and makes it visible and permanent in stone or brass. You see nothing in me, but merely Piso as he walks the streets. Periander sees another within, bearing no more resemblance to me--yet as much--than does this, to Aurelian.'

'That, I simply conceive, to be so much sophistry,' rejoined the poet, 'which no man would be guilty of, except he had been for the very purpose, as one must think, of degrading his intellect, to the Athenian schools. Still, as I said and think, the statue is made to commemorate the man represented, not the artist.'

'It is made for that. But, oftentimes, the very name of the man commemorated is lost, while that of the artist lives forever. In my judgment there is as much of Periander in the statue as there is of Aurelian.'

'I know not what the fame of this great Periander may be ages hence. It has not till now reached my ear.'

'It is not easy to reach the ear of some who dwell in the via coeli.' I could not help saying that.

'My rooms, sir, I would inform you,' he rejoined sharply, 'are on the third floor.'

'Then I do wonder you should not have heard of Periander.'

'Greater than Aurelian! and I must wonder too. A poet may be greater than a general or an emperor, I grant: he is one of the family of the gods; but how a worker in brass or marble can be, passes my poor understanding. It is vain to attempt to raise the mere artist, to the level of the historian or poet.'

'I think that too. I only said he was greater than Aurelian--'

'Than Aurelian,' replied Spurius, 'who has extended the bounds of the empire!'

'But narrowed those of human happiness,' I answered. 'Which is of more consequence, empire or man? But now, man was the great object! I grant you he is, and for that reason a man who, like an artist of genius, adds to the innocent sources of human enjoyment, is greater than the soldier and conqueror, whose business is the annoyance and destruction of life. Aurelian has slain hundreds of thousands. Periander never injured a worm. He dwells in a calm and peaceful world of his own, and his works are designed to infuse the same spirit that fills himself into all who behold them. You must confess the superior power of art, and of the artist, in this very figure. Who thinks of conquest, blood, and death, as he looks upon these flowing outlines, this calm, majestic form--upon that still face? The artist here is the conqueror of the conqueror, and makes him subserve his own purposes; purposes, of a higher nature than the mere soldier ever dreamed of. No one can stand and contemplate this form, without being made a lover of beauty rather than of blood and death; and beauty is peace.'

'It must be impossible,' replied the bitter spirit, 'for one who loves Palmyra better than his native Rome, to see much merit in Aurelian. It is a common saying, Piso is a Palmyrene. The report is current too that Piso is about to turn author, and celebrate that great nation in history.'

'I wish I were worthy to do so,' I answered, 'I might then refute certain statements in another quarter. Yet events have already refuted them.'

'If my book,' replied Spurius, 'be copied a thousand times, the statements shall stand as they are. They are founded upon indisputable evidence and philosophical inferences.'

'But, Spurius, they are every one contradicted by the late events.'

'No matter for that, if they were ever true they must always be true. Reasoning is as strong as fact. I found Palmyra a vulgar, upstart, provincial city; the most distasteful of all spots on earth to a refined mind; such I left it, and such I have shown it to the world.'

'Yet,' I urged, 'if the Palmyrenes in the defence of their country showed themselves a brave, daring, and dangerous foe, as they certainly were magnanimous; if so many facts and events prove this, and all Rome admits it, it will seem like little else than malice for such pages to circulate in your book. Besides, as to a thousand other things I can prove you to have seen amiss.'

'Because I have but one eye, am I incapable of vision? Am I to be reproached with my misfortunes? One eye is the same as two; who sees two images except he squint? I can describe that wain, loaded down with wine casks, drawn by four horses with scarlet trappings, the driver with a sweeping Juno's favor in his cap, as justly as you can. Who can see more?'

'I thought not, Spurius, of your misfortune, though I must think two eyes better for seeing than one, but only of favorable opportunities for observation. You were in Palmyra from the ides of January to the nones of February, and lived in a tavern. I have been there more than half a year, and dwelt among the citizens themselves. I knew them in public and in private, and saw them under all circumstances most favorable to a just opinion, and I can affirm that a more discolored picture of a people was never drawn than yours.'

'All the world,' said the creature, 'knows that Spurius is no flatterer. I have not only published travels among the Palmyrenes, but I intend to publish a poem also--yes, a satire--and if it should be entitled "Woman's pride humbled," or "The downfall of false greatness" or "The gourd withered in a day," or "Mushrooms not oaks," or "Ants not elephants," what would there be wonderful in it?--or, if certain Romans should figure largely in it, eh?'

'Nothing is less wonderful, Spurius, than the obstinacy and tenaciousness of error?'

'Periander greater than Aurelian!' rejoined he, moving off; 'that is a good thing for the town.'

As I turned, intending to visit the shop of Demetrius, to see what progress he was making in his silver Apollo, I was accosted by the consul, Marcellinus.

'A fair morning to you, Piso,' said he; 'and I see you need the salutation and the wish, for a black cloud has just drifted from you, and you must still feel as if under the shadow. Half the length of the street, as I slowly approached, have I witnessed your earnest discourse with one whom, I now see, to have been Spurius. But I trust your Christian principles are not about to make an agrarian of you? Whence this sudden intimacy with one like Spurius?'

'One need not, I suppose, be set down as a lover of an east wind because they both sometimes take the same road, and can scarcely separate if they would? But, to speak the truth, a man is to me a man, and I never yet have met one of the race from whom I could not gain either amusement, instruction, or warning. Spurius is better than a lecture from a philosopher, upon the odiousness of prejudice. To any one inclined to harbor prejudices would I recommend an hour's interview with Spurius, sooner far than I would send him to Cleanthes the Stoic, or Silius the Platonist, or, I had almost said Probus the Christian.'

'May I ask, Piso, if you have in sober earnest joined yourself to the community of the Christians, or, are you only dallying for awhile with their doctrines, just as our young men are this year infected by the opinions of Cleanthes, the next followers of Silius, the third of the nuisance Crito, and the fourth, adrift from all, and the fifth, good defenders, if not believers, of the popular superstitions? I presume I may believe that such is the case with you. I trust so, for the times are not favorable for the Christians, and I would like to know that you were not of them.'

'I am however of them, with earnestness. I have been a Christian ever since I first thoroughly comprehended what it meant.'

'But how can it be possible that, standing as you do at the head as it were of the nobility and wealth of Rome, you can confound yourself with this obscure and vulgar tribe? I know that some few of reputation are with them beside yourself; but how few! Come, come, disabuse yourself of this error and return to the old, safe, and reputable side.'

'If mere fancy, Marcellinus, had carried me over to the Christians, fancy or whim might bring me away from them. But if it be, on the other hand, a question of truth, then it is clear, fashion and respectability, and even what is safest, or most expedient, are arguments not to be so much as lisped.'

'No more, no more! I see how it is. You are fairly gone from us. Nevertheless, though it may be thought needful to check the growth of this sect, I shall hope that your bark may sail safely along. But this reported disappearance of Aurelia shows that danger is not far off.'

'Do you then credit the rumor?'

'I can do no otherwise. It is in every part of the town. I shall learn the truth at the capitol. I go to meet the senate.'

'One moment: Is my judgment of the senate a right one in this, that it would not second Aurelian in an attack upon the privileges, property, or lives of the Christians?'

'I think it is. Although, as I know, there are but few Christians in the body--how many you know surely better than I--yet I am persuaded it would be averse to acts of intolerance and persecution. Will you not accompany me to the sitting?'

'Not so early. I am first bound elsewhere.'

'You know, Fausta, that I avoid the senate. Being no longer a senate, a Roman senate, but a mere gathering of the flatterers of the reigning Emperor, whoever he may be, neither pleasure nor honor can come of their company. There is one aspect however, at the present moment, in which this body is to be contemplated with interest. It is not, in matters of religion, a superstitious body. Here it stands, between Aurelian with the populace on his side, and the Christians, or whatever religious body or sect there should be any design to oppress or exterminate. It consists of the best and noblest, and richest, of Rome; of those who have either imbibed their opinions in philosophy and religion from the ancient philosophers or their living representatives, or are indifferent and neglectful of the whole subject; which is the more common case. In either respect they are as a body tolerant of the various forms which religion or superstition may assume. The only points of interest or inquiry with them would be, whether any specified faith or ceremonies tended to the injury of the state? whether they affected to its damage the existing order of civil affairs? These questions being answered favorably on the part of the greater number, there would be no disposition to interfere. Of Christianity, the common judgment in that body, and among those in the capital who are of the same general rank, is for the most part favorable. It is commended for its modesty, for the quiet and unostentatious manner in which its religious affairs are managed, and for the humble diligence with which it concerns itself with the common people and the poor, carefully instructing them in the doctrines of their religion, and relieving liberally their necessities. I am persuaded, that any decision of the senate concerning the Christians, would be indulgent and paternal, and that it would, in opinion and feeling, be opposed to any violence whatever on the part of Aurelian. But then, alas! it is little that they can do with even the best purposes. The Emperor is absolute--the only power, in truth, in the state. The senate exists but in name and form. It has even less independent power than that of Palmyra had under Zenobia. Yours, indeed, was dependent through affection and trust, reposing in a higher wisdom than its own. This, through fear and the spirit of flattery. So many members too were added, after the murderous thinning of its seats in the affair of the mint, that, now, scarce a voice would be raised in open opposition to any course the Emperor might adopt. The new members being moreover of newer families, nearer the people, are less inclined than the others to resist any of his measures. Still, it is most evident that there is an under current of ill-will, opposition, jealousy, distrust, running through the body, which, if the opportunity should present itself, and there were courage enough for the work, may show itself and make itself felt and respected. The senate, in a word, though slavish and subservient, is not friendly.

But I am detaining you from the company of Demetrius, of which you were always fond. I soon reached his rich establishment, and being assured that he of Palmyra was within, I entered. First passing through many apartments, filled with those who were engaged in some one of the branches of this beautiful art, I came to that which was sacred to the labors of the two brothers, who are employed in the invention of the designs of their several works, in drawing the plans, in preparing the models, and then in overseeing the younger artists at their tasks, themselves performing all the higher and more difficult parts of the labor. Demetrius was working alone at his statue; the room in which he was, being filled either with antiquities in brass, ivory, silver, or gold, or with finished specimens of his own and his brother's skill, all disposed with the utmost taste, and with all the advantages to be derived from the architecture of the room, from a soft and mellowed light resembling moonlight which came through alabaster windows, from the rich cloths, silks, and other stuffs, variously disposed around, and from the highly ornamented cabinets in which articles of greatest perfection and value were kept and exhibited. Here stood the enthusiast, applying himself so intently to his task, that he neither heard the door of the apartment as it opened, nor the voice of the slave who announced my name. But, in a moment, as he suddenly retreated to a dark recess to observe from that point the effect of his touches as he proceeded, he saw me, and cried out,

'Most glad to greet you here, Piso; your judgment is, at this very point, what I shall be thankful for. Here, if it please you, move to the very spot in which I now am in, and tell me especially this, whether the finger of the right hand should not be turned a line farther toward the left of the figure. The metal is obstinate, but still it can be bent if necessary. Now judge, and speak your judgment frankly, for my sake.'

I sank back into the recess as desired, and considered attentively the whole form, rough now and from the moulds, and receiving the first finishing touches from the rasp and the chisel. I studied it long and at my leisure, Demetrius employing himself busily about some other matter. It is a beautiful and noble figure, worthy any artist's reputation of any age, and of a place in the magnificent temple for which it is designed. So I assured Demetrius, giving him at length my opinion upon every part. I ended with telling him I did not believe that any effect would be gained by altering the present direction of the finger. It had come perfect from the moulds.

'Is that your honest judgment, Piso? Christians, they say, ever speak the exact truth. Fifty times have I gone where you now are to determine the point. My brother says it is right. But I cannot tell. I have attempted the work in too much haste; but Aurelian thinks, I believe, that a silver man may be made as easily as a flesh one may be unmade. Rome is not Palmyra, Piso. What a life there for an artist! Calm as a summer sea. Here! by all the gods and goddesses! if one hears of anything but of blood and death! Heads all on where they should be to-day, to-morrow are off. To-day, captives cut up on the altars of some accursed god, and to-morrow thrown to some savage beast, no better and no worse, for the entertainment of savages worse than either or all. The very boys in the streets talk of little else than of murderous sports of gladiators or wild animals. I swear to you, a man can scarce collect or keep his thoughts here. What's this about the Christians too? I marvel, Piso, to see you here alive! They say you are to be all cut up root and branch. Take my advice, and fly with me back to Palmyra! Not another half year would I pass among these barbarians for all the patronage of the Emperor, his minions, and the senate at their heels. What say you?'

'No, Demetrius, I cannot go; but I should not blame you for going. Rome is no place, I agree with you, for the life contemplative, or for the pure and innocent labors of art. It is the spot for intense action; but--'

'Suffering you mean--'

'That too, most assuredly, but of action too. It is the great heart of the world.'

'Black as Erebus and night.'

'Yes, but still a great one, which, if it can be once made to beat true, will send its blood, then a pure and life-giving current, to the remotest extremities of the world, which is its body. I hope for the time to come when this will be true. There is more goodness in Rome, Demetrius, than you have heard, or known of. There is a people here worth saving: I, with the other Christians, am set to this work. We must not abandon it.'

''Twill be small comfort though, should you all perish doing it.'

'Our perishing might be but the means of new and greater multitudes springing up to finish what we had begun, but left incomplete. There is great life in death. Blood, spilled upon the ground, is a kind of seed that comes up men. Truth is not extinguished by putting out life. It then seems to shine the more brightly, as if the more to cheer and comfort those who are suffering and dying for it.'

'That may, or may not be,' said the artist, 'here and there; but, in my judgment, if this man-slayer, this world-butcher once fastens his clutches upon your tribe, he will leave none to write your story. How many were left in Palmyra?--Just, Piso, resume your point of observation, and judge whether this fold of the drapery were better as it is, or joined to the one under it, an alteration easily made.'

I gave him my opinion, and he went on filing and talking.

'And now, Piso, if I must tell you, I have conceived a liking for you Christians, and it is for this reason partly I would have you set about to escape the evil that is at least threatened. Here is my brother, whose equal the world does not hold, is become a Christian. Then, do you know, here is a family, just in the rear of our shop, of one Macer, a Christian and a preacher, that has won upon us strangely. I see much of them. Some of his boys are in a room below, helping on by their labor the support of their mother and those who are younger, for I trow, Macer himself does little for them, whatever he may be doing for the world at large, or its great heart as you call it. But, what is more still,' cried he with emphasis, and a jump at the same moment, throwing down his tools, 'do you know the Christians have some sense of what is good in our way? they aspire to the elegant, as well as others who are in better esteem.'

And as he finished, he threw open the doors of a small cabinet, and displayed a row of dishes, cups, and pitchers, of elegant form and workmanship.

'These,' he went on, 'are for the church of Felix, the bishop of the Christians. What they do with them I know not; but, as I was told by the bishop, they have a table or altar of marble, on which, at certain times, they are arranged for some religious rite or other. They are not of gold, as they seem, but of silver gilded. My brother furnished the designs, and put them into the hands of Flaccus, who wrought them. Neither I nor my brother could labor at them, as you may believe, but it shows a good ambition in the Christians to try for the first skill in Rome or the world,--does it not? They are a promising people.'

Saying which, he closed the doors and flew to his work again.

At the same moment the door of the apartment opened, and the brother Demetrius entered accompanied by Probus. When our greetings were over, Probus said, continuing as it seemed a conversation just broken off,

'I did all I could to prevent it, but the voice of numbers was against me, and of authority too, and, both together, they prevailed. You, I believe, stood neuter, or indeed, I may suppose, knew nothing about the difference?'

'As you suppose,' replied the elder Demetrius, 'I knew nothing of it, but designed the work and have completed it. Here it is.' And going to the same cabinet, again opened the doors and displayed the contents. Probus surveyed them with a melancholy air, saying, as he did so,

'I could bear that the vessels, used for the purpose to which these are destined, should be made of gold, or even of diamond itself, could mines be found to furnish it, and skill to hollow it out. For, we know, the wine which these shall hold is that which, in the way of symbol, shadows forth the blood of Christ which, by being shed on the cross, purchased for us this Christian truth and hope; and what should be set out with every form of human honor, if not this?'

'I think so,' replied Demetrius; 'to that which we honor and reverence in our hearts we must add the outward sign and testimony; especially moreover if we would affect, in the same way that ours are, the minds of others. Paganism understands this; and it is the pomp and magnificence of her ceremony, the richness of the temple service, the grandeur of her architecture, and the imposing array of her priests in their robes, ministering at the altars or passing through the streets in gorgeous procession, with banners, victims, garlands, and music, by which the populace are gained and kept. That must be founded on just principles, men say, on which the great, the learned, and the rich, above all the State itself, are so prompt to lavish so much splendor and wealth.'

'But here is a great danger,' Probus replied. 'This, carried too far, may convert religion into show and ostentation. Form and ceremony, and all that is merely outward and material, may take the place of the moral. Religion may come to be a thing apart by itself, a great act, a tremendous and awful rite, a magnificent and imposing ceremony, instead of what it is in itself, simply a principle of right action toward man and toward God. This is at present just the character and position of the Roman religion. It is a thing that is to be seen at the temples, but nowhere else; it is a worship through sacrifices and prayers, and that is all. The worshipper at the temple may be a tyrant at home, a profligate in the city, a bad man everywhere, and yet none the less a true worshipper. May God save the religion of Christ from such corruption! Yet is the beginning to be discerned. A decline has already begun. Rank and power are already sought with an insane ambition, even by ministers of Christ. They are seeking to transfer to Christianity the same outward splendor, and the same gilded trappings, which, in the rites and ceremonies of the popular faith, they see so to subdue the imagination, and lead men captive. Hence, Piso and Demetrius, the golden chair of Felix, and his robes of audience, on which there is more gold, as I believe, than would gild all these cups and pitchers; hence, too, the finery of the table, the picture behind it, and, in some churches, the statues of Christ, of Paul, and Peter. These golden vessels for the supper of Christ's love, I can forgive--I can welcome them--but in the rest that has come, and is coming, I see signs of danger.'

'But, most excellent Probus,' said the younger Demetrius, 'I like not to hear the arts assailed and represented dangerous. I have just been telling Piso, that you are a people to be respected, for you were beginning to honor the arts. Yet here now you are denouncing them. But, let me ask, what harm could it do any good man among you, to come and look at this figure of Apollo, or a statue of your Paul or Peter, as you name them--supposing they were just men and benefactors of their race?'

'There ought to be none,' Probus replied. 'It ought to be a source of innocent pleasure, if not of wholesome instruction, to gaze upon the imitated form of a good man--of a reformer, a benefactor, a prophet. But man is so prone to religion,--it is an honorable instinct--that you can scarce place before him an object of reverence but he will straightway worship it. What were your gods but once men, first revered, then worshipped, and now their stone images deemed to be the very gods themselves? Thus the original idea--the effect, we may believe, of an early revelation--of one supreme Deity has been almost lost out of the world. Let the figure of Christ be everywhere set before the people in stone or metal, and, what with the natural tendency of the mind to idolatry, and the force of example in the common religion, I fear it would not be long before he, whom we now revere as a prophet, would soon be worshipped as a god; and the disciples whom you have named, in like manner, would no longer be remembered with gratitude and affection as those who devoted their lives to the service of their fellow-men, but be adored as inferior Deities, like your Castor and Pollux. I can conceive that, in the lapse of ages, men shall be so redeemed from the gross conceptions that now inthrall them concerning both God and his worship, and so nourished up to a divine strength by the power of truth, they shall be in no danger from such sources; but shall reap all the pleasure and advantage which can be derived from beautiful forms of art and the representation of great and excellent characters, without ever dreaming that any other than the infinite and invisible Spirit of the universe is to be worshipped, or held divine. The religion of Christ will itself, if aught can do it, bring about such a period.'

'That then will be the time for artists to live, next after now,' said Demetrius of Palmyra. 'In the meantime, Probus, if Hellenism should decline and die, and your strict faith take its place, art will decline and perish. We live chiefly by the gods and their worship.'

'If our religion,' replied Probus, 'should suffer injury from its own professors, in the way it has, for a century or two more, it will give occupation enough to artists. Its corruptions will do the same for you that the reign of absolute and perfect truth would.'

'The gods then grant that the corruptions you speak of may come in season, before I die. I am tired of Jupiters, Mercurys, and Apollos. I have a great fancy to make a statue of Christ. Brother! what think you, should I reach it? Most excellent Probus, should I make you such an one for your private apartments I do not believe you would worship it, and doubtless it would afford you pleasure. If you will leave a commission for such a work, it shall be set about so soon as this god of the Emperor's is safe on his pedestal. What think you?'

'I should judge you took me, Demetrius, for the priest of a temple, or a noble of the land. The price of such a piece of sculpture would swallow up more than all I am worth. Besides, though I might not worship myself--though I say not but I might--I should give an ill example to others, who, if they furnished themselves or their churches with similar forms, might not have power over themselves, but relapse into the idolatry from which they are but just escaped.'

'All religions, as to their doctrine and precept, are alike to me,' replied Demetrius, 'only, as a general principle, I should ever prefer that which has the most gods. Rome shows excellent judgment in adopting all the gods of the earth, so that if the worship of one god will not bring prosperity to the nation, there are others in plenty to try their fortune with again. Never doubt, brother, that it is because you Christians have no gods, that the populace and others are so hostile to you. Only set up a few images of Christ, and some of the other founders of the religion, and your peace will be made. Otherwise I fear this man-killer will, like some vulture, pounce upon you and tear you piecemeal. What, brother, have you learned of Aurelia?'

'Nothing with certainty. I could find only a confirmation from every mouth, but based on no certain knowledge, of the rumor that reached us early in the morning. But what is so universally reported, generally turns out true. I should, however, if I believed the fact of her imprisonment, doubt the cause. I said that I could conceive of no other cause, and feared that if the fact were so, the religion of Aurelian was the reason of her being so dealt with. It was like Aurelian, if he had resolved upon oppressing the Christians to any extent whatever, that he should begin with those who were nearest to him; first with his own blood, and then with those of his household.'

With this, and such like conversation, I passed a pleasant hour at the rooms of Demetrius.

* * * * *

My wish was, as I turned from the apartments of Demetrius, to seek the Emperor or Livia, and learn from them the exact truth concerning the reports current through the city. But, giving way to that weakness which defers to the latest possible moment the confirmation of painful news, and the resolution of doubts which one would rather should remain as doubts than be determined the wrong way, in melancholy mood, I turned and retraced my steps. My melancholy was changed to serious apprehension by all that I observed and heard on my way to the Coelian. As the crowd in this great avenue, the Suburra, pressed by me, it was easy to gather that the Christians had become the universal topic of conversation and dispute. The name of the unhappy Aurelia frequently caught my ear. Threatening and ferocious language dropt from many, who seemed glad that at length an Emperor had arisen who would prove faithful to the institutions of the country. I joined a little group of gazers before the window of the rooms of Periander, at which something rare and beautiful is always to be seen, who, I found, were looking intently at a picture, apparently just from the hands of the artist, which represented Rome under the form of a beautiful woman--Livia had served as the model--with a diadem upon her head, and the badges of kingly authority in her hands, and at her side a priest of the Temple of Jupiter, "Greatest and Best", in whose face and form might plainly be traced the cruel features of Fronto. The world was around them. On the lowest earth, with dark shadows settling over them, lay scattered and broken, in dishonor and dust, the emblems of all the religions of the world, their temples fallen and in ruins. Among them, in the front ground of the picture, was the prostrate cross, shattered as if dashed from the church, whose dilapidated walls and widespread fragments bore testimony not so much to the wasting power of time as to the rude hand of popular violence; while, rearing themselves up into a higher atmosphere, the temples of the gods of Rome stood beautiful and perfect, bathed in the glowing light of a morning sun. The allegory was plain and obvious enough. There was little attractive, save the wonderful art with which it was done. This riveted the eye; and that being gained, the bitter and triumphant bigotry of the ideas set forth had time to make its way into the heart of the beholder, and help to change its warm blood to gall. Who but must be won by the form and countenance of the beautiful Livia? and, confounding Rome with her, be inspired with a new devotion to his country, and its religion, and its lovely queen? The work was inflaming and insidious, as it was beautiful. This was seen in what it drew from those among whom I stood.

'By Jupiter!' said one, 'that is well done. They are all down, who can deny it! Those are ruins not to be built up again. Who, I wonder, is the artist? He must be a Roman to the last drop of his blood, and the last hair of his beard.'

'His name is Sporus,' replied his companion, 'as I hear, a kinsman of Fronto, the priest of Apollo.'

'Ah, that's the reason the priest figures here,' cried the first, 'and the Empress too; for they say nobody is more at the Gardens than Fronto. Well, he's just the man for his place. If any man can bring up the temples again, it's he. Religion is no sham at the Temple of the Sun. The priests are all what they pretend to be. Let others do so, and we shall have as much reason to thank the Emperor for what he has done for the gods--and so for us all--as for what he has done for the army, the empire, and the city.'

'You say well,' rejoined the other. 'He is for once a man, who, if he will, may make Rome what she was before the empire, a people that honored the gods. And this picture seems as if it spoke out his very plans, and I should not wonder if it were so.'

'Never doubt it. See, here lies a Temple of Isis flat enough; next to it one of the accursed tribe of Jews. And what ruder pile is that?'

'That must be a Temple of the British worship, as I think. But the best of all, is this Christian church: see how the wretches fly, while the work goes on! In my notion, this paints what we may soon see.'

'I believe it! The gods grant it so! Old men, in my judgment, will live to see it all acted out. Do you hear what is said? That Aurelian has put to death his own niece, the princess Aurelia?'

'That's likely enough,' said another, 'no one can doubt it. 'Tis easy news to believe in Rome. But the question is what for?'

'For what else but for her impiety, and her aims to convert Mucapor to her own ways.'

'Well, there is no telling, and it's no great matter; time will show. Meanwhile, Aurelian forever! He's the man for me!'

'Truly is he,' said one at his side, who had not spoken before, 'for thy life is spent at the amphitheatres, and he is a good caterer for thee, sending in ample supplies of lions and men.'

'Whew! who is here? Take care! Your tongue, old man, has short space to wag in.'

'I am no Christian, knave, but I trust I am a man: and that is more than any can say of you, that know you. Out upon you for a savage!'

The little crowd burst into loud laughter at this, and with various abusive epithets moved away. The old man addressed himself to me, who alone remained as they withdrew,--

'Aurelian, I believe, would do well enough were he let alone. He is inclined to cruelty, I know: but nobody can deny that, cruel or not, he has wrought most beneficial changes both in the army and in the city. He has been in some sort, up to within the last half year, a censor, greater than Valerian; a reformer, greater and better than even he. Had he not been crazed by his successes in the East, and were he not now led, and driven, and maddened, by the whole priesthood of Rome, with the hell-born Fronto at their head, we might look for a new and a better Rome. But, as it is, I fear these young savages, who are just gone, will see all fulfilled they are praying for. A fair day to you.'

And he too turned away. Others were come into the same spot, and for a long time did I listen to similar language. Many came, looked, said nothing, and took their way, with paler face, and head depressed, silent under the imprecations heaped upon the atheists, but manifestly either of their side in sympathy, or else of the very atheists themselves.

I now sought my home, tired of the streets, and of all I had seen and heard. Many of my acquaintance, and friends passed me on the way, in whose altered manner I could behold the same signs which, in ruder form, I had just seen at the window of Periander. Not, Fausta, that all my friends of the Roman faith are summer ones, but that, perhaps, most are. Many among them, though attached firmly as my mother to the existing institutions, are yet, like her, possessed of the common sentiments of humanity, and would venture much or all to divert the merest shadow of harm from my head. Among these, I still pass some of my pleasantest and most instructive hours-- for with them the various questions involved in the whole subject of religion, are discussed with the most perfect freedom and mutual confidence. Varus, the prefect, whom I met among others, greeted me with unchanged courtesy. His sweetest smile was on his countenance as he swept by me, wishing me a happy day. How much more tolerable is the rude aversion, or loud reproaches of those I have told you of, than this honied suavity, that means nothing, and would be still the same though I were on the way to the block.

As I entered my library, Solon accosted me, to say, that there had been one lately there most urgent to see me. From his account, I could suppose it to be none other than the Jew Isaac, who, Milo has informed me, is now returned to Rome, which he resorts to as his most permanent home. Solon said that, though assured I was not at home, he would not be kept back, but pressed on into the house, saying that 'these Roman nobles often sat quietly in their grand halls, while they were denied to their poor clients. Piso was an old acquaintance of his when in Palmyra, and he had somewhat of moment to communicate to him, and must see him.'

'No sooner,' said Solon, 'had he got into the library, the like of which, I may safely affirm, he had never seen before, for his raiment betokened a poor and ragged life, than he stood, and gazed as much at his ease as if it had been his own, and then, by Hercules! unbuttoning his pack, for he was burdened with one both before and behind, he threw his old limbs upon a couch, and began to survey the room! I could not but ask him, If he were the elder Piso, old Cneius Piso, come back from Persia, in Persian beard and gown?--'Old man,' said he, 'your brain is turned with many books, and the narrow life you lead here, shut out from the living world of man. One man is worth all the books ever writ, save those of Moses. Go out into the streets and read him, and your senses will come again. Cneius Piso! Take you me for a spirit? I am Isaac the Jew, citizen of the world, and dealer in more rarities and valuables than you ever saw or dreamed of. Shall I open my parcels for thee?' No, said I, I would not take thy poor gewgaws for a gift. One worm-eaten book is worth them all.--'God restore thy reason!' said he, 'and give thee wisdom before thou diest; and that, by thy wrinkles and hairless pate must be soon.' What more of false he would have added I know not, for at that moment he sprang from where he sat like one suddenly mad, exclaiming, 'Holy Abraham! what do my eyes behold, or do they lie? Surely that is Moses! Never was he on Sinai, if his image be not here! Happy Piso! and happy Isaac to be the instrument of such grace! Who could have thought it? And yet many a time, in my dreams, have I beheld him, with a beard like mine, his hat on his head, his staff in his hand, as if standing at the table of the Passover, the princess with him, and--dreams will do such things--a brood of little chickens at their side. And now--save the last--it is all come to pass. And here, too, who may this be? who, but Aaron, the younger and milder! He was the speaker, and lo! his hand is stretched out! And this young Joseph is at his knee the better to interpret his character to the beholder. Moses and Aaron in the chief room of a Roman senator, and he, a Piso! Now, Isaac, thou mayest tie on thy pack, and take thy leave with a merry heart, for God, if never before, now accepteth thy works.' And much more, noble sir, in the same raving way, which was more dark to my understanding than the darkest pages of Aristotle.'

I gathered from Solon, that he would return in the evening in the hope to see me, for he had that to impart which concerned nearly my welfare.

I was watching with Julia, from the portico which fronts the Esquiline and overlooks the city, the last rays of the declining sun, as they gilded the roofs and domes of the vast sea of building before us, lingering last upon, and turning to gold the brazen statues of Antonine and of Trajan, when Milo approached us, saying that Isaac had returned. He was in a moment more with us.

'Most noble Piso,' said he, 'I joy to see thee again; and this morning, I doubt not, I should have seen thee, but for the obstinacy of an ancient man, whose wits seem to have been left behind as he has gone onward. I seek thee, Piso, for matters of moment. Great princess,' he suddenly cried, turning to Julia with as profound a reverence as his double burden would allow, 'glad am I to greet thee in Rome; not glad that thou wert forced to flee here, but glad that if, out of Palmyra, thou art here in the heart of all that can best minister to thy wants. Not a wish can arise in the heart but Rome can answer it. Nay, thou canst have few for that which is rare and costly, but even I can answer them. Hast thou ever seen, princess, those diamonds brought from the caves of mountains a thousand miles in the heart of India, in which there lurks a tint, if I may so name it, like this last blush of the western sky? They are rarer than humanity in a Roman, or apostacy in a Jew, or truth in a Christian. I shall show thee one.' And he fell to unlacing his pack, and drawing forth its treasures.

Julia assured him, she should see with pleasure whatever he could show her of rich or rare.

'There are, lady, jewelers, as they name themselves in Rome, who dwell in magnificent houses, and whose shops are half the length of a street, who cannot show you what Isaac can out of an old goatskin pack. And how should they? Have they, as I have, traveled the earth's surface and trafficked between crown and crown? What king is there, whose necessities I have not relieved by purchasing his rarest gems; or whose vanity I have not pleased by selling him the spoils of another? Old Sapor, proud as he was, was more than once in the grasp of Isaac. There! it is in this case--down, you see, in the most secret part of my pack--but who would look for wealth under this sordid covering? as who, lady, for a soul within this shriveled and shattered body? yet is there one there. In such outside, both of body and bag, is my safety. Who cares to stop the poor man, or hold parley with him? None so free of the world and its high ways as he; safe alike in the streets of Rome, and on the deserts of Arabia. His rags are a shield stouter than one of seven-fold bull's hide. Never but in such guise could I bear such jewels over the earth's surface. Here, lady, is the gem; never has it yet pressed the finger of queen or subject. The stone I brought from the East, and Demetrius, here in Rome, hath added the gold. Give me so much pleasure--'

And he placed it upon Julia's finger. It flashed a light such as we never before saw in stone. It was evidently a most rare and costly gem. It was of great size and of a hue such as I had never before seen.

'This is a queen's ring, Isaac,' said Julia--'and for none else.'

'It well becomes the daughter of a queen'--replied the Jew, 'and the wife of Piso--specially seeing that--Ah, Piso! Piso! how was I overjoyed to-day to see in thy room the evidence that my counsels had not been thrown away. The Christian did not gain thee with all his cunning--'

'Nay, Isaac'--I here interrupted him--'you must not let your benevolent wishes lead you into error. I am not yet a Jew. Those images that caught your eye were not wholly such as you took them for.'

'Well, well,' said the philosophic Jew, 'rumor then has for once spoken the truth. She has long, as I learn, reported thee Christian: but I believed it not. And to-day, when I looked upon those statues, I pleased myself with the thought that thou, and the princess, like her august mother, had joined themselves to Israel. But if it be not so, then have I an errand for thee, which, but now, I hoped I might not be bound to deliver. Piso, there is danger brewing for thee, and for all who hold with thee!'

'So I hear, Isaac, on all sides, and partly believe it. But the rumor is far beyond the truth, I do not doubt.'

'I think not so,' said Isaac. 'I believe the truth is beyond the rumor. Aurelian intends more and worse than he has spoken; and already has he dipt his hand in blood!'

'What say you? how is it you mean?' said Julia.

'Whose name but Aurelia's has been in the city's ears these many days? I can tell you, what is known as yet not beyond the Emperor's palace and the priest's, Aurelia is dead!'

'Sport not with us, Isaac!'

'I tell you, Piso, the simple truth. Aurelia has paid with her life for her faith. I know it from more than one whose knowledge in the matter is good as sight. It was in the dungeons of the Fabrician bridge, that she was dealt with by Fronto the priest of Apollo.'

'Aurelian then,' said Julia, 'has thrust his sickle into another field of slaughter, and will not draw it out till he swims in Christian blood, as once before in Syrian. God help these poor souls.' 'What, Isaac, was the manner of her death, if you have heard so much?'

'I have heard only,' replied Isaac, 'that, after long endeavor on the part of Aurelian and the priest to draw her from her faith while yet at the palace, she was conveyed to the prisons I have named, and there given over to Fronto and the executioners, with this only restriction, that if neither threats, nor persuasions, nor the horrid array of engines, could bend her, then should she be beheaded without either scourging or torture. And so it was done. She wept, 'tis said, as it were without ceasing, from the time she left the gardens; but to the priest would answer never a word to all his threats, entreaties, or promises; except once, when that wicked minister said to her, 'that except she in reality and truth would curse Christ and sacrifice, he would report that she had done so, and so liberate her and return her to the palace:'--at which, 'tis said, that on the instant her tears ceased, her eyes flashed lightning, and with a voice, which took the terrific tones of Aurelian himself, she said, 'I dare thee to it, base priest! Aurelian is an honorable man--though cruel as the grave--and my simple word, which never yet he doubted, would weigh more than oaths from thee, though piled to heaven! Do thy worst then, quick!' Whereupon the priest, white with wrath, first sprang toward her as if he had been a beast set to devour her, drawing at the same moment a knife from his robes; but, others being there, he stopped, and cried to the executioner to do his work--raving that he had it not in his power first to torment her. Aurelia was then instantly beheaded.'

We were silent as he ended, Julia dissolved in tears Isaac went on.

'This is great testimony, Piso, which is borne to thy faith. A poor, weak girl, alone, with not one to look on and encourage, in such a place, and in the clutches of such a hard-hearted wretch, to die without once yielding to her fears or the weakness of her tender nature--it is a thing hardly to be believed, and full of pity. Piso, thou wilt despise me when I say that my tribe rejoices at this, and laughs; that the Jew is seen carrying the news from house to house, and secretly feeding on it as a sweet morsel! And why should he not? Answer me that, Roman! Answer me that, Christian! In thee, Piso, and in every Roman like thee, there is compacted into one the enmity that has both desolated my country, and--far as mortal arm may do so--dragged down to the earth, her altars and her worship. Judea was once happy in her ancient faith; and happier than all in that great hope inspired by our prophets in endless line, of the advent, in the opening ages, of one who should redeem our land from the oppressor, and give to her the empire of the world. Messiah, for whom we waited, and while we waited were content to bear the insults and aggressions of the whole earth--knowing the day of vengeance was not far off--was to be to Judea more than Aurelian to Rome. He was to be our prophet, our priest, and our king, all in one; not man only, but the favored and beloved of God, his Son; and his empire was not to be like this of Rome, hemmed in by this sea and that, hedged about by barbarians on one side and another, bounded by rivers and hills, but was to stretch over the habitable earth, and Rome itself to be swallowed up in the great possession as a little island in the sea. And then this great kingdom was never to end. It could not be diminished by an enemy taking from it this province and another, as with Rome, nor could there be out of it any power whatever that could assail it; for, by the interference of God, through the right arm of our great Prince, fear, and the very spirit of submission, were to fall on every heart. All was to be Judea's, and Judea's forever; the kingdom was to be over the whole earth; and the reign forever and ever. And in those ages peace was to be on the earth, and universal love. God was to be worshipped by all according to our law, and idolatry and error to cease and come to an end. In this hope, I say, we were happy, in spite of all our vexations. In every heart in our land, whatever sorrows or sufferings might betide, there was a little corner where the spirit could retire and comfort itself with this vision of futurity. Among all the cities of our land, and far away among the rocks and vallies by Jordan and the salt sea, and the mountains of Lebanon, there were no others to be found than men, women, and children, happy in this belief, and by it bound into one band of lovers and friends. And what think you happened? I need not tell you. There came, as thou knowest, this false prophet of Gallilee, and beguiled the people with his smooth words, and perverted the sense of the prophets, and sowed difference and discord among the people; and the cherished vision, upon which the nation had lived and grown, fled like a dream. The Gallilean impostor planted himself upon the soil, and his roots of poison struck down, and his broad limbs shot, abroad, and half the nation was lost. Its unity was gone, its peace lost, its heart broken, its hope, though living still, yet obscured and perplexed. Canst thou wonder then Piso, or thou, thou weeping princess, that the Jew stands by and laughs when the Christian's turn comes, and the oppressor is oppressed, the destroyer destroyed? And when, Piso, the Christian had done his worst, despoiling us of our faith, our hope, our prince, and our God; not satisfied, he brought the Roman upon us, and despoiled us of our country itself. Now, and for two centuries, all is gone. Judea, the beautiful land, sits solitary and sad. Her sons and daughters wanderers over the earth, and trodden into the dust. When shall the light arise! and he, whom we yet look for, come and turn back the flood that has swept over us, and reverse the fortunes befallen to one and the other? The chariot of God tarries; but it does not halt. The wheels are turning, and when it is not thought of, it will come rolling onward with the voice of many thunders, and the great restoration shall be made, and a just judgment be meted out to all. What wonder, I say then, Piso, if my people look on and laugh, when this double enemy is in straits? when the Christian and Roman in one, is caught in the snare and can not escape? That laugh will ring through the streets of Rome, and will out-sound the roaring of the lions and the shouts of the theatre. Nature is strong in man, Piso, and I do not believe thou wilt think the worse of our people, if bearing what they have, this nature should break forth. Hate them not altogether, Roman, when thou shalt see them busy at the engines or the stake, or the theatres. Remember the cause! Remember the cause! But we are not all such. I wish, Piso, thou couldst abandon this faith. There will else be no safety to thee, I fear, ere not many days. What has overtaken the lady Aurelia, of the very family of the Emperor, will surely overtake others. Piso, I would fain serve thee, if I may. Though I hate the Roman, and the Christian, and thee, as a Jew, yet so am I, that I cannot hate them as a man, or not unto death; and thee do I love. Now it is my counsel, that thou do in season escape. Now thou canst do it; wait but a few days, and, perhaps, thou canst no longer. What I say is, fly! and, it were best, to the farthest east; first, to Palmyra, and then, if need be, to Persia. This, Piso, is what I am come for.'

'Isaac, this all agrees with the same goodness--'

'I am a poor, miserable wretch, whom God may forgive, because his compassions never fail, but who has no claim on his mercy, and will be content to sit hereafter where he shall but just catch, now and then, a glimpse of the righteous.'

'I must speak my thoughts, not yours, Isaac. This all agrees with what we have known of you; and, with all our hearts, you have our thanks. But we are bound to this place by ties stronger than any that bind us to life, and must not depart.'

'Say not so! Lady, speak! Why should ye remain to add to the number that must fall? Rank will not stand in the way of Aurelian.'

'That we know well, Isaac,' said Julia. 'We should not look for any shield such as that to protect us, nor for any other. Life is not the chief thing, Isaac. What is life, without liberty? Would you live, a slave? and is not he the meanest slave, who bends his will to another? who renounces the thoughts he dearly cherishes for another's humor? Who will beggar the soul, to save, or serve, the body?'

'Alas, princess, I fear there is more courage in thee, woman as thou art, than in this old frame! I love my faith, too, princess, and I labor for it in my way; but, may the God of Abraham spare me the last trial! And wouldst thou give up thy body to the tormentors and the executioner, to keep the singleness of thy mind, so that merely a few little thoughts, which no man can see, may run in and out of it, as they list?'

'Even so, Isaac.'

'It is wonderful,' exclaimed the Jew, 'what a strength there is in man! how, for an opinion, which can be neither bought, nor sold, nor weighed, nor handled, nor seen--a thing, that, by the side of lands, and gold, and houses, seems less than the dust of the balance--men and women, yea, and little children, will suffer and die; when a word, too, which is but a little breath blown out of the mouth, would save them!'

'But, it is no longer wonderful,' said Julia, 'when we look at our whole selves, and not only at one part. We are all double, one part, of earth, another, of heaven; one part, gross body, the other, etherial spirit; one part, life of the body, the other, life of the soul. Which of these parts is the better, it is not hard to determine. Should I gain much by defiling the heavenly, for the sake of the earthly? by injuring the mind, for the preservation of the body; by keeping longer the life I live now, but darkening over the prospect of the life that is hereafter? If I possess a single truth, which I firmly believe to be a truth, I cannot say that it is a lie, for the sake of some present benefit or deliverance, without fixing a stain thereby, not on the body, which by and by perishes, but on the soul, which is immortal; and which would then forever bear about with it the unsightly spot.'

'It is so; it is as you say, lady; and rarely has the Jew been known to deny his name and his faith. Since you have spoken, I find thoughts called up which have long slept. Despise me not, for my proposal, yet I would there were a way of escape! Flight now, would not be denial, or apostacy.'

'It would not,' said Julia. 'And we may not judge with harshness those whose human courage fails them under the apprehension of the sufferings which often await the persecuted. But, with my convictions, and Piso's, the guilt and baseness of flight or concealment would be little less than that of denial or apostacy. We have chosen this religion for its divine truth, and its immortal prospects; we believe it a good which God has sent to us; we believe it the most valuable possession we hold; we believe it essential to the world's improvement and happiness. Believing it thus, we must stand by it; and, if it come to this--as I trust in Heaven it will not, notwithstanding the darkness of the portents--that our regard for it will be questioned except we die for it--then we will die.'

Isaac rose, and began to fasten on his pack. As he did so, he said,

'Excellent lady, I grieve that thou shouldst be brought from thy far home, and those warm and sunny skies, to meet the rude shocks of this wintry land.

It was enough to see what thou didst there, and to know what befell thy ancient friends. The ways of Providence, to our eyes, are darker than the Egyptian night, brought upon that land by the hand of Moses. It is darkness solid and impenetrable. The mole sees farther toward the earth's centre, than does my dim eye into the judgments of God. And what wonder? when he is God looking down upon earth and man's ways as I upon an ant-hill, and seeing all at once. To such an eye, lady, that may be best which to mine is worst.'

'I believe it is often so, Isaac,' replied Julia. 'Just as in nauseous drugs or rankest poisons there is hidden away medicinal virtue, so is there balm for the soul, by which its worst diseases are healed and its highest health promoted, in sufferings, which, as they first fall upon us, we lament as unmitigated evil. I know of no state of mind so proper to beings like us, as that indicated by a saying of Christ, which I shall repeat to you, though you honor not its source, and which seems to me to comprehend all religion and philosophy, "Not my will, but thine, O God, be done!" We never take our true position, and so never can be contented and happy, till we renounce our own will, and believe all the whole providence of God to be wisest and best, simply because it is his. Should I dare, were the power this moment given me, to strike out for myself my path in life, arrange its events, fix my lot? Not the most trivial incident can be named that I should not tremble to order otherwise than as it happens.'

'There is wisdom, princess, in the maxim of thy prophet, and its spirit is found in many of the sayings of truer prophets who went before him, whose words are familiar to thy royal mother, though, I fear, they are not to thee; a misfortune, wholly to be traced to that misadventure of thine, Piso, in being thrown into the company of the Christian Probus on board the Mediterranean trader. Had I been alone with thee on that voyage, who can say that thou wouldst not now have been what, but this morning, I took thee for, as I looked upon those marble figures?'

'But, Isaac, forget not your own principles,' said Julia. 'May you, who cannot, as you have said, see the end from the beginning, and whose sight is but a mole's, dare to complain of the providence which threw Piso into the society of the Christian Probus? I am sure you would not, on reflection, re-arrange those events, were it now permitted you. And seeing, Isaac, how much better things are ordered by the Deity than we could do it, and how we should choose voluntarily to surrender all into his hands, whose wisdom is so much more perfect, and whose power is so much more vast, than ours, ought we not, as a necessary consequence of this, to acquiesce in events without complaint, when they have once occurred? If Providence had made both Piso and Probus Christians, then ought you not to complain, but acquiesce; and, more than that, revere the Providence that has done it, and love those none the less whom it has directed into the path in which it would have them go. True piety, is the mother of charity.'

'Princess,' rejoined Isaac, 'you are right. The true love of God cannot exist, without making us true lovers of man; and Piso I do love, and think none the worse of him for his Christian name. But, touching Probus, and others, I experience some difficulty. Yet may I perhaps, escape thus--I may love them as men, yet hate them as Christians; just as I would bind up the wounds of a thief or an assassin, whom I found by the wayside, and yet the next hour bear witness against him, and without compunction behold him swinging upon the gibbet! It is hard, lady, for the Jew to love a Christian and a Roman.--But how have I been led away from what I wished chiefly to say before departing! When I spake just now of the darkness of Providence, I was thinking, Piso, of my journey across the desert for thy Persian brother, Calpurnius. That, as I then said to thee, was dark to me. I could not comprehend how it should come to pass that I, a Jew, of no less zeal than Simon Ben Gorah himself, should tempt such dangers in the service of thee, a Roman, and half a Christian.'

'And is the enigma solved at length?' asked Julia.

'I could have interpreted it by saying that the merit of doing a benevolent action was its solution.'

'That was little or nothing, princess. But I confess to thee, that the two gold talents of Jerusalem were much. Still, neither they, nor what profit I made in the streets of Ecbatana, and even out of that new Solomon the hospitable Levi, clearly explained the riddle. I have been in darkness till of late. And how, think you, the darkness has been dispersed?'

'We cannot tell.'

'I believe not. Piso! princess! I am the happiest man in Rome.'

'Not happier, Isaac, than Civilis the perfumer.'

'Name him not, Piso. Of all the men--he is no man--of all the living things in Rome I hold him meanest. Him, Piso, I hate. Why, I will not tell thee, but thou mayest guess. Nay, not now. I would have thee first know why I am the happiest man in Rome. Remember you the woman and the child, whom, in the midst of that burning desert, we found sitting, more dead than alive, at the roots of a cedar--the wife, as we afterwards found, of Hassan the cameldriver--and how that child, the living resemblance of my dead Joseph, wound itself round my heart, and how I implored the mother to trust it to me as mine, and I would make it richer than the richest of Ecbatana?'

'We remember it all well.'

'Well, rejoice with me! Hassan is dead!'

'Rejoice in her husband's death? Nay, that we cannot do. Milo will rejoice with thee.'

'Rejoice with me, then, that Hassan, being dead by the providence of God, Hagar and Ishmael are now mine!'--and the Jew threw down his pack again in the excess of his joy, and strode wildly about the portico.

'This is something indeed,' said Julia. 'Now, we can rejoice sincerely with you. But how happened all this? When, and how, have you obtained the news?'

'Hassan,' replied Isaac, 'as Providence willed it, died in Palmyra. His disconsolate widow, hearing of his death, in her poverty and affliction bethought herself of me, and applied, for intelligence of me, to Levi; from whom a letter came, saying that Hagar had made now on her part the proposal that had once been made on mine--that Ishmael should be mine, provided, he was not to be separated from his mother and a sister older than he by four years. I, indeed, proposed not for the woman, but for the child only--nor for the sister. But they will all be welcome. They must, by this, be in Palmyra on their way to Rome. Yes, they will be all welcome! for now once more shall the pleasant bonds of a home hold me, and the sounds of children's voices--sweeter to my ear than will ever be the harps of angels though Gabriel sweep the strings. Already, in the street Janus, where our tribe most resort, have I purchased me a house; not, Roman, such a one as I dwelt in in Palmyra, where thou and thy foolish slave searched me out, but large and well-ordered, abounding with all that woman's heart could most desire. And now what think you of all this? whither tends it? to what leads all this long and costly preparation? what think you is to come of it? I have my own judgment. This I know, it cannot be all for this, that a little child of a few years should come and dwell with an old man little removed from the very borders of the grave! Had it been only for this, so large and long a train of strange and wild events would not have been laid. This child, Piso, is more than he seems! take that and treasure it up. It is to this the finger of God has all along pointed. He is more than he seems! What he will be I say not, but I can dimly--nay clearly guess. And his mother! Piso, what will you think when I say that she is a Jewess! and his father--what will you think when I tell you that he was born upon the banks of the Gallilean lake?--that misfortunes and the love of a wandering life drew him from Judea to the farther East, and to a temporary, yet but apparent apostacy, I am persuaded, from his proper faith? This to me is all wonderful. Never have I doubted, that by my hand, by me as a mediator, some great good was to accrue to Jerusalem. And now the clouds divide, and my eye sees what has been so long concealed. It shall all come to pass, before thy young frame, princess, shall be touched by years.'

'We wish you all happiness and joy, Isaac,' replied Julia; 'and soon as this young family shall have reached your dwelling, we shall trust to see them all, specially this young object of thy great expectations.'

Isaac again fastened on his pack, and taking leave of us turned to depart, but ere he did so, he paused--fixed his dark eyes upon us--hesitated--and then said,

'Lady, if trouble flow in upon you here in Rome, and thou wilt not fly, as I have counseled, to Palmyra; but thou shouldst by and by change thy mind and desire safety, or Piso should wish thee safe--perhaps, that by thy life thou mightest work more mightily for thy faith than thou couldst do by thy death-- for oftentimes it is not by dying that we best serve God, or a great cause, but by living--then, bethink thee of my dwelling in the street Janus, where, if thou shouldst once come, I would challenge all the blood-hounds in Rome, and what is more and worse, Fronto and Varus leagued, to find thee. Peace be with you.'

And so saying, he quickly parted from us.

All Rome, Fausta, holds not a man of a larger heart than Isaac the Jew. For us, Christians as we are, there is I believe no evil to himself he would not hazard, if, in no other way, he could shield us from the dangers that impend. In his conscience he feels bound to hate us, and, often, from the language he uses, it might be inferred that he does so. But in any serious expression of his feelings, his human affections ever obtain the victory over the obligations of hatred, which his love of country, as he thinks, imposes upon him, and it would be difficult for him to manifest a warmer regard toward any of his own tribe, than he does toward Julia and myself. He is firmly persuaded, that providence is using him as an instrument, by which to effect the redemption and deliverance of his country; not that he himself is to prove the messiah of his nation--as they term their great expected prince--but that through him, in some manner, by some service rendered or office filled, that great personage will manifest himself to Israel. No disappointment damps his zeal, or convinces him of the futility of expectations resting upon no other foundation than his own inferences, conjectures, or fanciful interpretation of the dark sayings of the prophets. When in the East, it was through Palmyra, that his country was to receive her king; through her victories, that redemption was to be wrought out for Israel. Being compelled to let go that dear and cherished hope, he now fixes it upon this little "Joseph," and it will not be strange if this child of poverty and want should in the end inherit all his vast possessions, by which, he will please himself with thinking, he can force his way to the throne of Judea. Portia derives great pleasure from his conversation, and frequently detains him long for that purpose; and of her Isaac is never weary uttering the most extravagant praise. I sometimes wonder that I never knew him before the Mediterranean voyage, seeing he was so well known to Portia; but then again do not wonder, when I remember by what swarms of mendicants, strangers, and impostors of every sort, Portia was ever surrounded, from whom I turned instinctively away; especially did I ever avoid all intercourse with Christians and Jews. I held them, of all, lowest and basest.

* * * * *

We are just returned from Tibur, where we have enjoyed many pleasant hours with Zenobia. Livia was there also. The day was in its warmth absolutely Syrian, and while losing ourselves in the mazes of the Queen's extensive gardens, we almost fancied ourselves in Palmyra. Nicomachus being of the company, as he ever is, and Vabalathus, we needed but you, Calpurnius, and Gracchus, to complete the illusion.

The Queen devotes herself to letters. She is rarely drawn from her favorite studies, but by the arrival of friends from Rome. Happy for her is it that, carried back to other ages by the truths of history, or transported to other worlds by the fictions of poetry, the present and the recent can be in a manner forgotten; or, at least, that, in these intervals of repose, the soul can gather strength for the thoughts and recollections which will intrude, and which still sometimes overmaster her. Her correspondence with you is another chief solace. She will not doubt that by and by a greater pleasure awaits her, and that instead of your letters she shall receive and enjoy yourself. Farewell.

LETTER VII.

FROM PISO TO FAUSTA.

The body of the Christians, as you may well suppose, Fausta, is in a state of much agitation. Though they cannot discern plainly the form of the danger that impends, yet they discern it; and the very obscurity in which it is involved adds to their fears. It is several days since I last wrote, yet not a word has come from the palace. Aurelian is seen as usual in all public places; at the capitol, taking charge of the erection and completion of various public edifices; or, if at the palace, he rides as hard as ever, and as much, upon his Hippodrome; or, if at the Pretorian camp, he is exact and severe as ever in maintaining the discipline of the Legions. He has issued no public order of any kind that bears upon us. Yet not only the Christians, but the whole city, stand as if in expectation of measures of no little severity, going at least to the abridgement of many of our liberties, and to the deprivation of many of our privileges. This is grounded chiefly, doubtless, upon the reported imprisonment of Aurelia; for, though some have little hesitation in declaring their belief, that she has been made way with, others believe it not at all; and none can assign a reason for receiving one story rather than another. How Isaac came to be possessed of his information I do not know, but it bore all the marks of truth. He would inform me neither how he came by it, nor would he allow it to be communicated. But it would never be surprising to discover, that of my most private affairs he has a better knowledge than myself.

Do not, from what I have said, conceive of the Christians as giving any signs of unmanly fear. They perceive that danger threatens, but they change not their manner of life, not turn from the daily path of their pursuits. Believing in a providence, they put their trust in it. Their faith stands them in stead as a sufficient support and refuge. They cannot pretend, any more than Isaac, to see through the plans and purposes of Heaven. They pretend not to know, nor to be able to explain to another, why, if what they receive is the truth, and they are true believers in a true religion, they should be exposed to such sufferings for its sake; and that which is false, and injurious as false, should triumph. It is enough for them, they say, to be fully persuaded; to know, and possess, the truth. They can never relinquish it; they will rather die. But, whether Christianity die with them or not, they cannot tell--that they leave to God. They do not believe that it will--prophecy, and the present condition of the world, notwithstanding a present overhanging cloud, give them confidence in the ultimate extension and power of their faith. At any rate it shall receive no injury at their hands. They have professed it during twenty years of prosperity, and have boasted of it before the world--they shall profess it with the same boldness, and the same grateful attachment, now that adversity approaches. They are fixed--calm--unmoved. Except for a deeper tone of earnestness and feeling when you converse with them, and a cast of sadness upon the countenance, you would discern no alteration in their conduct or manner.

I might rather say that, in a very large proportion, there are observable the signs of uncommon and almost unnatural exhilaration. They even greet the coming of trouble as that which shall put their faith to the test, shall give a new testimony of the readiness of Christians to suffer, and, like the former persecution, give it a new impulse forwards. They seek occasions of controversy and conversation with the Pagans at public places, at their labor, and in the streets. The preachers assume a bolder, louder tone, and declaim with ten times more vehemence than ever against the enormities and abominations of the popular religions. Often at the market-places, and at the corners of the streets, are those to be seen, not authorized preachers perhaps, but believers and overflowing with zeal, who, at the risk of whatever popular fury and violence, hold forth the truth in Christ, and denounce the reigning idolatries and superstitions.

At the head of these is Macer; at their head, both as respects the natural vigor of his understanding, and the perfect honesty and integrity of his mind, and his dauntless courage. Every day, and all the day, is he to be found in the streets of Rome, sometimes in one quarter, sometimes in another, gathering an audience of the passengers or idlers, as it may be, and sounding in their ears the truths of the new religion. That he, and others of the same character, deserve in all they do the approbation of the Christian body, or receive it, is more than can be said. They are often, by their violences in the midst of their harangues, by harsh and uncharitable denunciations, by false and exaggerated statements, the causes of tumult and disorder, and contribute greatly to increase the general exasperation against us. With them it seems to be a maxim, that all means are lawful in a good cause. Nay, they seem rather to prefer the ruder and rougher forms of attack. They seem possessed of the idea that the world is to be converted in a day, and that if men will not at once relinquish the prejudices or the faith of years, they are fit but for cursings and burnings. In setting forth the mildest doctrine the world ever knew, delivered to mankind by the gentlest, the most patient and compassionate being it ever saw they assume a manner and use a language so entirely at variance with their theme, that it is no wonder if prejudices are strengthened oftener than they are set loose, incredulity made more incredulous, and the hardened yet harder of heart. They who hear notice the discrepancy, and fail not to make the use of it they may. When will men learn that the mind is a fortress that can never be taken by storm? You may indeed enter it rudely and by violence, and the signs of submission shall be made: but all the elements of opposition are still there. Reason has not been convinced; errors and misconceptions have not been removed, by a wise and logical and humane dealing, and supplanted by truths well proved, and shown to be truths;--and the victory is one in appearance only. And, what is more, violence, on the part of the reformer and assailant, begets violence on the other side. The whole inward man, with all his feelings, prejudices, reason, is instantly put into a posture of defence; not only of defence, for that were right, but of angry defence, which is wrong. Passion is up, which might otherwise have slept; and it is passion, never reason, which truth has to fear. The intellect in its pure form, the advocate of truth would always prefer to meet, for he can never feel sure of a single step made till this has been gained. But intellect, inflamed by passion, he may well dread, as what there is but small hope even of approaching, much less of convincing.

Often has Probus remonstrated with this order of men, but in vain. They heed him not, but in return charge him with coldness and indifference, worldliness, and all other associated faults. Especially has he labored to preserve Macer from the extremes to which he has run; for he has seen in him an able advocate of Christian truth, could he but be moderated and restrained. But Macer, though he has conceived the strongest affection for Probus, will not allow himself in this matter to be influenced by him. He holds himself answerable to conscience and God alone for the course he pursues. As for the consequences that may ensue, either to himself or his family, his mind cannot entertain them. It is for Christ he lives, and for Christ he is ready to die.

I had long wished to meet him and witness his manner both of acting and of preaching, and yesterday I was fortunate enough to encounter him. I shall give you, as exactly as I can, what took place; it will show you better than many letters could do what, in one direction, are our present position and prospects.

I was in the act of crossing the great avenue, which, on the south, leads to the Forum, when I was arrested by a disorderly crowd, such as we often see gathered suddenly in the street of a city about a thief who has been caught, or a person who has been trodden down on the pavement. It moved quickly in the direction of the tribunal of Varus, and, what was my surprise, to behold Macer, in the midst, with head aloft, and inflamed countenance, holding in his grasp, and dragging onwards, one, who would willingly have escaped. The crowd seemed disposed, as I judged by the vituperations that were directed against Macer, to interfere, but were apparently deterred by both the gigantic form of Macer and their vicinity to the tribunal, whither he was going. Waiting till they were at some distance in advance of me, I then followed, determined to judge for myself of this singular man. I was with them in the common hall before the prefect had taken his seat. When seated at his tribunal, he inquired the cause of the tumult, and who it was that wished to appeal to him.

'I am the person,' said Macer; 'and I come to drag to justice this miscreant--'

'And who may you be?'

'I should think Varus might recognize Macer.'

'It is so long since I met thee last at the Emperor's table, that thy features have escaped me.'

At which, as was their duty, the attendant rabble laughed.

'Is there any one present,' continued the prefect, 'who knows this man?'

'Varus need apply to no other than myself,' said Macer. 'I am Macer, the son of that Macer who was neighbor of the gladiator Pollex,--'

'Hold, I say,' interrupted the prefect; 'a man witnesses not here of himself. Can any one here say that this man is not crazy or drunk?'

'Varus! prefect Varus--' cried Macer, his eyes flashing lightning, and his voice not less than thunder; but he was again interrupted.

'Peace, slave! or rods shall teach thee where thou art.' And at the same moment, at a sign from Varus, he was laid hold of with violence by officials of the place armed with spears and rods, and held.

'What I wish to know then,' said Varus, turning to the crowd, 'is, whether this is not the street brawler, one of the impious Gallileans, a man who should long ago have been set in the stocks to find leisure for better thoughts?'

Several testified, as was desired, that this was he.

'This is all I wish to know,' said the prefect. 'The man is either without wits, or they are disordered, or else the pestilent faith he teaches has made the nuisance of him he is, as it does of all who meddle with it. It is scarcely right that he should be abroad. Yet has he committed no offence that condemns him either to scourging or the prison. Hearken therefore, fellow! I now dismiss thee without the scourging thou well deservest; but, if thou keep on thy wild and lawless way, racks and dungeons shall teach thee what there is in Roman justice. Away with him!'

'Romans! Roman citizens!' cried Macer; 'are these your laws and this your judge?--'

'Away with him, I say!' cried the prefect; and the officers of the palace hurried him out of the hall.

As he went, a voice from the crowd shouted,

'Roman citizens, Macer, are long since dead. 'Tis a vain appeal.'

'I believe you,' replied Macer; 'tyrant and slave stand now for all who once bore the proud name of Roman.'

This violence and injustice on the part of Varus must be traced--for though capricious, and imperious, this is not his character--to the language of Macer in the shop of Publius, and to his apprehension lest the same references to his origin, which he would willingly have forgotten, should be made, and perhaps more offensively still, in the presence of the people. Probus, on the former occasion, lamented deeply that Macer should have been tempted to rehearse in the way he did some of the circumstances of the prefect's history, as its only end could be to needlessly irritate the man of power, and raise up a bitterer enemy than we might otherwise have found in him.

Upon leaving the tribunal, I was curious to watch still further the movements of the Christian. The crowd about him increased rather than diminished, as he left the building and passed into the street. At but a little distance from the hall of the prefect, stands the Temple of Peace, with its broad and lofty flights of steps. When Macer had reached it he paused, and looked round upon the motley crowd that had gathered about him.

'Go up! go up!' cried several voices. 'We will hear thee.'

'There is no prefect here,' cried another.

Macer needed no urging, but quickly strode up the steps, till he stood between the central columns of the temple and his audience had disposed themselves below him in every direction, when he turned and gazed upon the assembled people, who had now--by the addition of such as passed along, and who had no more urgent business than to attend to that of any others whom they might chance to meet,--grown to a multitude. After looking upon them for a space, as if studying their characters, and how he could best adapt his discourse to their occasions, he suddenly and abruptly broke out--

'You have asked me to come up here; and I am here; glad for once to be in such a place by invitation. And now I am here, and am about to speak, you will expect me to say something of the Christians.'

'Yes yes.'

'But I shall not--not yet. Perhaps by and by. In the meantime my theme shall be the prefect! the prefect Varus!'

'A subject full of matter,' cried one near Macer.

'Better send for him,' said another. 'Twere a pity he lost it.'

'Yes,' continued Macer, 'it is a subject full of matter, and I wish myself he were here to see himself in the mirror I would hold before him; he could not but grow pale with affright. You have just had a sample of Roman justice! How do you like it, Romans? I had gone there to seek justice; not for a Christian, but against a Christian. A Christian master had abused his slave with cruelty, I standing by; and when to my remonstrance--myself feeling the bitter stripes he laid on--he did but ply his thongs the more, I seized the hardened monster by the neck, and wrenching from his grasp the lash, I first plied it upon his own back, and then dragged him to the judgment-seat of Varus,--'

'O fool!'

'You say well--fool that I was, crying for justice! How I was dealt with, some of you have seen. There, I say, was a sample of Roman justice for you! So in these times does power sport itself with poverty. It was not so once in Rome. Were Cincinnatus or Regulus at the tribunal of Varus, they would fare like the soldier Macer. And who, Romans, is this Varus? and why is he here in the seat of authority? At the tribunal, Varus did not know me. But what if I were to tell you there was but a thin wall between the rooms where we were born, and that when we were boys we were ever at the same school!--not such schools as you are thinking of, where the young go for letters and for Greek, but the school where many of you have been and are now at, I dare say, the school of Roman vice, which you may find always open all along the streets, but especially where I and Varus were, in one of the sinks near the Flavian. Pollex, the gladiator, was father of Varus!--not worse, but just as bad, as savage, as beastly in his vices, as are all of that butcher tribe. My father--Macer too--I will not say more of him than that he was keeper of the Vivaria of the amphitheatre, and passed his days in caging and uncaging the wild beasts of Asia and Africa; in feeding them when there were no games on foot, and starving them when there were. Varus, the prefect, Romans, and I, were at this school till I joined the legions under Valerian, and he, by a luckier fortune, as it would be deemed, found favor in the eyes of Gallienus, to whom, with his fair sister Fannia, he was sold by those demons Pollex and Cecina. I say nothing of how it fared with him in that keeping. Fannia has long since found the grave. Is Varus one who should sit at the head of Rome? He is a man of blood, of crime, of vice, such as you would not bear to be told of! I say not this as if he were answerable for his birth and early vice, but that, being such, this is not his place. He could not help it, nor I, that we were born and nurtured where we were; that the sight of blood and the smell of it, either of men or beasts, was never out of our eyes and nostrils, during all our boyhood and youth; that to him, and me, the sweetest pleasure of our young life was, when the games came on, and the beasts were let loose upon one another, and,--O the hardening of that life!--when, specially, there were prisoners or captives, on which to glut their raging hunger! Those were the days and hours marked whitest in our calendar. And, whitest of all, were the days of the Decian persecution, when the blood of thrice cursed Christians, as I was taught to name them, flowed like water. Every day then Varus and I had our sport; working up the beasts, by our torments, to an unnatural height of madness ere they were let loose, and then rushing to the gratings, as the doors were thrown open, to see the fury with which they would spring upon their defenceless victims too, and tear them piecemeal. The Romans required such servants--and we were they. They require them now, and you may find any number of such about the theatres. But if there must be such there, why should they be taken thence and put upon the judgment-seat? save, for the reason, that they may have been thoroughly purged, as it were, by fire-- which Varus has not been. What with him was necessary and forced when young, is now chosen and voluntary. Vice is now his by election. Now, I ask, why has the life of Varus been such? and why, being such, is he here? Because you are so! Yes, because you are all like him! It is you, Roman citizens, who rear the theatres, the circuses, and the thousand temples of vice, which crowd the streets of Rome,--'

'No, no! it is the emperors.'

'But who make the emperors? You Romans of these times, are a race of cowards and slaves, and it is therefore that tyrants rule over you. Were you freemen, with the souls of freemen in you, do you think you would bear as you do--and love and glory in the yoke--this rule of such creatures as Varus, and others whom it were not hard to name? I know what you are--for I have been one of you. I have not been, nor am I now, hermit, as you may think, being a Christian. A Christian is a man of the world--a man of action and of suffering--not of rest and sleep. I have ever been abroad among men, both before I was a Christian and since; and I know what you are. You are of the same stamp as Varus! nay, start not, nor threaten with your eyes,--I fear you not. If you are not so, why, I say, is Varus there? You know that I speak the truth. The people of Rome are corrupt as their rulers! How should it be much otherwise? You are fed by the largesses of the Emperor, you have your two loaves a day and your pork, and you need not and so do not work. You have no employment but idleness, and idleness is not so much a vice itself as the prolific mother of all vices. When I was one of you, it was so; and so it is now. My father's labor was nothing; he was kept by the state. The Emperor was not more a man of pleasure than he, nor the princes, than I and Varus. Was that a school of virtue? When I left the service of the amphitheatre I joined the Legions. In the army I had work, and I had fighting, but my passions, in the early days of that service, raged like the sea; and during all the reign of Valerian's son there was no bridle upon them;--for I served under the general Carinus, and what Carinus was and is, most of you know. O the double horrors of those years! I was older, and yet worse and worse. God! I marvel that thou didst not interpose and strike me dead! But thy mercy spared me, and now the lowest, lowest hell shall not be mine.' Tears, forced by these recollections, flowed down his cheeks, and for a time he was speechless.

'Such, Romans, was I once. What am I now? I am a changed man--through and through. There is not a thought of my mind, nor a fibre of my body, what they were once. You may possibly think the change has been for the worse, seeing me thus thrust forth from the tribunal of the prefect with dishonor, when I was once a soldier and an officer under Aurelian. I would rather a thousand times be what I am, a soldier of Jesus Christ. And I would that, by anything I could do, you, any one of you, might be made to think so too; I would that Varus might, for I bear him no ill will.

'But what am I now? I am so different a man from what I once was, that I can hardly believe myself to be the same. The life which I once led, I would not lead again--no--not one day nor hour of it, though you would depose Aurelian to day and crown me Caesar to-morrow. I would no more return to that life, than I would consent to lose my nature and take a swine's, and find elysium where as a man I once did, in sinks and sties. I would not renounce for the wealth of all the world, and its empire too, that belief in the faith of Christ, the head of the Christians, which has wrought so within me.

'And what has made me so--would make you so--if you would but hearken to it. And would it not be a good thing if the flood of vice, which pours all through the streets of Rome, were stayed? Would it not be a happy thing, if the misery which dwells beneath these vaulted roofs and these humbler ones equally, the misery which drunkenness and lust, the lust of money, and the love of place, and every evil passion generates, were all wiped away, and we all lived together observant of the rights of one another, helping one another; not oppressing; loving, not hating; showing in our conduct as men, the virtues of little children? Would it not be happier if all this vast population were bound together by some common ties of kindred; if all held all as brethren; if the poor man felt himself to be the same as Aurelian himself, because he is a man like him and weighs just as much as he in the scales of God, and that it is the vice in the one or the other, and that only that sinks him lower? Would it not be better, if you all could see in the presiding power of the universe, one great and good Being, who needs not to be propitiated by costly sacrifices of oxen or bulls, nor by cruel ones of men,--but is always kindly disposed towards you, and desires nothing so much as to see you living virtuously, and is never grieved as he is to see you ruining your own peace,--not harming him--by your vices? for you will bear witness with me that your vices are never a cause of happiness. Would it not be better if you could behold such a God over you, in the place of those who are called gods, and whom you worship, as I did once, because I feared to do otherwise, and yet sin on never the less: who are your patterns not so much in virtue as in all imaginable vice?'

'Away with the wicked!'--'Away with the fellow!' cried several voices; but others predominated, saying, 'Let him alone!'--'He speaks well! We will hear him!'--'We will defend him! go on, go on!'

'I have little or nothing more to say,' continued Macer. 'I will only ask you whether you must not judge that to be a very powerful principle of some kind that drew me up out of that foul pit into which I was fallen, and made me what I am now? Which of you now feels that he has motive strong enough to work out such a deliverance for him? What help in this way do you receive from your priests, if perchance you ever apply to them? What book of instructions concerning the will of the gods have you, to which you can go at any time and all times? Only believe as I do, Romans, and you will hate sin as I do. You cannot help it. Believe in the God that I do, and in the revealer of his will, the teacher whom he sent into the world to save us from our heathen errors and vices, and you will then be more than the Romans you once were. You are now, and you know it, infinitely less. Then you will be what the old Romans were and more. You will be as brave as they, and more just. You will be as generous and more gentle. You will love your own country as well, but you will love others too. You will be more ready to offer up your lives for your country, for it will be better worth dying for; every citizen will be a brother; every ruler a brother; it will be like dying for your own little household. If you would see Rome flourish, she must become more pure. She can stagger along not much longer under this mountain weight of iniquity that presses her into the dust. She needs a new Hercules to cleanse her foul chambers. Christ is he; and if you will invite him, he will come and sweep away these abominations, so that imperial Rome shall smell fragrantly as a garden of spices.'

Loud exclamations of approval here interrupted Macer. The great proportion of those who were present were now evidently with him, and interested in his communications.

'Tell us,' cried one, as soon as the noise subsided, 'how you became what you are? What is to be done?'

'Yes,' cried many voices, 'tell us.'

'I will tell you gladly,' answered Macer. 'I first heard the word of truth from the lips of Probus, a preacher of the Christians, whom you too may hear whenever you will, by seeking him out on the days when the Christians worship. Probus was in early life a priest of the temple of Jupiter, and if any man in Rome can place the two religions side by side, and make the differences plain, it is he. Go to him such of you as can, and you will never repent it. But if you would all learn the first step toward Christian truth, and all truth, it is this; lay aside your prejudices, be willing to see, hear, and judge for yourselves. Take not rumor for truth. Do not believe without evidence both for and against. You would not, without evidence and reason, charge Aurelian with the death of Aurelia, though ten thousand tongues report it. Charge not the Christians with worse things then, merely because the wicked and ill-disposed maliciously invent them and spread them. If you would know the whole truth and doctrine of Christians; if you would ascend to the fountain-head of all Christian wisdom, take to your homes our sacred books and read them. Some of you at least can obtain them. Let one purchase, and then twenty or fifty read. One thing before I cease. Believe not the wicked aspersions of the prefect. He charges me as a brawler, a disturber of the peace and order of the city. Romans, believe me, I am a lover of peace, but I am a lover of freedom too. Because I am a lover of peace, and would promote it, do I labor to teach the doctrines of Christ, which are doctrines of peace and love, both at home and abroad, in the city and throughout the world; and because I am the friend of freedom, do I open my mouth at all times and in every place, wherever I can find those who, like you, are ready to hear the words of salvation. When in Rome I can no longer speak--no longer speak for the cause of what I deem truth, then will I no longer be a Roman. Then will I that day renounce my name and my country. Thanks to Aurelian, he has never chained up the tongue. I have fought and bled under him, and never was there a braver man, or who honored courage more in others. I do not believe he will ever do so cowardly a thing as to restrain the freedom of men's speech. Aurelian is some things, but he is not others. He is severe and cruel, but not mean. Cut Aurelian in two, and throw the worser half away, and t'other is as royal a man as ever the world saw.

'One thing more, good friends and citizens: If I am sometimes carried away by my passions to do that which seems a disturbance of the common order, say that it is the soldier Macer that does it, not his Christian zeal--his human passions, not his new-adopted faith. It is not at once and perfectly that a man passes from one life to another; puts off one nature and takes another. Much that belonged to Macer of the amphitheatre, and Macer the soldier, cleaves to him now. But make not his religion amenable for that. You who would see the law of Christ written, not only on a book but in the character and life of a living man, go read the Christian Probus.'

As he said these words he began to descend the steps of the temple; but many crowded round him, assailing him, some with reproaches, and others with inquiries put by those who seemed anxious to know the truth. The voices of his opponents were the most violent and prevailed, and made me apprehensive that they would proceed to greater length than speech. But Macer stood firm, nothing daunted by the uproar. One, who signalized himself by the loudness and fierceness of his cries, exclaimed, 'that he was nothing else than an atheist like all the rest of the Christians; they have no gods; they deny the gods of Rome, and they give us nothing in their stead.'

'We deny the gods of Rome, I know,' replied Macer, 'and who would not, who had come to years of discretion? who had so much as left his nurse's lap? A fouler brotherhood than they the lords of Heaven, Rome does not contain. Am I to be called upon to worship a set of wretches chargeable with all the crimes and vices to be found on earth? It is this accursed idolatry, O Romans, that has sunk you so low in sin! They are your lewd, and drunken, and savage deities, who have taught you all your refinement in wickedness; and never, till you renounce them, never till you repent you of your iniquities--never till you turn and worship the true God will you rise out of the black Tartarean slough in which you are lying. These two hundred years and more has God called to you by his Son, and you have turned away your ears; you have hardened your hearts; the prophets who have come to you in his name have you slain by the sword or hung upon the accursed tree. Awake out of your slumbers! These are the last days. God will not forbear forever. The days of vengeance will come; they are now at hand: I can hear the rushing of that red right arm hot with wrath--'

'Away with him! away with him!' broke from an hundred voices!--'Down with the blasphemer!'--'Who is he to speak thus of the gods of Rome?'--'Seize the impious Gallilean, and away with him to the prefect'--These, and a thousand exclamations of the same kind, and more savage, were heard on every side; and, at the same moment, their denial and counter-exclamations, from as many more.

'He has spoken the truth!'--'He is a brave fellow!' 'He shall not be touched except we fall first!'--came from a resolute band who encompassed the preacher, and seemed resolved to make good their words by defending him against whatever assault might be made. Macer, himself a host in such an affray, neither spoke nor moved, standing upright and still as a statue; but any one might see the soldier in his kindling eye, and that a slight cause would bring him upon the assailants with a fury that would deal out wounds and death. He had told them that the old Legionary was not quite dead within him, and sometimes usurped the place of the Christian; this they seemed to remember, and after showering upon him vituperation and abuse in every form, one after another they withdrew and left him with those who had gathered immediately around him. These too soon took their leave of him, and Macer, unimpeded and alone, turned towards his home.

When I related to Probus afterwards what I had heard and witnessed, he said that I was fortunate in hearing what was so much more sober and calm than that which usually fell from him; that generally he devoted himself to an exposition of the absurdities of the heathen worship, and the abominations of the mysteries, and the vices of the priesthood; and he rarely ended without filling with rage a great proportion of those who heard him. Many a time had he been assaulted; and hardly had escaped with his life. You will easily perceive, Fausta, how serious an injury is inflicted upon us by rash and violent declaimers like Macer. There are others like him; he is by no means alone, though he is far the most conspicuous. Together they help to kindle the flame of active hostility, and infuse fresh bitterness into the Pagan heart. Should the Emperor carry into effect the purposes now ascribed to him, these men will be sure victims, and the first.

* * * * *

Upon my return after hearing Macer, I found Livia seated with Julia, to whom she often comes thus, and then together--I often accompanying--we visit Tibur. She had but just arrived. It was easy to see that the light-heartedness, which so manifested itself always in the beaming countenance and the elastic step, was gone; the usual signs of it at least were not visible. Her whole expression was serious and anxious; and upon her face were the traces of recent grief. For a long time, after the first salutations and inquiries were through, neither spoke. At length Livia said,

'I am come now, Julia, to escape from what has become of late little other than a prison. The Fabrician dungeons are not more gloomy than the gardens of Sallust are now. No more gaiety; no feasting by day and carousal by night; the gardens never illuminated; no dancing nor music. It is a new life for me: and then the only creatures to be seen, that hideous Fronto and the smiling Varus; men very well in their place, but no inmates of palaces.'

'Well' said Julia; 'there is the greater reason why we should see more of each other and of Zenobia. Aurelian is the same?'

'The same? There is the same form, and the same face, and the same voice; but the form is motionless, save when at the Hippodrome,--the face black as Styx, and his voice rougher than the raven's. That agreeable humor and sportiveness, which seemed native to him, though by reason of his thousand cares not often seen, is now wholly gone. He is observant as ever of all the forms of courtesy, and I am to him what I have ever been; but a dark cloud has settled over him and all the house, and I would willingly escape if I could. And worse than all, is this of Aurelia! Alas, poor girl!'

'And what, Livia, is the truth?' said Julia; 'the city is filled with rumors, but they are so at variance one with another, no one knows which to believe, or whether none.'

'I hardly know myself,' replied Livia. 'All I know with certainty is, that I have lost my only companion--or the only one I cared for--and that Aurelian merely says she has been sent to the prisons at the Fabrician bridge. I cannot tell you of our parting. Aurelia was sure something terrible was designed against her, from the sharpness and violence of her uncle's language, and she left me as if she were never to see me again. But I would believe no such thing, and so I told her, and tried to give to her some of the courage and cheerfulness which I pretended to have myself: but it was to no purpose. She departed weeping as if her heart were broken. I love her greatly, notwithstanding her usual air of melancholy and her preference of solitude, and I have found in her, as you know, my best friend and companion. Yet I confess there is that in her which I never understood, and do not now understand. I hope she will comply with the wishes of Aurelian, and that I shall soon see her again. The difficulty is all owing to this new religion. I wish, Julia, there were no such thing. It seems to me to do nothing but sow discord and violence.'

'That, dear Livia,' said Julia, 'is not a very wise wish; especially seeing you know, as you will yourself confess, so little about it.'

'But,' quickly added Livia, 'was it not better as it was at Palmyra? who heard then of these bitter hostilities? who were there troubled about their worship? One hardly knew there was such a thing as a Christian. When Paul was at the palace, it was still all the same only, if anything, a little more agreeable. But here, no one at the gardens speaks of Christians but with an assassin air that frightens one. There must surely be more evil in them than I ever dreamed of.'

'The evil, Livia,' answered her sister, 'comes not from the Christians nor Christianity, but from those who oppose them. There were always Christians in Palmyra, and, as you say, even in the palace, yet there was always peace and good-will too. If Christianity were in itself an element of discord and division, why were no such effects seen there? The truth is, Livia, the division and discord are created, not by the new religion, but by those who resist it, and will not suffer people to act and think as they please about it. Under Zenobia, all had liberty to believe as they would. And there was under her the reign of universal peace and good-will. Here, on the other hand, it has been the practice of the state to interfere, and say what the citizens shall believe and whom they shall worship, and what and whom they shall not. How should it be otherwise than that troubles should spring up, under legislation so absurd and so wicked? Would it not be a certain way to introduce confusion, if the state--or Aurelian--should prescribe our food and drink? or our dress? And if confusion did arise, and bitter opposition, you could not justly say it was owing to the existence of certain kinds of food, or of clothes which people fancied, but to their being interfered with. Let them alone, and they will please themselves and be at peace.'

'Yes,' said Livia, 'that may be. But the common people are in no way fit judges in such things, and it seems to me if either party must give way, it were better the people did. The government has the power and they will use it.'

'In so indifferent a matter as food or dress,' rejoined the sister, 'if a government were so foolish as to make prohibitory and whimsical laws, it were better to yield than contend. But in an affair so different from that as one's religion, one could not act in the same way. I may dress in one kind of stuff as well as another; it is quite a possible thing: but is it not plainly impossible, if I think one kind of stuff is of an exquisite fineness and color, for me to believe and say at the same time, that its texture is coarse and its hue dull? The mind cannot believe according to any other laws than those of its own constitution. Is it not then the height of wickedness to set out to make people believe and act one way in religion? The history of the world has shown that, in spite of men's wickedness, there is nothing on earth they value as they do their religion. They will die rather than change or renounce it. Men are the same now. To require that any portion of the people shall renounce their religion is to require them to part with that which they value most--more than life itself--and is it not in effect pronouncing against them a sentence of destruction? Some indeed will relinquish it rather than die; and some will play the hypocrite for a season, intending to return to a profession of it in more peaceful times: but most, and the best, will die before they will disown their faith.'

'Then if that is so,' said Livia, 'and I confess what you say cannot be denied, I would that Aurelian could be prevailed upon to recede from a position which he appears to be taking. His whole nature now seems to have been set on fire by this priest Fronto. Superstition has wholly seized and possessed him. His belief is that Rome can never be secure and great till the enemies of the gods, as well as of the state, shall perish; and pushed on by Fronto, so far as can be gathered from their discourse, is now bent on their injury or destruction. I wish he could be changed back again to what he was before this notion seized him. Piso, have you seen him? Have you of late conversed with him?'

'Only, Livia, briefly; and on this topic only at intervals of other talk; for he avoids it, at least with me. But from what we all know of Aurelian, it is not one's opinion nor another's that can alter his will when once bent one way.'

'How little did I once deem,' said Livia, 'when I used to wish so for greatness and empire, that they could be so darkened over. I thought that to be great was necessarily to be happy. But I was but a child then.'

'How long since was that?' asked Julia, smiling.

'Ah! you would say I am little better than that now.'

'You are young yet, Livia, for much wisdom to have come; and you must not wonder if it come slowly, for you are unfortunately placed to gain it. An idol on its pedestal can rarely have but two thoughts--that it is an idol, and that it is to be worshipped. The entrance of all other wisdom is quite shut out.'

'How pleasant a thing it is, Piso, to have an elder sister as wise as Julia! But come, will you to Tibur? I must have Faustula, now I have lost Aurelia.'

'O no, Livia,' said Julia; 'take her not away from Zenobia. She can ill spare her.'

'But there is Vabalathus.'

'Yes, but he is now little there. He is moreover preparing for his voyage. Faustula is her all.'

'Ah, then it cannot be! Yes, it were very wrong. But, this being so, I see not then but I must go to her, or come live with you. Only think of one's trying to escape from the crown of Rome? I can hardly believe I am Livia; once never to be satisfied with power and greatness--now tired of them! No, not that exactly--'

'You are tired, only, Livia, of some little attendant troubles; you like not that overhanging cloud you just spoke of; but for the empire itself, you love that none the less. To believe that, it is enough to see you.'

'I suppose you are right. Julia is always right, Piso.'

So our talk ran on; sometimes into graver and then into lighter themes--often stopping and lingering long over you, and Calpurnius, and Gracchus. You wished to know more of Livia and her thoughts, and I have given her to you in just the mood in which she happened to be.

* * * * *

The wife of Macer has just been here, seeking from Julia both assistance and comfort. She implores us to do what we may to calm and sober her husband.

'As the prospect of danger increases,' she said to Julia, 'he grows but the more impetuous and ungovernable. He is abroad all the day and every day, preaching all over Rome, and brings home nothing for the support of the family; and if it were not for the Emperor's bounty, we should starve.'

'And does that support you?'

'O no, lady! it hardly gives us food enough to subsist upon. Then we have besides to pay for our lodging and our clothes. But I should mind not at all our labor nor our poverty, did I not hear from so many that my husband is so wild and violent in his preaching, and when he disputes with the gentiles, as he will call them. I am sure it is a good cause to suffer in, if one must suffer; but if our dear Macer would only work half the time, there would be no occasion to suffer, which we should now were it not for Demetrius the jeweler--who lives hard by, and who I am sure has been very kind to us--and our good Celia.'

'You do not then,' I asked, 'blame your religion nor weary of it?'

'O, sir, surely not. It is our greatest comfort. We all look out with expectation of our greatest pleasure, when Macer returns home, after his day's labors,--and labors they surely are, and will destroy him, unless he is persuaded to leave them off. For when he is at home the children all come round him, and he teaches them in his way what religion is. Sometimes it is a long story he gives them of his life, when he was a little boy and knew nothing about Christ, and what wicked things he did, and sometimes about his serving as a soldier under the Emperor. But he never ends without showing them what Christ's religion tells them to think of such ways of life. And then, sir, before we go to bed he reads to us from the gospels--which he bought when he was in the army, and was richer than he is now--and prays for us all, for the city, and the Emperor, and the gentiles. So that we want almost nothing, as I may say, to make us quite contented and happy.'

'Have you ever been disturbed in your dwelling on Macer's account?'

'O yes, sir, and we are always fearing it. This is our great trouble. Once the house was attacked by the people of the street, and almost torn down--and we escaped, I and the children, through a back way into the shop of the good Demetrius. There we were safe; and while we were gone our little cabin was entered, and everything in it broken in pieces. Macer was not at home, or I think he would have been killed.

'Did you apply to the prefect?'

'No, sir, I do not believe there would be much use in that: they say he hates the Christians so.'

'But he is bound to preserve order in the city.'

'Yes, sir; but for a great man like him it's easy to see only one way, and to move so slowly that it does no good. That is what our people say of him. When the Christians are in trouble he never comes, if he comes at all, till it is too late to do them any service. The best way for us is, I think, to live quietly, and not needlessly provoke the gentiles, nor believe that we can make Christians of them all in a day. That is my husband's dream. He thinks that he must deliver his message to people, whether they will or not, and it almost seems as if the more hostile they were, the more he made it his duty to preach to them, which certainly was not the way in which Christ did, as he reads his history to us. It was just the other way. It almost makes me believe that some demon has entered into him, he is so different from what he was, and abroad from what he is at home. Do you think that likely, sir? I have been at times inclined to apply to Felix to see if he could not exorcise him.'

'No, I do not think so certainly; but many may. I believe he errs in his notion of the way in which to do good; but under some circumstances it is so hard to tell which the best way is, that we must judge charitably of one another. Some would say that Macer is right; others that the course of Probus is wisest; and others, that of Felix. We must do as we think right, and leave the issue to God.'

'But you will come and see us? We dwell near the ruins, and behind the shop of Demetrius. Every body knows Demetrius.'

I assured her I would go.

I almost wish, Fausta, that Julia was with you. All classes seem alike exposed to danger. But I suppose it would be in vain to propose such a step to her, especially after what she said to Isaac. You now, after your storm, live at length in calm: not exactly in sunshine; for you would say the sun never can seem to shine that falls upon the ruins of Palmyra. But calm and peace you certainly have, and they are much. I wish Julia could enjoy them with you. For here, every hour, so it now seems to me, the prospect darkens, and it will be enough for one of us to remain to encounter the evil, whatever it may be, and defend the faith we have espoused. This is an office more appropriate to man than to woman; though emergencies may arise, as they have, when woman herself must forget her tenderness and put on soldiers' panoply; and when it has come, never has she been found wanting. Her promptness to believe that which is good and pure, has been equalled by her fortitude and patience in suffering for it.

You will soon see Vabalathus. He will visit you before he enters upon his great office. By him I shall write to you soon again. Farewell.

* * * * *

AURELIAN;

ROME IN THE THIRD CENTURY

* * * * *

LETTER VIII.

FROM PISO TO FAUSTA.

Marcus and Lucilia are inconsolable. Their grief, I fear, will be lasting as it is violent. They have no resource but to plunge into affairs and drive away memory by some active and engrossing occupation. Yet they cannot always live abroad; they must at times return to themselves and join the company of their own thoughts. And then, memory is not to be put off; at such moments this faculty seems to constitute the mind more than any other. It becomes the mind itself. The past rises up in spite of ourselves, and overshadows the present. Whether its scenes have been prosperous or afflictive, but especially if they have been shameful, do they present themselves with all the vividness of the objects before us and the passing hour, and infinitely increase our pains. We in vain attempt to escape. We are prisoners in the hands of a giant. To forget is not in our power. The will is impotent. The effort to forget is often but an effort to remember. Fast as we fly, so fast the enemy of our peace pursues. Memory is a companion who never leaves us--or never leaves us long. It is the true Nemesis. Tartarean regions have no worse woes, nor the Hell of Christians, than memory inflicts upon those who have done evil. My friends struggle in vain. They have not done evil indeed, but they have suffered it. The sorest calamity that afflicts mortals has overtaken them; their choicest jewel has been torn from them; and they can no more drown the memory of their loss than they can take that faculty itself and tear it from their souls. Comfort cannot come from that quarter. It can come only from being re-possessed of that which has been lost hereafter, and from enjoying the hope of that felicity now. See how Marcus writes. After much else, he says,

'I miss you, Piso, and the conversations which we had together. I know not how it is, but your presence acted as a restraint upon my hot and impatient temper. Since your departure I have been little less than mad, and so far from being of service to Lucilia, she has been compelled to moderate her own grief in the hope to assuage mine. I have done nothing but rave, and curse my evil fortune. And can anything else be looked for? How should a man be otherwise than exasperated when the very thing he loves best in the wide universe is, without a moment's warning, snatched away from him? A man falls into a passion if his seal is stolen, or his rings, or his jewels, if his dwelling burns down, or his slaves run away or die by some pestilence. And why should he not much more when the providence of the gods, or the same power whatever it may be that gave as a child, tears it from us again; and just then when we have so grown into it that it is like hewing us in two? I can believe in nothing but capricious chance. We live by chance, and so we die. Such events are otherwise inexplicable. For what reason can by the most ingenious be assigned for giving life for a few years to a being like Gallus, and who then, before he is more than just past the threshold of life, before a single power of his nature has put itself forth, but at the moment when he is bound to his parents by ties of love which never afterwards would be stronger--is struck dead? We can give no account of it. It is irreconcilable with the hypothesis of an intelligent and good Providence. It has all the features of chance upon it. A god could not have done it unless he had been the god of Tartarus. Dark Pluto might, or the avenging Furies, were they supreme. But away with all such dreams! The slaves who were his proper attendants, have been scourged and crucified. That at first gave me some relief; but already I repent it. So it is with me; I rush suddenly upon what at the moment I think right, and then as suddenly think and feel that I have done wrong, and so suffer. I see and experience nothing but suffering, whichever way I turn. Truly we are riddles. Piso, you cannot conceive of my loss. It was our only child--and the only one we shall ever know. I wish that I believed in the gods that I might curse them.'

And much more in the same frantic way. Time will blunt his grief; but it will bring him I fear no other or better comfort. He hopes for oblivion of his loss; but that can never be. He may cease to grieve as he grieves now; but he can never cease to remember. I trust to see him again ere long, and turn his thoughts into a better channel.

* * * * *

I did not forget to keep my promise to the wife of Macer. In truth I had long regarded it as essential to our safety almost, certainly to our success, that this man, and others of the same character, should be restrained in some way in their course of mistaken zeal; and had long intended to use what influence to that end I might possess. Probus had promised to accompany me, and do what in him lay, to rescue religion from this peril at the hands of one of her best friends. He joined me toward the evening of the same day on which I had seen the wife of Macer, and we took our way toward his dwelling.

It was already past the hour of twilight when we reached the part of the city where Macer dwells, and entered the ruins among which his cabin stands. These ruins are those of extensive and magnificent baths destroyed a long time ago, and to this day remaining as the flames left them. At the rear of them, far from the street and concealed from it by arches and columns and fragments of wall, we were directed by the rays of a lamp streaming from a window, to the place we sought. We wound our way among these fallen or still standing masses of stone, which frequently hid from us the object of our search, till, as we found ourselves near the spot, we were arrested by the sound of a single voice uttering itself with vehemence and yet solemnity. We paused, but could not distinguish the words used; but the same conviction possessed us as to its cause. It was Macer at prayer. We moved nearer, so that, without disturbing the family, we might still make ourselves of the number of hearers. His voice, loud and shrill, echoed among the ruins and conveyed to us, though at some distance, every word that he uttered. But for the noise of carriages and passengers it would have penetrated even to the streets. The words we caught were such as these--

--'If they hear thee not, O Lord, nor reverence thy messengers, but deny thee and turn upon those whom thou sendest the lip of scorn and the eye of pride, and will none of their teachings, and so do despite to the spirit of thy grace, and crucify the Lord afresh, then do thou, O Lord, come upon them as once upon the cities of the plain in the times of thine anger. Let fire from Heaven consume them. Let the earth yawn and swallow them up. Tear up the foundations of this modern Babylon; level to the earth her proud walls; and let her stand for a reproach, and a hissing, and a scorn; through all generations; so that men shall say as they pass by, lo! the fate of them that held to their idols rather than serve the living God; their proud palaces are now dwellings of dragons, and over her ruins the trees of the forest are now spreading their branches. But yet, O Lord, may this never be; but may a way of escape be made for them through thy mercy. And to this end may we thy servants, to whom thou hast given the sword of the spirit, gird it upon our sides, lift up our voices and spare not, day and night, morning and evening, in the public place, and at the corners of the streets; in all places, and in every presence, proclaiming the good news of salvation. Let not cowardice seal our lips. Whether before gentile or jew, emperor or slave, may we speak as becomes the Lord's anointed. Warm the hearts of the cold and dead; put fire into them; fire from thine own altar. The world, O Lord, and its honors and vanities, seduce thine own servants from thee. They are afraid, they are cold, they are dead, and the enemy lifts himself up and triumphs. For this we would mourn and lament. Give us, O Lord, the courage and the zeal of thine early apostles and teachers so that no fear of tortures and death may make us traitors to Christ and thee.'

It was a long time that he went on in this strain, inveighing, with heat and violence, against all who withdrew their hand from the work, or abated their zeal. When he had ceased, and we stood waiting to judge whether the service were wholly ended, the voices of the whole family apparently, were joined together in a hymn of praise--Macer's now more gentle and subdued, as if to hear himself the tones of the children and of his wife who accompanied him. The burden of the hymn was also a prayer for a spirit of fidelity and a temper of patience, in the cause of truth and Christ. It was worship in the highest sense, and none within the dwelling could have joined more heartily than we did who stood without.

When it was ended, and with it evidently the evening service, we approached, and knocked for admittance. Macer appeared holding a light above his head, and perceiving who his guests were, gave us cordial welcome, at the same time showing us into his small apartment and placing stools for our accommodation. The room in which we were was small and vaulted, and built of stone in the most solid manner. I saw at once that it was one of the smaller rooms of the ancient bath, which had escaped entire destruction and now served as a comfortable habitation. A door on the inner side appeared to connect it with a number of similar apartments. A table in the centre and a few stools, a shelf on which were arranged the few articles which they possessed both for cooking and eating their food, constituted the furniture of the room. In the room next beyond I could see pallets of straw laid upon the floor, which served for beds. Macer, his wife, and six children, composed the family then present; the two elder sons being yet absent at their work, in the shop of Demetrius. The mother held at her breast an infant of a year or more; one of three years sprang again upon his father's lap, as he resumed his seat after our entrance, whence he had apparently been just dislodged; the rest, sitting in obscure parts of the room, were at first scarcely visible. The wife of Macer expressed heartily her pleasure at seeing us, and said even more by her flushed and animated countenance than by her words. The severe countenance of Macer himself relaxed and gave signs of satisfaction.

'I owe you, Piso,' he said, 'many thanks for mercies shown to my wife and my little ones here, and I am glad to see you among us. We are far apart enough as the world measures such things, but in Christ we are one. At such times as these, when the Prince of Darkness rules, we ought if ever to draw toward each other, that so we may make better our common defence. I greet you as a brother--I trust to love you as one.'

I told him that nothing should be wanting on my part toward a free and friendly intercourse; that from all I had heard of him I had conceived a high regard for him, and owed him more thanks for what he had done in behalf of our religion, than he could me for any services I had rendered him.

'Me?' said he, and his head fell upon his bosom. 'What have I done for Christ to deserve the thanks of any? I have preached and I have prayed; I have opposed heresies and errors; I have wrestled with the enemies and corrupters of our faith within our own body and without; but the fruit seems nothing. The gentile is still omnipotent--heresy and error still abound.'

'Yes, Macer,' I replied, 'that is certainly so, and may be so for many years to come, but still we are gaining. He who can remember twenty years can count a great increase. After the testimony borne by the martyrs of the Decian persecution to their faith, and all the proof they gave of sincere attachment to the doctrine of Christ, crowds have entered the church, an hundred for every one whose blood then flowed.'

'And now,' said Macer, his eye kindling with its wild fires, 'the church is dead! The truest prayer that the Christian can now offer is, that it would please God to try us again as it were by fire! We slumber, Piso! The Christians are not now the Nazarites they were in the first age of the church. Divisions have crept in; tares have been sown with the wheat, and have come up, and are choking the true plants of God. I know not but that the signs of terror which are scaring the heavens ought rather to be hailed as tokens of love. Better a thousand perish on the rack or by the axe, than that the church itself faint away and die.'

'It will not do,' said Probus, 'always to depend upon such remedies of our sloth and heresies. Surely it were better to prosper in some other and happier way. All I think we can say of persecution, and of the oppositions of our enemies, is this, that if it be in the providence of God that they cannot be avoided, we have cause to bless him that their issue is good rather than evil; that they serve as tests by which the genuine is tried and proved; that they give the best and highest testimony to the world that man can give, of his sincerity; that they serve to bind together into one compact and invincible phalanx the disciples of our common master, however in many things they may divide and separate. But, were it not better, if we could attain an equal good without the suffering?'

'I believe that to be impossible,' said Macer. 'Since Jesus began his ministry, persecution has been the rod that has been laid upon the church without sparing, and the fruit has been abundant. Without it, like these foolish children, we might run riot in all iniquity.'

'I do not say that the rod has not been needed,' answered Probus, 'nor that good has not ensued; but only, that it would be better, wiser, and happier, to reach the same good without the rod; just as it is better when your children, without chastisement, fulfil your wishes and perform their tasks. We hope and trust that our children will grow up to such virtue, that they will no longer need the discipline of suffering to make them better. Ought we not to look and pray for a period to arrive in the history of the church, when men shall no longer need to be lashed and driven, but shall of themselves discern what is best and cleave to it?'

'That might indeed be better,' replied the other; 'but the time is not come for it yet. The church I say is corrupt, and it cries out for another purging. Christians are already lording it over one another. The bishop of Rome sets himself up, as a lord, over subjects. A Roman Caesar walks it not more proudly. What with his robes of state, and his seat of gold, and his golden rod, and his altar set out with vessels of gold and silver, and his long train of menials and subordinates, poor simple Macer, who learned of Christ, as he hopes, is at a loss to discern the follower of the lowly Jesus, but takes Felix, the Christian servant, for some Fronto of a Heathen temple! Were the power mine, as the will is, never would I stay for Aurelian, but my own arm should sweep from the places they pollute the worst enemies of the Saviour. Did Jesus die that Felix might flaunt his peacock's feathers in the face of Rome?'

'We cannot hope, Macer,' answered Probus, 'to grow up to perfection at once. I see and bewail the errors at which you point as well as you. But if, to remove them, we bring down the heavy arm of Rome upon our heads--the remedy may prove worse than the disease.'

'No. That could not be! Let those who with open eyes abuse the gifts of God, perish! If this faith cannot be maintained undefiled by Heathen additions, let it perish!'

'But God dealeth not so with us,' continued Probus; 'he beareth long and patiently. We are not destroyed because in the first years of our life we do not rise to all virtue, but are spared to fourscore. Ought we not to manifest a like patience and forbearance? By waiting patiently we shall see our faults, and one by one correct them. There is still some reason and discernment left among us. We are not all fools and blind. And the faults which we correct ourselves, by our own action, and the conviction of our own minds acting freely and voluntarily, will be more truly corrected, than if we are but frightened away from them for a time by the terrors of the Roman sword. I think, Macer, and so thinks Piso, that, far from seeking to inflame the common mind, and so drawing upon us the evils which are now with reason apprehended, we should rather aim to ward them off.'

'Never!' cried Macer with utmost indignation. 'Shall the soldier of the cross shrink--'

'No, Macer, he need not shrink. Let him stand armed in panoply complete; prompt to serve, willing to die; but let him not wantonly provoke an enemy who may not only destroy him, that were a little thing, but, in the fury of the onset, thousands with him, and, perhaps, with them the very faith for which they die! The Christian is not guiltless who--though it be in the cause of Christ--rushes upon unnecessary death. You, Macer, are not only a Christian and soldier of Jesus Christ, but a man, who, having received life from the Creator, have no right wantonly to throw it away. You are a husband, and you are bound to live for your wife;--these are your children, and you are bound to live for them.'

'He,' said Macer, solemnly, 'who hateth not father and mother and wife and children and brethren and sister, yea and his own life also, cannot be my disciple.'

'Yes,' replied Probus, 'that is true; we are to be ready and willing to suffer for Christ and truth; but not to seek it. He who seeks martyrdom is no martyr. Selfish passions have then mingled their impure current with that of love to God, and the sacrifice is not without spot and blemish. Jesus did not so; nor his first followers. When the Lord was persecuted in one city, he staid not there to inflame it more and more; he fled to another. Paul and Peter and Barnabas stood ever for their rights; they suffered not wrong willingly. When the ark of truth is intrusted to few hands, they must bear it forward boldly, but with care, else are they at a blow cut off, and the ark with its precious burden borne away and lost--or miracles alone can rescue it. But when the time comes that no prudence or care will avail, then they may not refuse the issue, but must show that life is nothing in comparison of truth and God.'

'Probus,' said Macer, 'I like not your timid counsels. 'Tis not by such that Christ's cause shall ever advance, or that period ever come when he, the long-looked and waited for, shall descend, and the millenial reign begin. Life is nothing to me and less than nothing. I hold it as dirt and dross. And if by throwing it away I can add such a commentary to my preaching as shall strike a single Pagan heart, I shall not have died in vain; and if the blood that shall flow from these veins, may serve but as a purge, to carry off the foul humors that now fester and rage in the body of the church, thrice happy shall I be to see it flow. And for these--let them be as the women and children of other times, and hold not back when their master calls. Arria! do thou set before thee St. Blandina, and if the Lord let thee be as her, thou wilt have cause to bless his name.'

'Never, Macer, would I shrink from any trial to which the Lord in his wisdom might call me--that you know. But has not Probus uttered a truth, when he says, that we are not innocent, and never glorious, when we seek death? that he who seeks martyrdom is no martyr? Listen, Macer, to the wisdom of Probus and the noble Piso. Did you not promise that you would patiently hear them?'

'Woman--I have heard them--their words are naught, stark naught, or worse. Where would have been the blessed gospel at this hour, had it been committed to such counsels? Even under Nero would it have died for want of those who were willing to die for it. I am a soldier of the cross, whose very vocation it is to fight and die. And if I may but die, blessed Jesus, for thee! then may I hope that thou wilt deal mercifully with thy servant at thy judgment-seat. I hear thy voice ever sounding in my ear, reproving me for my cowardice. Have patience with me, and I will give thee all. And if labor, and torture, and death, would but cancel sin!--But alas! even they may not suffice.'

'Then, dear father,' said one of his daughters who had drawn near and seated herself at his knee, while the others had gathered round, 'then will we add ourselves to the sacrifice.'

'Would you?' said Macer--in an absent, musing way--as if some other thought were occupying him.

Thinking that his love of his children, evidently a very strong affection in him, might be made to act as a restraint, I said, 'that I feared he greatly exposed his little family to unnecessary danger. Already had his dwelling been once assailed, and the people were now ripe for any violence. This group of little ones can ill encounter a rude and furious mob.'

'They can die, can they not?' said Macer. 'Is that difficult, or impossible? If the Lord need them, they are his. I can ask no happier lot for them than that by death they may glorify God. And what is it to die so, more than in another way? Let them die in their beds, and whom do they benefit? They die then to themselves, and no one is the gainer; let them die by the sword of Varus, or by the stones of the populace, and then they become themselves stones in the foundation of that temple of God, of which Jesus is the chief corner-stone, and they are glorious forever. What say you, Cicer, will you die for Christ?'

The little fellow hid his head in his father's bosom at this sudden appeal, but soon drew it out and said,

'I would rather die for you, father.'

'Ah!' said Macer, 'how am I punished in my children! Cicer, would you not die for Christ?'

'I would die for him if you wish it.'

'Macer,' said Probus, 'do you not see how God has bound you and this family into one? and he surely requires you not to separate yourself, their natural protector, from them forever; still less, to involve them in all the sufferings which, taking the course you do, may come upon them at any hour.'

'Probus! their death would give me more pleasure than their life, dying for Christ. I love them now and here, fondly as ever parent loved his children,--but what is now, and here? Nothing. The suffering of an hour or of a moment joins us together again, where suffering shall be no more, and death no more. To-morrow! yes, to-morrow! would I that the wrath of these idol-worshippers might be turned against us. Rome must be roused; she sleeps the sleep of death; and the church sleeps it too; both need that they who are for the Lord should stand forth, and, not waiting to be attacked, themselves assail the enemy, who need but to be assailed with the zeal and courage of men, who were once to be found in the church, to be driven at all points.'

'But, father,' said the daughter who had spoken before, 'other Christians think not so. They believe for the most part, as I hear, with Probus and Piso, that on no account should we provoke the gentiles, or give them cause of complaint against us; they think that to do so would greatly harm us; that our duty is to go on the even tenor of our way, worshipping God after our own doctrine, and in our own manner, and claiming and exercising all our rights as citizens, but abstaining from every act that might rouse their anger, or needlessly irritate them--irritated, necessarily, almost beyond bearing, by the wide and increasing prosperity of our faith, and the daily falling away of the temple worshippers. Would it be right, dearest father, to do that which others approved not, and the effect of which might be, not only to draw down evil upon your and our heads, but upon thousands of others? We cannot separate ourselves from our brethren; if one suffer all will suffer--'

'Celia, my daughter, there is a judge within the breast, whom I am bound to obey rather than any other counsellor, either man or woman. I cannot believe, because another believes, a certain truth. Neither can I act in a certain way because others hold it their duty to act so. I must obey the inward voice, and no other. If I abandon this, I am lost--I am on the desert without sun, moon or stars to guide me. All the powers of the earth could not bribe nor drag me from that which I hold to be the true order of conduct for me; shown by the finger of God to be such.'

'But, father,' continued the daughter, pursuing her object, 'are we not too lately entered among the Christians to take upon us a course which they condemn? It is but yesterday that we were among the enemies of this faith. Are we to-day to assume the part of leaders? Would not modesty teach us a different lesson?'

'Modesty has nothing to do with truth,' said Macer. 'He who is wholly a Christian to-day, is all that he can be to-morrow, or next year. I am as old in faith and zeal as Piso, Probus, or Felix. No one can believe more, or more heartily, by believing longer. Nay, it is they who are newly saved who are most sensible to the blessing. Custom in religion as in other things dulls the soul. Were I a Christian much longer before God called me to serve him by suffering or death, I fear I should be then spiritually dead, and so worse than before I believed. Let it be to-morrow, O Lord, that I shall glorify thee!'

It was plain that little impression was to be made upon the mind of Macer. But we ceased not to urge him farther, his wife and elder children uniting with us in importunate entreaty and expostulation. But all in vain. In his stern and honest enthusiasm he believed all prudence, cowardice; all calculation, worldliness; all moderation and temperance, treason to the church and Christ. Yet none of the natural current of the affections seemed to be dried up or poisoned. No one could be more bound to his wife and children; and, toward us, though in our talk we spared him not, he ever maintained the same frank and open manner--yielding never an inch of ground, and uttering himself with an earnestness and fury such as I never saw in another; but, soon as he had ceased speaking, subsiding into a gentleness that seemed almost that of a woman, and playfully sporting with the little boy that he held on his knee.

Soon as our conversation was ended, Macer, turning to his wife, exclaimed,

'But what hinders that we should set before our visiters such hospitality as our poor house affords? Arria, have we not such as may well enough entertain Christians?'

Celia, at a word from her mother, and accompanied by her sister, immediately busied themselves in the simple rites of hospitality, and soon covered the table which stood in the centre of the room with bread, lettuces, figs, and a flask of wine. While they were thus engaged, I could not but observe the difference in appearance of the two elder sisters, who, with equal alacrity, were setting out the provisions for our repast. One was clad like the others of the family in the garments common to the poor. The other--she who had spoken--was arrayed, not richly, but almost so, or, I should rather say, fancifully, and with studied regard to effect. While I was wondering at this, and seeking in my own mind for its explanation, I was interrupted in my thoughts by Macer.

'Thanks to Aurelian, Piso, we are able, though poor, as you see, and dwelling in these almost subterranean vaults, to live above the fear of absolute want. But especially are we indebted for many of our comforts, and for such luxury as this flask of Massican, to my partly gentile daughter, Celia, whom you behold moving among us, as if by her attire she were not of us--but Cicer's heart is not truer--and who will, despite her faith and her father's bidding, dance and sing for the merriment of these idolaters. Never before, I believe, had Christian preacher a dancing-girl for a daughter.'

A deep blush passed over the features of the daughter as she answered,

'But, father, you know that in my judgment--and whose in this matter is so to be trusted?--I am in no way injured by my art, and it adds somewhat to the common stock. I see not why I need be any the less a Christian, because I dance; especially, as with me, it is but one of the forms of labor. Were it forbidden by our faith, or could it be shown to be to me an evil, I would cease. But most sure I am it is neither. Let me now appeal to Probus for my justification, and to Piso.'

'Doubtless,' said Probus, 'those Christians are right who abstain from the theatres, the amphitheatres, the circuses, and from the places of public amusement where sights and sounds meet ear and eye such as the pure should never hear or see, and such as none can hear or see and maintain their purity. The soul is damaged in spite of herself. But for these arts of music and dancing, practised for the harmless entertainment of those who feast their friends,--where alone I warrant Celia is found--who can doubt that she is right? Were not the reception of the religion of Christ compatible with indulgence in innocent amusement, or the practice of harmless arts such as these, few, I fear, would receive it. Christianity condemns many things, which, by Pagans, are held to be allowable, but not everything.'

'Willingly would I abandon my art,' said Celia,' did I perceive it to injure the soul; or could I in other ways buy bread for our household. So dearly do I prize this new-found faith, that for its sake, were it to be retained in no other way, would I relinquish it, and sink into the deeper poverty that would then be ours, or drudge at some humbler toil.'

'Do it, do it, Celia,' said Macer; 'and the Lord will love thee all the more. 'Tis the only spot on thy white and glistering robes. The Lord loves not more than I to see thee wheeling and waving to and fro, to supply mirth to those, who, mayhap, would crucify thee the next hour, as others crucified thy master.'

Tears fell from the eyes of the fair girl as she answered,

'Father, it shall be as you wish. Not willingly, but by constraint, have I labored as I have. God will not forsake us, and will, I cannot doubt, open some new path of labor for me--if indeed the disorders of the times do not first scatter or destroy us.'

I here said to Macer and his daughter, that there need be no hesitation about abandoning the employment in question, from any doubt concerning a future occupation; if Celia would but accompany her mother, when next she went to visit Julia, I could assure her of obtaining there all she could desire.

At this the little boy, whom Macer held, clapped his hands and cried out with joy--'Ah! then will Celia be always with us and go away no more;' and flying to his sister was caught by her in her arms.

The joy diffused throughout the little circle at this news was great. All were glad that Celia was to dance and sing no more, for all wished her at home, and her profession had kept her absent almost every day. The table was now spread, and we sat down to the frugal repast, Macer first offering a prayer to God.

'It is singular,' said he, when we were seated, 'that in my Heathen estate, I ever asked the blessing of the gods before I ate. Nay, and notwithstanding the abominations of my life, was often within the temples a worshipper. I verily believe there are many Christians who pray less than the Heathen, and less after they become Christian than before.'

'I can readily believe it,' said Probus. 'False religions multiply outward acts; and for the reason, that they make religion to consist in them. A true faith, which places religion in the inward disposition, not in services, will diminish them. More prayers were said, and more rites performed in the temple of Jupiter, where my father was priest, than the Christian church, where I serve, ever witnesses. But what then? With the Pagan worshipper religion ended when the service closed, and he turned from the temple to the world. With the Christian, the highest service only then commences when he leaves the church. Religion, with him, is virtuous action, more than it is meditation or prayer. He prays without ceasing, not by uttering without cessation the language of prayer, but by living holily. Every act of every hour, which is done conscientiously is a prayer, as well as the words we speak, and is more pleasing to God, for the reason that practice is better than mere profession-- doing better than saying.'

'That is just, Probus,' replied Macer. 'When I prayed as an idolater, it was because I believed that the gods required such outward acknowledgment, and that some evil or other might befall me through their vengeance, if I did not. But when I had ended that duty I had ended my religion, and my vices went on none the less prosperously. Often indeed my prayers were for special favors,--wealth, or success in some affair--and when, after wearying myself with repeating them a thousand times, the favors were not bestowed, how have I left the temple in a rage, cursing the gods I had just been worshipping, and swearing never more to propitiate them by prayer or sacrifice. Sometimes I repented of such violence, but oftener kept my word and tried some other god. You, Probus, were, I may believe, of a more even temper?'

'Yes, perhaps so. My father was one of the most patient and gentle of men, and religious after the manner of our remoter ancestors of the days of the republic. He was my instructor; and from him I learned truths which were sufficient for my happiness under ordinary circumstances. I was a devout and constant worshipper of the gods. My every-day life may then have been as pure as it has been since I have been a Christian; and my prayers as many or more. The instincts of my nature, which carried up the soul toward some great and infinite being, which I could not resist, kept me within the bounds of that prudent and virtuous life which I believed would be most acceptable to them. But when a day of heavy and insupportable calamity came upon me, and I was made to look after the foundations of what I had been believing, I found there were none. I was like a ship tossed about by the storms, without rudder or pilot. I then knew not whether there were gods or not; or if there were any, who, among the multiplicity worshipped in Rome, the true ones were. In my grief, I railed at the heavens and their rulers, for not revealing themselves to us in our darkness and weakness; and cursed them for their cruelty. Soon after I became a Christian. The difference between my state then, and now, is this. I believed then; but it was merely instinctive. I could give no reason to myself nor to others for my faith. It was something and yet nothing. Now, I have somewhat to stand upon. I can prove to myself, and to others, my religion, as well as other things. I have knowledge as well as blind belief. It is good to believe in something, and in some sort, though one can give no account of his faith; but it is better to believe in that which we know, as we know other things. I have now, as a Christian, the same strength of belief in God, providence, and futurity, that I have in any facts attested by history. Jesus has announced them or confirmed them, and they are susceptible of proof. I differed from you, Macer, in this; that I cursed not the gods in my passion, or caprice; I was for years and years their humble, and contented, and patient worshipper. I rebelled not till I suffered cruel disappointment, and in my faith could find no consolation or light. One real sorrow, by which the foundations of my earthly peace were all broken up, revealed to me the nothingness of my so called religion. Into what a new world, Macer, has our new faith introduced us! I am now happier than ever I was, even with my wife and children around me.'

'Some of our neighbors,' said Auria, 'wonder what it is that makes us so light of heart, notwithstanding our poverty and the dangers to which we are so often exposed. I tell them that they, who, like us, believe in the providence of a God, who is always near us and within us, and in the long reign with Christ as soon as death is past, have nothing to fear. That which they esteem the greatest evil of all, is, to us, an absolute gain. Upon this they either silently wonder, or laugh and deride. However, many too believe.'

'Probus, we are all ready to be offered up,' the enthusiast rejoined. 'God's mercy to me is beyond all power of mine to describe, in that he has touched and converted the hearts of every one under my roof. Now if to this mercy he will but add one more, that we may glorify him by our death as well as in our life, the cup of his servant will be full and running over.'

Probus did not choose again to engage with his convert upon that theme, knowing him to be beyond the reach of influence and control. We could not but marvel to see to what extent he had infused his own enthusiasm into his family. His wife indeed and elder daughters would willingly see him calmer and less violent when abroad, but like him, being by nature of warm temperament, they are like him Christians warm and zealous beyond almost any whom I have seen. They are as yet also so recently transferred from their Heathen to their Christian state, that their sight is still dazzled, and they see not objects in their true shapes and proportions. In their joy they seem to others, and perhaps often are, greatly extravagant in the expression of their feelings and opinions.

When our temperate repast was ended, Macer again prayed, and we then separated. Our visit proved wholly ineffectual as to the purpose we had in view, but by no means so when I consider the acquaintance which it thus gave me with a family in the very humblest condition, who yet were holding and equally prizing the same opinions, at which, after so much research and labor, I had myself arrived. I perceived in this power of Christianity to adapt itself to minds so different in their slate of previous preparation, and in their ability to examine and sift a question which was offered to them; in the facility and quickness with which it seized both upon the understanding and the affections; in the deep convictions which it produced of its own truth and excellence, and the scorn and horror with which it filled the mind for its former superstitions--I saw in this an element of strength, and of dominion, such as even I had hardly conceived, and which assures me that this religion is destined to a universal empire. Not more certainly do all men need it than they will have it. When in this manner, with everything against it, in the habits, lives, and prejudices of men--with itself almost against itself in its strictness and uncompromising morality--it nevertheless forces its way into minds of every variety of character, and diffuses wherever it goes the same inward happiness;--its success under such circumstances is at once an argument for its truth, and an assurance that it will pause in its progress not till it shall have subdued the world to its dominion.

Julia was deeply interested in all that I told her of the family of Macer, and will make them all her special charge. 弟ia will I hope become in some capacity a member of our household.

I ought to tell you that we have often of late been at the Gardens, where we have seen both Livia and Aurelian. Livia is the same, but the Emperor is changed. A gloomy horror seems to sit upon him, which both indisposes him to converse as formerly, and others to converse with him. Especially has he shown himself averse to discussion of any point that concerns the Christians, at least with me. When I would willingly have drawn him that way, he has shrunk from it with an expression of distaste, or with more expressive silence, or the dark language of his terrific frown. For me however he has no terrors, and I have resolved to break through all the barriers he chooses to set up around him, and learn if I can what his feelings and purposes precisely are. One conversation may reveal them in such a way, as may make it sufficiently plain what part he means to act, and what measure of truth there may be in the current rumors; in which, for my own part, I cannot bring myself to place much reliance. I doubt even concerning the death of Aurelia, whether, even if it has taken place, it is not to be traced to some cause other than her religion.

* * * * *

A day has passed. I have seen the Emperor, as I was resolved to do, and now I no longer doubt what his designs are, nor that they are dark as they have been represented; yea, and darker, even as night is darker than day.

Upon reaching the palace, I was told that the Emperor was exercising at the hippodrome, toward which I then bent my steps. It lies at some distance from the palace, concealed from it by intervening groves. Soon as I came in sight of it, I beheld Aurelian upon his favorite horse running the course as if contending for a prize, plying, the while, the fierce animal he bestrode with the lash, as if he were some laggard who needed rousing to his work. Swifter than the wind he flew by me, how many times I know not, without noting apparently that any one was present beside the attendant slaves; nor did he cease till the horse, spent and exhausted, no longer obeyed the will of even the Emperor of the world. Many a noble charger has he in this manner rode till he has fallen dead. So long used has this man been to the terrific game of war, and the scenes and sights which that reveals, stirring to their depths all the direst passions of our nature, that now, at home and at peace, life grows stale and flat, and needs the artificial stimulants which violent and extreme modes of action can alone supply. The death of a horse on the course, answers now for a legion slain in battle; an unruly, or disobedient, or idle slave hewn in two, affords the relief which the execution of prisoners has been accustomed to yield. Weary of inaction, he pants for the day to arrive when, having completed the designs he has set on foot in the city, he shall again join the army, now accumulating in huge masses in Thrace, and once more find himself in the East, on the way to new conquests and fresh slaughter.

As he threw himself from his horse, now breathing hard and scarcely supporting himself, the foam rolling from him like snow, he saluted me in his usual manner.

'A fair and fortunate day to you, Piso! And what may be the news in the city? I have rode fast and far, but have heard nothing. I come back empty as I went out, save the heat which I have put into my veins. This horse is he I was seen upon from the walls of Palmyra by your and other traitor eyes. But for first passing through the better part of my leg and then the saddle, the arrow that hit me then had been the death of him. But death is not for him, nor he for death; he and his rider are something alike, and will long be so, if auguries ever speak truth. And if there be not truth in auguries, Piso, where is it to be found among mortals? These three mornings have I rode him to see if in this manner he could be destroyed, but thou seest how it issues; I should destroy myself before him. But what, I say, is the news? How does the lady Julia? and the Queen?'

Replying first to these last inquiries, I then said that there was little news I believed in the city. The only thing, perhaps, that could be treated as news, was the general uneasiness of the Christians.

'Ah! They are uneasy? By the gods, not wholly without reason. Were it not for them I had now been, not here chafing my horse and myself on a hippodrome, but tearing up instead the hard sands of the Syrian deserts. They weigh upon me like a nightmare! They are a visible curse of the gods upon the state--but, being seen, it can be removed. I reckon not you among this tribe, Piso, when I speak of them. What purpose is imputed?'

'Rumor varies. No distinct purpose is named, but rather a general one of abridging some of their liberties--suppressing their worship, and silencing their priests.'

'Goes it no further?'

'Not with many; for the people are still willing to believe that Aurelian will inflict no needless suffering. They see you great in war, severe in the chastisement of the enemies of the state, and just in the punishment inflicted upon domestic rebels; and they conceive that in regard to this simple people you will not go beyond the rigor I have just named.'

'Truly they give me credit,' replied Aurelian, 'for what I scarcely deserve. But an Emperor can never hear the truth. Piso! they will find themselves deceived. One or the other must fall--Helenism or Christianity! I knew not, till my late return from the East, the ravages made by this modern superstition, not only throughout Rome, but the world. In this direction I have for many years been blind. I have had eyes only for the distant enemies of my country, and the glories of the battle-field. But now, upon resting here a space in the heart of the empire, I find that heart eaten out and gone; the religion of ancient Rome, which was its very life, decaying, and almost dead, through the rank growth of this overshadowing poison-tree that has shot up at its side. It must be cut up by the roots--the branches hewn away--the leaves stripped and scattered to the winds--nay, the very least fibre that lurks below the surface with life in it, must be wrenched out and consumed. We must do thus by the Christians and their faith, or they will do so by us.'

'I am hardly willing,' I replied, 'to believe what I have heard; nor will I believe it. It were an act, so mad and unwise, as well as so cruel, that I will not believe it though coming from the lips of Aurelian!'

'It is true, Piso, as the light of yonder sun! But if thou wilt not believe, wait a day or two and proof enough shall thou have--proof that shall cure thy infidelity in a river of Christian blood.'

'Still, Aurelian,' I answered. 'I believe not: nor will, till that river shall run down before my eyes red and thick as the Orontes!'

'How, Piso, is this? I thought you knew me!'

'In part I am sure I do. I know you neither to be a madman nor a fool, both which in one would you be to attempt what you have now threatened.'

'Young Piso, you are bold!'

'I make no boast of courage,' I replied; 'I know that in familiar speech with Aurelian, I need not fear him. Surely you would not converse on such a subject with a slave or a flatterer. A Piso can be neither. I can speak, or I can be silent; but if I speak--'

'Say on, say on, in the name of the gods!'

'What I would say to Aurelian then is this, that slaughter as he may, the Christians cannot be exterminated; that though he decimated, first Rome and then the empire, there would still be left a seed that would spring up and bear its proper harvest. Nay, Aurelian, though you halved the empire, you could not win your game. The Christians are more than you deem them.'

'Be it so,' replied the Emperor; 'nevertheless I will try. But they are not so many as you rate them at, neither by a direct nor an indirect enumeration.'

'Let that pass, then,' I answered. 'Let them be a half, a quarter, a tenth part of what I believe them to be, it will be the same; they cannot be exterminated. Soon as the work of death is done, that of life will begin again, and the growth will be the more rank for the blood spilled around. Outside of the tenth part, Aurelian, that now openly professes this new religion, there lies another equal number of those who do not openly profess it, but do so either secretly, or else view it with favor and with the desire to accept it. Your violence, inflicted upon the open believers, reaches not them, for they are an invisible multitude; but no sooner has it fallen and done its work of ruin, than this other multitude slowly reveals itself, and stands forth heirs and professors of the persecuted faith, and ready, like those who went before them, to live for it and die for it.'

'What you say may be so,' answered Aurelian; 'I had thought not of it. Nevertheless, I will try.'

'Moreover,' I continued, 'in every time of persecution, there are those-- sincere believers, but timid--who dare not meet the threatened horrors. These deny not their faith, but they shrink from sight; they for a season disappear; their hearts worship as ever, but their tongues are silent; and search as they may, your emissaries of blood cannot find them. But soon as the storm is over-past, then do they come forth again, as insects from the leaves that sheltered them from the storm, and fill again the forsaken churches.'

'Nevertheless I will try for them.'

'Then will you be, Aurelian, as one that sheds blood, because he will shed it-- seeing that the end at which you aim cannot in such way be reached. Confiscation, imprisonment, scourging, fires, torture, and death, will all be in vain; and with no more prospect that by such oppression Christianity can be annihilated, than there would be of rooting out poppies from your fields when as you struck off the heads or tore up the old roots, the ripe seeds were scattered abroad over the soil, a thousand for every parent stalk that fell. You will drench yourself in the blood of the innocent, only that you may do it-- while no effect shall follow.'

'Let it be so then; even so. Still I will not forbear. But this I know, Piso, that when a disaffection has broken out in a legion, and I have caused the half thereof, or its tenth, to be drawn forth and cut to pieces by the other part, the danger has disappeared. The physic has been bitter, but it has cured the patient! I am a good surgeon; and well used to letting blood. I know the wonders it works and shall try it now, not doubting to see some good effects. When poison is in the veins, let out the blood, and the new that comes in is wholesome. Rome is poisoned!'

'Great Emperor,' I replied, 'you know nothing, allow me to say, whereof you affirm. You know not the Christians, and how can you deem them poison to the state? A purer brotherhood never has the world seen. I am but of late one among them, and it is but a few months since I thought of them as you now do. But I knew nothing of them. Now I know them. And knowledge has placed them before me in another light. If, Aurelian--'

'I know nothing of them, Piso, it is true; and I wish to know nothing--nothing more, than that they are Christians! that they deny the good gods! that they aim at the overthrow of the religion of the state--that religion under whose fostering care Rome has grown up to her giant size--that they are fire-brands of discord and quarrel in Rome and throughout the world! Greater would my name be, could I extirpate this accursed tribe than it would be for triumphing over both the East and West, or though I gained the whole world.'

'Aurelian,' I replied, 'this is not the language I used to hear from your lips. Another spirit possesses you and it is not hard to tell whence it comes.'

'You would say--from Fronto.'

'I would. There is the rank poison, that has turned the blood in the veins of one, whom justice and wisdom once ruled, into its own accursed substance.'

'I and Rome, Piso,' said Aurelian, 'owe much to Fronto. I confess that his spirit now possesses me. He has roused the latent piety into action and life, which I received with my mother's milk, but which, the gods forgive me! carried away by ambition, had well nigh gone quite out in my soul. My mother--dost thou know it?--was a priestess of Apollo, and never did god or goddess so work by unseen influence to gain a mortal's heart, as did she to fill mine with reverence of the deities of heaven--specially of the great god of light. I was early a wayward child. When a soldier in the legions I now command, my life was what a soldier's is--a life of action, hardship, peril, and blood. The deities of Heaven soon became to me as if they were not. And so it has been for well nigh all the years of my life. But, the gods be thanked, Fronto has redeemed me! and since I have worn this diadem have I toiled, Rome can testify with what zeal, to restore to her gods their lost honors--to purge her worship of the foul corruptions that were bringing it into contempt--and raise it higher than ever in the honor of the people, by the magnificence of the temples I have built; by the gifts I have lavished upon them; by the ample riches wherewith I have endowed the priesthood. And more than once, while this work has been achieving, has the form of my revered parent, beautiful in the dazzling robes of her office, stood by my bedside--whether in dream, or in vision, or in actual presence, I cannot tell--and blessed me for my pious enterprise--"The gods be thanked," the lips have said, or seemed to say, "that thy youth lasts not always but that age has come, and with it second childhood in thy reverence of the gods, whose worship it was mine to put into thy infant heart. Go on thy way, my son! Build up the fallen altars, and lay low the aspiring fanes of the wicked. Finish what thou hast begun, and all time shall pronounce thee greatest of the great." Should I disobey the warning? The gods forbid! and save me from such impiety. I am now, Piso, doubly armed for the work I have taken in hand--first by the zeal of the pious Fronto, and second, by the manifest finger of Heaven pointing the way I should go. And, please the Almighty Ruler! I will enter upon it, and it shall not be for want of a determined will and of eyes too used to the shedding of blood to be frightened now though an ocean full were spilled before them, if this race be not utterly swept from the face of the earth, from the suckling to the silver head, from the beggar to the prince--and from Rome all around to the four winds, as far as her almighty arms can reach.'

My heart sunk within me as he spoke, and my knees trembled under me. I knew the power and spirit of the man, and I now saw that superstition had claimed him for her own; that he would go about his work of death and ruin, armed with his own cruel and bloody mind, and urged behind by the fiercer spirit still of Pagan bigotry. It seemed to me, in spite of what I had just said myself, and thought I believed, as if the death-note of Christianity had now been rung in my ear. The voice of Aurelian as he spoke had lost its usual sharpness, and fallen into a lower tone full of meaning, and which said to me that his very inmost soul was pouring itself out, with the awful words he used. I felt utterly helpless and undone--like an ant in the pathway of a giant--incapable of resistance or escape. I suppose all this was visible in my countenance. I said nothing; and Aurelian, after pausing a moment, went on.

'Think me not, Piso, to be using the words of an idle braggart in what I have said. Who has known Aurelian, when once he has threatened death, to hold back his hand? But I will give thee earnest of my truth!'

'I require it not, Aurelian. I question not thy truth.'

'I will give it notwithstanding, Piso. What will you think--you will think as you ever have of me--if I should say that already, and upon one of my own house, infected with this hell-begotten atheism, has the axe already fallen!'

Hearing the horrible truth from his own lips, it seemed as if I had never heard it before. I hardly had believed it.

'Tyrant!' I exclaimed, 'it cannot be! What, Aurelia?'

'Yes, Aurelia! Keep thy young blood cool, Piso. Yes, Aurelia! Ere I struck at others, it behoved me to reprove my own. It was no easy service, as you may guess, but it must be done. And not only was Aurelia herself pertinaciously wedded to this fatal mischief, but she was subduing the manly mind of Mucapor too, who, had he been successfully wrought upon, were as good as dead to me and to Rome--and he is one whom our legions cannot spare. We have Christians more than enough already in our ranks: a Christian general was not to be borne. This was additional matter of accusation against Aurelia, and made it right that she should die. But she had her free choice of life, honor, rank, riches, and, added to all, Mucapor, whose equal Rome does not hold, if she would but take them. One word spoken and they were all her own; with no small chance that she should one day be what Livia is. But that one word her obstinate superstition would not let her speak.'

'No, Aurelian; there is that in the Christian superstition that always forbids the uttering of that one word. Death to the Christian is but another word for life. Apostacy is the true death. You have destroyed the body of Aurelia, but her virtuous soul is already with God, and it is you who have girded upon her brow a garland that shall never fade. Of that much may you make your boast.'

'Piso, I bear with you, and shall; but there is no other in Rome who might say so much.'

'Nay, nay, Aurelian, there I believe you better than you make yourself. To him who is already the victim of the axe or the beasts do you never deny the liberty of the tongue,--such as it then is.'

'Upon Piso, and he the husband of Julia, I can inflict no evil, nor permit it done.'

'I would take shelter, Aurelian, neither behind my own name, my father's, nor my wife's. I am a Christian--and such fate as may befall the rest, I would share. Yet not willingly, for life and happiness are dear to me as to you--and they are dear to all these innocent multitudes whom you do now, in the exercise of despotic power, doom to a sudden and abhorred death. Bethink yourself, Aurelian, before it be too late--'

'I have bethought myself of it all,' he replied--'and were the suffering ten times more, and the blood to be poured out a thousand times more, I would draw back not one step. The die has been cast; it has come up as it is, and so must be the game. I listen to no appeal.'

'Not from me,' I replied; 'but surely you will not deny a hearing to what these people may say in their own defence. That were neither just nor merciful; nor were it like Aurelian. There is much which by their proper organs they might say to place before you their faith in the light of truth. You have heard what you have received concerning it, chiefly from the lips of Fronto; and can he know what he has never learned? or tell it unperverted by prejudices black as night?'

'I have already said,' rejoined the Emperor, 'that I would hear them, and I will. But it can avail them no more than words uttered in the breath of the tempest that is raging up from the north. Hear them! This day have I already heard them--from one of those madmen of theirs who plague the streets of Rome. Passing early by the temple of Aculapius--that one which stands not an arrow's flight from the column of Trajan--I came upon a dense crowd of all sorts of persons listening to a gaunt figure of a man who spoke to them. Soon as I came against him, and paused on my horse for the crowd to make way, the wild beast who was declaiming, shouted at me at the top of his voice, calling on me to 'hear the word of God which he would speak to me.' Knowing him by such jargon to be a Christian, I did as he desired, and there stood, while he, for my especial instruction, laid bare the iniquities and follies of the Roman worship; sent the priesthood and all who entered their temples to the infernal regions; and prophesied against Rome--which he termed Babylon--that ere so many centuries were gone, her walls would lie even with the ground, her temples moulder in ruins, her language become extinct, and her people confounded with other nations and lost. And all this because, I, whom he now called, if I remember the names aright, Ahaz and now Nebuchadnezzar, oppressed the children of God and held them in captivity: while in the same breath he bid me come on with my chains, gibbets, beasts, crosses, and fires, for they were ready, and would rejoice to bear their testimony in the cause of Christ. As I turned to resume my way, his words were; 'Go on, thou man of pride and blood; go on thy way! The gates of hell swing open for thee! Already the arm of the Lord is bared against thee! the winged lightning struggles in his hand to smite thee! I hear thy cry for mercy which no one answers--' and more, till I was beyond the reach of his owl's voice. There was an appeal, Piso, from this people! What think you of it?'

'He whom you heard,' I replied, 'I know, and know him to be honest and true; as loyal a subject too as Rome holds. He is led away by his hot and hasty temper both to do and say what injures not only him, but all who are joined with him, and the cause he defends. He offends the Christians hardly less than others. Judge not all by him. He stands alone. If you would hear one whom all alike confide in, and who may fitly represent the feelings and principles of the whole body of Christians, summon Probus. From him may you learn without exaggeration or concealment, without reproach of others or undue boasting of themselves, what the Christians are in their doctrines and their lives, as citizens of Rome and loyal subjects of Aurelian, and what, as citizens of heaven and loyal followers of Jesus Christ.'

The Emperor promised to consider it. He had no other reason to deny such favor, but the tedium of listening to what could profit neither him nor others.

We then turned toward the palace, where I saw Livia; now as silent and sad as, when in Palmyra, she was lively and gay. Not that Aurelian abates the least of his worship, but that the gloom which overshadows him imparts itself to her, and that knowing what has befallen Aurelia, she cannot but feel it to be a possible thing for the blow to fall elsewhere and nearer. Yet is there the same outward show as ever. The palace is still thronged, with not Rome only, but by strangers from all quarters of the empire, anxious to pay their homage at once to the Empress of Rome, to the most beautiful woman in the world-- such is the language--and to a daughter of the far-famed Zenobia.

The city is now crowded with travelers of all nations, so much so that the inns can scarce receive them; and hardly ever before was private hospitality so put to all its resources. With all, and everywhere, in the streets, at the public baths, in the porticos, at the private or public banquet, the Christians are the one absorbing topic. And, at least, this good comes with the evil, that thus the character of this religion, as compared with that of Rome and other faiths, is made known to thousands who might otherwise never have heard of it, or have felt interest enough in it to examine its claims. It leads to a large demand for, and sale of, our sacred books. The copyists can hardly supply them so fast as they are wanted. For in the case of any dispute or conversation, it is common to hear the books themselves referred to, and then to be called in as witnesses for or against a statement made. And pleasant enough is it to see how clear the general voice is on our side-- especially with the strangers--how indignant they are, for the most part, that violence, to the extreme of another Decian persecution, should be so much as dreamed of. Would that the same could be said of our citizens and countrymen! A large proportion of them indeed embrace the same liberal sentiments, but a greater part, if not for extreme violence, are yet for oppression and suppression; and I dare not say how many, for all that Aurelian himself designs. Among the lower orders, especially, a ferocious and blood-thirsty spirit breaks out in a thousand ways that fills the bosom both with grief and terror.

The clouds are gathering over us, Fausta, heavy and black with the tempest pent up within. The thunders are rolling in the distance, and each hour coming nearer and nearer. Whom the lightnings shall strike--how vain to conjecture! Would to God that Julia were anywhere but here! For, to you I may say it, I cannot trust Aurelian--yes--Aurelian himself I may; but not Aurelian the tool of Fronto. Farewell.

LETTER IX.

FROM PISO TO FAUSTA.

When I turned from the palace of Aurelian and again took my way towards the Coelian, I did it in the belief that before the day should end, edicts against the Christians would be published. I found, as I conversed with many whom I met in the way, that from other sources the same opinion had become common. In one manner or another it had come abroad that measures had been resolved upon by the Emperor, and would soon be put in force. Many indeed do not give the least credit to the rumors, and believe that they all spring from the violent language of Fronto, which has been reported as that of Aurelian. You may wonder that there should be such uncertainty respecting a great design like this. But you must remember that Aurelian has of late shrouded himself in a studied obscurity. Not a despot, in the despotic lands of Asia, keeps more secret counsel than he, or leans less upon the opinion or advice of others. All that is done throughout the vast compass of the empire, springs from him alone--all the affairs of foreign and dependent kingdoms are arranged and determined by him. As for Italy and the capital, they are mere playthings in his hand. You ask if the senate does not still exist? I answer, it does; but, as a man exists whom a palsy has made but half alive; the body is there, but the soul is gone, and even the body is asleep. The senators, with all becoming gravity, assemble themselves at the capitol, and what time they sleep not away the tedious hours in their ivory chairs, they debate such high matters as, 'whether the tax which this year falls heavy upon Capua, by reason of a blast upon the grapes, shall be lightened or remitted!' or 'whether the petition of the Milanese for the construction at the public expense of a granary shall be answered favorably!' or 'whether V. P. Naso shall be granted a new trial after defeat at the highest court!' Not that there is not virtue in the senate, some dignity, some respect and love for the liberties of Rome--witness myself--but that the Emperor has engrossed the whole empire to himself, and nothing is left for that body but to keep alive the few remaining forms of ancient liberty, by assembling as formerly, and taking care of whatever insignificant affairs are intrusted to them. In a great movement like this against the Christians, Aurelian does not so much as recognize their existence. No advice is asked, no cooperation. And the less is he disposed to communicate with them in the present instance perhaps, from knowing so well that the measure would find no favor in their eyes; but would, on the contrary, be violently opposed. Everything, accordingly, originates in the sovereign will of Aurelian, and is carried into effect by his arm wielding the total power of this boundless empire--being now, what it has been his boast to make it, coextensive with its extremest borders as they were in the time of the Antonines. There is no power to resist him; nor are there many who dare to utter their real opinions, least of all, a senator, or a noble. A beggar in the street may do it with better chance of its being respected, if agreeable to him, and of escaping rebuke or worse, if it be unpalatable. To the people, he is still, as ever, courteous and indulgent.

* * * * *

There is throughout the city a strange silence and gloom, as if in expectancy of some great calamity; or of some event of dark and uncertain character. The Christians go about their affairs as usual, not ceasing from any labors, nor withdrawing from the scene of danger; but with firm step and serious air keep on their way as if conscious of the great part which it is theirs to act, and resolved that it shall not suffer at their hands. Many with whom I have spoken, put on even a cheerful air as they have greeted me, and after the usual morning's salutation, have passed on as if things were in their usual train. Others with pale face and quivering lip confessed the inward tumult, and that, if they feared naught for themselves, there were those at home, helpless and exposed, for whom the heart bled, and for whom it could not but show signs of fear.

I met the elder Demetrius. His manly and thoughtful countenance--though it betrayed nothing of weakness--was agitated with suppressed emotion. He is a man full of courage, but full of sensibility too. His affections are warm and tender as those of a girl. He asked me 'what I could inform him of the truth of the rumors which were now afloat of the most terrific character.' I saw where his heart was as he spoke, and answered him, as you may believe, with pain and reluctance. I knew, indeed, that the whole truth would soon break upon him--it was a foolish weakness--but I could hardly bring myself to tell him what a few hours would probably reveal. I told him, however, all that I had just learned from Aurelian himself, and which, as he made no reserve with regard to me, nor enjoined concealment, I did not doubt was fully resolved upon, and would be speedily put in force. As I spoke, the countenance of the Greek grew pale beyond its usual hue of paleness. He bent his head, as in perplexed and anxious thought; the tears were ready to overflow as he raised it, after a moment, and said,

'Piso, I am but recently a Christian. I know nothing of this religion but its beauty and truth. It is what I have ever longed for, and now that I possess it I value it far more than life. But,'--he paused a moment--'I have mingled but little with this people; I know scarcely any; I am ignorant of what they require of those who belong to their number in such emergences. I am ready to die myself, rather than shrink from a bold acknowledgment of what in my heart I believe to be the divinest truth; but--my wife and my children!--must they too meet these dangers? My wife has become what I am; my children are but infants; a Greek vessel sails to-morrow for Scio, where dwells, in peaceful security, the father of my wife, from whom I received her, almost to his distraction; her death would be his immolation. Should I offend'--

'Surely not,' I replied. 'If, as I believe will happen, the edicts of the Emperor should be published to-day, put them on board to-night, and let to-morrow see them floating on the Mediterranean. We are not all to stand still and hold our throats to the knife of this imperial butcher.'

'God be thanked!' said Demetrius, and grasping my hand with fervor turned quickly and moved in the direction of his home.

Soon after, seated with Julia and Probus--he had joined me as I parted from Demetrius--I communicated to her all that I had heard at the palace. It neither surprised nor alarmed her. But she could not repress her grief at the prospect spread out before us of so much suffering to the innocent.

'How hard is this,' said she, 'to be called to bear such testimony as must now be borne to truth! These Christian multitudes, so many of whom have but just adopted their new faith and begun to taste of the pleasures it imparts, all enjoying in such harmony and quietness their rich blessings--with many their only blessings--how hard for them, all at once, to see the foundations of their peace broken up, and their very lives clamored for! rulers and people setting upon them as troops of wild beasts! It demands almost more faith than I can boast, to sit here without complaint a witness of such wrong. How strange, Probus, that life should be made so difficult! That not a single possession worth having can be secured without so much either of labor or endurance! I wonder if this is ever to cease on earth?'

'I can hardly suppose that it will,' said Probus. 'Labor and suffering, in some of their forms, seem both essential. My arm would be weak as a rush were it never moved; but exercised, and you see it is nervous and strong; plied like a smith's, and it grows to be hard as iron and capable of miracles. So it is with any faculty you may select; the harder it is tasked the more worthy it becomes; and without tasking at all, it is worth nothing. So seems to me it is with the whole man. In a smooth and even lot our worth never would be known, and we could respect neither ourselves nor others. Greatness and worth come only of collision and conflict. Let our path be strewed with roses, and soft southern gales ever blow, and earth send up of her own accord our ready prepared nutriment, and mankind would be but one huge multitude of Sybarites, dissolved in sloth and effeminacy. If no difficulty opposed, no labor exacted, body and mind were dead. Hence it is, we may believe, that man must everywhere labor even for the food which is necessary to mere existence. Life is made dear to us by an instinct--we shrink from nothing as we do from the mere thought of non-existence--but still it is death or toil; that is the alternative. So that labor is thus insured wherever man is found, and it is this that makes him what he is. Then he is made, moreover, so as to crave not only food but knowledge as much, and also virtue; but between him and both these objects there are interposed, for the same reason doubtless, mountains of difficulty, which he must clamber up and over before he can bask in the pleasant fields that lie beyond, and then ascend the distant mountain-tops, from which but a single step removes him from the abode of God. Doubt it not, lady, that it is never in vain and for naught that man labors and suffers; but that the good which redounds is in proportion to what is undergone, and more than a compensation. If, in these times of darkness and fear, suffering is more, goodness and faith are more also. There are Christians, and men, made by such trials, that are never made elsewhere nor otherwise-- nor can be; just as the arm of Hercules could not be but by the labors of Hercules. What says Macer? Why even this, that God is to be thanked for this danger, for that the church needs it! The brief prosperity it has enjoyed since the time of Valerian and Macrianus, has corrupted it, and it must be purged anew, and tried by fire! I think not that; but I think this; that if suffering ever so extreme is ordained, there will be a virtue begotten in the souls of the sufferers, and abroad through them, that shall prove it not to have been in vain.'

'I can believe what you say,' said Julia, 'at least I can believe in the virtue ascribed to labor, and the collision with difficulty. Suffering is passive; may it not be that we may come to place too much merit in this?'

'It is not to be doubted that we may,' replied Probus. 'The temptation to do so is great. It is easy to suffer. In comparison with labor and duty--life-long labor and duty--it is a light service. Yet it carries with it an imposing air, and is too apt to take to itself all the glory of the Christian's course. Many who have lived as Christians but indifferently have, in the hour of persecution, and in the heat of that hour, rushed upon death and borne it well, and before it extremest torture, and gained the crown of martyrdom and the name of saint--a crown not always without spot--a name not always honorable. He who suffers for Christ must suffer with simplicity--even as he has lived with simplicity. And when he has lived so, and endured the martyr's death at last, that is to be accounted but the last of many acts of duty which are essentially alike--unless it may be that in many a previous conflict over temptation and the world and sin, there was a harder victory won, and a harder duty done, than when the flames consumed him, or the beasts tare him limb from limb.'

'Yet, Probus,' continued Julia, 'among the humble and the ignorant, where we cannot suppose that vanity could operate, where men have received Christianity only because it seemed to them just the faith they needed, and who then when it has been required that they renounce it, will not do so, but hold steadfastly to what they regard the truth of God, and for it take with meekness and patience all manner of torture, and death itself--there is surely here great virtue! Suffering here has great worth and sets upon the soul the seal of God. Is it not so?'

'Most assuredly it is,' answered Probus. 'O there is no virtue on earth greater than theirs! When dragged from their quiet homes--unknown, obscure, despised, solitary, with not one pitying eye to look on upon their sufferings, with none to record their name, none to know it even--they do, nevertheless, without faltering, keep true to their faith, hugging it to them the closer the more it is tried to tear them asunder--this, this is virtue the greatest on earth! It is a testimony borne to the truth of whatever cause is thus supported, that is daily bringing forth its fruits in the conviction and conversion of multitudes. It is said, that in the Decian persecution, it was the fortitude and patience under the cruelest sufferings of those humble Christians whom no one knew, who came none knew whence, and who were dying out of a pure inward love of the faith they professed, that fell upon the hearts of admiring thousands with more than the force of miracle, and was the cause of the great and sudden growth of our numbers which then took place. Still, suffering and dying for a faith is not unimpeachable evidence of its truth. There have been those who have died and suffered for idolatries the most abhorred. It is proof, indeed, not at all of truth itself, but only of the deep sincerity of him who professes it.'

'Yes,' replied Julia, 'I see that it is so. But then it is a presumption in behalf of truth, strong almost as miracles done for it, when so many--multitudes--in different ages, in the humblest condition of life, hesitate not to die rather than renounce their faith in a religion like this of Christianity; which panders to not one of man's passions, appetites or weaknesses, but is the severest censor of morals the world has ever seen; which requires a virtue and a purity in its disciples such as no philosopher ever dared to impose upon his scholars; whose only promise is immortality--and that an immortality never to be separated from the idea of retribution as making a part of it. They, who will suffer and die for such a religion, do by that act work as effectively for it, as their master by the signs and wonders which he did. If Christianity were like many of the forms of Paganism; or if it ministered to the cravings of our sensual nature, as we can conceive a religion might do; if it made the work of life light, and the reward certain and glorious; if it relieved its followers of much of the suffering, and fear, and doubt, that oppress others--it would not be surprising that men should bear much for its sake; and their doing so, for what appealed so to their selfishness, would be no evidence, at all to be trusted, of its truth. But as it is, they who die for it afford a presumption in behalf of it, that appeals to the reason almost or quite with the force of demonstration. So, I remember well, my reason was impressed by what I used to hear from Paul of the sufferings of the early Christians.'

While Julia had been saying these things, it had seemed to me as if there was an unusual commotion in the streets; and as she ended I was about to look for the cause of it, when the hasty steps of several running through the hall leading from the main entrance of the house prevented me, and Milo breathless, followed by others of the household, rushed into the apartment where we sat, he exclaiming with every mark of fear and horror upon his countenance,

'Ah! sir, it is all just as I was told by Curio it would be; the edicts are published on the capitol. The people are going about the streets now in crowds, talking loud and furiously, and before night they say the Christians will all be delivered to their pleasure.'

Soon as Milo could pause, I asked him 'if he had read or seen the edicts?'

'No, I have not,' he answered; 'I heard from Curio what they were to be.'

I told Julia and Probus that such I did not believe was their tenor. It did not agree with usage, nor with what I had gathered from Aurelian of his designs. But that their import was probably, at present, no more than deprivation of a portion of their freedom and of some of their privileges. It was the purpose of Aurelian first to convert back again the erring multitudes to Paganism, for which time must be granted.

But my words had no effect to calm the agitation of our slaves, who, filled with terror at the reports of Milo, and at the confusion in the streets, had poured into the room, and were showing in a thousand ways their affection for us, and their concern. Some of this number are Christians, having been made so by the daily conversations which Julia has had with them, and the instruction she has given them in the gospels. Most however are still of that religion in which they were reared, as they are natives of the East, of the North, or of Africa. But by all, with slight differences, was the same interest manifested in our safety. They were ready to do anything for our protection; and chiefly urgent were they that we should that very night escape from Rome--they could remain in security and defend the palace. When they had thus in their simple way given free expression to their affections, I assured them that no immediate danger impended, but even if it did, I should not fly from it, but should remain where I was; that the religion for which I might suffer was worth to those who held it a great deal more than mere life--we could easily sacrifice life for it, if that should be required. Some seemed to understand this--others not; but they then retired, silent and calm, because they saw that we were so.

Soon as they were withdrawn, I proposed to Probus that we should go forth and learn the exact truth. We accordingly passed to the street, which, as it is one that forms the principal avenue from this part of the city to the capitol, we found alive with numbers greater than usual, with their faces turned toward that quarter. We joined them and moved with them in the same direction. It was a fearful thing, Fausta, even to me, who am rarely disturbed by any event, to listen to the language which fell on my ear on all sides from the lips of beings who wore the same form as myself, and with me have a right to the name of man. It was chiefly that of exultation and joy, that at length the power of the state was about to strike at the root of this growing evil--that one had taken hold of the work who would not leave it, as others had, half accomplished, but would finish it, as he had every other to which he had put his hand.

'Now we shall see,' cried one, 'what he whose hand bears the sword of a true soldier can do, and whether Aurelian, who has slain more foes of Rome abroad than emperor before ever did, cannot do as well by enemies at home.'

'Never doubt it,' said another. 'Before the ides of the month now just come in, not a Christian will be seen in the streets of Rome. They will be swept out as clean, as by Varus they now are of other filth. The Prefect is just the man for the times. Aurelian could not have been better matched.'

'Lucky this,' said still another as he hurried away, 'is it not? Three vessels arrived yesterday stowed thick with wild beasts from Africa and Asia. By the gods! there will be no starving for them now. The only fear will be that gorged so they will lose their spirit.'

'I don't fear that,' said his older companion. 'I remember well the same game twenty-five years ago. The fact was then that the taste of human blood whetted it for more and more, and, though glutted, their rage seemed but to become more savage still; so that, though hunger was fed to the full, and more, they fell upon fresh victims with increased fury--with a sort of madness as it were. Such food, 'tis said, crazes them.

Others were soon next us from whom I heard,

'Let every soul perish. I care not for that, or rather I do. Let all die I say; but not in this savage way. Let it be done by a proper accusation, trial, and judgment. Let profession of atheism be death by a law, and let the law be executed, and the name will soon die. Inevitable death under a law for any one who assumes the name, would soon do the work of extermination--better than this universal slaughter which, I hear, is to be the way. Thousands are then overlooked in the blind popular fury; the work by and by ceases through weariness; it is thought to be completed--when lo! as the first fury of the storm is spent, they come forth from their hiding-places, and things are but little better than before.'

'I think with you,' said the younger companion of him who had just spoken; 'and besides, Romans need not the further instruction in the art of assassination, which such a service would impart. Already nothing comes so like nature to a Roman as to kill; kill something--if not a beast, a slave--if there is no slave at hand, a Christian--if no Christian, a citizen. One would think we sucked in from our mothers not milk but blood--the blood too of our Parent Wolf. If the state cannot stand secure, as our great men say, but by the destruction of this people, in the name of the gods, let the executioners do the work, not our sons, brothers, and fathers. So too, I say, touching the accursed games at the Flavian and elsewhere. What is the effect but to make of us a nation of man-butchers? as, by the gods, we already are. If the gods send not something or somebody to mend us, we shall presently fall upon one another and exterminate ourselves.'

'Who knows but it is this very religion of the Christians that has been sent for that work?' said a third who had joined the two. 'The Christians are famed for nothing more than for their gentleness, and their care of one another--so, at least, I hear.'

'Who knows, indeed?' said the other. 'If it be so, pity it were not found out soon. Aurelian will make short work with them.'

In the midst of such conversation, which on every side caught our ears as we walked silently along, we came at length to the neighborhood of the capitol; but so great was the throng of the people, who in Rome, have naught else to do but to rush together upon every piece of news, that we could not even come within sight of the building, much less of the parchment.

We accordingly waited patiently to learn from some who might emerge from the crowd what the precise amount of the edicts might be. We stood not long, before one struggling and pushing about at all adventures, red and puffing with his efforts, extricated himself from the mass, and adjusting his dress which was half torn from his back, began swearing and cursing the Emperor and his ministers for a parcel of women and fools.

'What is it?' we asked, gathering about him. 'What have you seen? Did you reach the pillar?'

'Reach it? I did; but my cloak, that cost yesterday ten good aurelians, did not, and here I stand cloakless--'

'Well, but the edicts.'

'Well, but the edicts! Be not in a hurry, friend--they are worth not so much as my cloak. Blank parchment were just as good. I wonder old 'sword-in-hand didn't hang up a strip--'twould have saved the expense of a scrivener. If any of you hear of a cloak found hereabouts, or any considerable part of one, blue without, lined with yellow, and trimmed with gold, please to note the name sewed on beneath the left shoulder, and send it according to the direction and your labor shall not be lost.'

'But the edicts--the edicts.'

'O the edicts! why they are just this; the Christians are told that they must neither assemble together in their houses of worship to hear their priests, nor turn the streets into places of worship in their stead; but leave off all their old ways just as fast as they can and worship the gods. There's an edict for you!'

'Who is this?' said one to Probus.

'I do not know; he seems sadly disappointed at the Emperor's clemency as he deems it.'

But what Probus did not know, another who at the moment came up, did; exclaiming, as he slapped the disappointed man on the shoulder,

'What, old fellow, you here? always where mischief is brewing. But who ever saw you without Nero and Sylla? What has happened? and no cloak either?'

'Nero and Sylla are in their den--for my cloak I fear it is in a worse place. But come, give me your arm, and let us return. I thought a fine business was opening, and so ran up to see. But it's all a sham.'

'It's only put off,' said his companion, as they walked away; 'your dogs will have enough to do before the month is half out--if Fronto knows anything.'

'That is one, I see,' said he who had spoken to Probus, 'who breeds hounds for the theatres--I thought I had seen him before. His ordinary stock is not less than five hundred blood-hounds. He married the sister of the gladiator Sosia. His name is Hanno.'

Having heard enough, we turned away and sought again the Coelian. You thus see, Fausta, what Rome is made of, and into what hands we may all come. Do you wonder at my love of Christianity? at my zeal for its progress? Unless it prosper, unless it take root and spread through this people, their fate is sealed, to my mind, with the same certainty as if I saw their doom written upon the midnight sky in letters of fire. Their own wickedness will break them in pieces and destroy them. It is a weight beneath which no society can stand. It must give way in general anarchy and ruin. But my trust is that, in spite of Aurelian and of all other power, this faith will go on its way, and so infuse itself into the mass as never to be dislodged, and work out its perfect ultimate regeneration.

By this decree of the Emperor then, which was soon published in every part of the capital, the Christians are prohibited from assembling together for purposes of worship, their churches are closed, and their preachers silenced.

One day intervenes between this, and the first day of the week, the day on which the Christians as you may perhaps know assemble for their worship. In the meantime it will be determined what course shall be pursued.

* * * * *

Those days have passed, Fausta, and before I seal my letter I will add to it an account of them.

Immediately upon the publication of the Emperor's decrees, the Christians throughout the city communicated with each other, and resolved, their places of worship being all closed and guarded, to assemble secretly, in some spot to be selected, both for worship and to determine what was to be done, if anything, to shield themselves from the greater evils which threatened. The place selected was the old ruins where the house of Macer stands. 'There still remains,' so Macer urged, 'a vast circular apartment partly below and partly above the surface of the ground, of massy walls, without windows, remote from the streets, and so surrounded by fallen walls and columns as to be wholly buried from the sight. The entrance to it was through his dwelling, and the rooms beyond. Resorting thither when it should be dark, and seeking his house singly and by different avenues among the ruins, there would be little chance of observation and disturbance.' Macer's counsel was accepted.

On the evening of the first day of the week--a day which since I had returned from the East to Rome had ever come to me laden with both pleasure and profit--I took my way under cover of a night without star or moon, and doubly dark by reason of clouds that hung black and low, to the appointed place of assembly. The cold winds of autumn were driving in fitful blasts through the streets, striking a chill into the soul as well as the body. They seemed ominous of that black and bitter storm that was even now beginning to break in sorrow and death upon the followers of Christ. Before I reached the ruins the rain fell in heavy drops, and the wind was rising and swelling into a tempest. It seemed to me, in the frame I was then in, better than a calm. It was moreover a wall of defence against such as might be disposed to track and betray us.

Entering by the door of Macer's cell, I passed through many dark and narrow apartments, following the noise of the steps of some who were going before me, till at length I emerged into the vaulted hall spoken of by Macer. It was lofty and spacious, and already filled with figures of men and women, whom the dim light of a few lamps, placed upon the fragments of the fallen architecture, just enabled me to discern and distinguish from the masses of marble and broken columns which strewed the interior, which, when they afforded a secure footing, were covered with the assembled worshippers. The footsteps of those who were the last to enter soon died away upon the ear, and deep silence ensued, unbroken by any sound save that of the sighs and weeping of such as could not restrain their feelings.

It was interrupted by the voice of one who said,

'That the Christians of Rome were assembled here by agreement to consult together concerning their affairs, which now, by reason of the sudden hostility of Aurelian, set on by the Pagan priesthood, had assumed a dark and threatening aspect. It was needful so to consult; that it might be well ascertained whether no steps could be taken to ward off the impending evil, and if not, in what manner and to what extent we might be able to protect ourselves. But before this be done,' he continued, 'let us all first with one heart seek the blessing of God. To-day, Christians, for the first time within the memory of the younger portion of this assembly, have we by the wicked power of the state been shut out of those temples where we have been wont to offer up our seventh day worship. Here, in this deep cavern, there is none to alarm or interrupt. Let us give our first hour to God. So shall the day not be lost, nor the enemy wholly prevail.'

'That is right,' said another. 'It is what we all wish. Let Probus speak to us and pray for us.'

'Felix! Felix!' cried other voices in different parts of the room.

'Not so, but Probus! Probus!' shouted a far greater number.

'Who does not know,' cried a shrill voice elevated to its utmost pitch, 'that Probus is a follower of Paul of Samosata?'

'And who does not know,' responded he who had first spoken, 'that Felix follows after Plato and Plotinus? Pagans both!'

'And what,' said the sharp voice of Macer, 'what if both be true? who dare say that Felix is not a Christian?--who dare say that Probus is not a Christian? and if they are Christians, who shall dare to say they may not speak to Christians? Probus was first asked, and let Probus stand forth.'

The name of Probus was then uttered as it were by the whole assembly.

As he moved toward a more central and elevated spot, the same mean and shrill voice that had first charged him, again was heard, advising that no hymn nor chant be sung; 'the Roman watch is now abroad, and despite the raging of the storm their ears may catch the sound and the guard be upon us.'

'Let them come then!' shouted Macer. 'Let them come! Shall any fear of man or of death frighten us away from the worship of God? What death more glorious than if this moment those doors gave way and the legions of Aurelian poured in? Praise God and Christ, Christians, in the highest note you can raise, and let no cowardice seal your lips nor abate your breath.'

The voice of Probus, now heard in prayer, brought a deep silence upon the assembly, and I would fain believe, harmony and peace also into the spirits of all who were there. It was a service deeply moving and greatly comforting. Whatever any who were present might have thought of the principles of Probus, all must have been penetrated and healed by that devout and benevolent temper that was so manifest in the sentiments he uttered, and in the very tones of his voice.

No sooner had he ended his prayer than the voice of Macer broke forth, commencing a chant commonly heard in the churches and with which all were familiar. His voice, louder than that of the storm and shriller than the blast of a war-trumpet, rang through the vast apartment, and inspiring all who were there with the same courage that possessed himself, their voices were instinctively soon joined with his, and the hymn swelled upward with a burst of harmony that seemed as if it might reach Heaven itself. Rome and its legions were then as if they did not exist. God only was present to the mind, and the thoughts with which that hymn filled it. Its burden was like this:

'O God almighty, God of Christ our Lord, arise and defend thy people. The terrors of death are around us the enemies of truth and thy Son assail us, and we faint and are afraid. Their hosts are encamped against us; they are ready to devour us. Our hope is in thee: Strengthen and deliver us. Arise, O God, and visit us with thy salvation.'

These, and words like them, repeated with importunity and dwelt upon, the whole soul pouring itself out with the notes, while tears ran down the cheeks of those who sang--the sign not of weakness but of the strength of those affections which bound their hearts to God, to Christ, and to one another--it seemed as if such words and so uttered could not but draw a blessing down. As the hymn drew to a close and the sounds died away, deep silence again fell upon the assembly. The heart had been relieved by the service; the soul had been rapt and borne quite away; and by a common feeling an interval of rest ensued, which by each seemed to be devoted to meditation and prayer.

This, when it had lasted till the wants of each had been satisfied, was broken by the voice of Probus.

What he said was wonderfully adapted to infuse fresh courage into every heart, and especially to cheer and support the desponding and the timid. He held up before them the great examples of those who, in the earlier ages of the church, had offered themselves as sacrifices upon the same altar upon which the great head of the Christians had laid down his life. He made it apparent how it had ever been through suffering of some kind on the part of some, that great benefits had been conferred upon mankind; that they who would be benefactors of their race must be willing cheerfully to bear the evil and suffering that in so great part constitutes that office; and was it not a small thing to suffer, and that in the body only, and but for a moment, if by such means great and permanent blessings to the souls of men might be secured, and remotest ages of the world made to rejoice and flourish through the effects of their labors? Every day of their worship they were accustomed to hear sung or recited the praises of those who had died for Christ and truth; men of whom the world was not worthy, and who, beautiful with the crown of martyrdom, were now of that glorious company who, in the presence of God, were chanting the praises of God and the Lamb. Who was not ready to die, if it were so ordained, if by such death truth could be transmitted to other ages? What was it to die to-day rather than to-morrow--for that was all--or this year rather than the next, if one's death could be made subservient to the great cause of Christ and his gospel? What was it to die by the sword of a Roman executioner, or even to be torn by wild beasts, if by suffering so the soul became allied to reformers and benefactors of all ages? And besides, what evil after all was it in the power of their enemies to inflict? They could do no more than torment and destroy the body. They could not touch nor harm the soul. By the infliction of death itself they did but hasten the moment when they should stand clothed in shining garments in the presence of the Father. 'The time has come, Christians,' he then said, 'when, in the providence of God, you are called upon to be witnesses of the faith which you profess in Christ. After many years of calm, a storm has arisen, which begins already to be felt in the violence with which it beats upon our heads. Almost ever since the reign of Decius have we possessed our borders in quietness. Especially under Gallienus and Claudius, and during these nearly four years of Aurelian, have we enjoyed our faith and our worship with none to alarm or oppress us. The laws of the empire have been as a wall of defence between us and this fierce and bloody spirit of Pagan superstition. They who would have willingly assailed and destroyed us have been forcibly restrained by wise and merciful enactments. During this season of repose our numbers have increased, we have been prosperous and happy. Our churches have multiplied, and all the signs of an outward prosperity have been visible in all parts of this vast empire. Would to God I could say that while numbers and wealth have been added to the church, it had grown in grace and in the practice of the virtues of the gospel in the same proportion! But I cannot. The simplicity and purity of the first ages are no longer to be seen among us. We no longer emulate the early apostles and make them our patterns. We rather turn to the Pagan and Jewish priesthood, and in all that pertains to the forms of our worship mould ourselves upon them; and in all that pertains to opinion and doctrine we turn to the philosophers, and engraft, whatever of their mysteries and subtleties we can, upon the plain and simple truth of Jesus. We have departed far, very far, from the gospel standard, both in practice and in faith. We need, Christians, to be brought back. We have gone astray--we have almost worshipped other gods,--it is needful that we return in season to our true allegiance. I dare not say, Christians, that the calamity which now impends is a judgment of God upon our corruptions; we know not what events are of a judicial character, they have upon them no signature which marks them as such; but this we may say, that it will he no calamity, but a benefit and a blessing rather, if it have the effect to show us our errors, and cause us to retrace our steps. Aurelian, enemy though we call him, may prove our benefactor; he may scourge us, but the sufferings he inflicts may bring healing along with them, being that very medicine which the sick soul needs. Let us meet then this new and heavy trial as a part of the providence of God, as a part of that mysterious plan--the lines of which are in so great part hidden from our eyes--by which he educates his children, and at the same time, and by the same means, prepares and transmits to future generations the richest blessings. If we, Christians, suffer for the cause of truth, if our blood is poured out like water, let us remember that it serves to fertilize that soil out of which divine nutriment shall grow for generations yet unborn, whom it shall nourish up unto a better life. Let your hearts then be strong within you; faint not, nor fear; God will be with you and his Spirit comfort you.

'But why do I say these things? Why do I exhort you to courage? For when was it known that the followers of Christ shrunk from the path of duty, though it were evidently the path of death? When and in what age have those been wanting who should bear witness to the truth, and seal it with their blood? There have been those who in time of persecution have fallen away--but for one apostate there have been a thousand martyrs. We have been, I may rather affirm, too prodigal of life--too lavish of our blood. There has been, in former ages, not only a willingness, a readiness to die for Christ, but an eagerness. Christians have not waited to be searched for and found by the ministers of Roman power; they have thrust themselves forward; they have gone up of their own accord to the tribunal and proclaimed their faith, and invited the death at which nature trembles and revolts. But shall we blame this divine ardor? this more than human contempt of suffering and death? this burning zeal for the great cause of our Master? Let us rather honor and revere it as a temper truly divine and of more than mortal force. But let us be just to all. While we honor the courage and self-sacrificing love of so many, let us not require that all should be such, nor cast suspicion upon those who--loving Christ not less in their hearts--shrink from the sufferings in which others glory. Ye need not, Christian men and women, yourselves rush to the tribunal of Varus, ere you can feel that you are Christ's indeed. It is not needful that to be a Christian you must also be a martyr. Ye need not, ye ought not, impatiently seek for the rack and the cross. It is enough if, when sought and found and arraigned, you be found faithful; if then you deny not nor renounce your Lord, but glory in your name, and with your dying breath shout it forth as that for which you gladly encounter torture and death. Go not forth then seeking the martyr's crown! Wait till you are called. God knoweth, and he alone, whom he would have to glorify him by that death which is so much more to be coveted than life. Leave all in the hand of Providence. You that are not chosen, fear not that, though later, the gates of Heaven shall not be thrown open for you. Many are the paths that lead to those gates. Besides, shall all rush upon certain death? Were all martyrs, where then were the seed of the church? They who live, and by their life, consecrate to holiness and God, show that they are his, do no less for their Master and his cause than do they who die for that cause. Nay, 'tis easier to die well than to live well. The cross which we bear through a long life of faithful service, is a heavier one than that which we bear as we go up our Calvary. Leave all then, Christian men and women, in the hands of God. Seek not death nor life. Shun not life nor death. Say each, "Here, Lord, is thy servant, do with him as shall seem to thee good."

'And now, Christians, how shall we receive the edict of Aurelian? It silences our preachers, it closes our churches. What now is the duty of the Christians of Rome?'

Soon as this question was proposed by Probus, many voices from various parts of the room gave in their judgments. At first, the opinions expressed differed on many points: but as the discussion was prolonged the difference grew less and less, till unanimity seemed to be attained. It was agreed at length, that it was right to conform to the edict so far as this: 'That they would not preach openly in the streets nor elsewhere; they would, at first, and scrupulously, conform to the edict in its letter and spirit--until they had seen what could be done by appeals both to the Emperor and the senate; but, maintaining at the same time, that if their appeals were vain, if their churches were not restored to them with liberty to assemble in them as formerly and for the same purposes--then they would take the freedom that was not granted, and use it as before, and abide by the issue; no power of man should close their mouths as ambassadors of God, as followers of Christ and through him reformers of the world; they would speak--they would preach and pray, though death were the immediate reward.'

In this determination I heartily agreed as both moderate and yet firm; as showing respect for the powers that are over us, and at the same time asserting our own rights, and declaring our purpose to stand by them. But so thought not all. For no sooner was the opinion of the assembly declared than Macer broke forth:

'I have heard,' said he, 'the judgment which has been pronounced. But I like it not--I agree not to it. Shall the minister of Christ, the ambassador of God, a messenger from Heaven to earth, hold his peace at the behest of a man, though he be an emperor, or of ten thousand men, were all emperors? Not though every Christian in Rome subscribed to this judgment, not though every Christian in the world assented to it, would I. Is Christ to receive laws of Aurelian? Is the cause of God and truth to be postponed to that of the empire? and posterity to die of hunger because we refuse to till the earth? We are God's spiritual husbandmen--the heart of Rome is our field of labor--it is already the eleventh hour--the last days are at hand--and shall we forbear our toil? shall we withdraw our hand from the plough? shall we cease to proclaim the glad tidings of salvation because the doors of our churches are closed? Not so, Christians, by the blessing of God, shall it be with me. While the streets of Rome and her door-stones will serve me for church and pulpit, and while my tongue is left unwrenched from my mouth, will I not cease to declare Jesus Christ and him crucified! Think you Aurelian will abate his wrath or change his purposes of death, for all your humble sueing? that cringing and fawning will turn aside the messengers of death? Believe it not. Ye know not Aurelian. More would ye gain with him, did the faith of the peace-loving Jesus allow it, if ye went forth in battle array and disputed this great question in the streets of Rome sword in hand! More would ye gain now, if ye sent a word of defiance--denying his right to interpose between God and his people--between Christ and his church--and daring him to do his worst, than by this tame surrender of your rights--this almost base denial of your Master. No sooner shall tomorrow's sun have risen, than on the very steps of the capitol will I preach Christ, and hurl the damnation of God upon this bloody Emperor and his bloody people.'

'O, Macer, Macer! cease, cease!' cried a woman's voice from the crowd. 'You know not what you say! Already have your harsh words put new bitterness into Aurelian's heart. Forbear, as you love Christ and us.'

'Woman--' replied Macer, 'for such your voice declares you to be--I do love both Christ and you, and it is because I love you that I aim to set aside this faithless judgment of the Roman Christians. But when I say I love you and the believers in Rome, I mean your souls, not your bodies. I love not your safety, nor your peace, nor your outward comforts; your houses, nor your wealth, nor your children, nor your lives, nor anything that is yours which the eye can see or the hands handle. I love your souls, and, beside them, nothing. And while it is them I love, and for them am bound in the spirit as a minister of Christ, I may not hold my peace, nor hide myself, for that there is a lion in the path! As a soldier of the cross I will never flee. Though at the last day I hear no other word of praise from Him the judge--and no other shall I hear, for my Pagan sins weigh me down--down--help, Lord! or I perish!--' Macer's voice here took the tone of deepest agony; he seemed for a time wholly lost, standing still, with outstretched arms and uplifted eye. After a long pause he suddenly resumed. 'What did I say?--It was this: though I hear no other word of praise from my judge as I stand at his judgment-seat, I trust I shall hear this, that I did not flee nor hide myself, that I was no coward, but a bold and fearless soldier of the cross, ready at any time and at all times to suffer for the souls of my brethren.'

'Think not, Macer,' said Probus, 'that we shrink at the prospect of danger. But we would be not only bold and unshrinking, but wise and prudent. There is more than one virtue goes to make the Christian man. We think it right and wise first to appeal to the Emperor's love of justice. We think it might redound greatly to our advantage if we could obtain a public hearing before Aurelian, so that from one of our own side he, with all the nobility of Rome, might hear the truth in Christ, and then judge whether to believe so was hurtful to the state, or deserving of torture and death.'

'As well, Probus,' replied Macer, 'might you preach the faith of Christ in the ear of the adder! to the very stones of the highways! Aurelian turn from a settled purpose! ha! ha! you have not served, Probus, under him in Gaul and Asia as others have. Never did the arguments of his legions and his great officers on the other side, serve but to intrench him the more impregnably in his own. He knows not what the word change means. But were this possible, and of good hope, it shows not that plain and straight path to which my spirit points, and which therefore I must travel. Is it right to hearken to man rather than God? That to me is the only question. Shall Aurelian silence the ambassador of God and Christ? Shall man wrestle and dispute it with the Almighty? God, or Aurelian, which shall it be? To me, Christians, it would be a crime of deeper dye than the errors of my Pagan youth, did I chain my tongue, were it but for an hour, at the command of Aurelian. I have a light within, and it is that I must obey. I reason not--I weigh not probabilities--I balance not argument against argument--I feel! and that I take to be the instinct of God--the inspiration of his holy Spirit--and as I feel so am I bound to act.'

It was felt to be useless to reason with this impetuous and self-willed man. He must be left to work out his own path through the surrounding perils, and bear whatever evil his violent rashness might draw upon his head. Yet his are those extreme and violent opinions and feelings which are so apt to carry away the multitude, and it was easy to see that a large proportion of the assembly went with him. Another occasion was given for their expression.

When it had been determined that the edicts should be observed so far as to refrain from all public preaching and all assembling together, till the Emperor had been first appealed to, it then became a question in what manner he should be approached, and by whom, in behalf of the whole body.

And no sooner had Macer ceased, than the same voice which had first brought those charges against Probus was again heard--the voice as I have since learned of a friend of Felix, and an exorcist.

'If it be now determined,' said the voice, 'that we appeal to the clemency of the Emperor in order to avert from our heads the evil that seems to be more than threatened, let it be done by some one who in his faith may nay represent the great body of Christ's followers. Whether the Emperor shall feel well inclined toward us or not, will it not greatly depend upon the manner in which the truth in Christ shall be set forth, and whether by means of the principles and doctrines that shall be shown to belong to it and constitute it, it shall be judged by him to be of hurtful or beneficial tendency? Now it is well known to all how variously Christ is received and interpreted in Rome. As received by some, his gospel is one thing; as received by others, it is another and quite a different thing. Who can doubt that our prospect of a favorable hearing with Aurelian will be an encouraging one in the proportion that he shall perceive our opinions to agree with those which have already been advanced in the schools of philosophy--especially in that of the divine Plato. This agreement and almost identity has, ever since the time of Justin, been pointed out and learnedly defended. They who perceive this agreement, and rest in it as their faith, now constitute the greater part of the Christian world. Let him then who is to bespeak for us the Emperor's good-will be, as in good sooth he ought to be, of these opinions. As to the declaration that has been made that one is as much a Christian as another, whatever the difference of faith may be, I cannot receive it; and he who made the declaration, I doubt would scarce abide by it, since as I learn he is a worshipper and follower of that false-hearted interloper Novatian. The puritans least of all are apt to regard with favor those who hold not with them. Let Felix then, who, if any now living in Rome may stand forward as a specimen of what Christ's religion is in both its doctrine and its life--let Felix plead our cause with Aurelian.'

The same difference of feeling and opinion manifested itself as before. Many voices immediately cried out, 'Yes, yes, Felix, let Felix speak for us.' While others from every part of the room were heard shouting out, 'Probus, Probus, let Probus be our advocate!'

At length the confusion subsided as a single voice made itself heard above the others and caught their attention, saying,

'If Felix, O Christians, as has just been affirmed, represents the opinions which are now most popular in the Christian world, at least here in Rome, Probus represents those which are more ancient--' He was instantly interrupted.

'How long ago,' cried another, 'lived Paul of Samosata?'

'When died the heretic Sabellius?' added still another.

'Or Praxeas?' said a third, 'or Theodotos? or Artemon?'

'These,' replied the first, soon as he could find room for utterance--'these are indeed not of the earliest age, but they from whom they learned their faith are of that age, namely, the apostles and the great master of all.'

'Heresy,' cried out one who had spoken before, 'always dates from the oldest; it never has less age nor authority than that of Christ.'

'Christians! Christians!' Macer's stentorian voice was now heard towering above the tumult, 'what is it ye would have? What are these distinctions about which ye dispute? What have they to do with the matter now in hand? How would one doctrine or the other in such matters weigh with Aurelian more than straws or feathers? But if these are stark naught, and less than naught, there are other questions pertinent to the time, nay, which the time forces upon us, and about which we should be well agreed. A new age of persecution has arisen, and the church is about to be sifted, and the wheat separated from the chaff--the first to be gathered into the garners of God, the last to be burnt up in fire unquenchable. Now is it to be proved who are Christ's, and who are not--who will follow him bearing their cross to some new Calvary, and who, saving their lives, shall yet lose them. Who knows not the evil that, in the time of Decius, yes, and before and since too, fell upon the church from the so easy reception and restoration of those who, in an hour of weakness and fear, denied their master and his faith, and bowed the knee to the gods of Rome? Here is the danger against which we are to guard; from this quarter--not from any other of vain jargon concerning natures, essences, and modes of being--are we to look for those fatal inroads to be made upon the purity of the gospel, that cannot but draw along with them corruption and ruin. Of what stuff will the church then be made, when they who are its ministers, deacons and bishops, shall be such as, when danger showed itself, relapsed into idolatry, and, soon as the clouds had drifted by, and the winds blew soft, came forth again into the calm sunshine, renounced their idolatry, and again professing Christ, were received to the arms of the church, and even to the communion of the body and blood of our Lord? Christians, the great Novatian is he to whom we owe what purity the church yet retains, and it is in allegiance to him--'

'The great Novatian!' exclaimed a priest of the Roman church, 'great only in his infamy! Himself an apostate once, he sought afterwards, having been received himself back again to the church upon his repentance, to bury his shame under a show of zeal against such as were guilty of the same offence. His own weakness or sin, instead of teaching him compassion, served but to harden his heart. Is this the man to whose principles we are to pledge ourselves? Were his principles sound in themselves, we could hardly take them from such a source. But they are false. They are in the face of the spirit and letter of the gospel. What is the character of the religion of Christ, if it be not mercy? Yet this great Novatian, to those who like Peter have fallen--Peter whom his master received and forgave--denies all mercy! and for one offence, however penitence may wring the soul, cuts them off forever like a rotten branch from the body of Christ! Is this the teacher whose follower should appeal for us to the Roman Emperor?'

'I seek not,' Macer began to say, 'to defend the bishop of Rome--'

'Bishop!' cried the other, 'bishop! who ever heard that Novatian was bishop of Rome? But who has not heard that that wicked and ambitious man through envy of Cornelius, and resolved to supplant him, caused himself to be ordained bishop by a few of that order, weak and corrupt men, whom he bribed to the bad work, but who, corrupt as they were, and bribed as they were, it was first needful to make drunk before conscience would allow them by such act eternally to disgrace themselves and the church--'

'Lies and slanders all,' cried Macer and others with him, in the same breath and with their utmost voice. The greatest confusion prevailed. A thousand contradictory cries were heard. In the midst of the uproar the name of Macer was proclaimed by many as that of one who would best assert and defend the Christian cause before Aurelian. But these were soon overborne and silenced by a greater number, who now again called upon Probus to fill that office.

Probus seemed not sorry that, his name being thus tumultuously called out, he had it again in his power to speak to the assembly. Making a sign accordingly that he would be heard, he said,

'That he coveted not the honorable office of appealing for them to the Emperor of Rome. It would confer more happiness a thousand fold, Christians, if I could by any words of mine put harmony and peace into your hearts, than if I might even convert a Roman emperor. What a scene of confusion and discord is this, at such an hour, when, if ever, our hearts should be drawn closer together by this exposure to a common calamity. Why is it that when at home, or moving abroad in the business of life, your conversation so well becomes your name and faith, drawing upon you even the commendation of your Pagan foes, you no sooner assemble together, as now, than division and quarrel ensue, in such measure, as among our Heathen opponents is never seen? Why is it, Christians, that when you are so ready to die for Christ, you will not live at peace for him? Honor you not him more by showing that you are of his spirit, that for his name's sake you are willing to bear patiently whatever reproach may be laid upon you, than you do even by suffering and dying for him? The questions you have here agitated are not for this hour and place. What now does it signify whether one be a follower of Paul, of Origen, of Sabellius, or Novatian, when we are each and all so shortly to be called upon to confess our allegiance to neither of these--but to a greater, even Jesus, the master and head of us all! And what has our preference for some of the doctrines of either of these to do with our higher love of Christ and his truth? By such preference is our superior and supreme regard for Jesus and his word vitiated or invalidated? Nay, what is it we then do when we embrace the peculiar doctrine of some great or good man, who has gone before, but embrace that which in a peculiar sense we regard as the doctrine of Christ? We receive the peculiar doctrine of Paul, or Justin, or Origen, not because it is theirs, but because we think they have shown it to be eminently the doctrine of Christ. In binding upon us then the dogmas of any teacher, we ought not to be treated other than as those who, in doing so, are seeking to do the highest honor, not to such teacher, but to Christ. I am charged as a disciple of the bishop of Antioch, and the honored Felix as a disciple of Plato. If I honor Paul of Samosata, Christians, for any of his truth, it is because I deem him to have discerned clearly the truth as it is in Jesus. My faith is not in him, but in Jesus. And if Felix honor Plato or Plotinus, it is but because in them he beholds some clearer unfolding--clearer than elsewhere--of the truth in Christ. Are not we then, and all who do the same thing, to be esteemed as those who honor Christ? not deny nor forsake him. And as we all hold in especial reverence some one or another of a former age, through whom as a second master we receive the doctrines of the gospel, ought we not all to love and honor one another, seeing that in the same way we all love and honor Christ? Let love, Christians, mutual honor and love, be the badge of our discipleship, as it was in the first age of the church. Soon, very soon, will you be called to bear testimony to the cause you have espoused, and perhaps seal it with your blood. Be not less ready to show your love to those around you by the promptness with which you lend your sympathy, or counsel, or aid, as this new flood of adversity flows in upon them. But why do I exhort you? The thousand acts of kindness, of charity, of brotherly love, which flow outwards from you in a perpetual stream toward Heathen not less than Christian, and have drawn upon you the admiration even of the Pagan world, is sufficient assurance that your hearts will not be cold when the necessities of this heavier time shall lay upon you their claims. It is only in the public assembly, and in the ardor of debate, that love seems cold and dead. Forget then, now and tomorrow, that you are followers of any other than Christ. Forget that you call yourselves after one teacher or another, and remember only that you are brethren, members of one family, of the same household of faith, owning one master, worshipping one and the same God and Father of us all. And now, Christians, if you would rather that Felix should defend you before Aurelian, I would also. There is none among us who loves Christ more or better than he, or would more readily lay down his life for his sake.'

Felix however joined with all the others--for all now, after these few words of Probus, seemed of one opinion--in desiring that Probus should appear for the Christians before the Emperor; which he then consented to do. Harmony was once more restored. The differences of opinion, which separated them, seemed to be forgotten, and they mingled as friends and fellow-laborers in the great cause of truth. They who had been harshest in the debate--which was at much greater length, and conducted with much more vehemence than as I have described it--were among the most forward to meet with urbanity those who were in faith the most distantly removed from them. A long and friendly interview then took place, in which each communed with each, and by words of faith or affection helped to supply the strength which all needed for the approaching conflict. One saw no longer and heard no longer the enthusiastic disputant more bent upon victory than truth, and heedless of the wounds he gave to the heart, provided he convinced the head or silenced the tongue, but instead, those who now appeared no other than a company of neighbors and friends engaged in the promotion of some common object of overwhelming interest.

When in this manner and for a considerable space of time a fit offering had been laid upon the altar of love, the whole assembly again joined together in acts of prayer, and again lifted up their voices in song of praise. This duty being performed, we separated and sought the streets. The storm which had begun in violence, had increased, and it was with difficulty that beset by darkness, wind, and rain, I succeeded without injury in finding my way to the Coelian.

Julia was waiting for me with anxious impatience.

After relating to her the events of the evening, she said,

'How strange, Lucius, the conduct of such men at such a time! How could Christians, with the Christian's faith in their hearts, so lose the possession of themselves--and so violate all that they profess as followers of Jesus! I confess, if this be the manner in which Christianity is intended to operate upon the character, I am as yet wholly ignorant of it, and desire ever to remain so. But it is not possible that they are right. Nay, they seem in some sort to have acknowledged themselves to have been in the wrong by the last acts of the meeting. This brings to my mind what Paul has often told me of the Christians of the same kind, at which I was then amazed, but had forgotten. I do not comprehend it. I have read and studied the character and the teachings of Jesus, and it seems to me I have arrived at some true understanding--for surely there is little difficulty in doing so--of what he himself was, and of what he wished his followers to be. Would he have recognized his likeness in those of whom you have now told me?'

'Yet,' I replied, 'there was more of it there in those very persons than at first we might be inclined to think; and in the great multitude of those who were present, it may have been all there, and was in most, I cannot doubt. We ought not to judge of this community by the leaders of the several divisions which compose it. They are by no means just specimens, from which to infer the character of all. They are but too often restless, ambitious, selfish men; seeking their own aggrandizement and their party's, rather than the glory of Christ and his truth. I can conceive of a reception of Christian precept and of the Christian spirit being but little more perfect and complete, than I have found it among the humbler sort of the Christians of Rome. Among them there is to be seen nothing of the temper of violence and bigotry that was visible this evening in the language of so many. They, for the most part, place the religion of Jesus in holy living, in love of one another, and patient waiting for the kingdom of God. And their lives are seen to accord with these great principles of action. Even for their leaders, who are in so many points so different from them, this may be said in explanation and excuse--that from studying the record more than the common people, they come to consider more narrowly in what the religion of Jesus consists, and arriving, after much labor, at what they believe in their hearts to be the precise truth--truth the most vital of any to the power and success of the gospel--this engrosses all their affections, and prompts all their labor and zeal. In the dissemination of this do they alone behold the dissemination of Christianity itself--this being denied or rejected, the gospel itself is. With such notions as fundamental principles of action, it is easy to see with what sincere and virtuous indignation they would be filled toward such as should set at nought and oppose that, which they cherish as the very central glory and peculiarity of Christianity. These things being so, I can pity and forgive a great deal of what appears to be, and is, so opposite to the true Christian temper, on account of its origin and cause. Especially as these very persons, who are so impetuous, and truculent almost, as partizans and advocates, are, as private Christians, examples perhaps of extraordinary virtue. We certainly know this to be the case with Macer. An apostle was never more conscientious nor more pure. Yet would he, had he power equal to his will, drive from the church all who bowed not the knee to his idol Novatian.'

'But how,' asked Julia, 'would that agree with the offence he justly took at those who quarreled with Probus and Felix on account of their doctrine?'

'There certainly would be in such conduct no agreement nor consistency. It only shows how easy it is to see a fault in another, to which we are stone-blind in ourselves. In the faith or errors of Probus and Felix he thought there was nothing that should injure their Christian name, or unfit them for any office. Yet in the same breath he condemned as almost the worst enemies of Christ such as refused honor and adherence to the severe and inhuman code of his master Novatian.'

'But how far removed, Lucius, is all this from the spirit of the religion of Jesus! Allowing all the force of the apologies you may offer, is it not a singular state for the minds and tempers of those to have arrived at, who profess before the world to have formed themselves after the doctrine, and, what is more, after the character of Christ? I cannot understand the process by which it has been done, nor how it is that, without bringing upon themselves public shame and reproach, such men can stand forth and proclaim themselves not only Christians, but Christian leaders and ministers.'

'I can understand it, I confess, quite as little. But I cannot doubt that as Christianity outgrows its infancy, especially when the great body of those who profess it shall have been formed by it from their youth, and shall not be composed, as now, of those who have been brought over from the opposite and uncongenial regions of Paganism, with much of their former character still adhering to them, Christians will then be what they ought to be who make the life and character of Jesus their standard. Nothing is learned so slowly by mankind as those lessons which enforce mutual love and respect, in which the gospels so abound. We must allow not only years, but hundreds of years, for these lessons to be imprinted upon the general heart of men, and to be seen in all their character and intercourse. But when a few hundred years shall have elapsed, and that is a long allowance for this education to be perfected in, I can conceive that the times of the primitive peace and love shall be more than restored, and that such reproaches as to-night were heard lavished upon one and another will be deemed as little compatible with a Christian profession as would be violence and war. All violence and wrong must cease, as this religion is received, and the ancient superstitions and idolatries die out.'

'What a privilege, to be born and live,' said Julia, 'in those fast approaching years, when Christianity shall alone be received as the religion of this large empire, when Paganism shall have become extinct in Rome war and slavery shall cease, and all our people shall be actuated by the same great principles of faith and virtue that governed both Christ and his apostles! A few centuries will witness more and better than we now dream of.'

So we pleased ourselves with visions of future peace and happiness, which Christianity was to convert to reality. To me they are no longer mere visions, but as much realities to be experienced, as the future towering oak is, when I look upon an acorn planted, or as the future man is, when I look upon a little child. If Christianity grows at all, it must grow in such direction. If it do not, it will not be Christianity that grows, but something else that shall have assumed its name and usurped its place. The extension of Christianity is the extension and multiplication as it were of that which constituted Christ himself--it is the conversion of men into his image--or else it is nothing. Then, when this shall be done, what a paradise of peace, and holiness, and love, will not the earth be! Surely, to be used as an instrument in accomplishing such result, one may well regard as an honor and privilege, and be ready to bear and suffer much, if need be, in fulfilling the great office.

I hope I shall not have wearied you by all this exactness. I strictly conform to your injunctions, so that you can complain only of yourself.

We often wish that the time would allow us to escape to you, that we might witness your labors and share them in the rebuilding and reesbelishing of the city. Rome will never be a home to Julia. Her affections are all in Syria. I can even better conceive of Zenobia becoming a Roman than Julia. Farewell.

* * * * *

Finding among the papers of Piso no letter giving any account of what took place immediately after the meeting of the Christians, which, in his last letter, he has so minutely described, I shall here supply, as I may, the deficiency; and I can do it at least with fidelity, since I was present at the scenes of which I shall speak.

No one took a more lively interest in the condition and affairs of the Christians than Zenobia; and it is with sorrow that I find among the records of Piso no mention made of conversations had at Tibur while these events were transpiring, at which were present himself, and the princess Julia, the Queen, and, more than once, Aurelian and Livia. While I cannot doubt that such record was made, I have in vain searched for it among those documents which he intrusted to me.

It was by command of the Queen that on the day following that on which the Christians held their assembly at the baths, I went to Rome for the very purpose to learn whatever I could, both at the Gardens and abroad in the city, concerning the condition and probable fate of that people, she desiring more precise information than could be gathered from any of the usual sources of intelligence.

It was apparent to me as I entered the city, and penetrated to its more crowded parts, that somewhat unusual had taken place, or was about to happen. There were more than the common appearances of excitement among those whom I saw conversing and gesticulating at the corners of streets or the doors of the public baths. This idle and corrupt population seemed to have less than on other occasions to employ their hands, and so gave their time and their conversation to one another, laying no restraint upon the quantity of either. It is an indisputable fact that Rome exists to this day, for any one who will come into Italy may see it for himself, and he cannot reject the testimony of his eyes and ears. But how it exists from year to year, or from day to day, under such institutions, it would puzzle the wisest philosopher, I believe, to tell. Me, who am no philosopher, it puzzles as often as I reflect upon it. I cannot learn the causes that hold together in such apparent order and contentment so idle and so corrupt a people. I have supposed it must be these, but they seem not sufficient: the Priorian camp without the walls, and the guard, in league with them, within, and the largesses and games proceeding from the bounty of the Emperor. These last, though they are the real sources of their corruption and must end in the very destruction of the city and people, yet, at present, operate to keep them quiet and in order. So long as these bounties are dispensed, so long, such is our innate love of idleness and pleasure, will the mass think it foolish to agitate any questions of right or religion, or any other, by which they might be forfeited. Were these suddenly suspended, all the power of the Priorian cohorts, I suppose, could not keep peace in Rome. They were now I found occupied by the affairs of the Christians, and waiting impatiently for the orders which should next issue from the imperial will. The edicts published two days before gave them no employment, nor promised much. They merely laid restraints upon the Christians, but gave no liberty of assault and injury to the Roman.

'That does not satisfy the people,' said one to me, at the door of a shop, of whom I had made some inquiry on the subject. 'More was looked for from the Emperor, for it is well known that he intends the extremest measures, and most are of opinion that, before the day is out, new edicts will be issued. Why he took the course he did of so uncommon moderation 'tis hard to say. All the effect of it is to give the Christians opportunity to escape and hide themselves, so that by the time the severer orders against them are published, it will be impossible to carry them into execution.'

'Perhaps,' I said, 'it was after all his intention to give them a distant warning, that some might, if they saw fit to do so, escape.'

'I do not believe that,' he replied; 'it will rather, I am of the opinion, be found to have proceeded from the advice of Fronto and Varus, to give to the proceedings a greater appearance of moderation; which shows into the hands of what owls the Emperor has suffered himself to fall. Nobody ever expected moderation in Aurelian, nor do any but a few as bad as themselves think these wretches deserve it. The only consequence of the present measures will be to increase their swelling insolence and pride, thinking that Aurelian threatens but dares not execute. Before another day, I trust, new edicts will show that the Emperor is himself. The life of Rome hangs upon the death of these.'

Saying which, with a savage scowl, which showed how gladly he would turn executioner or tormentor in such service, he turned and crossed the street.

I then sought the palace of Piso. I was received in the library, where I found the lady Julia and Piso.

They greeted me as they ever did, rather as if I were a brother than but the servant of Zenobia. But whatever belongs to her, were it but so much as a slave of the lowest office, would they treat with affection at least, if not with reverence. After answering their inquiries after the welfare of the Queen and Faustula, I made mine concerning the condition of the city and the affairs of the Christians, saying, 'that Zenobia was anxious to learn what ground there was, or whether any, to feel apprehension for the safety of that people?'--Piso said, 'that now he did not doubt there was great ground for serious apprehension. It was believed by those who possessed the best means of intelligence, that new edicts of a much severer character would be issued before another day. But that Zenobia need be under no concern either as to himself or Julia, since the Emperor in conversation with him as much as assured him that, whatever might befal others, no harm should come to them.'

He then gave me an account of what the Christians had done in their assembly, agreeing with what is now to be found in the preceding letter.

I then asked whether he thought that the Christian Macer would keep to the declaration he had made, that he would to-day, the edicts notwithstanding, preach in the streets of Rome! He replied, that he did not doubt that he would, and that if I wished to know what some of the Christians were, and what the present temper of the people was towards them, I should do well to seek him and hear him.'

'Stand by him, good Nicomachus,' said Julia, 'if at any moment you find that you can be of service to him. I have often heretofore blamed him, but since this murder of Aurelia, and the horrors of the dedication, I hold him warranted, and more than that, in any means he may use, to rouse this guilty people. Perhaps it is only by the use of such remedies as he employs, that the heart of Rome--hardened by ages of sin--can be made to feel. To the milder treatment of Probus, and others like him, it seems for the most part utterly insensible and dead. At least his sincerity, his zeal, and his courage, are worthy of all admiration.'

I assured her that I would befriend him if I could do so with any prospect of advantage, but it was little that one could do against the fury of a Roman mob. I then asked Piso if he would not accompany me; but he replied, that he had already heard Macer, and was, besides, necessarily detained at home by other cares.

As there was no conjecturing in what part of the city this Christian preacher would harangue the people, and neither the Princess nor Piso could impart any certain information, I gave little more thought to it, but, as I left the palace on the Coelian, determined to seek the gardens of Sallust, where, if I should not see Aurelian, I might at least pass the earlier hours of the day in an agreeable retreat. I took the street that leads from the Coelian to the Capitol Hill, as affording a pleasanter walk--if longer. On the way there, I observed well the signs which were given in the manner and conversation of those whom I met, or walked with, of the events which were near at hand. There is no better index of what a despotic ruler, and yet at the same time a 'people's' despot, will do, than the present will of the people. It was most apparent to me that they were impatient for some quick and vigorous action, no matter how violent, against the Christians. Language the most ferocious met my ear. The moderation and tardiness of the Emperor--of him who had in every thing else been noted for the rapidity of his movements--were frequent subjects of complaint.

'It is most strange,' they said, 'that Aurelian should hesitate in this matter, in truth as if he were afraid to move. Were it not for Fronto, it is thought that nothing would be done after all. But this we may feel sure of, that if the Emperor once fairly begins the work of extermination, he is not the man to stop half way. And there is not a friend of the ancient institutions of religion, but who says that their very existence depends upon--not the partial obstruction of this sect--but upon its actual and total extermination. Who does not know that measures of opposition and resistance, which go but part way and then stop, through a certain unwillingness as it were to proceed to extremes, do but increase the evil they aim to suppress. Weeds that are but mown, come up afterwards only the more vigorously. Their very roots must be torn up and then burned.' Such language was heard on all sides, uttered with utmost violence--of voice and gesture.

I paused, among other curious and busy idlers, at the door of a smith's shop, which, as I passed slowly by, presented a striking view of a vast and almost boundless interior, blazing with innumerable fires, where laborers half naked--and seeming as if fire themselves, from the reflection from their steaming bodies of the red glare of the furnaces--stood in groups, some drawing forth the bars of heated metal and holding them, while others wielding their cyclopean hammers made the anvils and the vast interior ring with the blows they gave. All around the outside of the shop and in separate places within stood the implements and machines of various kinds which were either made, or were in the process of being put together. Those whom I joined were just within the principal entrance looking upon a fabric of iron consisting of a complicated array of wheels and pulleys, to which the workmen were just in the act of adding the last pieces. The master of the place now approaching and standing with us, while he gave diverse orders to the men, I said to him,

'What new device may this be? The times labor with new contrivances by which to assist the laborer in his art, and cause iron to do what the arm has been accustomed to perform. But after observing this with care I can make nothing of it. It seems not designed to aid any manufacture of which I have any knowledge.'

The master looked at me with a slighting expression of countenance as much as to say 'you are a wise one! You must have just emerged from the mountains of Helvetia, or the forests of the Danube.' But he did not content himself with looks.

'This, sir?' said he. 'This, if you would know it, is a rack--a common instrument of torture--used in all the prisons of the empire, the use of which is to extract truth from one who is unwilling to speak except compelled; or, sometimes, when death is thought too slight a punishment, to give it an edge with, just as salt and pepper are thrown into a fresh wound. Some crimes, you must know, were too softly dealt with, were a sharp axe the only instrument employed. Caesar! just bring some wires of a good thickness, and we will try this. Now shall you see precisely how it would fare with your own body, were you on this iron frame and Varus standing where I am. There,-- Caesar having in a few moments brought the wires--the body you perceive is confined in this manner.--You observe there can be no escape and no motion. Now at the word of the judge, this crank is turned. Do you see the effect upon the wire? Imagine it your body and you will have a lively idea of the instrument. Then at another wink or word from Varus, these are turned, and you see that another part of the body, the legs or arms as it may be, are subjected to the same force as this wire, which as the fellow keeps turning you see--strains, and straightens, and strains, till--crack!--there!--that is what we call a rack. A most ingenious contrivance and of great use. This is going up within the hour to the hall of the Prefect.'

'It seems,' I remarked, 'well contrived indeed for its object. And what,' I asked, 'are these which stand here? Are they for the same or a similar purpose?'

'Yes--these, sir, are different and yet the same. They are all for purposes of torture, but they vary infinitely in the ingenuity with which they severally inflict pain and death. That is esteemed in Rome the most perfect instrument which, while it inflicts the most exquisite torments, shall at the same time not early, assail that which is a vital part, but, you observe, prolong life to the utmost. Some, of an old-fashioned structure, with a clumsy and bungling machinery--here are some sent to me as useless--long before the truth could be extracted, or much more pain inflicted than would accompany beheading, destroyed the life of the victim. Those which I build--and I build for the State--are not to be complained of in that way. Varus is curious enough, I can assure you, in such things. All these that you see here, of whatever form or make, are for him and the hall of justice. They have been all refitted and repaired--or else they are new.'

'How is it possible,' I asked, 'so many could be required in one place?'

'Surely,' said the master, 'you must just have dropt down in Rome from Britain, or Scythia, or the moon! Didst ever hear of a people called Galilean or Christian? Perhaps the name is new to you.'

'No, I have heard it.'

'Well, these are for them. As you seem new in the city and to our Roman ways, walk a little farther in and I will show you others, which are for the men and the boys at such time as the slaughter of this people shall become general. For you must know,--although it is not got widely abroad yet--that by and by the whole city is to be let loose upon them. That is the private plan of the Emperor. Every good citizen, it will be expected, will do his share in the work, till Rome shall be purged. Aurelian does nothing by halves. It is in view of such a state of things that I have prepared an immense armory--if I may call it so--of every sort of cheap iron tool--I have the more costly also--to meet the great demand that will be made. Here they are! commend now my diligence, my patriotism, and my foresight! Some of my craft will not engage in this work: but it exactly jumps with my humor. Any that you shall choose of these, sir, you shall have cheap, and they shall be sent to your lodgings.'

I expressed my gratitude, but declined the offer.

After wandering a little longer around the huge workshop, I took my leave of its humane master, still entreating me to purchase, and, as I entered again the street, turned towards the capitol. My limbs were sympathising with those wires throughout the rest of the day.

I had forgotten Macer, and almost my object in coming abroad, and was revolving various subjects in my mind, my body only being conscious of the shocks which now and then I received from persons meeting or passing me, when I became conscious of a sudden rush along the street in the direction of the capitol, which was now but a furlong from where I was. I was at once awake. The people began to run, and I ran with them by instinct. At length it came into my mind to ask why we were running? One near me replied,

'O, it's only Macer the Christian, who, 'tis said, in spite of the edict, has just made for the steps of the capitol, followed by a large crowd.'

On the instant I outstripped my companion, and turning quickly the corner, where the street in which I was crossed the hill, I there beheld an immense multitude gathered around the steps of the capitol, and the tall form of Macer just ascending them. Resolved to be near him, I struggled and forced my way into the mass till I found myself so far advanced that I could both hear and be heard by him, if I should find occasion to speak, and see the expression of his countenance. It was to me, as he turned round toward the people, the most extraordinary countenance I ever beheld. It seemed as if once it had been fiercer than the fiercest beast of the forest, while through that was now to be discerned the deep traces of grief, and an expression which seemed to say, "I and the world have parted company. I dwell above." His two lives and his two characters were to be read at once in the strong and deep-sunk lines of a face that struck the beholder at once with awe, with admiration, and compassion.

The crowd was restless and noisy; heaving to and fro like the fiery mass of a boiling crater. A thousand exclamations and imprecations filled the air. I thought it doubtful whether the rage which seemed to fill a great proportion of those around me would so much as permit the Christian to open his mouth. It seemed rather as if he would at once be dragged from where he stood to the Prefect's tribunal, or hurled from the steps and sacrificed at once to the fury of the populace. But, as the cries of his savage enemies multiplied, the voices of another multitude were lifted up in his behalf, which were so numerous and loud, that they had the effect of putting a restraint upon the others. It was evident that Macer could not be assailed without leading to a general combat. All this while Macer stood unmoved, and calm as the columns of the capitol itself--waiting till the debate should be ended and the question decided--a question of life or death to him. Upon the column immediately on his right hand hung, emblazoned with gold, and beautiful with all the art of the chirographer, the edict of Aurelian. It was upon parchment, within a brazen frame.

Soon as quiet was restored, so that any single voice could be heard, one who was at the foot of the steps and near the preacher cried out to him,

'Well, old fellow, begin! thy time is short.'

'Young man,' he replied, 'I was once old in sin, for which God forgive me!--now I am old in the love of Christ, for which God be thanked!--but in years I am but forty. As for time!--I think only of eternity.'

'Make haste, Macer!' cried another voice from the crowd. 'Varus will soon be here.'

'I believe you,' replied the soldier; 'but I am ready for him. I love life no longer than I can enjoy free speech. If I may not now and here speak out every thought of my heart, and the whole truth in Christ, then would I rather die; and whether I die in my own bed, or upon the iron couch of Varus, matters little. Romans!' turning now and addressing the crowd, 'the Emperor in his edict tells me not to preach to you. Not to preach Christ in Rome, neither within a church nor in the streets. Such is this edict. Shall I obey him? When Christ says, 'Go forth and preach the gospel to every creature,' shall I give ear to a Roman Emperor, who bids me hold my peace? Not so, not so, Romans. I love God too well, and Christ too well, and you too well, to heed such bidding. I love Aurelian too, I have served long under him, and he was ever good to me. He was a good as well as great general, and I loved him. I love him now, but not so well as these; not so well as you. And if I obeyed this edict, it would show that I loved him better than you, and better than these, which would be false. If I obeyed this edict I should never speak to you again of this new religion, as you call it. I should leave you all to perish in your sins, without any of that knowledge, or faith, or hope in Christ, which would save you from them, and form you after the image of God, and after death carry you up to dwell with him and with just men forever and ever. I should then, indeed, show that I hated you, which I can never do. I love you and Rome I cannot tell how much--as much as a child ever loved a mother, or children one another. And therefore it is that no power on earth--nor above it, nor under it--no power, save that of God, shall hinder me from declaring to you the doctrine which I think you need, nay, without which your souls will perish and dwell for ever and ever, not with God, but in fires eternal of the lowest hell. For what can your gods do for you? what are they doing? They lift you not up to themselves--they push you down rather to those fires. Christ, O Romans, if you will receive him, will save you from them, and from those raging fires of sorrow and remorse, which here on earth do constitute a hell hot as any that burns below. It is your sins which kindle those fires, and with which Christ wages war--not with you. It is your sins with which I wage war here in the streets of Rome, not with you. Only repent of your sins, Romans, and believe in Christ the son of God, and O how glorious and happy were then this great and glorious city. I have told you before, and I tell you now, your vices are undermining the foundations of this great empire. There is no power to cure these but in Jesus Christ. And when I know this, shall I cease to preach Christ to you because a man, a man like myself, forbids me? Would you not still prepare for a friend or a child the medicine that would save his life, though you were charged by another never so imperiously to forbear? The gospel is the divine medicament that is to heal all your sicknesses, cure all your diseases, remove all your miseries, cleanse all your pollutions, correct all your errors, confirm within you all necessary truth. And when it is this healing draught for which your souls cry aloud, for which they thirst even unto death, shall I the messenger of God, sent in the name of his Son to bear to your lips the cup, of which if you once drink you will live forever, withhold from you that cup, or dash it to the ground? Shall I, a mediator between God and man, falter in my speech, and my tongue hang palsied in my mouth, because Aurelian speaks? What to me, O Romans, is the edict of a Roman Emperor? Down, down, accursed scrawl! nor insult longer both God and man.'

And saying that, he reached forth his hand, and seizing the parchment wrenched it from its brazen frame, and rending it to shreds strewed them abroad upon the air.

It was done in the twinkling of an eye. At first, horror-struck at the audacity of the deed, and while it was doing, the crowd stood still and mute, bereft, as it were, of all power to move or speak. But soon as the fragments of the parchment came floating along upon the air, their senses returned, and the most violent outcries, curses, and savage yells rose from the assembled multitude, and at the same moment a movement was made to rush upon the Christian, with the evident purpose to sacrifice him on the spot to the offended majesty of the empire. I supposed that their purpose would be easily and instantly accomplished, and that whatever I might attempt to do in his defence would be no more than a straw thrown in the face of a whirlwind. But here a new wonder revealed itself. For no sooner was it evident, from the rage and tumultuous tossings of the crowd, and their ferocious cries, that the last momenta of Macer had arrived, than it was apparent that all in the immediate neighborhood of the building, on whose steps he stood, were either Christians, or Romans, who, like myself, were well disposed towards that people, and would promptly join them in their defence of Macer. These, and they amounted to a large and dense mass, at once, as those cries arose, sent forth others as shouts of defiance, and facing outwards made it known that none could assail Macer but by first assailing them.

I could not doubt that it was a preconcerted act by which the Christian was thus surrounded by his friends--not, as I afterward found, with his knowledge, but done at their own suggestion--so that if difficulty should arise, they, by a show of sufficient power, might rescue him, whom all esteemed in spite of his errors, and also serve by their presence to deter him from any further act, or the use of any language, that should give needless offence to either the Prefect or his friends. Their benevolent design was in part frustrated by the sudden, and, as it seemed, unpremeditated movement of Macer in tearing down the edict. But they still served as a protection against the immediate assaults of the excited and enraged mob.

But their services were soon ended, by the interference of a power with which it was in vain to contend. For when the populace had given over for a moment their design, awed by the formidable array of numbers about the person of Macer, he again, having never moved from the spot where he had stood, stretched out his long arm as if he would continue what he had scarcely as yet begun, and to my surprise the people, notwithstanding what had occurred, seemed not indisposed to hear him. But just at that moment-- just as a deep silence had at length succeeded the late uproar--the distant sound, in the direction of the Prefect's, of a troop of horse in rapid movement over the pavements, caught the ears of the people. No one doubted for a moment what it signified.

'Your hour is come, Macer,' cried a voice from the crowd.

'It can never come too soon,' answered the preacher, 'in the service of God. But remember, Roman citizens, what I have told you, that it is for you and for Rome, that I incur the wrath of the wicked Varus, and may so soon at his hands meet the death of a Christian witness.'

As Macer spoke, the Roman guard swept rapidly round a corner, and the multitude giving way in every direction left him alone upon the spot where he had been standing. Regardless of life and limb, the horse dashed through the flying crowds, throwing down many and trampling them under foot, till they reached the Christian, who, undismayed and fearless, maintained his post. There was little ceremony in their treatment of him. He was seized by a band of the soldiers, his hands strongly bound behind him, and placed upon a horse--when, wheeling round again, the troop at full speed vanished down the same avenue by which they had come, bearing their victim, as we doubted not, to the tribunal of Varus.

Determined to see all I could, and the last if it must be so, of this undaunted spirit, I hastened at my utmost speed in the wake of the flying troop. Little as I had heard or seen of this strange man, I had become as deeply concerned in his fate as any could have been who had known him more intimately, or believed both in him and with him. I know not what it was, unless it were the signatures of sincerity, of child-like sincerity and truth stamped upon him, that so drew me toward him, together with that expression of profound sadness, or rather of inward grief, which, wherever we see it and in whomsoever, excites our curiosity and engages our sympathy. He was to me a man who deserved a better fate than I feared he would meet. He seemed like one who, under fortunate circumstances, might have been of the number of those great spirits whose iron will and gigantic force of character bear down before them all opposition, and yoke nations to their car. Of fear he evidently had no comprehension whatever. The rustling of the autumn breeze in his gown alarmed him as much, as did the clang of those horses' hoofs upon the pavements, though he so well knew it was the precursor of suffering and death.

With all the speed I could use I hurried to the hall of the Prefect. The crowds were pouring in as I reached it, among whom I also rushed along and up the flights of steps, anxious only to obtain an entrance and a post of observation, whence I could see and hear what should take place. I soon entered the room of justice. Varus was not yet in his seat: but before it at some little distance stood Macer, his hands still bound, and soldiers of the palace on either side.

I waited not long before Varus appeared at the tribunal; and following him, and placed near him, Fronto, priest of the Temple of the Sun. Now, poor Christian! I thought within myself, if it go not hard with thee it will not be for want of those who wish thee ill. The very Satan of thy own faith was never worse than these. Fronto's cruel eyes were fixed upon him just as a hungry tiger's are upon the unconscious victim upon whom he is about to spring. Varus seemed as if he sat in his place to witness some holiday sport, drawing his box of perfume between his fingers, or daintily adjusting the folds of his robe. When a few preliminary formalities were gone through, Varus said, addressing one of the officials of the place,

'Whom have we here?'

'Noble Prefect, Macer the Christian.'

'And why stands he at my tribunal?' continued Varus.

'For a breach of the late edict of the Emperor, by which the Christians were forbidden to preach either within their temples or abroad in the streets and squares.'

'Is that all?' asked the Prefect.

'Not only,' it was replied, 'hath he preached abroad in the streets, but he hath cast signal contempt upon both the Emperor and the empire, in that he hath but now torn down from its brazen frame the edict which he had first violated, and scattered it in fragments upon the streets.'

'If these things are so, doubtless he hath well earned his death. How is this, Galilean? dost thou confess these crimes, or shall I call in other witnesses of thy guilt?'

'First,' replied Macer, 'will it please the Prefect to have these bonds removed? For the sake of old fellowship let them be taken off, that, while my tongue is free to speak, my hands may be free also. Else am I not a whole man.'

'Unbind them,' said the Prefect; 'let him have his humor. Yet shall we fit on other bracelets anon that may not sit so easy.'

'Be that as it may,' answered the Christian; 'in the meanwhile I would stand thus. I thank thee for the grace.'

'Now, Christian, once more if thou art ready. Is it the truth that hath been witnessed?'

'It is the truth,' replied Macer; 'and I thank God that it is so.'

'But knowest thou, Christian, that in saying that, thou hast condemned thyself to instant death? Was not death the expressed penalty for violation of that law?'

'Truly it was,' answered Macer; 'and what is death to me?'

'I suppose death to be death,' replied Varus.

'Therein thou showest thyself to be in the same darkness as all the rest of this idolatrous city. Death to the Christian, Prefect, is life! Crush me by thy engines, and in the twinkling of an eye is my soul dwelling with God, and looking down with compassion upon thy stony heart.'

'Verily, Fronto,' said Varus, 'these Christians are an ingenious people. What a wonderful fancy is this. But, Christian,' turning to Macer, 'it were a pity surely for thee to die. Thou hast a family as I learn. Would not thy life be more to them than thy death?'

'Less,' said the Christian, 'a thousand fold! were it not a better vision to them of me crowned with a victor's wreath and sitting with Christ, than dwelling here in this new Sodom, and drinking in its pestilential air? The sight of me there would be to them a spring of comfort and a source of strength which here I can never be.'

'But,' added the Prefect, 'it is but right that thou shouldst for the present, if it may be, live here and take care of thy family. They will want thee.'

'God,' replied Macer, 'who feeds the birds of the air, and through all their wanderings over the earth from clime to clime still brings them back to the accustomed home, will watch over those whom I love, and bring them home. Such, Prefect, are the mercies of Rome toward us who belong to Christ, that they will not be left long to bewail my loss.'

'Do thy family then hold with thee?' said Varus.

'Blessed be God, they do.'

'That is a pity--' responded the Prefect.

'Say not so, Varus; 'tis a joy and a triumph to me in this hour, and to them, that they are Christ's.'

'Still,' rejoined the Prefect, 'I would willingly save thee, and make thee live: and there is one way in which it may be done, and thou mayest return in joy to thy home.'

'Let me then know it,' said Macer.

'Renounce Christ, Macer, and sacrifice; and thy life is thine, and honor too.'

Macer's form seemed to dilate to more than its common size, his countenance seemed bursting with expression as he said,

'Renounce Christ? save life by renouncing Christ? How little, Varus, dost thou know what a Christian is! Not though I might sit in thy seat or Aurelian's, or on the throne of a new universe, would I renounce him. To Christ, Varus, do I owe it that I am not now what I was, when I dwelt in the caves of the Flavian. To Christ do I owe it that I am not now what I was when in the ranks of Aurelian. To Christ do I owe it that my soul, once steeped in sin as thy robe in purple dye, is now by him cleansed and, as I trust, thoroughly purged. To Christ do I owe it that once worshipping the dumb idols of Roman superstition, I now bow down to the only living God--' 'Away with him to the tormentors!' came from an hundred voices--'to Christ do I owe it, O Prefect, that my heart is not now as thine, or his who sits beside thee, or as that of these, hungering and thirsting--never after righteousness--but for the blood of the innocent. Shall I then renounce Christ? and then worship that ancient adulterer, Jupiter greatest and best?--' The hall here rang with the ferocious cries of those who shouted--

'Give him over to us!'--'To the rack with him!'--'Tear out the tongue of the blaspheming Galilean!'

'Romans,' cried Varus, rising from his chair, 'let not your zeal for the gods cause you to violate the sanctity of this room of Justice. Fear not but Varus, who, as you well know, is a lover of the gods, his country, and the city, will well defend their rights and honors against whoever shall assail them.'

He then turned to Macer and said,

'I should ill perform my duty to thee, Christian, did I spare any effort to bring thee to a better mind--ill should I perform it for Rome did I not use all the means by the State entrusted to me to save her citizens from errors that, once taking root and growing up to their proper height, would soon overshadow, and by their poisonous neighborhood kill, that faith venerable through a thousand years, and of all we now inherit from our ancestors of greatest and best, the fruitful and divine spring.'

'There, Romans, spoke a Roman,' exclaimed Fronto.

As Varus ended--at a sign and a word from him, what seemed the solid wall of the room in which we were, suddenly flew up upon its screaming pulleys, and revealed another apartment black as night, save here and there where a dull torch shed just light enough to show its great extent, and set in horrid array before us, engines of every kind for tormenting criminals, each attended by its half-naked minister, ready at a moment's warning to bind the victim, and put in motion the infernal machinery. At this sight a sudden faintness overspread my limbs, and I would willingly have rushed from the hall--but it was then made impossible. And immediately the voice of the Prefect was again heard:

'Again, Christian, with Rome's usual mercy, I freely offer to thee thy life, simply on the condition, easily fulfilled by thee, for it asks but one little word from thy lips, that thou do, for thy own sake and for the sake of Rome, which thou sayest thou lovest, renounce Christ and thy faith.'

'I have answered thee once, O Prefect; dost thou think so meanly of me as to suppose that what but now I affirmed, I will now deny, and only for this show of iron toys and human demons set to play them? It is not of such stuff Aurelian's men are made, much less the soldiers of the cross. For the love I bear to Rome and Christ, and even thee, Varus, I choose to die.'

'Be assured, Christian, I will not spare thee.'

'I ask it not, Prefect--do thy worst--and the worst is but death, which is life.'

'Pangs that shall keep thee hours dying,' cried the Prefect--'thy body racked and rent--torn piecemeal one part from another--this is worse than death. Bethink thee well. Do not believe that Varus will relent.'

'That were the last thing to find faith with one who knows him as well as Macer does,' replied the Christian.

A flush of passion passed over the face of Varus. But he proceeded in the same even tone,

'Is thy election made, Macer?'

'It is made.'

'Slaves,' cried the Prefect, 'away with him to the rack, and ply it well.'

'Yes,' repeated Pronto, springing with eager haste from his seat, that he might lose nothing of what was to be seen or heard, 'away with him to the rack, and ply it well.'

Unmoved and unresisting, his face neither pale nor his limbs trembling, did Macer surrender himself into the hands of those horrid ministers of a cruel and bloody faith, who then hastily approached him, and seizing him dragged him toward their worse than hell. Accomplished in their art, for every day is it put to use, Macer was in a moment thrown down and lashed to the iron bars; when, each demon having completed the preparation, he stood leaning upon his wheel for a last sign from the Prefect. It was instantly given, and while the breath even of every being in the vast hall was suspended, through an intense interest in the scene, the creating of the engine, as it began to turn, sounded upon the brain like thunder. Not a groan nor a sigh was heard from the sufferer. The engine turned till it seemed as if any body or substance laid upon it must have been wrenched asunder. Then it stopt. And the minutes counted to me like hours or ages ere the word was given, and the wheels unrestrained flew back again to their places. Macer was then unbound. He at first lay where he was thrown upon the pavement. But his life was yet strong within his iron frame. He rose at length upon his feet, and was again led to the presence of his judges. His eye had lost nothing of its wild fire, nor his air any thing of its lofty independence.

Varus again addressed him.

'Christian, you have felt what there is in Roman justice. Reject not again what Roman mercy again offers thee--life freely, honor too, and office, if thou wilt return once more to the bosom of the fond mother who reared thee.'

'Yes,' said Fronto, 'thy mother who reared thee! Die not with the double guilt of apostacy and ingratitude upon thy soul.'

'Varus,' said Macer, 'art thou a fool, a very fool, to deem that thy word can weigh more with me than Christ? Make not thyself a laughingstock to me and such Christians as may be here. The torments of thy importunity are worse to me than those of thy engines.'

'I wish thee well, Macer; 'tis that which makes me thus a fool,'

'So, Varus, does Satan wish his victim well, to whom he offers his luscious baits. But what is it when the bait is swallowed, and hell is all that has been gained? What should I gain, but to live with thee, O greater fool?'

'Think, Macer, of thy wife and children.'

At those names, Macer bent his head and folded his hands upon his breast, and tears rolled down his cheeks. Till then there had been, as it seemed, a blessed forgetfulness of all but himself and the scene before him. Varus, misinterpreting this his silence, and taking it for the first sign of repentance, hastily cried out,

'There is the altar, Macer.--Slave! hold to him the sacred libation; he will now pour it out.'

Instantly a slave held out to him a silver ladle filled with wine.

Macer at the same instant struck it with his sinewy arm and sent it whirling to the ceiling.

'Bind him again to the rack,' cried the Prefect, leaping from his seat; 'and let him have it till the nerves break.'

Macer was again seized and stretched upon the iron bed--this time upon another, of different construction, and greater power. Again the infernal machine was worked by the naked slaves, and, as it was wound up, inflicting all that it was capable of doing without absolutely destroying life, groans and screams of fierce agony broke from the suffering Christian. How long our ears were assailed by those terrific cries, I cannot say. They presently died away, as I doubted not, only because Macer himself had expired under the torment. When they had wholly ceased, the engine was reversed and Macer again unbound. He fell lifeless upon the floor. Varus, who had sat the while conversing with Fronto, now said,

'Revive him, and return him hither.'

Water was then thrown upon him, and powerful drinks were forced down his throat. They produced in a little while their intended effect, and Macer gave signs of returning life. He presently gazed wildly around him, and came gradually to a consciousness of where and what he was. His limbs refused their office, and he was supported and partly lifted to the presence of Varus.

'Now, Galilean,' cried Varus, 'again, how is it with thee?'

'Better than with thee, I trust in God.'

'Wilt thou now sacrifice?'

'I am myself, O Varus, this moment a sacrifice, well pleasing and acceptable to the God whom I worship, and the Master whom I serve.'

'Why, Varus,' said Fronto, 'do we bear longer his insults and impieties? Let me strike him dead.' And he moved his hand as if to grasp a concealed weapon, with which to do it.

'Nay, nay, hold, Fronto! let naught be done in haste or passion, nor in violation of the law, but all calmly and in order. We act for those who are not present as well as for ourselves.'

A voice from a dark extremity of the room shouted out,

'It is Macer, O Prefect, who acts for us.'

The face of Macer brightened up, as if he had suddenly been encompassed by a legion of friends. It was the first token he had received, that so much as one heart in the whole assembly was beating with his. He looked instantly to the quarter whence the voice came, and then, turning to the Prefect, said,

'Yes, Varus, I am now and here preaching to the people of Rome, though I speak never a word. 'Tis a sermon that will fall deeper into the heart than ten thousand spoken ones.'

The Prefect commanded that he who had spoken should be brought before him. But upon the most diligent search he could not be found.

'Christian,' said Varus, 'I have other pains in store, to which what thou hast as yet suffered is but as the scratching of the lion's paw. It were better not to suffer them. They will leave no life in thee. Curse Christ--'tis but a word--and live.'

Macer bent his piercing eye upon the Prefect, but answered not.

'Curse Christ, and live.'

Macer was still silent.

'Bring in then,' cried the Prefect, 'your pincers, rakes and shells; and we will see what they may have virtue to bring forth.'

The black messengers of death hastened at the word from their dark recesses, loaded with those new instruments of torture, and stood around the miserable man.

'Now, Macer,' said Varus once more, 'acknowledge Jupiter Greatest and Best, and thou shalt live.'

Macer turned round to the people, and with his utmost voice cried out,

'There is, O Romans, but One God; and the God of Christ is he--'

No sooner had he uttered those words than Fronto exclaimed,

'Ah! hah! I have found thee then! This is the voice, thrice accursed! that came from the sacred Temple of the Sun! This, Romans, is the god whose thunder turned you pale.'

'Had it been my voice alone, priest, that was heard that day, I had been accursed indeed. I was out the humble instrument of him I serve--driven by his spirit. It was the voice of God, not of man.'

'These,' said Fronto, 'are the Christian devices, by which they would lead blindfold into their snares you, Romans, and your children. May Christ ever employ in Rome a messenger cunning and skilful as this prating god, and Hellenism will have naught to fear.'

'And,' cried Macer, 'let your priests be but like Fronto, and the eyes of the blindest driveler of you all will be unsealed. Ask Fronto into whose bag went the bull's heart, that on the day of dedication could not be found--

'Thou liest, Nazarene--'

'Ply him with your pincers,' cried Varus,--and the cruel irons were plunged into his flesh. Yet he shrunk not--nor groaned; but his voice was again heard in the midst of the torture,

'Ask him from whose robe came the old and withered heart, the sight of which so unmanned Aurelian--'

'Dash in his mouth,' shrieked Fronto, 'and stop those lies blacker than hell.'

But Macer went on, while the irons tore him in every part.

'Ask him too for the instructions and the bribes given to the haruspices, and to those who led the beasts up to the altar. Though I die, Romans, I have left the proof of all this in good hands. I stood the while where I saw it all.'

'Thou liest, slave,' cried the furious priest; and at the same moment springing forward and seizing an instrument from the hands of one of the tormentors, he struck it into the shoulder of Macer, and the lacerated arm fell from the bleeding trunk. A piercing shriek confessed the inflicted agony.

'Away with him!' cried Varus, 'away with him to the rack, and tear him joint from joint!'

At the word he was borne bleeding away, but not insensible nor speechless. All along as he went his voice was heard calling upon God and Christ, and exhorting the people to abjure their idolatries.

He was soon stretched again upon the rack, which now quickly finished its work; and the Christian Macer, after sufferings which I knew not before that the human frame could so long endure and live, died a martyr to the faith he had espoused; the last words which were heard throughout the hall being these;

'Jesus, I die for thee, and my death is sweet!'

When it was announced to the Prefect that Macer was dead, he exclaimed,

'Take the carcass of the Christian dog and throw it upon the square of the Jews: there let the dogs devour it.'

Saying which, he rose from his seat, and, accompanied by Fronto, left by the same way he had before entered the hall of judgment.

Soon as he had withdrawn from the apartment, the base rabble that had filled it, and had glutted their savage souls upon the horrors of that scene, cried out tumultuously for the body of the Christian, which, when it was gladly delivered to them by those who had already had enough of it, they thrust hooks into, and rushed out dragging it toward the place ordained for it by the Prefect. As they came forth into the streets the mob increased to an immense multitude of those, who seemed possessed of the same spirit. And they had not together proceeded far, filling the air with their cries and uttering maledictions of every form against the unhappy Christians, before a new horror was proclaimed by that blood-thirsty crew. For one of them, suddenly springing up upon the base of one of the public statues, whence he could be heard by the greater part, cried out,

'To the house of Macer! To the house of Macer!'

'Aye, aye,' shouted another, 'to the house of Macer, in the ruins behind the shop of Demetrius!'

'To the house of Macer!' arose then in one deafening shout from the whole throng; and, filled with this new frenzy, maddened like wild beasts at the prospect of fresh blood, they abandoned there, where they had dragged it, the body of Macer, and put new speed into their feet in their haste to arrive at the place of the expected sport. I knew not then where the ruins were, or it was possible that I might have got in advance of the mob, and given timely warning to the devoted family. Neither did I know any to whom to apply to discharge such a duty. While I deplored this my helplessness and weakness, I suffered myself to be borne along with the rushing crowd. Their merciless threats, their savage language, better becoming barbarians than a people like this, living in the very centre of civilization, filled me with an undefinable terror. It seemed to me that within reach of such a populace, no people were secure of property or life.

'The Christians,' said one, 'have had their day and it has been a long one, too long for Rome. Let its night now come.'

'Yes,' said another, 'we will all have a hand in bringing it on. Let every Roman do his share, and they may be easily rooted out.'

'I understand,' said another, 'that it is agreed upon, that whatever the people attempt after their own manner, as in what we are now about, they are not to be interfered with. We are to have free pasturage, and feed where, and as we list.'

'Who could suppose,' said the first, 'it should be different? It is well known that formerly, though there has been no edict to the purpose, the people have not only been permitted, they have been expected, to do their part of the business without being asked or urged. I dare say if we can do up this family of--who is it?'

'Macer, the Christian Macer,' interrupted the other;--'we shall receive the thanks of Aurelian, though they be not spoken, as heartily as Varus. That was a tough old fellow though. They say he has served many years under the Emperor, and when he left the army was in a fair way to rise to the highest rank. Curses upon those who made a Christian of him! It is they, not Varus, who have put him on the rack. But see! are not these the ruins we seek? I hope so, for I have run far enough.'

'Yes,' replied his companion; 'these are the old baths! Now for it!'

The crowd thereupon abandoning the streets, poured itself like an advancing flood among the ruins, filling all the spaces and mounting up upon all the still standing fragments of walls and columns. It was not at all evident where the house of the Christian was. It all seemed a confusion of ruins and of dead wall.

'Who can show us,' cried out one who took upon himself the office of leader, 'where the dwelling of Macer is?'

'I can,' responded the slender voice of a little boy; 'for I have often been there before they became Christians.'

'Show us then, my young urchin; come up hither. Now, lead the way, and we will follow.'

'You need go no further,' replied the boy; 'that is it?'

'That? It is but a stone wall!'

'Still it is the house,' replied the child; 'but the door is of stone as well as the walls.'

At that the crowd began to beat upon the walls, and shout to those who were within to come forth. They had almost wearied themselves out, and were inclined to believe that the boy had given them false information, when, upon a sort of level roof above the projecting mass which served as the dwelling, a female form suddenly appeared, and, advancing to the edge--not far above, yet beyond, the reach of the mob below--she beckoned to them with her hand, as if she would speak to them.

The crowd, soon as their eyes caught this new object, ceased from their tumultuous cries and prepared to hear what she who approached them thus might have to say. Some, indeed, immediately began to hurl missiles, but they were at once checked by others, who insisted that she should have liberty to speak. And these wretches would have been more savage still than I believed them, if the fair girl who stood there pleading to them had not found some favor. Hers was a bright and sparkling countenance, that at once interested the beholder. Deep blushes spread over her face and bosom, while she stood waiting the pleasure of the heaving multitude before her.

'Ah! hah!' cried one; 'who is she but the dancing girl Celia! she is a dainty bit for us. Who would have thought that she was the daughter of a Christian!'

'I am sorry for her,' cried another; 'she is too pretty to be torn in pieces. We must save her.'

'Say on! say on!' now cried one of the leaders of the crowd as silence succeeded; 'we will hear you.'

'Whom do you seek?' then asked Celia, addressing him who had spoken.

'You know well enough, my pretty girl,' replied the other. 'We seek the house and family of Macer the Christian. Is this it? and are you of his household?'

'This,' she replied, 'is the house of Macer, and I am his daughter. My mother with all her children are below. And now why do you seek us thus?'

'We seek,' replied the savage, 'not only you but your lives. All you have to do is to unbar this door and let us in.'

Though Celiia could have supposed that they were come for nothing else, yet the brutal announcement of the terrible truth drove the color from her cheeks, and caused her limbs to tremble. Yet did it not abate her courage, nor take its energy from her mind.

'Good citizens and friends,' said she, 'for I am sure I must have some friends among you, why should you do us such wrong? We are poor and humble people, and have never had the power, if the will had been ours, to injure you. Leave us in safety, and, if you require it, we will abandon our dwelling and even our native Rome--for we are all native Romans.'

'That, my young mistress, will not serve our turn. Are you not, as you said, the family of the Christian Macer?'

'Yes, we are.'

'Well,' answered the other, 'that is the reason we seek you, and mean to have you.'

'But,' replied the girl, 'there must be many among you who would not willingly harm either Macer or anything that is his. Macer is not only a Christian, Romans, but he is a good warm-hearted patriot as ever was born within the compass of these walls. Brutus himself never loved freedom nor hated tyrants more than he.'

'That's little to the purpose now-a-days,' cried one from the crowd.

'There is not a single possession he has,' continued Celia, 'save only his faith as a Christian, which he would not surrender for the love he bears to Rome and to everything that is Roman. Ever since he was strong enough to draw and wield a sword, has he been fighting for you the battles of our country. If you have seen him, you have seen how cruelly the weapons of the enemy have hacked him. On every limb are there scars of wounds received in battle; and twice, once in Gaul and once in Asia, has he been left for dead upon the field. It was once in Syria, when the battle raged at its highest, and Carinus was suddenly beset by more than he could cope with, and had else fallen into the enemy's hands a prisoner, or been quickly despatched, that Macer came up and by his single arm saved his general--'

'A great pity that,' cried many from the crowd.

'Macer,' continued Celia, 'only thought that Carinus then represented Rome, and that his life, whatever it was, and however worthless in itself, was needful for Rome, and he threw himself into the breach even as he would have done for Aurelian or his great captain Probus. Was not his virtue the greater for that? Was he to feed his own humor, and leave Carinus to perish, when his country by that might receive detriment? Macer has never thought of himself. Had he been ambitious as some, he had now been where Mucapor is. But when in the army he always put by his own interests. The army, its generals and Rome were all in all with him, himself, nothing. How, citizens, can you wish to do him harm? or anything that is his? And, even as a Christian--for which you reproach him and now seek him--it is still the same. Believe me when I say, that it is because of his love of you and Rome that he would make you all as he is. He honestly thinks that it is the doctrine of Christ, which can alone save Rome from the destruction which her crimes are drawing down upon her. He has toiled from morning till night, all day and all night--harder than he ever did upon his marches either in Africa or in Asia--that you might be made to know what this religion of Christ is; what it means; what it will bestow upon you if you will receive it; and what it will save you from. And he would not scruple to lose his life, if by so doing he could give any greater efficacy to the truth in which he believes. I would he were here now, Romans, to plead his own cause with you. I know you would so esteem his honesty, and his warm Roman heart, that you would be more ready to serve than to injure him.'

Pity stood in some eyes, but impatience and anger in more.

'Be not so sure of that,' cried he who had spoken before. 'No true Roman can love a Christian. Christians are the worst enemies of the state. As for Macer, say no more of him; he is already done for. All you have to do is to set open the door.'

'What say you of Macer?' cried the miserable girl, wringing her hands. 'Has any evil befallen him?'

'What he will never recover from,' retorted the barbarian. 'Varus has just had him on one of his iron playthings, and his body we have but now left in the street yonder. So hasten.'

'O worse than demons to kill so good a man,' cried Celia, the tears rolling down her cheeks. 'But if he is dead, come and take us too. We wish not now to live; and ready as he was to die for Christ, so ready are we also. Cease your blows; and I will open the door.'

But her agency in that office was no longer needed. A huge timber had been brought in the meantime from the ruins, and, plied by an hundred hands with noisy uproar, the stone door soon gave way, just as Celia descended and the murderous crew rushed in.

The work of death was in part quickly done. The sons of Macer, who, on the uproar, had instantly joined their mother in spite of all the entreaties of Demetrius, were at once despatched, and dragged forth by ropes attached to their feet. The two youngest, transfixed by spears, were seen borne aloft as bloody standards of that murderous rout. The mother and the other children, placed in a group in the midst of the multitude, were made to march on, the savages themselves being divided as to what should be their fate. Some cried out, 'To the Tiber!'--some, 'Crucify them beyond the walls!--others, 'Give 'em the pavements!' But the voice of one more ingenious in cruelty than the rest prevailed.

'To the square by Hanno's with them!'

This proposition filled them with delight.

'To Hanno's! to Hanno's!' resounded on all sides. And away rushed the infuriated mass to their evil sport.

'And who is Hanno?' I asked of one near me.

'Hanno? know you not Hanno? He is brother of Sosia the gladiator, and breeds dogs for the theatres. You shall soon see what a brood he will turn out. There is no such breeder in Rome as he.'

Sick at heart as I was, I still pressed on, resolved to know all that Christian heroism could teach me. We were soon at the square, capable of holding on its borders not only thousands but tens of thousands, to which number it seemed as if the throng had now accumulated. Hanno's extensive buildings and grounds were upon one side of the square, to which the people now rushed, calling out for the great breeder to come forth with his pack.

He was not slow in obeying the summons. He himself appeared, accompanied, as on the day when Piso saw him on the Capitol Hill, by his two dogs Nero and Sylla. After first stipulating with the ringleaders for a sufficient remuneration, he proceeded to order the game. He was at first for separating the victims, but they implored to be permitted to suffer together, and so much mercy was shown them. They were then set together in the centre of the square, while the multitude disposed themselves in an immense circle around--the windows of the buildings and the roofs of all the neighboring dwellings being also thronged with those who both looked on and applauded. Before the hounds were let loose, Hanno approached this little band, standing there in the midst and clinging to one another, and asked them,

'If they had anything to say, or any message to deliver, for he would faithfully perform what they might enjoin.'

The rest weeping, she answered, 'that she wished to say a few words to the people who stood around.'

'Speak then,' replied Hanno, 'and you shall not be disturbed.'

She then turned toward the people, and said. 'I can wish you, Romans, before I die, no greater good than that, like me and those who are with me, you may one day become Christians. For you will then be incapable of inflicting such sufferings and wrongs upon any human being. The religion of Jesus will not suffer you to do otherwise than love others as you do yourselves; that is the great Christian rule. Be assured that we now die, as Christians, in full faith in Christ and in joyful hope of living with him, so soon as these mortal bodies shall have perished; and that, though a single word of denial would save us, we would not speak it. Ye have cruelly slaughtered the good Macer; do so now by us, if such is your will, and we shall then be with him where he is.'

With these words she again turned, and throwing her arms around her mother and younger sisters, awaited the onset of the furious dogs, whose yellings and strugglings could all the while be heard. She and they waited but a moment, when the blood-hounds, fiercer than the fiercest beasts of the forest, flew from their leashes, and, in less time than would be believed, naught but a heap of bones marked where the Christian family had stood.

The crowds, then fully sated as it seemed with the rare sport of the morning, dispersed, each having something to say to another of the firmness and patriotism of Varus and Fronto,--and of the training and behavior of the dogs.

* * * * *

From the earliest period of reflection have I detested the Roman character; and all that I have witnessed with my own eyes has served but to confirm those early impressions. They are a people wholly destitute of humanity. They are the lineal descendants of robbers, murderers, and warriors--which last are but murderers under another name--and they show their parentage in every line of their hard-featured visages, and still more in all the qualities of the soul. They are stern,--unyielding, unforgiving--cruel. A Roman heart dissected would be found all stone. Any present purpose of passion, or ambition, or party zeal, will extinguish in the Roman all that separates him from the brute. Bear witness to the truth of this, ye massacres of Marius and Sylla! and others, more than can be named, both before and since--when the blood of neighbors, friends, and fellow-citizens, was poured out as freely as if it had been the filthy stream that leaks its way through the public sewers! And, in good sooth, was it not as filthy? For those very ones so slain, had the turn of the wheel--as in very deed has often happened--set them uppermost, would have done the same deed upon the others. Happy is it for the peace of the earth and the great cause of humanity, that this faith of Christ, whether it be true or false, is at length beginning to bear sway, and doing somewhat to soften, what more than twelve centuries have passed over and left in its original vileness.

When, like the rest of that Roman mob, I had been filled with the sights and sounds of the morning, I turned and sought the palace of Piso.

Arriving there I found Portia, Julia, and Piso sitting together at the hour of dinner. I sat with them. Piso had not left the palace, since I had parted from him. They had remained at peace within, and as ignorant of what had happened in the distant parts of the huge capital, as we all were of what was then doing in another planet. When, as the meal drew to a close, I had related to them the occurrences of which I had just been the witness, they could scarce believe what they heard, though it was but what they and all had every reason to look for, from the language which Aurelian had used, and the known hostility of the Prefect. Portia, the mother, was moved more, if it could be so, than even Piso or Julia. When I had ended, she said,

'Think not, Nicomachus, that although, as thou knowest, I am of Aurelian's side in religion, I defend these inhuman wrongs. To inflict them can make no part of the duty of any worshipper of the gods, however zealous he may be. I do not believe that the gods are propitiated by any acts which occasion suffering to their creatures. I have seen no justification under any circumstances of human sacrifices--much less can I see any of sacrifices like those you have this morning witnessed. Aurelian, in authorizing or conniving at such horrors, has cut himself loose from the honor and the affections of all those in Rome whose esteem is worth possessing. He has given himself up to the priesthood, and to the vulgar rabble over whom it exercises a sway more strict than an Eastern despot. He is by these acts turning the current of the best Roman sympathy toward the Christians, and putting off by a long remove the hour when he might hope to see the ancient religion of the state delivered from its formidable rival.'

'It is the purpose of Aurelian,' I said, 'not so much to persecute and annoy the Christians, as to exterminate them. He is persuaded that by using the same extreme and summary measures with the Christians, which he has been accustomed to employ in the army, he can root out this huge evil from the state, as easily as those lesser ones from the camp;--without reflecting that it must be impossible to discover all, or any very large proportion of those who profess Christianity, and that therefore his slaughter of a half or a quarter of the whole number, will be to no purpose. It will have been but killing so many--there will be no other effect; unless, indeed, it have the effect to convince new thousands of the power, and worth, and divinity of that faith, for which men are so willing to die.'

'I mourn,' said Portia, 'that the great head of the state, and the great high priest of our religion should have taken the part he has. Measures of moderation and true wisdom, though they might not have obtained for him so great a name for zeal and love of the gods, nor made so sudden and deep an impression upon the common mind and heart, would have secured with greater probability the end at which he has aimed.'

'It is hard.' said I, 'to resist nature, especially so when superstition comes in to its aid. Aurelian, by nature a savage, is doubly one through the influence of his religion and the priesthood. Moderation and humanity are so contrary to every principle of the man and his faith, that they are not with more reason to be looked for from him than gentleness in a famished wolf.'

Portia looked as if I had assailed the walls and capitol of Rome.

'I know not, Greek,' she quickly said, 'on what foundation it is you build so heavy a charge against the time-honored faith of Rome. It has served Rome well these thousand years, and reared men whose greatness will dwell in the memory of the world while the world lasts.'

'Great men have been reared in Rome,' I replied; 'it can by none be denied. But it has been by resisting the influences of their religion, not by courting them. They have left themselves in this to the safer tutelage of nature, as have you, lady; and they have escaped the evils, which the common superstition would have entailed upon them, had they admitted it to their bosoms. Who can deny that the religion of Rome, so far as it is a religion for the common people, is based up on the characters of the gods, as they through history and tradition are held up to them--especially as they are painted by the poets? Say if there be any other books of authority on this great theme than the poets? What book of religious instruction and precept have you, or have you ever had, corresponding to the volume of the Christians, called their gospels?'

'We have none,' said Portia, as I paused compelling a rejoinder. 'It is true, we have but our historians and our poets, with what we find in the philosophers.'

'And the philosophers,' I replied, 'it will be seen at once can never be in the hands of the common people. Whence then do they receive their religious ideas, but from tradition, and the character of the deities of heaven, as they are set forth in the poets? And if this be so, I need not ask whether it be possible that the religion of Rome should be any other than a source of corruption to the people. So far as the gods should be their models, they can do no otherwise than help to sink their imitators lower and lower in all filth and vice. Happily for Rome and the world, lady, men instinctively revolt at such examples, and copy instead the pattern which their own souls supply. Had the Romans been all which the imitation of their gods would have made them, this empire had long ago sunk under the deep pollution. Fronto and Aurelian--the last at least sincere--aim at a restoration of religion. They would lift it up to the highest place, and make it the sovereign law of Rome. In this attempt, they are unconsciously digging away her very foundations; they are leveling her proud walls with the earth. Suppose Rome were made what Fronto would have her? Every Roman were then another Fronto--or another Aurelian. Were that a world to live in? or to endure? These, lady, are the enemies of Rome, Aurelian and Fronto. The only hope for Rome lies, in the reception of some such principles as these of the Christians. Whether true or false, as a revelation from Heaven, they are in accordance with the best part of our nature, and, once spread abroad and received, they would tend by a mighty influence to exalt it more and more. They would descend, as it is of the nature of absolute truth to do, and lay hold of the humblest and lowest and vilest, and in them erect their authority, and bring them into the state, in which every man should be, for the reason that he is a man. Helenism cannot do this.'

'Notwithstanding what I have heard, Nicomachus, I think you must yourself be a Christian. But whether you are or not, I grant you to understand well what religion should be. And I must say that it has ever been such to me. I, from what I have read of our moralists and philosophers, and from what I have reflected, have arrived at principles not very different from such as you have now hinted at--'

'And are those of Fronto or Varus like yours, lady?'

'I fear not,' said Portia.

'Yours then, let me say, are the religion, which you have first found within your own breast, a gift from the gods, and then by meditation have confirmed and exalted; theirs, the common faith of Rome. Could your faith rejoice in or permit the horrors I have this day witnessed and but now described? Yet of theirs they are the legitimate fruit, the necessary product.'

'Out of the best,' replied Portia, 'I believe, Nicomachus, may often come the worst. There is naught so perfect and so wise, but human passions will mar and pervert it. I should not wonder if, in ages to come, this peace-loving faith of the Christians, should it survive so long, should itself come to preside over scenes as full of misery and guilt as those you have to-day seen in the streets of Rome.'

'It may be,' I rejoined. 'But it is nevertheless our duty, in the selection of our principles, to take those which are the purest, the most humane, the most accordant with what is best in us, and the least liable to perversion and abuse. And whether, if this be just, it be better that mankind should have presented for their imitation and honor the character and actions of Jesus Christ, or those of Jupiter "Greatest and Best," may be left for the simplest to determine.'

Portia is so staunch a Roman, that one cannot doubt that as she was born and has lived, so she will die--a Roman. And truth to say, were all like her, there were little room for quarrel with the principles that could produce such results. But for one such, there are a thousand like Varus, Fronto, and Aurelian.

As after this interview, which was prolonged till the shades of evening began to fall, I held communion with myself on the way to the quiet retreats of Tibur, I could not but entertain apprehensions for the safety of the friends I had just left. I felt that where such men as Varus and Fronto were at the head of affairs, wielding, almost as they pleased, the omnipotence of Aurelian, no family nor individual of whatever name or rank could feel secure of either fortune or life. I had heard indeed such expressions of regard fall from the Emperor for Piso and his beautiful wife, that I was sure that if any in Rome might feel safe, it was they. Yet why should he, who had fallen with fatal violence upon one of his own household, and such a one as Aurelia, hesitate to strike the family of Piso, if thereby religion or the state were to be greatly benefited? I could see a better chance for them only in the Emperor's early love of Julia, which still seemed to exercise over him a singular power.

The Queen, I found, upon naming to her the subject of my thoughts, could entertain none of my apprehensions. It is so difficult for her nature to admit the faintest purpose of the infliction of wanton suffering, that she cannot believe it of others. Notwithstanding her experience of the harsh and cruel spirit of Aurelian, notwithstanding the unnecessary destruction, for any national or political object, of the multitudes of Palmyra, still she inclines to confide in him. He has given so many proofs of regret for that wide ruin, he has suffered so much for it--especially for his murder of Longinus--in the opinion of all Rome, and of the highest and best in all nations, that she is persuaded he will be more cautious than ever whom he assails, and where he scatters ruin and death. Still, such is her devotion to Julia and her love of Piso--so entirely is her very life lodged in that of her daughter, that she resolved to seek the Emperor without delay, and if possible obtain an assurance of their safety, both from his own arm and that of popular violence. This I urged upon her with all the freedom I might use; and not in vain; for the next day, at the gardens of Sallust, she had repeated interviews with Aurelian--and afterward at her own palace, whither Aurelian came with Livia, and where, while Livia ranged among the flowers with Faustula, the Emperor and the Queen held earnest discourse--not only on the subject which chiefly agitated Zenobia, but on the general principles on which he was proceeding in this attempted annihilation of Christianity. Sure I am, that never in the Christian body itself was there one who pleaded their cause with a more winning and persuasive eloquence.

LETTER X.

FROM PISO TO FAUSTA.

I write to you, Fausta, by the hands of Vabalathus, who visits Palmyra on his way to his new kingdom. I trust you will see him. The adversities of his family and the misfortunes of his country have had most useful effects upon his character. Though the time has been so short, he has done much to redeem himself. Always was he, indeed, vastly superior to his brothers; but now, he is not only that, but very much more. Qualities have unfolded themselves, and affections and tastes warmed into life, which we none of us, I believe, so much as suspected the existence of. Zenobia has come to be devotedly attached to him, and to repose the same sort of confidence in him as formerly in Julia. All this makes her the more reluctant to part with him; but, as it is for a throne, she acquiesces. He carries away from Rome with him one of its most beautiful and estimable women--the youngest daughter of the venerable Tacitus--to whom he has just been married. In her you will see an almost too favorable specimen of Roman women.

Several days have elapsed since I wrote to you, giving an account of the sufferings and death of the Christian Macer--as I learned them from those who were present--for a breach of the late edicts, and for sacrilegiously, as the laws term it, tearing down the parchment containing them from one of the columns of the capitol. During this period other horrors of the same kind have been enacted in different parts of the city. Macer is not the only one who has already paid for his faith with his life. All the restraints of the law seem to be withdrawn, not confessedly but virtually, and the Christians in humble condition--and such for the most part we are--are no longer safe from violence in the streets of Rome. Although, Fausta, you believe not with us, you must, scarcely the less for that, pity us in our present straits. Can the mind picture to itself, in some aspects of the case, a more miserable lot! Were the times, even at the worst, so full of horror in Palmyra as now here in

Rome? There, if the city were given up to pillage, the citizen had at least the satisfaction of dying in the excitement of a contest, and in the defence of himself and his children. Here the prospect is--the actual scene is almost arrived and present--that all the Christians of Rome will be given over to the butchery, first, of the Prefect's court, and others of the same character, established throughout the city for the express purpose of trying the Christians--and next, of the mob commissioned with full powers to search out, find, and slay, all who bear the hated name. The Christians, it is true, die for a great cause. In that cause they would rather die than live, if to live, they must sacrifice any of the interests of truth. But still death is not preferred; much less is death, in the revolting and agonizing form, which, chiefly, these voluntary executioners choose, to be viewed in any other light than an evil too great almost to be endured.

It would astonish you, I think, and give you conceptions of the power of this religion such as you have never had as yet, could you with me look into the bosoms of these thousand Christian families, and behold the calmness and the fortitude with which they await the approaching calamities. There is now, as they believe, little else before them but death--and death, such as a foretaste has been given of, in the sufferings of Macer. Yet are they, with wonderfully few exceptions, here in their houses prepared for whatever may betide, and resolved that they will die for him unto whom they have lived. This unshrinking courage, this spirit of self-sacrifice, is the more wonderful, as it is now the received belief that they would not forfeit their Christian name or hope by withdrawing, before the storm bursts, from the scene of danger.

There have been those in the church, and some there are now, who would have all, who in time of persecution seek safety in flight, or by any form of compromise, visited with the severest censures the church can inflict, and forever after refused readmission to the privileges which they once enjoyed. Paying no regard to the peculiar temperament and character of the individual, they would compel all to remain fixed at their post, inviting by a needless ostentation of their name and faith, the search and assault of the enemy. Macer was of this number. Happily they are now few: and the Christians are left free--free from the constraint of any tyrant opinion, to act according to the real feeling of the heart. But does this freedom carry them away from Rome? Does it show them to the world hurrying in crowds by day, or secretly flying by night, from the threatened woes? No so. All who were here when these troubles first began, are here now, or with few and inconsiderable exceptions--fewer than I could wish. All who have resorted to me under these circumstances for counsel or aid have I advised, if flight be a possible thing to them, that they should retreat with their children to some remote and secluded spot, and wait till the tempest should have passed by. Especially have I so advised and urged all whom I have known to be of a sensitive and timid nature, or bound by ties of more than common interest and necessity to large circles of relatives and dependents. I have aimed to make them believe, that little gain would accrue to the cause of Christ from the addition of them and theirs to the mass of sufferers--when that mass is already so large; whereas great and irreparable loss would follow to the community of their friends, and of the Christians who should survive. They would do an equal service to Christ and his church by living, and, on the first appearance of calmer times, reassuming their Christian name and profession; being then a centre about which there might gather together a new multitude of believers. If still the enemies of Christ should prevail, and a day of rest never dawn nor arise, they might then, when hope was dead, come forth and add themselves to the innumerable company of those, born of Heaven, who hold life and all its joys and comforts as dross, in comparison with the perfect integrity of the mind. By such statements have I prevailed with many. Probus too has exerted his power in the same direction, and has enjoyed the happiness of seeing safely embarked for Greece, or Syria, many whose lives in the coming years will be beyond price to the then just-surviving church.

Yet do not imagine, Fausta, that we are an immaculate people; that the weaknesses and faults which seem universal to mankind, are not to be discovered in us that we are all, what by our acknowledged principles we ought to be. We have our traitors and our renegades, our backsliders, and our well-dissembling hypocrites--but so few are they, that they give us little disquiet, and bring slight discredit upon us with the enemy. And beside these, there will now be those, as in former persecutions, who, as the day of evil approaches, will, through the operation simply of their fears, renounce their name and faith. Of the former, some have already made themselves conspicuous--conspicuous now by their cowardly and hasty apostasy, as they were before by a narrow, contentious, and restless zeal. Among others, the very one, who, on the evening when the Christians assembled near the baths of Macer, was so forward to assail the faith of Probus, and who ever before, on other occasions, when a display could by any possibility be made of devotion to his party, or an ostentatious parade of his love of Christ, was always thrusting himself upon the notice of our body and clamoring for notoriety, has already abandoned us and sought safety in apostacy. Others of the same stamp have in like manner deserted us. They are neither lamented by us nor honored by the other party. It is said of him whom I have just spoken of, that soon as he had publicly renounced Christ, and sacrificed, hisses and yells of contempt broke from the surrounding crowds. He, doubtless it occurred to them, who had so proved himself weak, cowardly, and faithless, to one set of friends, could scarcely be trusted as brave and sincere by those to whom he then joined himself. There are no virtues esteemed by the Romans like courage and sincerity. This trait in their character is a noble one, and is greatly in our favor. For, much as they detest our superstitions, they so honor our fortitude under suffering, that a deep sympathy springs up almost unconsciously in our behalf. Half of those who, on the first outbreak of these disorders, would have been found bitterly hostile, if their hearts could be scanned now or when this storm shall have passed by, would be found most warmly with us--not in belief indeed, but in a fellow-feeling, which is its best preparation and almost certain antecedent. Even in such an inhuman rabble as perpetrated the savage murder of the family of Macer, there were thousands who, then driven on by the fury of passion, will, as soon as reflection returns, bear testimony in a wholly altered feeling toward us, to the power with which the miraculous serenity and calm courage of those true martyrs have wrought within them. No others are now spoken of in Rome, but Macer and his heroic wife and children.

* * * * *

Throughout the city it is this morning current that new edicts are to be issued in the course of the day. Milo, returning from some of his necessary excursions into the more busy and crowded parts of the city, says that it is confidently believed. I told him that I could scarcely think it, as I had reason to believe that the Emperor had engaged that they should not be as yet.

'An Emperor surely,' said Milo, 'may change his mind if he lists. He is little better than the rest of us, if he have not so much power as that. I think, if I were Emperor, that would be my chief pleasure, to do and say one thing to-day and just the contrary thing to-morrow, without being obliged to give a reason for it. If there be anything that makes slavery it is this rendering a reason. In the service of the most noble Gallienus, fifty slaves were subject to me, and never was I known to render a reason for a single office I put them to. That was being nearer an Emperor than I fear I shall ever be again.'

'I hope so, Milo,' I said. 'But what reason have you to think,--if you will render a reason,--that Aurelian has changed his mind?'

'I have given proof,' answered Milo, 'have I not, that if anything is known in Rome, it is known by Curio?'

'I think you have shown that he knows some things.'

'He was clearly right about the sacrifices,' responded Milo, 'as events afterwards declared. Just as many suffered as he related to me. What now he told me this morning was this, "that certain persons would find themselves mistaken--that some knew more than others--that the ox led to the slaughter knew less than the butcher--that great persons trusted not their secrets to every one--Emperors had their confidants--and Fronto had his."'

'Was that all?' I patiently asked.

'I thought, noble sir,' he replied, 'that it was--for upon that he only sagaciously shook his head and was silent. However, as I said nothing, knowing well that some folks would die if they retained a secret, though they never would part with it for the asking, Curio began again, soon as he despaired of any question from me, and said "he could tell me what was known but to three persons in Rome." His wish was that I should ask him who they were, and what it was that was known but to so few; but I did not, but began a new bargain with a man for his poultry--for, you must know, we were in the market. He then began himself and said, "Who think you they were?" But I answered not. "Who," he then whispered in my ear, "but Aurelian, Fronto, and myself!" Then I gratified him by asking what the secret was, for if it had anything to do with the Christians I should like to know it. "I will tell it to thee," he said, "but to no other in Rome, and to thee only on the promise that it goes in at thy ear but not out at thy mouth." I said that I trusted that I, who had kept, I dared hardly say how many years, and kept them still, the secrets of Gallienus, should know how to keep and how to reveal anything he had to say. Whereupon, without any more reserve, he assured me that

Fronto had persuaded the Emperor to publish new and more severe edicts before the sixth hour, telling him as a reason for it, that the Christians were flying from Rome in vast numbers; that every night--they having first passed the gates in the day--multitudes were hastening into the country, making for Gaul and Spain, or else embarking in vessels long prepared for such service on the Tiber; that, unless instantly arrested, there would be none or few for the edicts to operate upon, and then, when all had become calm again, and he--Aurelian--were dead, and another less pious upon the throne, they would all return, and Rome swarm with them as before. Curio said that, when the Emperor heard this, he broke out into a wild and furious passion. He swore by the great god of light--which is an oath Curio says he never uses but he keeps--that you, sir, Piso, had deceived him--had cajoled him; that you had persuaded him to wait and hear what the Christians had to say for themselves before they were summarily dealt with, which he had consented to do, but which he now saw was a device to gain time by which all, or the greater part, might escape secretly from the capital. He then, with Fronto and the secretaries, prepared and drew up new edicts, declaring every Christian an enemy of the state and of the gods, and requiring them everywhere to be informed against, and upon conviction of being Christians, to be thrown into prison and await there the judgment of the Emperor. These things, sir, are what I learned from Curio, which I make no secret of, for many reasons. I trust you will believe them, for I heard the same story all along the streets, and mine is better worthy of belief only because of where and whom it comes from.'

I told Milo that I could not but suppose there was something in it, as I had heard the rumor from several other sources; that, if Curio spoke the truth, it was worse than I had apprehended.

Putting together what was thus communicated by Milo, and what, as he said, was to be heard anywhere in the streets, I feared that some dark game might indeed be playing by the priest against us, by which our lives might be sacrificed even before the day were out.

'Should you not,' said Julia, 'instantly seek Aurelian? If what Milo has said possess any particle of truth, it is most evident the Emperor has been imposed upon by the lies of Fronto. He has cunningly used his opportunities: and you, Lucius, except he be instantly undeceived, may be the first to feel his power.'

While she was speaking, Probus, Felix, and others of the principal Christians of Rome entered the apartment. Their faces and their manner, and their first words, declared that the same conviction possessed them as us.

'We are constrained,' said Felix, 'thus with little ceremony, noble Piso, to intrude upon your privacy But in truth the affair we have come upon admits not of ceremony or delay.'

'Let there be none then, I pray, and let us hear at once what concerns us all.'

'It is spread over the city,' replied the bishop, 'that before the sixth hour edicts are to be issued that will go to the extreme we have feared--affecting the liberty and life of every Christian in Rome. We find it hard to believe this, however, as it is in the face of what Aurelian has most expressly stipulated. It is therefore the wish and prayer of the Christians that you, being nearer to him than any, should seek an interview with him, and then serve our cause in such manner and by such arguments as you best can.'

'This is what we desire, Piso,' said they all.

I replied, that I would immediately perform that which they desired, but that I would that some other of our number should accompany me. Whereupon Felix was urged to join me; and consenting, we, at the moment, departed for the palace of Aurelian.

On arriving at the gardens, it was only by urgency that I obtained admission to the presence of the Emperor. But upon declaring that I came upon an errand that nearly concerned himself and Rome, I was ordered to be brought into his private apartment.

As I entered, Aurelian quickly rose from the table, at which he had been sitting, on the other side of which sat Fronto. None of the customary urbanity was visible in his deportment; his countenance was dark and severe, his reception of me cold and stately, his voice more harsh and bitter than ever. I could willingly have excused the presence of the priest.

'Ambassadors,' said Aurelian inclining toward us, 'I may suppose from the community of Christians.'

'We came at their request,' I replied; 'rumors are abroad through the city, too confidently reported, and too generally credited to be regarded as wholly groundless, yet which it is impossible for those who know Aurelian to believe, asserting that to-day edicts are to be issued affecting both the liberty and the lives of the Christians--'

'I would, Piso, that rumor were never farther from the truth than in this.'

'But,' I rejoined, 'has not Aurelian said that he would proceed against them no further till he had first heard their defence from their own organs?'

'Is it one party only in human affairs, young Piso,' he sharply replied,'that must conform to truth and keep inviolate a plighted word? Is deception no vice when it is a Christian who deceives? I indeed said that I would hear the Christians, though, when I made that promise, I also said that 'twould profit them nothing; but I then little knew why it was that Piso was so urgent.'

'Truth,' I replied, 'cannot be received from some quarters, any more than sweet and wholesome water through poisoned channels. Even, Aurelian, if Fronto designed not to mislead, no statement passing through his lips--if it concerned the Christians--could do so, without there being added to it, or lost from it, much that properly belonged to it. I have heard that too, which, I may suppose, has been poured into the mind of Aurelian, to fill it with a bitterer enmity still toward the Christians--that the Christians have sought this delay only that they might use the opportunities thus afforded, to escape from his power--and that, using them, they have already in the greater part fled from the capital, leaving to the Emperor but a few old women and children upon whom to wreak his vengeance. How does passion bring its film over the clearest mind! How does the eye that will not see, shut out the light though it be brighter than that of day! It had been wiser in Aurelian, as well as more merciful, first to have tried the truth of what has thus been thrust upon his credulity ere he made it a ground of action. True himself, he suspects not others; but suspicion were sometimes a higher virtue than frank confidence. Had Aurelian but looked into the streets of Rome, he could not but have seen the grossness of the lie that has been palmed upon his too willing ear. Of the seventy thousand Christians who dwelt in Rome, the same seventy thousand, less by scarce a seventieth part, are now here within their dwellings waiting the will of Aurelian. Take this on the word of one whom, in former days at least, you have found worthy of your trust. Take it on the word of the venerable head of this community who stands here to confirm it either by word or oath--and in Rome it needs but to know that Felix, the Christian, has spoken, to know that truth has spoken too.'

'The noble Piso,' added Felix 'has spoken what all who know aught of the affairs and condition of the Christians know to be true. There is among us, great Emperor, too much, rather than too little, of that courage that meets suffering and death without shrinking. Let your proclamations this moment be sounded abroad calling upon the Christians to appear for judgment upon their faith before the tribunals of Rome, and they will come flocking up as do your Pagan multitudes to the games of the Flavian.'

While we had been speaking, Fronto sat, inattentive as it seemed to what was going on. But at these last words he was compelled to give ear, and did it as a man does who has heard unwelcome truths. As Felix ended, the Emperor turned toward him without speaking, and without any look of doubt or passion, waiting for such explanation as he might have to give.

Fronto, instantly re-assuring himself, rose from his seat with the air of a man who doubts not the soundness of his cause, and feels sure of the ear of his judge.

'I will not say, great Emperor, that I have not in my ardor made broader the statements which I have received from others. It is an error quite possible to have been guilty of. My zeal for the gods is warm and oft-times outruns the calm dictates of reason. But if what has now been affirmed as true, be true, it is more I believe than they who so report can make good--or than others can, be they friends or enemies of this tribe. Who shall now go out into this wilderness of streets, into the midst of this countless multitude of citizens and strangers--men of all religions and all manners--and pick me out the seventy thousand Christians, and show that all are close at home? Out of the seventy thousand, is it not palpable that its third or half may have fled, and yet it shall be in no man's power to make it so appear--to point to the spot whence they have departed, or to that whither they have gone? But beside this, I must here and now confess, that it was upon no knowledge of my own gathered by my own eyes and ears that I based the truth, now charged as error; but upon what came to me through those in whose word I have ever placed the most sacred trust, the priests of the temple, and, more than all, my faithful servant--friend I may call him--Curio, into whom drops by some miracle all that is strange or new in Rome.'

I said in reply, 'that it were not so difficult perhaps as the priest has made it seem, to learn what part of the Christians were now in Rome, and what part were gone. There are among us, Aurelian, in every separate church, men who discharge duties corresponding to those which Fronto performs in the Temple of the Sun. We have our priests, and others subordinate to them, who fill offices of dignity and trust. Beside these, there are others still, who, for their wealth or their worth, are known well, not among the Christians only, but the Romans also. Of these, it were an easy matter to learn, whether or not they are now in Rome. And if these are here, who, from the posts they fill would be the first victims, it may be fairly supposed that the humbler sort and less able to depart--and therefore safer--are also here. Here I stand, and here stands Felix; we are not among the missing! And we boast not of a courage greater than may be claimed for the greater part of those to whom we belong.'

'Great Emperor,' said Fronto, 'I will say no more than this, that in its whole aspect this bears the same front, as the black aspersions of the wretch Macer, whose lies, grosser than Cretan ever forged, poured in a foul and rotten current from his swollen lips; yea, while the hot irons were tearing out his very heart-strings, did he still belch forth fresh torrents blacker and fouler as they flowed longer, till death came and took him to other tortures worse a thousand-fold--the just doom of such as put false for true. That those were the malignant lies I have said they are, Aurelian can need no other proof, I hope, than that which has been already given.'

'I am still, Fronto, as when your witnesses were here before me, satisfied with your defence. When indeed I doubt the truth of Aurelian, I may be found to question that of Fronto. Piso--hold! We have heard and said too much already. Take me not, as if I doubted, more than Fronto, the word which you have uttered, or that of the venerable Felix. You have said that which you truly believe. The honor of a Piso has never been impeached, nor, as I trust, can be. Yet, has there been error, both here and there, and, I doubt not, is. Let it be thus determined then. If, upon any, blame shall seem to rest, let it be upon myself. If any shall be charged with doing to-day what must be undone to-morrow, let the burden be upon my shoulders. I will therefore recede; the edicts, which, as you have truly heard, were to-day to have been promulged, shall sleep at least another day. To-morrow, Piso, at the sixth hour, in the palace on the Palatine, shall Probus--if such be the pleasure of the Christians-- plead in their behalf. Then and there will I hear what this faith is, from him, or from whomsoever they shall appoint. And now no more.'

With these words on the part of Aurelian, our audience closed, and we turned away--grieving to see that a man like him, otherwise a Titan every way, should have so surrendered himself into the keeping of another; yet rejoicing that some of that spirit of justice that once wholly swayed him still remained, and that our appeal to it had not been in vain.

To-morrow then, at the sixth hour, will Probus appear before Aurelian. It is not, Fausta, because I, or any, suppose that Aurelian himself can be so wrought upon as to change any of his purposes, that we desire this hearing. He is too far entered into this business--too heartily, and, I may add, too conscientiously--to be drawn away from it, or diverted from the great object which he has set up before him. I will not despair, however, that even he may be softened, and abate somewhat of that raging thirst for our blood, for the blood of us all, that now seems to madden him. But, however this may be, upon other minds impressions may be made that may be of service to us either directly or indirectly. We may suppose that the hearing of the Christians will be public, that many of great weight with Aurelian will be there, who never before heard a word from a Christian's lips, and who know only that we are held as enemies of the state and its religion. Especially, I doubt not, will many, most or all, of the Senate be there; and it is to that body I still look, as, in the last resort, able perhaps to exert a power that may save us at least from absolute annihilation.

* * * * *

To-day has Probus been heard; and while others sleep, I resume my pen to describe to you the events of it, as they have occurred.

It was in the banqueting hall of the imperial palace on the Palatine, that Probus was directed to appear, and defend his cause before the Emperor. It is a room of great size, and beautiful in its proportions and decorations. A row of marble pillars adorns each longer side of the apartment. Its lofty ceiling presents to the eye in allegory, and in colors that can never fade, Rome victorious over the world. The great and good of Rome's earlier days stand around, in marble or brass, upon pedestals, or in niches, sunk into the substance of the walls. And where the walls are not thus broken, pictures wrought upon them, set before the beholder many of the scenes in which the patriots of former days achieved or suffered for the cause of their country. Into this apartment, soon as it was thrown open, poured a crowd both of Christians and Pagans, of Romans and of strangers from every quarter of the world. There was scarcely a remote province of the empire that had not there its representative; and from the far East, discernible at once by their costume, were many present, who seemed interested not less than others in the great questions to be agitated. Between the two central columns upon the western side, just beneath the pedestal of a colossal statue of Vespasian, the great military idol of Aurelian, upon a seat slightly raised above the floor, having on his right hand Livia and Julia, sat the Emperor. He was surrounded by his favorite generals and the chief members of the senate, seated, or else standing against the columns or statues which were near him. There too, at the side of, or immediately before, Aurelian, but placed lower, were Porphyrius, Varus, Fronto, and half the priesthood of Rome. A little way in front of the Emperor, and nearly in the centre of the room, stood Probus.

If Aurelian sat in his chair of gold, looking the omnipotent master of all the world, as if no mere mortal force could drive him from the place he held and filled--Probus, on his part, though he wanted all that air of pride and self-confidence written upon every line of Aurelian's face and form, yet seemed like one, who, in the very calmness of an unfaltering trust in a goodness and power above that of earth, was in perfect possession of himself, and fearless of all that man might say or do. His face was pale; but his eye was clear. His air was that of a man mild and gentle, who would not injure willingly the meanest thing endowed with life; but of a man too of that energy and inward strength of purpose, that he would not on the other hand suffer an injury to be done to another, if any power lodged within him could prevent it. It was that of a man to be loved, and yet to be feared; whose compassion you might rely upon; but whose indignation at wrong and injustice might also be relied upon, whenever the weak or the oppressed should cry out for help against the strong and the cruel.

No sooner had Aurelian seated himself, and the thronged apartment become still, than he turned to those who were present and said,

'That the Christians had desired this audience before him and the sacred senate, and he had therefore granted them their request. And he was now here, to listen to whatever they might urge in their behalf. But,' said he, 'I tell them now, as I have told them before, that it can be of no avail. The acts of former Emperors, from Nero to the present hour, have sufficiently declared what the light is in which a true Roman should view the superstition that would supplant the ancient worship of the gods. It is enough for me, that such is the acknowledged aim, and asserted tendency and operation of this Jewish doctrine. No merits of any kind can atone for the least injury it might inflict upon that venerable order of religious worship which, from the time of Romulus, has exercised over us its benignant influence, and, doubtless, by the blessings it has drawn down upon us from the gods, crowned our arms with a glory the world has never known before--putting under our feet every civilized kingdom from the remotest East to the farthest West, and striking terror into the rude barbarians of the German forests. Nevertheless, they shall be heard; and if it is from thee, Christian, that we are to know what thy faith is, let us now hear whatever it is in thy heart to say. There shall no bridle be put upon thee; but thou hast freest leave to utter what thou wilt. There is nothing of worst concerning either Rome or her worship, her rulers or her altars, her priesthood or her gods, but thou mayest pour it forth in such measure as shall please thee, and no one shall say thee nay. Now say on; the day and the night are before thee.'

'I shall require, great Emperor,' replied Probus, 'but little of either; yet I thank thee, and all of our name who are here present thank thee, for the free range which thou hast offered. I thank thee too, and so do we all, for the liberty of frank and undisturbed speech, which thou hast assured to me. Yet shall I not use it to malign either the Romans or their faith. It is not with anger and fierce denunciation, O Emperor, that it becomes the advocate, of what he believes to be a religion from Heaven, to assail the adherents of a religion like this of Rome, descended to the present generation through so many ages, and which all who have believed it in times past, and all who believe it now, do hold to be true and woven into the very life of the state--the origin of its present greatness, and without which it must fall asunder into final ruin, the bond that held it together being gone. If the religion of Rome be false, or really injurious, it is not the generations now living who are answerable for its existence formerly or now, nor for the principles, truths, or rites, which constitute it. They have received it, as they have received a thousand customs which are now among them, by inheritance from the ancestors who bequeathed them, which they received at too early an age to judge concerning their fitness or unfitness, but to which, for the reason of that early reception, they have become fondly attached, even as to parents, brothers, and sisters, from whom they have never been divided. It becomes not the Christian, therefore, to load with reproaches those who are placed where they are, not by their own will, but by the providence of the Great Ruler. Neither does it become you of the Roman faith to reproach us for the faith to which we adhere; because the greater proportion of us also have inherited our religion, as you yours, from parents and a community who professed it before us, and all regard it as heaven-descended, and so proved to be divine, that without inexpiable guilt we may not refuse to accept it. It must be in the face of reason, then, and justice, in the face of what is both wise and merciful, if either should judge harshly of the other.

'Besides, what do I behold in this wide devotion of the Roman people to the religion of their ancestors, but a testimony, beautiful for the witness it bears, to the universality of that principle or feeling, which binds the human heart to some god or gods, in love and worship? The worship may be wrong, or greatly imperfect, and sometimes injurious; the god or gods may be so conceived of, as to act with hurtful influences upon human character and life; still it is religion; it is a sentiment that raises the thoughts of the humble and toilworn from the earthly and the perishing, to the heavenly and the eternal. And this, though accompanied by some or many rites shocking to humanity, and revolting to reason, is better than that men were, in this regard, no higher nor other than brutes; but received their being as they do theirs, they know not whence, and when they lose it, depart like them, they know not and care not whither. In the religious character of the Roman people--for religious in the earlier ages of this empire they eminently were, and they are religious now, though in less degree--I behold and acknowledge the providence of God, who has so framed us that our minds tend by resistless force to himself; satisfied at first with low and crude conceptions, but ever aspiring after those that shall be worthier and worthier.

'And now, O Emperor, for the same reason that we believe God the creator did implant in us all, of all tribes and tongues, this deep desire to know, worship, and enjoy him, so that no people have ever been wholly ignorant of him, do we believe that he has, in these latter years, declared himself to mankind more plainly than he did in the origin of things, or than he does through our own reason, so that men may, by such better knowledge of himself and of all necessary truth which he has imparted, be raised to a higher virtue on earth, and made fit for a more exalted life in heaven. We believe that he has thus declared himself by him whom you have heard named as the Master and Lord of the Christian, and after whom they are called, Jesus Christ. Him, God the creator, we believe, sent into the world to teach a better religion than the world had; and to break down and forever destroy, through the operation of his truth, a thousand injurious forms of false belief. It is this religion which we would extend, and impart to those who will open their minds to consider its claims, and their hearts to embrace its truths, when they have once been seen to be divine. This has been our task and our duty in Rome, to beseech you not blindly to receive, but strictly to examine, and, if found to be true, then humbly and gratefully to adopt this new message from above--'

'By the gods, Aurelian,' exclaimed Porphyrius, 'these Christians are kindly disposed! their benevolence and their philosophy are alike. We are obliged to them--'

'Not now, Porphyrius,' said Aurelian. 'Disturb not the Christian. Say on, Probus.'

'We hope,' continued Probus, nothing daunted by the scornful jeers of the philosopher, 'that we are sincerely desirous of your welfare, and so pray that in the lapse of years all may, as some have done, take at our hands the good we proffer them; for, sure we are, that would all so receive it, Rome would tower upwards with a glory and a beauty that should make her a thousand-fold more honored and beloved than now, and her roots would strike down, and so fasten themselves in the very centre of the earth, that well might she then be called the Eternal City. Yet, O Emperor, though such is our aim and purpose; though we would propagate a religion from God, and, in doing so, are willing to labor our lives long, and, if need be, die in the sacred cause, yet are we charged as atheists. The name by which we are known, as much as by that of Christian, is atheist--'

'Such, I have surely believed you,' said Porphyrius, again breaking in, 'and, at this moment, do.'

'But it is a name, Aurelian, fixed upon us ignorantly or slanderously; ignorantly, I am willing to believe. We believe in a God, O Emperor; it is to him we live, and to him we die. The charge of atheism I thus publicly deny, as do all Christians who are here, as would all throughout the world with one acclaim, were they also here, and would all seal their testimony, if need were, with their blood. We believe in God; not in many gods, some greater and some lesser, as with you, and whose forms are known and can be set forth in images and statues--but in one, one God, the sole monarch of the universe; whom no man, be he never so cunning, can represent in wood, or brass, or stone; whom, so to represent in any imaginary shape, our faith denounces as unlawful and impious. Hence it is, O Emperor, because the vulgar, when they enter our churches or our houses, see there no image of god or goddess, that they imagine we are without a God, and without his worship. And such conclusion may in them be excused. For, till they are instructed, it may not be easy for them to conceive of one God, filling Heaven and earth with his presence. But in others it is hard to see how they think us atheists on the same ground, since nothing can be plainer than that among you, the intelligent, and the philosophers especially, believe as we do in a great pervading invisible spirit of the universe. Plato worshipped not nor believed in these stone or wooden gods; nor in any of the fables of the Greek religion; yet who ever has charged him with atheism? So was it with the great Longinus. I see before me those who are now famed for their science in such things, who are the teachers of Rome in them, yet not one, I may venture to declare, believes other than as Plato and Longinus did in this regard. It is an error or a calumny that has ever prevailed concerning us; but in former times some have had the candor, when the error has been removed, to confess publicly that they had been subject to it. The Emperor Marcus Aurelius, to name no other, when, in the straits into which he was fallen at Cotinus, he charged his disasters upon the Christian soldiers, and, they praying prostrate upon the earth for him and his army and empire, he forthwith gained the victory, which before he had despaired of--did then immediately acknowledge that they had a God, and that they should no longer be reviled as atheists; since it was plain that men might believe in a God, and carry about the image of him in their own minds, though they had no visible one. It is thus we are all believers. We carry about with us, in the sanctuary of our own bosoms, our image of the great and almighty God whom we serve; and before that, and that only, do we bow down and worship. Were we indeed atheists, it were not unreasonable that you dealt with us as you now do, nay and much more severely; for, where belief in a God does not exist, it is not easy to see how any state can long hold together. The necessary bond is wanting, and, as a sheaf of wheat when the band is broken, it must fall asunder.

'The first principle of the religion of Christ is this belief in God; in his righteous providence here on earth, and in a righteous retribution hereafter. How then can the religion of Christ in this respect be of dangerous influence or tendency? It is well known to all, who are acquainted in the least with history or philosophy, that in the religion of the Jews, the belief and worship of one God almost constitutes the religion itself. Every thing else is inferior and subordinate. In this respect the religion of Jesus is like that of the Jews. It is exceeding jealous of the honor and worship of this one God--this very same God of the Jews; for Jesus was himself a Jew, and has revealed to us the same God whom we are required to worship, only with none of the ceremonies, rites, and sacrifices, which were peculiar to that people. It is this which has caused us, equally to our and their displeasure, frequently to be confounded together, and mistaken the one for the other. But the differences between us are, excepting in the great doctrine I have just named, very great and essential. This doctrine therefore, which is the chief of all, being so fundamental with us, it is not easy, I say, to see how we can on religious accounts be dangerous to the state. For many things are comprehended in and follow from this faith. It is not a barren, unprofitable speculation, but a practical and restraining doctrine of the greatest moral efficiency. If it be not this to us, to all and every one of us, it is not what it ought to be and we wrongly understand or else wilfully pervert it.

'We believe that we are everywhere surrounded by the presence of our God: that he is our witness every moment, and everywhere conscious, as we are ourselves, of our words, acts, and thoughts; and will bring us all to a strict account at last for whatever he has thus witnessed that has been contrary to that rigid law of holy living which he has established over us in Christ. Must not this act upon us most beneficially? We believe that in himself he is perfect purity, and that he demands of us that we be so in our degree also. We can impute to him none of the acts, such as the believers in the Greek and Roman religions freely ascribe to their Jove, and so have not, as others have, in such divine example, a warrant and excuse for the like enormities. This one God too we also regard as our judge, who will in the end sit upon our conduct throughout the whole of our lives, and punish or reward according to what we shall have been, just as the souls of men, according to your belief, receive their sentence at the bar of Minos and Rhadamanthus. And other similar truths are wrapt up with and make a part of this great primary one. Wherefore it is most evident, that nothing can be more false and absurd than to think and speak of us as atheists and for that reason a nuisance in the state.

'But it is not only that we are atheists, but that, through our atheism, we are to be looked upon as disorderly members of society, disturbers of the peace, disaffected and rebellious citizens, that we hear on every side. I do not believe that this charge has ever been true of any, much less of all. Or if any Christian has at any time and for any reason disobeyed the laws, withheld his taxes when they have been demanded, or neglected any duties which, as a citizen of Rome, he has owed to the Emperor, or any representative of him, then so far he has not been a Christian. Christ's kingdom is not of this world-- though, because we so often and so much speak of a kingdom, we have been thought to aim at one on earth--it is above; and he requires us while here below to be obedient to the laws and the rulers that are set up over us, so far as we deem them in accordance with the everlasting laws of God and of right; to pay tribute to whomsoever it is due; here in Rome to Cæsar; and, wherever we are, to be loyal and quiet citizens of the state. And the reception of his religion tends to make such of us all. Whoever adopts the faith of the gospel of Jesus will be a virtuous, and holy, and devout man, and therefore, both in Rome, in Persia, and in India, and everywhere, a good subject.

'We defend not nor abet, great Emperor, the act of that holy but impetuous and passionate man, who so lately, in defiance of the imperial edict and before either remonstrance or appeal on our part, preached on the very steps of the capitol, and there committed that violence for which he hath already answered with his life. We defend him not in that; but neither do we defend, but utterly condemn and execrate the unrighteous haste, and the more than demoniac barbarity of his death. God, we rejoice in all our afflictions to believe, is over all, and the wicked, the cruel, and the unjust, shall not escape.

'Yet it must be acknowledged that there are higher duties than those which we owe to the state, even as there is a higher sovereign to whom we owe allegiance than the head of the state, whether that head be king, senate, or emperor. Man is not only a subject and a citizen, he is first of all the creature of God, and amenable to his laws. When therefore there is a conflict between the laws of God and the king, who can doubt which are to be obeyed?--'

'Who does not see,' cried Porphyrius vehemently, 'that in such principles there lurks the blackest treason? for who but themselves are to judge when the laws of the two sovereigns do thus conflict? and what law then may be promulged, but to them it may be an offence?'

'Let not the learned Porphyrius,' resumed Probus, 'rest in but a part of what I say. Let him hear the whole, and then deny the principle if he can. I say, when the law of God and the law of man are opposite the one to the other, we are not to hesitate which to obey and which to break; our first allegiance is due to Heaven. And it is true that we ourselves are to be the judges in the case. But then we are judges under the same stern laws of conscience toward God, which compel us to violate the law of the empire, though death in its most terrific form be the penalty. And is it likely therefore that we shall, for frivolous causes, or imaginary ones, or none at all, hold it to be our duty to rebel against the law of the land? To think so were to rate us low indeed. They may surely be trusted to make this decision, whose fidelity to conscience in other emergences brings down upon them so heavy a load of calamity. I may appeal moreover to all, I think, who hear me, of the common faith, whether they themselves would not hold by the same principle? Suppose the case that your supreme god--"Jupiter greatest and best"--or the god beyond and above him, in whom your philosophers have faith--revealed a law, requiring what the law of the empire forbids, must you not, would you not, if your religion were anything more than a mere pretence, obey the god rather than the man? Although therefore, great Emperor, we blame the honest Macer for his precipitancy, yet it ought to be, and is, the determination of us all to yield obedience to no law which violates the law of

Heaven. We having received the faith of Christ in trust, to be by us dispensed to mankind, and believing the welfare of mankind to depend upon the wide extension of it, we will rather die than shut it up in our own bosoms--we will rather die, than live with our tongues tied and silent--our limbs fettered and bound! We must speak, or we will die--'

Porphyrius again sprang from his seat with intent to speak, but the Emperor restrained him.

'Contend not now, Porphyrius; let us hear the Christian. I have given him his freedom. Infringe it not.'

'I will willingly, noble Emperor,' said Probus, 'respond to whatsoever the learned Tyrian may propose. All I can desire is this only, that the religion of Christ may be seen, by those who are here, to be what it truly is; and it may be, that the questions or the objections of the philosopher shall show this more perfectly than a continued discourse.'

The Emperor, however, making a sign, he went on.

'We have also been charged, O Emperor, with vices and crimes, committed at both our social and our religious meetings, at which nature revolts, which are even beyond in grossness what have been ever ascribed to the most flagitious of mankind.'--Probus here enumerated the many rumors which had long been and still were current in Rome, and, especially by the lower orders, believed; and drew then such a picture of the character, lives, manners, and morals of the Christians, for the truth of which he appealed openly to noble and distinguished persons among the Romans then present,--not of the Christian faith, but who were yet well acquainted with their character and condition, and who would not refuse to testify to what he had said--that there could none have been present in that vast assembly but who, if there were any sense of justice within them, must have dismissed forever from their minds, if they had ever entertained them, the slanderous fictions that had filled them.

To report to you, Fausta, this part of his defence, must be needless, and could not prove otherwise than painful. He then also refuted in the same manner other common objections alleged against the Christians and their worship; the lateness of its origin; its beggarly simplicity; the low and ignorant people who alone or chiefly, both in Rome and throughout the world, have received it; the fierce divisions and disputes among the Christians themselves; the uncertainty of its doctrines; the rigor of its morality, as unsuited to mankind; as also its spiritual worship; the slowness of its progress, and the little likelihood that, if God were its author, he would leave it to be trodden under foot and so nearly annihilated by the very people to whom he was sending it; these and other similar things usually urged against the Christians, and now for the first time, it is probable, by most of the Romans present, heard, refuted, and explained, did Probus set forth, both with brevity and force; making nothing tedious by reason of a frivolous minuteness, nor yet omitting a single topic or argument, which it was due to the cause he defended, to bring before the minds of that august assembly. He then ended his appeal in the following manner:

'And now, great Emperor, must you have seen, in what I have already said, what the nature and character of this religion is; for in denying and disproving the charges that have been brought against it, I have, in most particulars, alleged and explained some opposite truth or doctrine, by which it is justly characterized. But that you may be informed the more exactly for what it is you are about to persecute and destroy us, and for what it is that we cheerfully undergo torture and death sooner than surrender or deny it, listen yet a moment longer. You have heard that we are named after Jesus, Jesus of Nazareth in Galilee, who, in the reign of Tiberius, was born in Judea, and there lived and taught, a prophet and messenger of God, till he was publicly crucified by his bitter enemies the Jews. We do not doubt, nay, we all steadfastly believe, that this Jesus was the Son of the Most High God, by reason of his wonderful endowments and his delegated office as the long-looked-for Messiah of the Jews. As the evidences of his great office and of his divine origin, he performed those miracles that filled with astonishment the whole Jewish nation, and strangers from all parts of the world; and so wrought even upon the mind of your great predecessor, the Emperor Tiberius, that he would fain receive him into the number of the gods of Rome. And why, O Emperor, was this great personage sent forth into the world, encircled by the rays of divine power and wisdom and goodness, an emanation of the self-existent and infinite God? And why do we so honor him, and cleave to him, that we are ready to offer our lives in sacrifice, while we go forth as preachers of his faith, making him known to all nations as the universal

Saviour and Redeemer? This Jesus came into the world, and lived and taught; was preceded by so long a preparation of prophetic annunciation, and accompanied by so sublime demonstrations of almighty power, to this end, and to this end only, that he might save us from our sins, and from those penal consequences in this world and in worlds to come, which are bound to them by the stern decrees of fate. Yes, Aurelian, Jesus came only that he might deliver mankind from the thraldom of every kind of wickedness, and raise them to a higher condition of virtue and happiness. He was a great moral and religious teacher and reformer, endowed with the wisdom and power of the supreme God. He himself toiled only in Judea; but he came a benefactor of Rome too--of Rome as well as of Judea. He came to purge it of its pollutions; to check in their growth those customs and vices which seem destined, reaching their natural height and size, to overlay and bury in final ruin the city and the empire; he came to make us citizens of Heaven through the virtues which his doctrine should build up in the soul, and so citizens of Rome more worthy of that name than any who ever went before. He came to heal, to mend, to reform the state; not to set up a kingdom in hostility to this, but in unison with it; an inward, invisible kingdom in every man's heart, which should be as the soul of the other.

'It was to reform the morals of the state, to save it from itself, that you, Aurelian, in the first years of your reign, applied those energies that have raised the empire to more than its ancient glory. You aimed to infuse a love of justice and of peace, to abate the extravagances of the times, to stem the tide of corruption that seemed about to bear down upon its foul streams the empire itself, tossing upon its surface a wide sea of ruin. It was a great work-- too great for man. It needed a divine strength and a more than human wisdom. These were not yours; and it is no wonder that the work did not go on to its completion. Jesus is a reformer; of Rome and of the world also. The world is his theatre of action; but with him there is leagued the arm and the power of the Supreme God; and the work which he attempts shall succeed. It cannot but succeed. It is not so much he, Jesus of Nazareth, who has come forth upon this great errand of mercy and love to mankind, as God himself in and through him. It is the Great God of the Universe, who, by Jesus Christ as his agent and messenger, comes to you, and would reform and redeem your empire, and out of that which is transitory, and by its inherent vice threatened with decay and death, make a city and an empire which, through the energy of its virtues, shall truly be eternal. Can you not, O Emperor, supposing the claims of this religion to a divine origin to be just, view it with respect? Nay, could you not greet its approach to your capital with pleasure and gratitude, seeing its aim is nothing else than this, to purify, purge, and reform the state, to heal its wounds, cleanse its putrifying members, and infuse the element of a new and healthier life? Methinks a true patriot and lover of Rome must rejoice when any power approaches and offers to apply those remedies that may, with remotest probability only, bid fair to cure the diseases of which her body is sick, nigh unto death.

'Such, Aurelian, was and is the aim of Jesus, in the religion which he brought. And of us, who are his ministers, his messengers--who go forth bearing these glad tidings of deliverance from sin and corruption, and of union with God-- our work is the same with his. We but repeat the lessons which he gave. Are we, in so doing, enemies of Rome? Are we not rather her truest friends? By making men good, just, kind, and honest, are we not at the same time making them the best citizens? Are there in Rome better citizens than the Christians?

'You will now perhaps, Aurelian, desire to be told by what instruments Christianity hopes to work such changes. It is simply, O Emperor, by the power of truth! The religion which we preach uses not force. Were the arm of Aurelian at this moment the arm of Probus, he could do no more than he now does with one, which, as the world deems, is in the comparison powerless as an infant's. In all that pertains to the soul, and its growth and purification, there must be utmost freedom. The soul must suffer no constraint. There must be no force laid upon it, but the force of reason and the appeal of divine truth. All that we ask or want in Rome is the liberty of speech--the free allowance to offer to men the truth in Christ, and persuade them to consider it. With that we will engage to reform and save the whole world. We want not to meddle with affairs of state, nor with the citizen's relations to the state; we have naught to do with the city, or its laws, or government, beyond what was just now stated. We desire but the privilege to worship God according to our consciences, and labor for the moral welfare of all who will hear our words.

'And if you would know what the truth is we impart, and by which we would save the souls of men, and reform the empire and the world, be it known to you that we preach Jesus Christ and him crucified, whom God raised up and sent into the world to save it by his doctrine and life, and whom--being by the

Jews hung upon a cross--God raised again from the dead. We preach him as the Son of God with power, by whom God has been revealed to mankind in his true nature and perfections, and through whom, he and he only is to be worshipped. In the place of Jupiter, we bring you a revelation of the God and Father of Christ Jesus our Lord--creator of the universe, who will call all men into judgment at last, rewarding or punishing according to what they have done. Through Jesus, we preach also a resurrection from the dead. We show, by arguments which cannot be refuted, that this Jesus, when he had been crucified and slain, and had lain three days in the tomb, was called again to life, and taken up to Heaven, as an example of what should afterwards happen to all his followers. Through him has immortality been plainly brought to light and proved, and this transporting truth we declare wherever we go. Through Jesus, we preach also repentance; we declare to men their wickedness; we show them what and how great it is; and exhort them to repentance, as what can alone save them from the wrath to come.

'This, O Emperor, is the great work which we, as apostles of Jesus, have to do, to convince the world how vile it is; how surely their wickedness, unrepented of, will work their misery and their ruin, and so lead them away from it, and up the safe and pleasant heights of Christian virtue. We find Rome sunk in sensuality and sin; nor only that, but ignorant of its own guilt, dead to the wickedness into which it has fallen, and denying any obligations to a different or better life. Such do we find, indeed, not Rome only, but the world itself, dead in trespasses and sin. We would rouse it from this sleep of death. We desire first of all, to waken in the souls of men a perception of the guilt of sin! a feeling of the wide departure of their lives from the just demands of the being who made them. The prospect of immortality were nothing without this. Longer life were but a greater evil were we not made alive to sin and righteousness. Life on earth, Aurelian, is not the best thing, but virtuous life: so life without end is not the best thing, but life without fault or sin. But to the necessity of such a life men are now insensible and dead. They love the prospect of an immortal existence, but not of that purity without which immortality were no blessing. But it is this moral regeneration--this waking up of men dead in sin, to the life of righteousness, which is the great aim of Christianity. Repentance! was the first word of its founder when he began preaching in Judea; it is the first word of his followers wherever they go, and should be the last. This, O Aurelian, in few words, is the gospel of Jesus--"Repent and live forever!"

'In the service of this gospel, and therefore of you and the world, we are content to labor while we live, to suffer injury and reproach, and if need be, and they to whom we go will not understand us, lay down our lives. Almost three hundred years has it appealed to mankind; and though not with the success that should have followed upon the labor of those who have toiled for the salvation of men, yet has it not been rejected everywhere, nor has the labor been in vain. The fruit that has come of the seed sown is great and abundant. In every corner of the earth are there now those who name the name of Christ. And in every place are there many more, than meet the eye, who read our gospels, believe in them, and rejoice in the virtue and the hope which have taken root in their souls. Here in Rome, O Aurelian, are there multitudes of believers, whom the ear hears not, nor the eye sees, hidden away in the security of this sea of roofs, whom the messengers of your power never could discover. Destroy us, you may; sweep from the face of Rome every individual whom the most diligent search can find, from the gray-haired man of fourscore to the infant that can just lisp the name of Jesus, and you have not destroyed the Christians; the Christian church still stands--not unharmed, but founded as before upon a rock, against which the powers of earth and hell can never prevail; and soon as this storm shall have overblown, those other, and now secret, multitudes, of whom I speak, will come forth, and the wilderness of the church shall blossom again as a garden in the time of spring. God is working with us, and who therefore can prevail against us!

'Bring not then, Aurelian, upon your own soul; bring not upon Rome, the guilt that would attend this unnecessary slaughter. It can but defer for an hour or a day the establishment of that kingdom of righteousness, which must be established, because it is God's, and he is laying its foundations and building its walls. Have pity too, great Emperor, upon this large multitude of those who embrace this faith, and who will not let it go for all the terrors of your courts and judges and engines; they will all suffer the death of Macer ere they will prove false to their Master. Let not the horrors of that scene be renewed, nor the greater ones of an indiscriminate massacre. I implore your compassions, not for myself, but for these many thousands, who, by my ministry, have been persuaded to receive this faith. For them my heart bleeds; them I would save from the death which impends. Yet it is a glorious and a happy death, to die for truth and Christ! It is better to die so, knowing that by such death the very church itself is profited, than to die in one's own bed, and only to one's self. So do these thousands think; and whatever compassion I may implore for them, they would each and all, were such their fate, go with cheerful step, as those who went to some marriage supper, to the axe, to the stake, or the cross. Christianity cannot die but with the race itself. Its life is bound up in the life of man, and man must be destroyed ere that can perish. Behold then, Aurelian, the labor that is thine!'

Soon as he had ceased, Porphyrius started from his seat and said,

'It is then, O Romans, just as it has ever been affirmed. The Galileans are atheists! They believe not in the gods of Rome, nor in any in whom mankind can ever have belief. I doubt not but they think themselves believers in a God. They think themselves to have found one better than others have; but upon any definition, that I or you could give or understand, of atheism, they are atheists! Their God is invisible; he is a universal spirit, like this circumambient air; of no form, dwelling in no place. But how can that without effrontery be called a being, which is without body and form; which is everywhere and yet nowhere; which, from the beginning of the world has never been heard of, till by these Nazarenes he is now first brought to light, or, if older, exists in the dreams of the dreaming Jews, whose religion, as they term it, is so stuffed with fable, that one might not expect, after the most exact and laborious search, to meet with so much as a grain of truth. Yet, whatever these Galileans may assert, their speech is hardly to be received as worthy of belief, when, in their very sacred records, such things are to be found as contradict themselves. For in one place--not to mention a thousand cases of the like kind--it is said that Jesus, the head of this religion, on a certain occasion walked upon the sea; when, upon sifting the narrative, it is found that it was but upon a paltry lake, the lake of Galilee, upon which he performed that great feat!--a thing to which the magic of which he is accused--and doubtless with justice--was plainly equal; while to walk upon the sea might well have been beyond that science. How much of what we have heard is to be distrusted also, concerning the love which these Nazarenes bear to Rome. We may well pray to be delivered from the affection of those, whose love manifests itself in the singular manner of seeking our destruction. He who loves me so well as to poison me that I may have the higher enjoyment of Elysium, I could hardly esteem as a well-wisher or friend. These Jewish fanatics love us after somewhat the same fashion. In the zeal of their affection they would make us heirs of what they call their heavenly kingdom, but in the meanwhile destroy our religion, deprive us of our ancient gods, and sap the foundations of the state.

'Romans, in spite of all you have heard of another sort, I hope you will still believe that experience is one of your most valuable teachers, and that therefore you will be slow to forsake opinions which have the sanction of venerable age, under which you have flourished so happily, and your country grown to so amazing a height of glory and renown. I think you would deserve the fate which this new-made religion would bring you to, if you abandoned the worship of a thousand years, for the presumptuous novelty of yesterday. Not a name of greatness or honor can be quoted of those who have adorned this foreign fiction; while all the great and good of Greece and Rome, philosophers, moralists, historians, and poets, are to be found on the side of Hellenism. If we cast from us that which we have experienced to be good, by what rule and on what principle can we afterward put our trust in anything else? And it is considerable, that which has ever been asserted of this people, and which I doubt not is true, that they have ever been prying about with their doctrines and their mysteries among the poor and humbler sort, among women, slaves, simple and unlearned folks, while they have never appealed to, nor made any converts of, the great and the learned, who alone are capable of judging of the truth of such things.

'Who are the believers here in Rome? Who knows them? Are the sacred Senate Christians? or any distinguished for their rank? No; with exceptions, too few to be noticed, those who embrace it are among the dregs of the people, men wholly incapable of separating true from false, and laying properly the safe foundations of a new religion--a work too great even for philosophers. And not only does this religion draw to itself the poor and humble and ignorant, but the base and wicked also; persons known, while of our way, to have been notorious for their vices, have all of a sudden joined themselves to the Christians; and whatever show of sanctity may then have been assumed, we may well suppose there has not been much of the reality. Long may it boast of such members, and while its brief life lasts make continually such converts from us. As to the amazing pretences they make of their benevolence in the care of the poor, and even of our poor, doing more offices of kindness toward them--so it is affirmed--than we ourselves--who does not see the motive that prompts so much charity, in the good opinion they build up for themselves in those whom they have so much obliged, and who cannot in decency do less afterward than oblige them in turn, by joining their superstitions--superstitions of which they know nothing before they adopt them, and as little afterward.

'But I will not, O Emperor, weary out your patience again--already so long tried--and will only say, that the fate which has all along and everywhere befallen these people, might well warn them that they are objects of the anger rather than the favor and love of the Lord of Heaven, of which they so confidently make their boast. For if he loved them would he leave them everywhere so to the rage and destruction of their enemies--to be reviled, trodden upon, and despised, all over the earth? If these be the signs of love, what are those of hate? And can it be that he, their Lord of Heaven, hath in store for them a world of bliss beyond this life, who gives them here on earth scarce the sordid shelter of a cabin? In truth, they seem to be a community living upon their imaginations. They fancy themselves favorites of Heaven--though all the world thinks otherwise. They fancy themselves the greatest benefactors the world has ever seen, while they are the only ones who think so. They have nothing here but persecution, contempt, and hatred, and yet are anticipating a more glorious Elysium than the greatest and best of earth have ever dared to hope for. We cannot but hope they may be at sometime the riddle to themselves which they are to us. This is a benevolent wish, for their entertainment would be great.'

When he had ended, and almost before, many voices were heard of those who wished to speak, and Probus rose in his place to reply to what had fallen from the philosopher, but all were alike silenced by the loud and stern command of Aurelian, who, evidently weary and impatient of further audience of what he was so little willing to hear at all, cried out, saying,

'The Christians, Romans, have now been heard, as they desired, by one whom they themselves appointed to set forth their doctrine. This is no school for the disputations of sophists or philosophers or fanatics. Let Romans and Christians alike withdraw.'

Whereupon, without further words or delay, the assembly broke up.

* * * * *

It was not difficult to see that the statements and reasonings of Probus had fallen upon many who heard them with equal surprise and delight. Every word that he uttered was heard with an eager attention I never before saw equaled. I have omitted the greater part of what he said, especially where he went with minuteness into an account of the history, doctrine, and precept of our faith, knowing it to be too familiar to you to make it desirable to have it repeated.

It was in part at least owing to an unwillingness to allow Probus again to address that audience, representing all the rank and learning of Rome, that the Emperor so hastily dissolved the assembly. Whatever effect the hearing of Probus may have upon him or upon us, there is reason to believe that its effects will be deep and abiding upon the higher classes of our inhabitants. They then heard what they never heard before--a full and an honest account of what Christianity is; and, from what I have already been informed, and gathered indeed from my own observation at the time, they now regard it with very different sentiments.

When, late in the evening of this day, we conversed of its events, Probus being seated with us, we indulged both in those cheering and desponding thoughts which seem to be strangely mingled together in our present calamities.

'No opinion,' said Julia, 'has been more strongly confirmed within me by this audience before Aurelian, than this, that it has been of most auspicious influence upon our faith. Not that some have not been filled with a bitterer spirit than before; but that more have been favorably inclined toward us by the disclosures, Probus, which you made; and whether they become Christians or not eventually, they will be far more ready to defend us in our claim for the common rights of citizens. Marcellinus, who sat near me, was of this number. He expressed frequently, in most emphatic terms, his surprise at what he heard, which, he said, he was constrained to admit as true and fair statements, seeing they were supported and corroborated by my and your presence and silence. At the close he declared his purpose to procure the gospels for his perusal.'

'And yet,' said I, 'the late consul Capitolinus, who was at my side, and whose clear and intelligent mind is hardly equaled here in Rome, was confirmed--

even as Porphyrius was, or pretended to be--in all his previous unfavorable impressions. He did not disguise his opinion, but freely said, that in his judgment the religion ought to be suppressed, and that, though he should by no means defend any measures like those which he understood Aurelian had resolved to put in force, he should advocate such action in regard to it, as could not fail to expel it from the empire in no very great number of years.'

'I could observe,' added Probus, 'the same differences of feeling and judgment all over the surface of that sea of faces. But if I should express my belief as to the proportion of friends and enemies there present, I should not hesitate to say--and that I am sure without any imposition upon my own credulity--that the greater part by far were upon our side--not in faith as you may suppose--but in that good opinion of us, and of the tendencies of our doctrine and the value of our services, that is very near it, and is better than the public profession of Christ of many others.'

'It will be a long time, I am persuaded,' said Julia, 'before the truths received then into many minds will cease to operate in our behalf. But what think you was the feeling of Aurelian? His countenance was hidden from me--yet that would reveal not much. It is immovable at those times, when he is deeply stirred, or has any motive to conceal his sentiments.'

'I cannot believe,' replied Probus, 'that any impression, such as we could wish, was made upon that hard and cruel heart. Not the brazen statue, against the base of which he leaned, stood in its place more dead to whatever it was that came from my lips than he. He has not been moved, we may well believe, to change any of his designs. Whatever yesterday it was in his intent to do, he will accomplish tomorrow. I do not believe we have anything to hope at his hands.'

'Alas, Lucius!' said Julia, 'that our faith in Christ, and our interest and concern for its progress in Rome, should after all come to this. How happy was I in Syria, with this belief as my bosom companion and friend; and free, too, to speak of it, to any and to all. How needless is all the misery which this rude, unlettered tyrant is about to inflict! How happily for all, would things take their course even here, might they but be left to run in those natural channels which would reveal themselves, and which would then conduct to those ends which the Divine Providence has proposed. But man wickedly interposes; and a misery is inflicted, which otherwise would have never fallen upon us, and which in the counsels of God was never designed. What now think you, Probus, will be the event?'

'I cannot doubt,' he replied, 'that tomorrow will witness all that report has already spread abroad as the purpose of Aurelian. Urged on by both Fronto and Varus, he will not pause in his course. Rome, ere the Ides, will swim in Christian blood. I see not whence deliverance is to come. Miracle alone could save us; and miracle has long since ceased to be the order of Providence. Having provided for us this immense instrument of moral reform in the authority and doctrine of Christ, we are now left, as doubtless it is on the whole best for our character and our virtues we should be, to our own unassisted strength, to combat with all the evils that may assail us, both from without and within. For myself, I can meet this tempest without a thought of reluctance or dread. I am a solitary man; having neither child nor relative to mourn my loss; I have friends indeed, whom I love, and from whom I would not willingly part; but, if any considerable purpose is to be gained by my death to that cause for which I have lived, neither I nor they can lament that it should occur. Under these convictions as to my own fate--and that of all, must I say and believe? no; I cannot, will not, believe that humanity has taken its final departure from the bosom of Aurelian--I turn to one bright spot, and there my thoughts dwell, and there my hopes gather strength, and that is here where you, Piso, and you, lady, will still dwell, too high for the aim of the imperial murderer to reach. Here I shall believe will there he an asylum for many a wearied spirit, a safe refuge from the sharp pelting of the storm without. And when a calm shall come again, from beneath this roof, as once from the ark of God, shall there go forth those who shall again people the waste-places of the church, and change the wilderness of death into a fruitful garden full of the plants of Heaven.'

'That it is the present purpose of Aurelian to spare me,' I answered, 'whatever provocation I may give him, I fully believe. He is true; and his word to that end, with no wish expressed on my part, has been given. But do not suppose that in that direction at least he may not change his purpose. Superstitiously mad as he now is, a mere plaything too in the bloody hands of Fronto--and nothing can well be esteemed as more insecure than even my life, privileged and secure as it may seem. If it should occur to him, in his day or his night visions and dreams, that I, more than others, should be an acceptable offering to his god, my life would be to him but that of an insect buzzing around his ear; and being dead by a blow, he would miss me no more. Still, let the mercy that is vouchsafed, whether great or little, be gratefully confessed.'

You then see, Fausta, the position in which your old friends now stand here in Rome. Who could have believed, when we talked over our dangers in Palmyra, that greater and more dreadful still awaited us in our own home. It has come upon us with such suddenness that we can scarce believe it ourselves. Yet are we prepared, with an even mind and a trusting faith, for whatever may betide.

It is happy for me, and for Julia, that our religion has fixed within us so firm a belief in a superintending Providence--who orders not only the greatest but the least events of life, who is as much concerned for the happiness and the moral welfare of the humblest individual, as he is for the orderly movement of a world--that we sit down under the shadows that overhang us, perfectly convinced that some end of good to the church or the world is to be achieved through these convulsions, greater than could have been achieved in any other way. The Supreme Ruler, we believe, is infinitely wise and infinitely good. But he would be neither, if unnecessary suffering were meted out to his creatures. This suffering then is not unnecessary. But through it, in ways which our sight now is not piercing enough to discern--but may hereafter be-- shall a blessing redound both to the individuals concerned, to the present generation, and a remote posterity, which could not otherwise have been secured. This we must believe; or we must renounce all belief.

Forget not to remember us with affection to Gracchus and Calpurnius.

* * * * *

I also was present at the hearing of Probus. But of that I need say nothing; Piso having so fully written concerning it to the daughter of Gracchus.

Early on the following day I was at the Gardens of Sallust, where I was present both with the Emperor and Livia, and with the Emperor and Fronto, and heard conversations which I here record.

When I entered the apartment, in which it was customary for the Empress to sit at this time of the day, I found her there engaged upon her embroidery, while the Emperor paced back and forth, his arms crossed behind him, and care and anxiety marked upon his countenance. Livia, though she sat quietly at her work, seemed ill at ease, and as if some thought were busy within, to which she would gladly give utterance. She was evidently relieved by my entrance, and immediately made her usual inquiries after the health of the Queen, in which Aurelian joined her.

Aurelian then turned to me and said,

'I saw you yesterday at the Palatine, Nicomachus; what thought you of the Christian's defence?'

'It did not convert me to his faith--'

'Neither, by the gods! did it me,' quickly interrupted Aurelian.

'But,' I went on, 'it seemed to show good cause why they should not be harshly or cruelly dealt with. He proved them to be a harmless people, if not positively profitable to the state.'

'I do not see that,' replied the Emperor. 'It is impossible they should be harmless who sap the foundations of religion; it is impossible they should be profitable who seduce from their allegiance the good subjects of the empire; and this religion of the Christians does both.'

'I agree that it is so,' I rejoined, 'if it is to be assumed in the controversy that the prevailing religion of the Romans is a perfect one, and that any addition or alteration is necessarily an evil. That seems to be the position of Porphyrius and others. But to that I can by no means assent. It seems to me that the religions of mankind are susceptible of improvement as governments are, and other like institutions; that what may be perfectly well suited to a nation in one stage of its growth, may be very ill adapted to another; that the gods in their providence accordingly design that one form of religious worship and belief should in successive ages be superseded by others, which shall be more exactly suited to their larger growth, and more urgent and very different necessities. The religion of the early days of Rome was perhaps all that so rude a people were capable of comprehending--all that they wanted. It worked well for them, and you have reason for gratitude that it was bestowed upon them, and has conferred so great benefits upon the preceding centuries. But the light of the sun is not clearer than it is that, for this present passing age, that religion is stark naught.'

The Emperor frowned, and stood still in his walk, looking sternly upon me; but I heeded him not.

'Most, of any intelligence and reflection,' I continued, 'spurn it away from them as fit but for children and slaves. Must they then be without any principle of this kind? Is it safe for a community to grow up without faith in a superintending power, from whom they come, to whom they are responsible? I think not. In any such community--and Rome is becoming such a one--the elements of disruption, anarchy, and ruin, are there at work, and will overthrow it. A society of atheists is a contradiction in terms. Atheists may live alone, but not together. Will you compel your subjects to become such? If a part remain true to the ancient faith, and find it to be sufficient, will you deny to the other part the faith which they crave, and which would be sufficient for them? I doubt if that were according to the dictates of wisdom and philosophy. And how know you, Aurelian, that this religion of Christ may not be the very principle which, and which alone, may save your people from atheism, and your empire from the ruin that would bring along in its train?'

'I cannot deny,' said the Emperor in reply, 'that there is some sense and apparent truth in what you have said. But to me it is shadowy and intangible. It is the speculation of that curious class among men, who, never satisfied with what exists, are always desiring some new forms of truth, in religion, in government, and all subjects of that nature. I could feel no more certain of going or doing right by conforming to their theories, than I feel now in adhering to what is already established. Nay, I can see safety nowhere but in what already is. There is the only certainty. Suppose some enthusiast in matters of government were to propose his system, by which the present established institutions were all to be abandoned and new ones set up, should I permit him to go freely among the people, puzzling their heads with what it is impossible they should understand, and by his sophistries alienating them from their venerable parent? Not so, by Hercules! I should ill deserve my office of supreme guardian of the honor and liberties of Rome, did I not mew him up in the Fabrician dungeons, or send him lower still to the Stygian shades.'

'But,' said Livia, who had seemed anxious to speak, 'though it may be right, and best for the interests of Rome, to suppress this new worship, yet why, Aurelian, need it be done at such expense of life? Can no way be devised by which the professors of this faith shall be banished, for instance, the realm, and no new teachers of it permitted to enter it afterward but at the risk of life, or some other appointed penalty? Sure I am, from what I heard from the Christian Probus, and what I have heard so often from the lips of Julia, this people cannot be the sore in the body of the state which Fronto represents them.'

'I cannot, Livia,' replied the Emperor, 'refuse to obey what to me have been warnings from the gods.'

'But may not the heavenly signs have been read amiss?' rejoined Livia.

'There is no truth in augury, if my duty be not where I have placed it,' answered Aurelian.

'And perhaps, Aurelian,' said the Empress, 'there is none. I have heard that the priests of the temples play many a trick upon their devout worshippers.'

'Livia, it has doubtless been so; but you would not believe that Fronto has trifled with Aurelian?'

'I believe Fronto capable of any crime by which the gods may be served. Have you not heard, Aurelian what fell from the dying Christian's lips?'

'I have, Livia; and have cast it from me as at best the coinage of a moonstruck mountebank. Shall the word of such a one as Macer the Christian, unseat my trust in such a one as Fronto? That were not reasonable, Livia.'

'Then, Aurelian, if not for any reason that I can give, for the love you bear me, withhold your hand from this innocent people. You have often asked me to crave somewhat which it would be hard for you to grant, that you might show how near you hold me. Grant me this favor, and it shall be more to me than if you gave me the one half the empire.'

The Emperor's stern countenance relaxed, and wore for a moment that softened expression, accompanied by a smile, that on his face might be termed beautiful. He was moved by the unaffected warmth and winning grace with which those words were spoken by Livia. But he only said,

'I love thee, Livia, as thou knowest,--but not so well as Rome or the gods.'

'I would not, Aurelian,' replied the Empress, 'that love of me should draw you away from what you owe to Rome--from what is the clear path of a monarch's duty; but this seems at best a doubtful case. They who are equally Roman in their blood differ here. It is not wrong to ask you, for my sake, to lean to the side of mercy.'

'You are never wrong, Livia. And were it only right to--'

'But are you not, Aurelian, always sure of being right in being merciful? Can it ever afterward repent you that you drew back from the shedding of blood?'

'It is called mercy, Livia, when he who has the power spares the culprit, forgives the offence, and sends him from the gibbet or the cross back to his weeping friends. The crowds throw up their caps and shout as for some great and good deliverance. But the mercy that returns upon the world a villain, whose crimes had richly earned for him his death, is hardly a doubtful virtue. Though, as is well known, I am not famed for mercy, yet were it clear to me what in this case were the truest mercy--for the pleasure, Livia, of pleasuring thee, I would be merciful. But I should not agree with thee in what is mercy. It were no mercy to Rome, as I judge, to spare these Christians, whatever the grace might be to them. Punishment is often mercy. In destroying these wretches I am merciful both to Rome and to the world, and shall look to have their thanks.'

'There comes, Aurelian.' said Livia, rising, 'thy evil genius--thy ill-possessing demon--who has so changed the kindly current of thy blood. I would that he, who so loves the gods, were with them. I cannot wait him.'

With these words Livia rose and left the apartment, just as Fronto entered in another direction.

'Welcome, Fronto!' said Aurelian. 'How thrive our affairs?'

'As we could wish, great Emperor. The city with us, and the gods with us,-- we cannot but prosper. A few days will see great changes.'

'How turns out the tale of Curio? What find you to be the truth? Are the Christians here, or are they fled?'

'His tale was partly false and partly true. More are fled than Piso or the Christians will allow; but doubtless the greater part, by large odds, remain.'

'That is well. Then for the other side of this great duty. Is thine own house purged? Is the temple, new and of milk-white marble, now as clean and white in its priesthood? Have those young sots and pimps yet atoned for their foul impieties?'

'They have,' replied Fronto. 'They have been dealt with; and their carcases swinging and bleaching in the wind will long serve I trust to keep us sweet. The temple, I now may believe, is thoroughly swept.'

'And how is it, Fronto, with the rest?'

'The work goes on. Your messengers are abroad; and it will be neither for want of power, will, nor zeal, if from this time Hellenism stands not before the world as beautiful in her purity as she is venerable in years and truth.'

'The gods be praised that I have been stirred up to this! When this double duty shall be done, Hellenism reformed, and her enemy extinct, then may I say that life has not been spent for naught. But meanwhile, Fronto, the army needs me. All is prepared, and letters urge me on. To-morrow I would start for Thrace. Yet it cannot be so soon.'

'No,' said the priest. 'Rome will need you more than Thrace, till the edicts have been published, and the work well begun. Then, Aurelian, may it be safely entrusted, so far as zeal and industry shall serve, to those behind.'

'I believe it, Fronto. I see myself doubly reflected in thee: and almost so in Varus. The Christians, were I gone, would have four Aurelians for one. Well, let us rejoice that piety is not dead. The sacrifice this morning was propitious. I feel its power in every thought and movement.'

'But while all things else seem propitious, Aurelian, one keeps yet a dark and threatening aspect.'

'What mean you?'

'Piso!--'

'Fronto, I have in that made known my will, and more than once. Why again dispute it?'

'I know no will, great Caesar, that may rightly cross or surmount that of the gods. They, to me, are supreme, not Aurelian.'

Aurelian moved from the priest, and paced the room.

'I see not, Fronto, with such plainness the will of Heaven in this.'

''Tis hard to see the divine will, when the human will and human affections are so strong.'

'My aim is to please the gods in all things,' replied the Emperor.

'Love too, Aurelian, blinds the eye, and softening the heart toward our fellow, hardens it toward the gods.' This he uttered with a strange significancy.

'I think, Fronto, mine has been all too hard toward man, if it were truly charged. At least, of late, the gods can have no ground of blame.'

'Rome,' replied the priest, 'is not slow to see and praise the zeal that is now crowning her seven hills with a greater glory than ever yet has rested on them. Let her see that her great son can finish what has been so well begun.'

'Fronto, I say it, but I say it with some inward pain, that were it plain the will of the gods were so--'

'Piso should die!' eagerly interrupted the priest.

'I will not say it yet, Fronto.'

'I see not why Aurelian should stagger at it. If the will of the gods is in this whole enterprise; if they will that these hundreds and thousands, these crowds of young and old, little children and tender youth, should all perish, that posterity by such sacrifice now in the beginning may be delivered from the curse that were else entailed upon them, then who can doubt, to whom truth is the chief thing, that they will, nay, and ordain in their sacred breasts, that he who is their chief and head, about whom others cluster, from whose station and power they daily draw fresh supplies of courage, should perish too; nay, that he should be the first great offering, that so, the multitudes who stay their weak faith on him, may, on his loss, turn again unharmed to their ancient faith. That too, were the truest mercy.'

'There may be something in that, Fronto. Nevertheless, I do not yet see so much to rest upon one life. If all the rest were dead, and but one alive, and he Piso, I see not but the work were done.'

'A thousand were better left, Aurelian, than Piso and the lady Julia! They are more in the ears and eyes of Rome than all the preachers of this accursed tribe. They are preaching, not on their holydays to a mob of beggarly knaves, men and women dragged up by their hot and zealous caterers from the lanes and kennels of the city, within the walls of their filthy synagogues, but they preach every day, to the very princes and nobles of the state--at the capitol to the Senate--here in thy palaces to all the greatest and best of Rome and, by the gods! as I believe, make more converts to their impieties than all the army of their atheistical priesthood. Upon Probus, Piso, and Julia, hang the Christians of Rome. Hew them away, end the branches die. Probus, ere tomorrow's sun is set, feeds the beasts of the Flavian--then--'

'Hold, Fronto! I will no more of it now. I have, besides, assured Piso of his safety.'

'There is no virtue like that of those, who, having erred, repent.'

Aurelian looked for the moment as if he would willingly have hurled Fronto, and his temple after him, to Tartarus. But the bold man heeded him not.

'Shall I,' he continued, 'say what it is that thus ties the hands of the conqueror of the world?'

'Say what thou wilt.'

'Rome says, I say it not--but Rome says, 'tis love.'

'What mean they? I take you not. Love?'

'Of the princess Julia, still so called.'

A deep blush burned upon the cheek of Aurelian. He paused a moment, as if for some storm within to subside. He then said, in his deep tone, that indicates the presence of the whole soul--but without passion--

'Fronto, 'tis partly true--truer than I wish it were. When in Syria my eye first beheld her, I loved her--as I never loved before, and never shall again. But not for the Emperor of the world would she part from young Piso. I sued, as man never sued before, but all in vain. Her image still haunts the chambers of my brain; yet, with truth do I say it, but as some pure vision sent from the gods. I confess, Fronto, it is she who stands between me and the will of Heaven. I know not what force, but that of all the gods, could make me harm her. To no other ear has this ever been revealed. She is to me god and goddess.'

'Now, Aurelian, that thou has spoken in the fullness of thy heart, do I hold thee redeemed from the invisible tyrant. In our own hearts we sin and err, as we dare not when the covering is off, and others can look in and see how weak we are. Thou canst not, great Caesar, for this fondness forget and put far from thee the vision of thy mother, whom, in dreams or in substantial shape, the gods sent down to revive thy fainting zeal! Let it not be that that call shall have been in vain.'

'Fronto, urge now no more. Hast thou seen Varus?'

'I have.'

'Are the edicts ready?'

'They are.'

'Again then at the hour of noon let them glare forth upon the enemies of Rome from the columns of the capitol. Let Varus be so instructed. Now I would be alone.'

Whereupon the priest withdrew, and I also rose from where I had sat, to take my leave, when the Emperor said,

'This seems harsh to thee, Nicomachus?'

'I cannot but pray the gods,' I said, 'to change the mind of Aurelian!'

'They have made his mind what it is, Nicomachus.'

'Not they,' I said, 'but Fronto.'

'But,' he quickly added, 'the gods made Fronto, and have put their mind in him, or it has never been known on earth. You know not the worth, Greek, of this man. Had Rome possessed such a one two hundred years ago, this work had not now to be done.'

Saying which, he withdrew into his inner apartment, and I sought again the presence of Livia.

LETTER XI.

FROM PISO TO FAUSTA.

A day has passed, Fausta, since the hearing of Probus, and I hasten to inform you of its events.

But, first of all, before I enter upon the dark chapter of our calamities, let me cheer you and myself by dwelling a moment upon one bright and sunny spot. Early in the day we were informed that Isaac was desirous to see us. He was at once admitted. As he entered, it was easy to see that some great good fortune had befallen him. His face shone through the effect of some inward joy, and his eyes sparkled in their deep sockets like burning tapers. When our customary salutations and inquiries were over, Julia said to him,

'I think, Isaac, you must have sold a jewel this morning to no less a person than Aurelian, if the face may be held as an index of good or evil fortune.'

'I have parted with no jewel, lady,' he replied, 'but there has fallen into my hands a diamond of inestimable value, drawn from those mines of the Orient, which I may say, not all the wealth of Aurelian could purchase of me. Whenever I shall receive such permission, it will give me highest delight to show it to thee.'

'Only a single jewel, Isaac?' said Julia. 'Is it but one stone that so transports thee, and makes thy face that of a young man?'

'Lady, to confess the truth, there are four--four living stories and precious--more precious than any that of old blazed upon the breastplate of our high-priest Princess, I have come to tell thee and Piso what none in Rome besides, as I think, would care to know--and strange it is that you Christians should be those whom I, a Jew, most love, and that I, an old and worn-out man, should fill any space, were it no bigger than a grain of wheat, in your regards--I have come to tell you what you have already discovered, that Hagar is arrived with the young Ishmael, and with them two dark-eyed daughters of Israel, who are as welcome as the others. There is not now, Piso, within the walls of Rome a dwelling happier than mine. Soon as leisure and inclination shall serve, come, if you will do us such grace, to the street Janus, and behold our contentment. Sorry am I that the times come laden to you with so many terrors. Piso,' continued he, in a more earnest tone, and bending toward me, 'rely upon the word of one who is rarely deceived, and who now tells thee, there is a sword hanging over thy head! Fronto thirsts for thy life, and thine, lady! and Aurelian, much as he may love you, is, as we have already seen, not proof against the violent zeal of the priest. Come to the street Janus, and I will warrant you safety and life. There is none for you here--nor in Rome--if Aurelian's hounds can scent you.'

We were again obliged to state, with all the force we could give to them, the reasons which bound us to remain, not only in Rome, but in our own dwelling, and await whatever the times might bring forth. He was again slow to be convinced, so earnestly does he desire our safety. But at length he was persuaded that he himself would take the same course were he called upon to defend the religion of his fathers. He then departed, having first exacted a promise that we would soon see his new family.

Soon as Isaac was gone I sought the streets.

Rome, Fausta, has put on the appearance of the Saturnalia. Although no license of destruction has yet been publicly given, the whole city is in commotion--the lower orders noisy and turbulent, as if they had already received their commission of death. Efforts have been made, both on the part of the senate and that of the nobles who are not of that body, joined by many of all classes, to arrest the Emperor in his murderous career, but in vain. Not the Seven Hills are more firmly rooted in the earth, than he in his purposes of blood. This is well known abroad; and the people are the more emboldened in the course they take. They know well that Aurelian is supreme and omnipotent; that no power in Rome can come in between him and his object, whatever it may be; and that they, therefore, though they should err through their haste, and in their zeal even go before the edicts, would find in him a lenient judge. No Christian was accordingly to be now seen in the streets--for nowhere were they safe from the ferocious language, or even the violent assaults, of the mob. These cruel executioners I found all along, wherever I moved, standing about in groups as if impatiently awaiting the hour of noon, or else gathered about the dwellings of well-known Christians, assailing the buildings with stones, and the ears of their pent-up inhabitants with all that variety of imprecation they so well know how to use. It was almost with sensations of guilt that I walked the streets of Rome in safety, bearing a sort of charmed life, while these thousands of my friends were already suffering more through their horrible anticipation, than they would when they should come to endure the reality. But, although I passed along uninjured by actual assault, the tongue was freely let loose upon me, and promises were abundantly lavished that, before many days were gone, not even the name of

Piso, nor the favor of Aurelian, should save me from the common doom.

As the hour of noon drew nigh, it seemed as if the entire population of Rome was pouring itself into the streets and avenues leading to the capitol. Not the triumph of Aurelian itself filled this people with a more absorbing, and, as it appeared, a more pleasing interest, than did the approaching calamities of the Christians. Expectation was written on every face. Even the boys threw up their caps as in anticipation of somewhat that was to add greatly to their happiness.

* * * * *

The sixth hour has come and is gone. The edicts are published, and the Christians are now declared enemies of the state and of the gods, and are required to be informed against by all good citizens, and arraigned before the Prefect and the other magistrates especially appointed for the purpose.

* * * * *

All is now confusion, uproar, and cruel violence.

* * * * *

No sooner was the purport of the edicts ascertained by the multitudes who on this occasion, as before, thronged the capitol, than they scattered in pursuit of their victims. The priests of the temples heading the furious crowds, they hastened from the hill in every direction, assailing, as they reached them, the houses of the Christians, and dragging the wretched inhabitants to the presence of their barbarous judges. Although in the present edicts the people are not let loose as authorized murderers upon the Christians, they are nevertheless exhorted and required to inform against them and bring them before the proper tribunals on the charge of Christianity, so that there is lodged in their hands a fearful power to harrass and injure--a power which is used as you may suppose Romans would use it. Every species of violence has this day been put in practice upon this innocent people; their perpetrators feeling sure that, in the confusion, deeds at which even Varus or Aurelian might take offence will be overlooked. The tribunals have been thronged from noon till night with Christians and their accusers. As the examination of those who have been brought up has rarely occupied but a few moments, the evidence always being sufficiently full to prove them Christians, and, when that has been wanting, their own ready confession supplying the defect--the prisons are already filling with their unhappy tenants, and extensive provisions are making to receive them in other buildings set apart for the time to this office. A needless provision. For it requires but little knowledge of Aurelian to know that his impatient temper will not long endure the tedious process of a regular accusation, trial, condemnation, and punishment. A year, in that case, would scarce suffice to make way with the Christians of Rome. Long before the prisons can be emptied in a legal way of the tenants already crowding them, will the Emperor resort to the speedier method of a general and indiscriminate massacre. No one can doubt this, who is familiar as I am with Aurelian, and the spirits who now rule him.

* * * * *

Let me tell you now of the fate of Probus.

He was seated within his own quiet home at the time the edicts were proclaimed from the steps of the capitol. The moment the herald who proclaimed them had pronounced the last word, and was affixing them to the column, the name of Probus was heard shouted from one side of the hill to the other, and, while the multitude scattered in every direction in pursuit of those who were known to them severally as Christians, a large division of it made on the instant for his dwelling. On arriving there, roused by the noise of the approaching throng, Probus came forth. He was saluted by cries and yells, that seemed rather to proceed from troops of wild beasts than men. He would fain have spoken to them, but no word would they hear. 'Away with the Christian dog to the Prefect!' arose in one deafening shout from the people; and on the instant he was seized and bound, and led unresisting away to the tribunal of Varus.

As he was dragged violently along, and was now passing the door which leads to the room where Varus sits, Felix, the bishop, having already stood before the Prefect, was leaving the hall, urged along by soldiers who were bearing him to prison.

'Be of good cheer, Probus!' exclaimed he; 'a crown awaits thee within. Rome needs thy life, and Christ thy soul.'

'Peace, dotard!' cried one of those who guarded and led him; and at the same moment brought his spear with such force upon his head that he felled him to the pavement.

'Thou hast slain thyself, soldier, by that blow rather than him,' said Probus. 'Thine own faith has torments in reserve for such as thee.'

'Thou too!' cried the enraged soldier; and he would have repeated the blow upon the head of the offender, but that the descending weapon was suddenly struck upwards, and out of the hand of him who wielded it, by another belonging to the same legion, who guarded Probus, saying as he did so,

'Hold, Mutius! it is not Roman to strike the bound and defenceless, Christians though they be. Raise that fallen old man, and apply such restoratives as the place affords.' And then, with other directions to those who were subordinate to him, he moved on, bearing Probus with him.

Others who had arrived before him, were standing in the presence of Varus, who was questioning them as to their faith in Christ. On the left hand of the Prefect, and on the right of those who were examined, stood a small altar surmounted by a statue of Jupiter, to which the Christians were required to sacrifice. But few words sufficed for the examination of such as were brought up. Upon being inquired of touching their faith, there was no waiting for witnesses, but as soon as the question was put, the arraigned person acknowledged at once his name and religion. He was then required to sacrifice and renounce his faith, and forthwith he should be dismissed in safety, and with honor. This the Christian refusing steadfastly to do, sentence of death was instantly pronounced against him, and he was remanded to the prisons to await the time of punishment.

Probus was now placed before the Prefect. When it was seen throughout the crowd which again filled the house, who it was that was arraigned for examination, there were visible signs of satisfaction all around, that he, who was in a manner the ringleader of the sect, was about to meet with his deserts. As the eye of Varus fell upon Probus, and he too became aware who it was that stood at his tribunal, he bent courteously towards him, and saluted him with respect.

'Christian,' said he, 'I sincerely grieve to see thee in such a pass. Ever since I met thee in the shop of the learned Publius have I conceived an esteem for thee, and would now gladly rescue thee from the danger that overhangs. Bethink thee now--thou art of too much account to die as these others. A better fate should be thine; and I will stand thy friend.'

'Were what thou sayest true,' replied Probus, 'which I am slow to admit--for nobler, purer souls never lived on earth than have but now left this spot where I stand--it would but be a reason of greater force to me, why I should lose my life sooner than renounce my faith. What sacrifice can be too holy for the altar of the God whom I serve? Would to God I were more worthy than I am to be offered up.'

'Verily,' said Varus, 'you are a wonderful people. The more fitted you are to live happily to yourselves, and honorably to others, the readier you are to die. I behold in you, Probus, qualities that must make you useful here in Rome. Rome needs such as thyself. Say but the word, and thou art safe.'

'Could I in truth, Varus, possess the qualities thou imputest to me, were I ready on the moment to abandon what I have so long professed to honor and believe--abjuring, for the sake of a few years more of life, a faith which I have planted in so many other hearts, and which has already brought them into near neighborhood of a cruel death? Couldst thou thyself afterward think of me but as of a traitor and a coward?'

'I never,' said Varus, 'could do otherwise than esteem one, who, however late, at length declared himself the friend of Rome; and, more than others should I esteem him, who, from being an enemy, became a friend. Even the Emperor, Probus, desires thy safety. It is at his instance that I press thee.'

Probus bent his head and remained silent. The people, taking it as a sign of acquiescence, cried out, many of them, 'See, he will sacrifice!'

Varus too said, 'It needs not that the outward sign be made. We will dispense with it. The inward consent, Probus, shall suffice. Soldiers!--'

'Hold, hold, Varus!' cried Probus, rousing himself from a momentary forgetfulness. 'Think not, O Prefect, so meanly of me! What have I said or done to induce such belief? I was but oppressed for a moment with grief and shame that I should be chosen out from among all the Christians in Rome as one whom soft words and bribes and the hope of life could seduce from Christ. Cease, Varus, then; these words are vain. Such as I have been, I am, and shall be to the end--a Christian!'

'To the rack with the Christian then!' shouted many voices from the crowd.

Varus enforced silence.

'Probus,' said he, as order was restored, 'I shall still hope the best for thee. Thou art of different stuff from him whom we first had before us, and leisure for reflection may bring thee to another mind. I shall not therefore condemn thee either to the rack or to death. Soldiers, bear him to the prisons at the Fabrician bridge.'

Whereupon he was led from the tribunal, and conducted by a guard to the place of his confinement.

* * * * *

The fate of Probus we now regard as sealed. In what manner he will finally be disposed of it is vain to conjecture, so various are the ways, each one more ingenious in cruelty than another, in which Christians are made to suffer and die. Standing as he does, as virtually the head of the Christian community, we can anticipate for him a death only of more refined barbarity.

Felix too, we learn, is confined in the same prison: and with him all the other principal Christians of Rome.

* * * * *

We have visited Probus in his confinement. You do not remember, Fausta, probably you never saw, the prison at the Fabrician bridge. It seems a city itself, so vast is it, and of so many parts, running upwards in walls and towers to a dizzy height, and downwards to unknown depths, where it spreads out in dungeons never visited by the light of day. In this prison, now crowded with the Christians, did we seek our friend. We were at once, upon making known our want, shown to the cell in which he was confined.

We found him, as we entered, seated and bending over a volume which he was reading, aided by the faint light afforded by a lamp which his jailer had furnished him. He received us with cheerfulness, and at his side on the single block of stone which the cell provided for its inmates, we sat and long conversed. I expressed my astonishment that the favor of a lamp had been allowed him. 'It is not in accordance,' I said, 'with the usages of this place.'

'You will be still more amazed,' he replied, 'when I tell you through whose agency I enjoy it.'

'You must inform us,' we said, 'for we cannot guess.'

'Isaac's;' he replied. 'At least I can think of no other to whom the description given me by the jailer corresponds. He told me upon bringing it to me, that a kind-hearted old man, a Jew, as he believed him, had made inquiry about me, and had entreated earnestly for all such privileges and favors, as the customs of the place would allow. He has even procured me the blessing of this friendly light--and what is more yet and which fills me with astonishment--has sent me this volume, which is the true light. Can it be that Isaac has done all this, who surely never has seemed to regard me with much favor.'

'Never doubt that it is he,' said Julia; 'he has two natures, sometimes one is seen, sometimes the other--his Jew nature, and his human nature. His human heart is soft as a woman's or a child's. One so full of the spirit of love I have never known. At times in his speech, you would think him a man bloody and severe as Aurelian himself; but in his deeds he is almost more than a Christian.'

'As the true circumcision,' said Probus, 'is that of the heart, and as he is a Jew who is one inwardly, so is he only a Christian who does the deeds of one and has the heart of one. And he who does those deeds, and has that heart--what matters it by what name he is called? Isaac is a Christian, in the only important sense of the word--and, alas! that it should be so, more than many a one who bears the name. But does this make Christ to be of none effect? Not so. The natural light, which lightens every man who cometh into the world will, here and there, in every place, and in every age, bring forth those who shall show themselves in the perfection of their virtues to be of the very lineage of Heaven--true heirs of its glory. Isaac is such a one. But what then? For one such, made by the light of nature, the gospel gives us thousands. But how is it, Piso, in the city? Are the wolves still abroad?'

'They are. The people have themselves turned informers, soldiers, and almost executioners. However large may be the proportion of the friendly or the neutral in the city, they dare not show themselves. The mob of those devoted to Aurelian constitutes now the true sovereignty of Rome--the streets are theirs--the courts are theirs--and anon the games will be theirs.'

'I am given to understand,' said Probus, 'that to-morrow I suffer; yet have I received from the Prefect no warning to that effect. It is the judgment of my keeper.'

'I have heard the same,' I answered, 'but I know not with what truth.'

'It can matter little to me,' he replied, 'when the hour shall come, whether to-morrow or to-night.'

'It cannot,' said Julia. 'Furnished with the whole armor of the gospel, it will be an easy thing for you to encounter death.'

'It will, lady, believe me. I have many times fought with enemies of a more fearful front. The enemies of the soul are those whom the Christian most dreads. Death is but the foe of life. So the Christian may but live to virtue and God, he can easily make his account with death. It is not the pain of dying, nor the manner of it, nor any doubts or speculations about the life to come, which, at an hour like this, intrude upon the Christian's thoughts.'

'And what then,' asked Julia, as Probus paused and fell back into himself, 'is it that fills and agitates the mind? for at such a moment it can scarcely possess itself in perfect peace.'

'It is this,' replied Probus. 'Am I worthy? Have I wrought well my appointed task? Have I kept the faith? And is God my friend and Jesus my Saviour? These are the thoughts that engross and fill the mind. It is busy with the past--and with itself. It has no thoughts to spare upon suffering and death--it has no doubts or fears to remove concerning immortality. The future life, to me, stands out in the same certainty as the present. Death is but the moment which connects the two. You say well, that at such an hour as this the mind can scarce possess itself in perfect peace. Yet is it agitated by nothing that resembles fear. It is the agitation that must necessarily have place in the mind of one to whom a great trust has been committed for a long series of years, at that moment when he comes to surrender it up to him from whom it was received. I have lived many years. Ten thousand opportunities of doing good to myself and others have been set before me. The world has been a wide field of action and labor, where I have been required to sow and till against the future harvest. Must I not experience solicitude about the acts and the thoughts of so long a career? I may often have erred; I must often have stood idly by the wayside; I must many times have been neglectful, and forgetful, and wilful; I must often have sinned; and it is not all the expected glory of another life, nor all the honor of dying in the cause of Christ, nor all the triumph of a martyr's fate, that can or ought to stifle and overlay such thoughts. Still I am happy. Happy, not because I am in my own view worthy or complete, but because through Jesus Christ I am taught, in God, to see a Father. I know that in him I shall find both a just and a merciful judge; and in him who was tempted even as we are, who was of our nature and exposed to our trials, shall I find an advocate and intercessor such as the soul needs. So that, if anxious as he who is human and fallible must ever be, I am nevertheless happy and contented. My voyage is ended; the ocean of life is crossed, and I stand by the shore with joyful expectations of the word that shall bid me land and enter into the haven of my rest.'

As Probus ended these words, a low and deep murmur or distant rumbling as of thunder caught our ears, which, as we listened, suddenly increased to a terrific roar of lions, as it were directly under our feet. We instinctively sprang from where we sat, but were quieted at once by Probus:

'There is no danger,' said he; 'they are not within our apartment, nor very near us. They are a company of Rome's executioners, kept in subterranean dungeons, and fed with prisoners whom her mercy consigns to them. Sounds more horrid yet have met my ears, and may yours. Yet I hope not.'

But while he yet spoke, the distant shrieks of those who were thrust toward the den, into which from a high ledge they were to be plunged headlong, were borne to us, accompanied by the oaths and lashes of such as drove them, but which were immediately drowned by the louder roaring of the imprisoned beasts as they fell upon and fought for their prey. We sat mute and trembling with horror, till those sounds at length ceased to reverberate through the aisles and arches of the building.

'O Rome!' cried Probus, when they had died away, 'how art thou drunk with blood! Crazed by ambition, drunk with blood, drowned in sin, hardened as a millstone against all who come to thee for good, how shalt thou be redeemed? where is the power to save thee?'

'It is in thee!' said Julia. 'It is thy blood, Probus, and that of these multitudes who suffer with thee, that shall have power to redeem Rome and the world. The blood of Jesus, first shed, startled the world in its slumbers of sin and death. Thine is needed now to sound another alarm, and rouse it yet once more. And even again and again may the same sacrifice be to be offered up.'

'True, lady,' said Probus; 'it is so. And it is of that I should think. Those for whom I die should fill my thoughts, rather than any concern for my own happiness. If I might but be the instrument, by my death, of opening the eyes of this great people to their errors and their guilt, I should meet death with gratitude and joy.'

With this and such like conversation, Fausta, did we fill up a long interview with Probus. As we rose from our seats to take leave of him, not doubting that we then saw him and spoke to him for the last time, he yielded to the force of nature and wept. But this was but for a moment. Quickly restored to himself--if indeed when shedding those tears he were not more truly himself--he bade us farewell, saying with firmness and cheerfulness as he did so,

'Notwithstanding, Piso, the darkness of this hour and of all the outward prospect, it is bright within. Farewell!--to meet as I trust in Heaven!'

We returned to the Coelian.

* * * * *

When I parted from Probus, at the close of this interview, it was in the belief that I should never see him more. But I was once again in his dungeon, and then heard from him what I will now repeat to you. It was thus.

Not long after we had withdrawn from his cell on our first visit, Probus, as was his wont when alone, sat reading by that dim and imperfect light which the jailer had provided him. He presently closed the volume and laid it away. While he then sat musing, and thinking of the morrow, and of the fate which then probably awaited him, the door of his cell slowly opened. He looked, expecting to see his usual visitant the jailer, but it was a form very different from his. The door closed, and the figure advanced to where Probus sat. The gown in which it was enveloped was then let fall, and the Prefect stood before the Christian.

'Varus!' said Probus. 'Do I see aright?'

'It is Varus,' replied the Prefect. 'And your friend.'

'I would, now at least, be at friendship with all the world,' responded Probus.

'Yet,' said Varus, 'your friends must be few, that you should be left in this place of horror, alone, to meet your fate.'

'I have no friend powerful enough, on earth at least, to cope with the omnipotence of Aurelian,' replied Probus.

'Thy friends, Christian, are more, and more potent than thou dreamest of. As I said to thee before, even Aurelian esteems thee.'

'Strange, that, if he esteems me, as thou sayest, he should thrust me within the lions' den, with prospect of no escape but into their jaws. And can I suppose that his esteem is worth much to me who crowds his prisons with those who are nearest to me, reserving them there for a death the most cruel and abhorred?'

'He may esteem thee, Probus, and not thy faith. 'Tis so with me. I like not thy faith, but truly do I say it, I like thee, and would fain serve and save thee. Nay, 'tis thy firmness and thy zeal in the cause thou hast espoused that wins me. I honor those virtues. But, Probus, in thee they are dangerous ones. The same qualities in a worthier cause would make thee great. That which thou hast linked thyself to, Christian, is a downward and a dying one. Its doom is sealed. The word of Aurelian is gone forth, and, before the Ides, the blood of every Christian in Rome shall flow--and not in Rome only, but throughout the empire. The forces are now disposing over the whole of this vast realm, which, at a sign from the great Head, shall fall upon this miserable people, and their very name shall vanish from the earth. It is vain to contend. It is but the struggling of a man with the will and the arm of Jove--'

'Varus!--' Probus began.

'Nay,' said the Prefect, 'listen first. This faith of thine, Christian, which can thus easily be destroyed, cannot be that divine and holy thing thou deemest it. So judges Porphyrius, and all of highest mark here in Rome. It is not to be thought of one moment as possible, that what a God made known to man for truth, he should afterward leave defenceless, to be trodden to the dust, and its ministers and disciples persecuted, tormented, and exterminated by human force. Christian, thou hast been deceived--and all thy fellows are in the like delusion. Do thou then save both thyself and them. It is in thy power to stop all this effusion of blood, and restore unity and peace to an empire now torn and bleeding in every part.'

'And how, Varus--seeing thou wouldst that I should hear all--how shall it be done?'

'Embrace, Probus, the faith of Rome--the faith of thy father, venerable for piety as for years--the faith of centuries, and of millions of our great progenitors and thou art safe, and all thine are safe.'

Probus was silent.

'Aurelian bids me say,' continued the Prefect, 'that doing this, there is not a wish of thy heart, for thyself, or for those who are dear to thee, but it shall be granted. Wealth, more than miser ever craved, office and place lower but little than Aurelian's own, shall be thine--'

'Varus! if there is within thee the least touch of humanity, cease! Thy words have sunk into these dead walls as far as into me; yet have they entered far enough to have wounded the soul through and through. Not, Varus, though to all thou hast said and promised thou shouldst add Rome itself and the empire, and still to that the subject kingdoms of the East and West, with their treasures, and the world itself, would I prove false to myself, my faith, and my God. Nor canst thou think me base enough for such a deed. This is no great virtue in me, Varus. I hold it not such; nor may you. Go through the secret chambers of these prisons with the same rich bribe upon thy tongue, and not one so fallen wouldst thou find that he would hear thee through as I have done. Varus, thou knowest not what a Christian is! Thou canst not conceive how little a thing life is in his regard set by the side of truth. I grieve that ever I should have been so esteemed by thee as to warrant the proffers thou hast made. This injures more and deeper than these bonds, or than all thine array of engines or of beasts.'

'Be not the fool and madman,' said the Prefect, 'to cast away from thee the mercy I have brought. Except on the terms I have now named, I say there is hope neither for thee, nor for one of this faith in Rome, how ever high their name or rank.'

'That can make no change in my resolve, Varus.'

'Consider, Probus, well. As by thy renunciation thou couldst save thyself, I now tell thee that the lives of those whom thou holdest nearest, hang also upon thy word. Assent to what I have offered, and Piso and Julia live! Reject it, and they die!'

Varus paused; but Probus spoke not. He went on.

'Christian, are not these dear to thee? Demetrius too, and Felix? Where are the mercies of thy boasted faith, if thy heart is left thus hard? Truly thou mightest as well have lived and died a Pagan.'

'Again I say, Varus, thou knowest not what a Christian is. We put truth before life; and if by but a word that should deny the truth in Christ, or any jot or tittle of it, I could save the life of Piso, Julia, Felix, Demetrius, nay, and all in Rome who hold this faith, my tongue should be torn from my mouth before that word should be spoken. And so wouldst thou find every Christian here in Rome. Why then urge me more? Did Macer hear thee?'

'I hold thee, Probus, a wiser man than he. All Rome knew him mad. Cast not away thy life. Live, and tomorrow's sun shall see thee First in Rome!'

'Varus! why is this urgency? Think me not a fool and blind. Thou knowest, and Fronto and Aurelian know, that one apostate would weigh more for your bad cause than a thousand headless trunks; and so with cruel and insulting craft you weave your snares and pile to Heaven your golden bribes. Begone, Varus, and say to Aurelian, if in truth he sent thee on thy shameful errand, that, in the Fabrician prison, in the same dungeon where he cast Probus the Christian, there still lives Probus the Roman, who reveres what he once revered and loved, truth, and whom his bribes cannot turn from his integrity.'

'Die then, idiot, in thy integrity! Thou hast thrown scorn upon one, who has power and the will to pay it back in a coin it may little please thee to take it in. If there be one torment, Galilean, sharper than another, it shall be thine tomorrow; and for one moment that Macer passed upon my irons, there shall be hours for thee. Not till the flesh be peeled inch by inch from thy bones, and thy vitals look through thy ribs, and thy brain boil in its hot case, and each particular nerve be stretched till it break, shall thy life be suffered to depart. Then, what the tormentors shall have left, the dogs of the streets shall devour. Now, Christian, let us see if thy God, beholding thy distress, will pity and deliver thee.'

Saying these words, his countenance transformed by passion to that of a demon, he turned and left the cell.

Never, Fausta, I feel assured, did Aurelian commission Varus with such an errand. Fallen though he be, he has not yet fallen to that lowest deep. Varus doubtless hoped to prevail over Probus by his base proposals, and by such triumph raise his fortunes yet higher with Aurelian. It was a game worth playing--so he judged, and perhaps wisely--and worth a risk. For doubtless one apostate of the rank of Probus would have been of more avail to them, as Probus said to him, than a thousand slain. For nothing do the judges so weary themselves, and exhaust their powers of persuasion, as to induce the

Christians who are brought before them to renounce their faith. So desirous are they of this, that they have caused, in many instances, those who were no Christians to be presented at their tribunals, who have then, after being threatened with torture and death, renounced a faith which they never professed. Once and again has this farce been acted before the Roman people. Their real triumphs of this sort have as yet been very few; and the sensation which they produced was swallowed up and lost in the glory--in the eyes even of the strangers who are in Rome--which has crowned us in the steadfast courage with which our people have remained quietly in their homes, throughout all this dreadful preparation, and then, when the hour of trial drew nigh, and they were placed at the bar of the judge, and were accused of their religion, confessed the charge, boasted of it, and then took their way to the prison, from which, they well knew, death only would deliver them.

* * * * *

That, Fausta, which we have long feared and looked for, has come to pass, and Probus, our more than friend, our benefactor, and almost our parent, is, by the Emperor, condemned to death; not, as from the words of Varus it might be supposed, to the same torments as those to which Macer was made subject; but to be thrown to the beasts in the Flavian, a death more merciful than that, but yet full of horror. How is it that, in the Roman, mercy seems dead, and the human nature, which he received from the gods, changed to that of the most savage beast!

Livia has been with us; and here, with us, would she now gladly remain. It is impossible, she says, for us to conceive the height of the frenzy to which Aurelian is now wrought up against the Christians. In his impatience, he can scarce restrain himself from setting his Legions in the neighboring camp at once to the work of slaughter. But he is, strange as it may seem, in this held back and calmed by the more bloody-minded, but yet more politic, Fronto. Fronto would have the work thoroughly accomplished; and that it may be so, he adheres to a certain system of order and apparent moderation, from which Aurelian would willingly break away and at once flood the streets of Rome in a new deluge of blood. Livia is now miserable and sad, as she was, but a few months ago, gay and happy. At the palace, she tells us, she hears no sounds but the harsh and grating voice of Fronto, or the smooth and silvery tones of Varus. As soon, she says, as Aurelian shall have departed for the East, shall she dwell either with us, or fly to the quiet retreat of Zenobia, at Tibur.

* * * * *

The day appointed for the death of Probus has arrived, and never did the sun shine upon a fairer one in Rome. It seems as if some high festival were come, for all Rome is afoot. Heralds parade the streets, proclaiming the death of Probus, Felix, and other Christians, in the Flavian, at the hour of noon. At the corner of every street, and at all the public places, the name of "Probus the Christian, condemned to the beasts," meets the eye. Long before the time of the sacrifice had come, the avenues leading to the theatre, and all the neighborhood of it, were crowded with the excited thousands of those who desired to witness the spectacle. There was little of beauty, wealth, fashion, or nobility in Rome that was not represented in the dense multitude that filled the seats of the boundless amphitheatre. Probus had said to me, at my last interview with him, 'Piso, you may think it a weakness in me, but I would that one at least, whose faith is mine, and whose heart beats as mine, might be with me at the final hour. I would, at that hour, meet one eye that can return the glance of friendship. It will be a source of strength to me, and I know not how much I may need it.' I readily promised what he asked, though, as you may believe, Fausta, I would willingly have been spared the trial. So that making part of that tide pouring toward the centre, I found myself borne along at the appointed hour to the scene of suffering and death.

As I was about to pass beneath the arched-way which leads to the winding passages within, I heard myself saluted by a well-known voice, and, turning to the quarter whence it came, beheld Isaac, but without his pack, and in a costume so different from that which he usually wears, that at first I doubted the report of my eyes. But the sound of his voice, as he again addressed me, assured me it could be no other than he.

'Did I not tell thee, Piso,' said he, 'that, when the Christian was in his straits, there thou wouldst see the Jew, looking on, and taking his sport? This is for Probus the very end I looked for. And how should it be otherwise? Is he to live and prosper, who aims at the life of that to which God has given being and authority? Shall he flourish in pride and glory who hath helped to pull down what God built up? Not so, Piso. 'Tis no wonder that the Christians are now in this plight. It could be no otherwise. And in every corner of this huge fabric wilt thou behold some of my tribe looking on upon this sight, or helping at the sacrifice. Yet, as thou knowest, I am not among them. There is no hope for Probus, Piso?'

'None, Isaac. All Rome could not save him.'

'Truly,' rejoined the Jew, 'he is in the lion's den. Yet as the prophet Daniel was delivered, so may it be to him. God is over all.'

'God is, indeed, over all,' I said; 'but he leaves us with our natural passions, affections, and reason, to work out our own way through the world. We are the better for it.'

'Doubtless,' said Isaac. 'Yet at times, when we look not for it, and from a quarter we dream not of, deliverance comes. So was it to Abraham, when he thought that by his own hand Isaac his son must be slain. But why to a Christian should I speak of these? Dost thou witness the sacrifice, Piso?'

'Yes, at the earnest entreaty of Probus himself.'

'I, too, shall be there. We shall both then see what shall come to pass.'

So saying, he moved away toward the lower vaults, where are the cages of the beasts, and I passed on and ascended the flight of steps leading to that part of the interior where it is the custom of Aurelian to sit. The Emperor was not as yet arrived, but the amphitheatre, in every part of it, was already filled with its countless thousands. All were seated idly conversing, or gazing about as at the ordinary sports of the place. The hum of so many voices struck the ear like the distant roar of the ocean. How few of those thousands--not one perhaps--knew for what it was that Probus and his companions were now about to suffer a most cruel and abhorred death! They knew that their name was Christian, and that Christian was of the same meaning as enemy of the gods and of the empire; but what it was which made the Christian so willing to die, why it was he was so ready to come to that place of horror and give up his body to the beasts--this they knew not. It was to them a riddle they could not read. And they sat and looked on with the same vacant unconcern, or with the same expectation of pleasure, as if they were to witness the destruction of murderers and assassins. This would not have been so, had that class of the citizens of Rome, or any of them, been present, who, regarding us with favor, and hoping that somewhat might yet come of our religion advantageous to the world, maintain a neutral position. These were not there; owing, both to their disinclination to witness scenes so brutalizing, and to apprehensions lest they should be betrayed into words or acts of sympathy, that might lead to their being confounded with the obnoxious tribe, and exposed to the like dangers. All, therefore, within the embrace of those wide-spreading walls were of one heart and one mind.

While I sat waiting the coming of the Emperor, and surrounded by those whom I knew not nor had ever seen, one who occupied a part of the same seat, accompanied by his wife and daughters, said to me,

"Tis to be hoped, sir, that so terrible an example as this will have its effect in deterring others from joining this dangerous superstition, and not only that, but strike so wholesome a terror into those who already profess it, that they shall at once abandon it, and so the general massacre of them not be necessary; which, indeed, I should be loth to witness in the streets of Rome.'

'If you knew,' I replied, 'for what it is these people are condemned to such sufferings, you would not, I am sure, express yourself in that manner. You know, I may presume, only what common report has brought to your ears.'

'Nothing else, I admit,' he replied. 'My affairs confine me from morning till night. I am a secretary, sir, in the office of the public mint. I have no time to inform myself of the exact truth of any thing but columns of figures. I am not afraid to say there is not a better accountant within the walls of Rome. But as for other things, especially as to the truth in matters of this sort, I know nothing, and can learn nothing. I follow on as the world leads.'

'I dare say,' I replied, 'you have spoken the truth. And every one here present, were he to speak, would make very much the same declaration. So here are eighty thousand citizens of Rome assembled to witness the destruction of men, of whose crime they know nothing, yet rejoicing in their death as if they were murderers or robbers! Were you charged with a false enumeration of your columns, would not you hold it basest injustice to suffer punishment before pains were taken to learn the exact truth in the case? But are you not acting the same unjust and cruel part--with all who are here--in looking on and approving the destruction of these men, about whose offence you know nothing, and have taken no pains to inquire?'

'By the gods!' exclaimed his wife, who seemed the sharper spirit of the two, 'I believe we have a Christian here! But however that may be, we should be prettily set to work, whenever some entertainment is in prospect, to puzzle ourselves about the right and the wrong in the matter. If we are to believe you, sir, whenever a poor wretch is to be thrown to the beasts, before we can be in at the sport we must settle the question--under the law I suppose-- whether the condemnation be just or not! Ha! ha! Our life were in that case most light and agreeable! The Prefect himself would not have before him a more engaging task. Gods! Cornelia dear, see what a pair of eyes!'

'Where, mother?'

'There! in that old man's head. They burn and twinkle like coals of fire. I should think he must be a Christian.'

I was not sorry that a new object had attracted the attention of this lady of the secretary; and looking where she pointed, I saw Isaac planted below us and near the arena. At the same moment the long peal of trumpets, and the shouts of the people without, gave note of the approach and entrance of the Emperor. In a moment more, with his swift step, he entered the amphitheatre, and strode to the place set apart for him, the whole multitude rising and saluting him with a burst of welcome that might have been heard beyond the walls of Rome. The Emperor acknowledged the salutation by rising from his seat and lifting the crown from his head. He was instantly seated again, and at a sign from him the herald made proclamation of the entertainments which were to follow. He who was named as the first to suffer was Probus.

When I heard his name pronounced, with the punishment which awaited him, my resolution to remain forsook me, and I turned to rush from the theatre. But my recollection of Probus's earnest entreaties that I would be there, restrained me and I returned to my seat. I considered, that as I would attend the dying bed of a friend, so I was clearly bound to remain where I was, and wait for the last moments of this my more than Christian friend; and the circumstance that his death was to be shocking and harrowing to the friendly heart was not enough to absolve me from the heavy obligation. I therefore kept my place, and awaited with patience the event.

I had waited not long when, from beneath that extremity of the theatre where I was sitting, Probus was led forth and conducted to the centre of the arena, where was a short pillar to which it was customary to bind the sufferers. Probus, as he entered, seemed rather like one who came to witness what was there than to be himself the victim, so free was his step, so erect his form. In his face there might indeed be seen an expression, that could only dwell on the countenance of one whose spirit was already gone beyond the earth, and holding converse with things unseen. There is always much of this in the serene, uplifted face of this remarkable man; but it was now there written in lines so bold and deep, that there could have been few in that vast assembly but must have been impressed by it, as never before by aught human. It must have been this, which brought so deep a silence upon that great multitude--not the mere fact that an individual was about to be torn by lions--that is an almost daily pastime. For it was so, that when he first made his appearance, and as he moved toward the centre, turned and looked round upon the crowded seats rising to the heavens, the people neither moved nor spoke, but kept their eyes fastened upon him as by some spell which they could not break.

When he had reached the pillar, and he who had conducted him was about to bind him to it, it was plain, by what at that distance we could observe, that Probus was entreating him to desist and leave him at liberty; in which he at length succeeded, for that person returned, leaving him alone and unbound. O sight of misery!--he who for the humblest there present would have performed any office of love, by which the least good should redound to them, left alone and defenceless, they looking on and scarcely pitying his cruel fate!

When now he had stood there not many minutes, one of the doors of the vivaria was suddenly thrown back, and bounding forth with a roar, that seemed to shake the walls of the theatre, a lion of huge dimensions leaped upon the arena. Majesty and power were inscribed upon his lordly limbs; and as he stood there where he had first sprung, and looked round upon the multitude, how did his gentle eye and noble carriage, with which no one for a moment could associate meanness, or cruelty, or revenge, cast shame upon the human monsters assembled to behold a solitary, unarmed man torn limb from limb! When he had in this way looked upon that cloud of faces, he then turned and moved round the arena through its whole circumference, still looking upwards upon those who filled the seats--not till he had come again to the point from which he started, so much as noticing him who stood, his victim, in the midst. Then--as if apparently for the first time becoming conscious of his presence--he caught the form of Probus; and moving slowly towards him, looked steadfastly up-upon him, receiving in return the settled gaze of the Christian. Standing there, still, awhile--each looking upon the other--he then walked round him, then approached nearer, making, suddenly and for a moment, those motions which indicate the roused appetite; but as it were in the spirit of self-rebuke, he immediately retreated a few paces and lay down in the sand, stretching out his head toward Probus, and closing his eyes as if for sleep.

The people, who had watched in silence, and with the interest of those who wait for their entertainment, were both amazed and vexed, at what now appeared to be the dulness and stupidity of the beast. When however he moved not from his place, but seemed as if he were indeed about to fall into a quiet sleep, those who occupied the lower seats began both to cry out to him and shake at him their caps, and toss about their arms in the hope to rouse him. But it was all in vain; and at the command of the Emperor he was driven back to his den.

Again a door of the vivaria was thrown open, and another of equal size, but of a more alert and rapid step, broke forth, and, as if delighted with his sudden liberty and the ample range, coursed round and round the arena, wholly regardless both of the people and of Probus, intent only as it seemed upon his own amusement. And when at length he discovered Probus standing in his place, it was but to bound toward him as in frolic, and then wheel away in pursuit of a pleasure he esteemed more highly than the satisfying of his hunger.

At this, the people were not a little astonished, and many who were near me hesitated not to say, "that there might be some design of the gods in this." Others said plainly, but not with raised voices, "An omen! an omen!" At the same time Isaac turned and looked at me with an expression of countenance which I could not interpret. Aurelian meanwhile exhibited many signs of impatience; and when it was evident the animal could not be wrought up, either by the cries of the people, or of the keepers, to any act of violence, he too was taken away. But when a third had been let loose, and with no better effect, nay, with less--for he, when he had at length approached Probus, fawned upon him, and laid himself at his feet--the people, superstitious as you know beyond any others, now cried out aloud, "An omen! an omen!" and made the sign that Probus should be spared and removed.

Aurelian himself seemed almost of the same mind, and I can hardly doubt would have ordered him to be released, but that Fronto at that moment approached him, and by a few of those words, which, coming from him, are received by Aurelian as messages from Heaven, put within him a new and different mind; for rising quickly from his seat he ordered the keeper of the vivaria to be brought before him. When he appeared below upon the sands, Aurelian cried out to him,

'Why, knave, dost thou weary out our patience thus--letting forth beasts already over-fed? Do thus again, and thou thyself shall be thrown to them. Art thou too a Christian?'

'Great Emperor,' replied the keeper, 'than those I have now let loose, there are not larger nor fiercer in the imperial dens, and since the sixth hour of yesterday they have tasted nor food nor drink. Why they have thus put off their nature 'tis hard to guess, unless the general cry be taken for the truth, "that the gods have touched them."'

Aurelian was again seen to waver, when a voice from the benches cried out,

'It is, O Emperor, but another Christian device! Forget not the voice from the temple! The Christians, who claim powers over demons, bidding them go and come at pleasure, may well be thought capable to change, by the magic imputed to them, the nature of a beast.'

'I doubt not,' said the Emperor, 'but it is so. Slave! throw up now the doors of all thy vaults, and let us see whether both lions and tigers be not too much for this new necromancy. If it be the gods who interpose, they can shut the mouths of thousands as of one.

At those cruel words, the doors of the vivaria were at once flung open, and an hundred of their fierce tenants, maddened both by hunger and the goads that had been applied, rushed forth, and in the fury with which in a single mass they fell upon Probus--then kneeling upon the sands--and burying him beneath them, no one could behold his fate, nor, when that dark troop separated and ran howling about the arena in search of other victims, could the eye discover the least vestige of that holy man.---- I then fled from the theatre as one who flies from that which is worse than death.

Felix was next offered up, as I have learned, and after him more than fourscore of the Christians of Rome.

Rome continues the same scene of violence, cruelty and blood. Each moment are the miserable Christians dragged through the streets either to the tribunals of the judges, or thence, having received their doom, to the prisons.

Seeing, Fausta, that the Emperor is resolved that we shall not be among the sufferers, and that he is also resolved upon the total destruction of all within the walls of Rome, from which purpose no human power can now divert him, we feel ourselves no longer bound to this spot, and are determined to withdraw from it, either to Tibur or else to you. Were there any office of protection or humanity, which it were in our power to perform toward the accused or the condemned, you may believe that we should remain fixed to the post of duty. But the fearful sweep which is making, and yet to be made, of every living soul in Rome, leaves nothing for us to do but to stand idle and horror-struck witnesses of sufferings and wrongs, which we can do nothing to avert or relieve. Portia shares our sorrows, and earnestly entreats us to depart, consenting herself to accompany us.

* * * * *

After seeing Zenobia at Tibur, and conversing with her and Livia, whom I found there, we have resolved upon Palmyra, and already have I engaged a vessel bound to Berytus. A brief interval will alone be needful for our preparations. Portia goes with us.

* * * * *

In the midst of these preparations, news is brought us by Milo that Aurelian, hastened by accounts of disturbances in the army, has suddenly started for Thrace. But I see not that this can interfere with our movements, unless indeed.... What can mean this sudden uproar in the streets?--and now within the house itself.... My fears are true....

* * * * *

Fausta, I am a prisoner in the hands of Fronto. I now write in chains, and Julia stands at my side bound also. I have obtained with difficulty this grace, to seal my letter, and bid you farewell.

* * * * *

Thus were Piso and Julia at length in the grasp of the cruel and relentless Fronto. Aurelian's sudden departure from Rome placed the whole conduct of the enterprise he had undertaken in the hands of Varus and the priest, who were left by the Emperor with full powers to carry on and complete the work which he had begun. It was his purpose however, so soon as the difficulties in the army should be composed, himself immediately to return, and remain till the task were ended--the great duty done. But, as many causes might conspire to prevent this, they were clothed with sovereign authority to do all that the welfare of the city and the defence and security of religion might require. I will not charge Aurelian with an unnecessary absence at this juncture, that so he might turn over to his tools a work, at which his own humanity and conscience, hardened as they were, revolted--or rather that they, voluntarily, and moved only by their own superstitious and malignant minds might then be free to do what they might feel safe in believing would be an acceptable service to their great master. I will still believe, that, had he intended the destruction of Piso and Julia, he would, with that courage which is natural to him, have fearlessly and unshrinkingly done the deed himself. I will rather suppose that his ministers, without warrant from him, and prompted by their own hate alone, ventured upon that dark attempt, trusting, when it should have once been accomplished, easily to obtain the pardon of him, who, however he might affect or feel displeasure for a moment, would secretly applaud and thank them for the deed.

However this may be, Aurelian suddenly departed from Rome, and Fronto and Varus filled his place; and their first act of authority was the seizure of Piso and the Princess. At Tibur we knew nothing of these events till they were passed; we caring not to hear of the daily horrors that were acted in the city, and feeling as secure of the safety of Piso and Julia as of our own.

It was on a gloomy winter evening when they were borne away from their home upon the Coelian to the dark vaults beneath the Temple of the Sun, Fronto's own province. But here again let Piso speak for himself, as I find recorded in the fragment of a letter.

* * * * *

* * * The darkness of the night scarce permitted me to see, he says, whither we were borne, but when the guard stopped and required us to alight from the carriage in which we had been placed, I perceived that we were at the steps of the temple--victims therefore in his own regions of a man, as much more savage than Aurelian, as he than a beast of the forest. We were denied the happiness of being confined in the same place, but were thrust into separate dungeons, divided by walls of solid rock. Here, when wearied out by watching, I fell asleep. How long this lasted I cannot tell; I was wakened by the withdrawing of the bolts of my door. One, bearing a dim light, slowly opening the door, entered. Forgetting my condition I essayed to rise, but my heavy chains bound me to the floor. Soon as the noise of my motion caught the ear of the person who had entered, he said,

'So; all is safe. I am not thy keeper, sir Piso, but 'tis my province to keep the keeper--that is--visit thee every hour to see that thou art here. Yet, by the gods! if you Christians have that power of magic, which is commonly reported of you, I see not of what use it were to watch you thus. How is it with thee, most noble Piso?'

'That is of little moment; but tell me, if there is anything human in thee, where is the Princess Julia, and what is her fate?'

'Be not too much concerned,' he replied. 'She is safe, I warrant you. None but Fronto deals with her.'

'Fronto!' I could only say.

'Yes, Fronto. Fear not, he is an honorable man and a holy priest.'

'Fronto!' I was about to add more, but held my peace; knowing well that what I might say could avail nothing for us, and might be turned against us. I only asked, 'why there was such delay in examining and condemning us?'

'That is a question truly,' he replied; 'but not so easy to be answered. Few know the reason, that I can say. But what is there in the heart of Pronto that is kept from Curio? Are thy chains easy, Piso?'

'I would that they might be lengthened. Here am I bound to the floor without so much as the power to stand upright. This is useless suffering.'

'Twas so ordered by Fronto; but then if there is one in Rome who can take a liberty with him, I know well who he is. So hold thou the lamp, Piso, and I will ease thee;' and, like one accustomed to the art, he soon struck apart the chain, and again uniting it left me room, both to stand and move.

'There,' said he, as he took again the lamp, 'for one who hates a Christian as he does death, that's a merciful deed. But I can tell thee one thing, that it will not ease thee long.'

'That I can believe. But why, once more, is there this delay?'

'I know not, Piso, whether I should tell thee, but as I doubt not Fronto would, were he here, I surely may do the same, for if there are two men in Rome, Piso, whose humors are the same and jump together, I and Fronto are they. There is a dispute then, noble Piso, between Varus and Fronto about the lady Julia--' and without heeding my cries the wretch turned and left the vault, closing after him the heavy door.

How many days, in the torture of a suspense and ignorance worse than death, I lay here, I cannot tell. Curio came as often as he said to see that all was safe, but there was little said by either; he would examine my chain and then depart. On the night--the last night I passed in that agony--preceding my examination by Varus and Fronto, I was disturbed from my slumbers by the entrance of Curio. He advanced with as it seemed to me an unusually cautious step, and I rose expecting some communication of an uncommon nature. But what was my amazement, as the light fell upon the face of him who bore it, to see not Curio but Isaac. His finger was on his lips, while in his hand he held the implements necessary for sawing apart my chains.

'Piso!' said he in a whispered tone, 'thou art now free,--I could not save Probus, but I can save thee--horses fleet as the winds await thee and the Princess beyond the walls, and at the Tiber's mouth a vessel takes you to Berytus. Curio lies drunk or dead, it matters little which, in a neighboring vault.' And he set down the lamp and seized my chain. The strange devotion of this man moved me; and, were it but to reward his love, I could almost have slipped my bonds. But other thoughts prevailed.

'Isaac, you have risked your life and that of your household in this attempt; and sorry am I that I can pay thee only with my thanks. I cannot fly.'

'Piso! thou surely art not mad? Why shouldst thou stay in the hands of these pagan butchers--'

'Were this, Isaac, but the private rage of Fronto, gladly would I go with thee--more gladly would I give Julia to thy care. But it is not so. It is, as thou knowest, for our faith that we are here and thus; and shall we shrink from what Probus bore?'

'Piso, believe me--'tis not for thy faith alone that thou art here, but for thy riches, and thy wife--'

'Isaac! thou hast been deceived. Sooner would they throw themselves into a lion's den for sport, than brave the wrath of Aurelian for such a crime. Thou hast been deceived.'

'I have it,' replied the Jew, 'from the mouth of the miscreant Curio, who has told me of fierce disputes, overheard by him, between Varus and Pronto concerning the lady Julia.'

'Their dispute has been, doubtless, whether she too should be destroyed; for to Fronto is well known the constant love which Aurelian still bears her. Curio is not always right.'

'And is this my answer, Piso?' said Isaac. 'And, if I cannot prevail with thee, shall I not still see thy wife? Over her perchance--'

'No, Isaac; it would be of no avail. Her answer would be the same as mine.'

'Nevertheless, Piso, I believe that what I have heard and surmised is so. Fronto and Varus, who have played with the great Aurelian as a toyman with his images, may carry even this.'

'Were it so, I put my trust in God, and to him commend myself and Julia. For this our faith are we ready to bear all that man can devise or do.'

Seeing that further argument was vain, Isaac, with eyes that overflowed as any woman's, embraced me and left the cell.

* * * * *

On the day which followed the visit of Isaac was I placed before Fronto and Varus.

It was in the great room of the temple that the Prefect and the Priest awaited their victims. It was dimly illuminated, so that the remoter parts were lost in thick darkness. So far as the eye could penetrate it, a crowd of faces could be discerned in the gloom, of those who were there to witness the scene. All, whom my sight could separate from the darkness, were of the Roman priesthood, or friends of Fronto. Not that others were excluded--it was broad day, and the act was a public one, and authorized by the imperial edict--but that no announcement of it had been made; and by previous concert the place had been filled with the priests and subordinate ministers of the Roman temples. I knew therefore that not a friendly eye or arm was there. Whatever it might please those cruel judges to inflict upon myself or Julia,--there was none to remonstrate or interpose. With what emotions, when I had first been placed before those judges, did I await the coming of Julia, from whom I had now been so long parted! Fervently did I pray that the mercy of Fronto would first doom her, that she might be sure of at least one sympathising and pitying heart.

On the right of the Prefect, upon a raised platform, were set the various instruments of torture and death, each attended by its half naked minister.

I had not stood long, when upon the other side of the room the noise of the dividing crowd told me that Julia was entering, and in a moment more she was standing at a little distance from me, and opposite Fronto--I being opposite the Prefect. Our eyes met once--and no more. As I could have desired, Fronto first addressed her.

'Woman! thou standest here charged with impiety and denial of the gods of Rome; in other words, with being a follower of Christ the Nazarene. That the charge is true, witnesses stand here ready to affirm. Dost thou deny the charge? Then will we prove its truth.'

'I deny it not,' responded Julia, 'but confess it. Witnesses are not needed. The Christian witnesses for himself.'

'Dost thou know the penalty that waits on such confession?'

'I know it, but do not fear it.'

'But for thee to die so, woman, is of ill example to all in Rome. We would rather change thee. We would not have thee die the enemy of the gods, of Rome, and of thyself. I ask thee then to renounce thy vain impiety!'

Julia answered not.

'I require thee, Christian, to renounce Christ!'

Still Julia made no reply.

'Know you not, woman, I have power to force from thee that, which thou wilt not say willingly?'

'Thou hast no such power, Priest. Thou wert else God.'

'Thy tender frame cannot endure the torture of those engines. It were better spared such suffering.'

'I would gladly be spared that suffering,' said Julia; 'but not at the expense of truth.'

'Think not that I will relent. Those irons shall rack and rend thee in every bone and joint, except thou dost renounce that foul impostor, whose curse now lies heavy upon Rome and the world.'

'Weary me not, Priest, with vain importunity. I am a Christian, and a Christian will I die.'

'Prepare then the rack!' cried Fronto, his passions rising; 'that is the medicine for obstinacy such as this. Now bind her to it.'

Hearing that, I wildly exclaimed,

'Priest! thou dar'st not do it for thy life! Touch but the hair of her head, and thy life shall answer it. Aurelian's word is pledged, and thou dar'st not break it.'

'Aurelian is far enough from here,' replied the priest. 'But were he where I am, thou wouldst see the same game. I am Aurelian now.'

'Is this then thy commission, had from Aurelian?'

'That matters not, young Piso. 'Tis enough for thee to know that Fronto rules in Rome. No more! Hold now thy peace! Where an Empress has sued in vain, there is no room for words from thee. Slaves! bind her, I say! To the rack with her!'

At that I sprang madly forward, thinking only of her rescue from those murderous fangs, but was at the same instant drawn violently back both by my chains and the arms of those who guarded me. The tormentors descended from their engines to fulfil the commands of Fronto, and, laying hold of Julia, bore her, without an opposing word, or look, or motion, toward their instruments of death. And they were already binding her limbs to the accursed wheels, while Fronto and Varus both drew nigh to gloat over her agonies, when a distant sound, as of the ocean lashed by winds, broke upon the ears of all within that hell. Even the tormentors paused in their work, and looked at each other and at Fronto, as if asking what it should mean.

The silence of death fell upon the crowd--every ear strained to catch the still growing sound and interpret it.

"Tis but the winter wind!' cried Fronto. 'On, cowards, with your work!'

But, ere the words had left his lips, or those demons could wind the wheels of their engine, the appalling tumult of a multitude rushing toward the temple became too fearfully distinct for even Pronto or Varus to pretend to doubt its meaning. But why it was, or for what, none could guess; only upon the terror-struck forms of both the Prefect and the Priest might be read apprehensions of hostility that from some quarter was aiming at themselves. Fronto's voice was again heard:

'Bar the great doors of the temple! let not the work of the gods be profanely violated.'

But the words were too late; for, while he was yet speaking, O Fausta, how shall I paint my agony of joy! there was heard from the street and from the porch of the temple itself the shouts of as it were ten thousand voices,

"Tacitus is Emperor!" "Long live the good Tacitus!"

Freedom and life were in those cries. The crowds from the streets swept in at the doors like an advancing torrent. Varus and Fronto, followed by their myrmidons, vanished through secret doors in the walls behind them, and among the first to greet me and strike the chains from my limbs were Isaac and Demetrius.

'And where is the lady Julia?' cried Isaac.

'There!'

He flew to the platform, and, turning back the wheels, Julia was once more in my arms.

'And now,' I cried, 'what means it all? Am I awake or do I dream?'

'You are awake,' replied Demetrius. 'The tyrant is dead! and the senate and people all cry out for Tacitus.'

I now looked about me. The mob of priests was fled, and around me I beheld a thousand well-known faces of those who already had been released from their dungeons. Christians, and the friends of Christians, now filled the temple.

'We were led hither,' continued Demetrius, 'by your fast friend and the friend I believe of all, Isaac. None but he, and those to whom he gave the tidings, knew where the place of your confinement was; nor was the day of your trial publicly proclaimed, although we found the temple open. But for him we should have been, I fear, too late. But no sooner was the news of Aurelian's assassination spread through the city, than Isaac roused your friends and led the way.'

As Demetrius ceased, the name of "Tacitus Emperor," resounded again throughout the temple, and the crowds then making for the streets, about which they careered mad with joy, we were at liberty to depart; and accompanied by Isaac and Demetrius, were soon beneath our own roof upon the Coelian.

With what joy then, in our accustomed place of prayer, did we pour forth our thanksgivings to the Overruling Providence, who had not only rescued ourselves from the very jaws of death, but had wrought out this great deliverance of his whole people! Never before, Fausta, was Christianity in such peril; never was there a man, who, like Aurelian, united to a native cruelty that could behold the shedding of blood with the same indifference as the flowing of water, a zeal for the gods and a love of country that amounted quite to a superstitious madness. Had not death interposed--judging as man-- no power could have stayed that arm that was sweeping us from the face of the earth.

The prisons have all been thrown open, and their multitudes again returned to their homes. The streets and squares of the capital resound with the joyful acclamations of the people. Our churches are once more unbarred, and with the voice of music and of prayer, our people testify before Heaven their gratitude for this infinite mercy.

The suddenness of this transition, from utter hopelessness and blank despair to this fulness of peace, and these transports of joy, is almost too much for the frame to bear. Tears and smiles are upon every face. We know not whether to weep or laugh; and many, as if their reason were gone, both laugh and cry, utter prayers and jests in the same breath.

* * * * *

Soon as we found ourselves quietly in possession again of our own home, surrounded by our own household, Portia sitting with us and sharing our felicity, the same feeling impelled us at once to seek Livia and Zenobia. The Empress was, as we had already learned, at Tibur, whither she had but this morning fled, upon finding all interference of no avail, hoping--but how vainly--that possibly her mother, than whose name in Rome none was greater, save Aurelian's--might prevail, where the words had fallen but upon deaf ears and stony hearts. Our chariot bore us quickly beyond the walls, and toward the palace of the Queen. As we reached the entrance, Zenobia at the same moment, accompanied by Livia, Nicomachus, and her usual train, was mounting her horse for Rome. Our meeting I need not describe. That day and evening were consecrated to love and friendship; and many days did we pass there in the midst of satisfactions of double worth, I suppose, from the brief interval which separated them from the agonies which but so lately we had endured.

All that we have as yet learned of Aurelian is this, that he has met the fate that has waited upon so many of the masters of the world. His own soldiers have revenged themselves upon him. Going forth, as it is reported, to quell a sudden disturbance in the camp, he was set upon by a band of desperate men--made so by threats of punishment which he ever keeps--and fell pierced by a hundred swords. When more exact accounts arrive, you shall hear again.

Tacitus, who has long been the idol of the Senate, and of the best part of the people of Rome, famed, as you know, for his wisdom and his mild virtues, distinguished too for his immense wealth and the elegance of his tastes, was at once, on the news of Aurelian's death, proclaimed Emperor; not so much, however, by any formal act of the Senate, as by the unanimous will of all--senators and people. For, in order that the chance of peace may be the greater, the Senate, before any formal and public decree shall be passed, will wait the pleasure of the army. But, in the meantime, he is as truly Emperor as was Aurelian--and was, indeed, at the first moment the news of the assassination arrived. His opinions concerning the Christians also, being well known, the proclamation of his name as Augustus, was at the same time one of safety and deliverance to our whole community. No name in Rome could have struck such terror into the hearts of Varus and Fronto, as that of Tacitus--"Tacitus Emperor!"

After our happy sojourn at Tibur, and we had once more regained our home upon the Coelian, we were not long, as you may believe, in seeking the street Janus, and the dwelling of Isaac. He was happily within, and greeted us with heartiest welcome.

'Welcome, most noble Piso,' he cried, 'to the street Janus!'

'And,' I added, 'to the house of a poverty-pinched Jew! This resembles it indeed!'

'Ah! are you there, Piso? Well, well, if I have seemed poor, thou knowest why it has been, and for what. Welcome too, Princess! enter, I pray you, and when you shall be seated I shall at once show you what you have come to see, I doubt not--my assortment of diamonds. Ah! the news of your arrival has spread, and they are before me--here, Piso, is the woman of the desert, and the young Ishmael, and here, lady, are two dark-eyed nymphs of Ecbatana. Children, this is the beautiful Princess of Palmyra, whose name you have heard more than once.'

It was a pretty little circle, Fausta, as the eye need behold; and gathered together here by how strange circumstances! The very sun of peace and joy seemed breaking from the countenance of Isaac. He caressed first one and then another, nor did he know how to leave off kissing and praising them.

When we had thus sat, and made ourselves known all around to each other, Julia said to Isaac, 'that she should hope often to see him and them in the same way; but however often it might be, and at whatever other times, she begged, that annually, on the Ides of January, she with Piso might be admitted to his house and board, to keep with them all a feast of grateful recollection. Whatever it is that makes the present hour so happy to us all, we owe, Isaac, to you.'

'Lady! to the providence of the God of Abraham!'

'In you, Isaac, I behold his providence.'

'Lady, it shall be as you say--on the Ides of January, will we, as the years go round, call up to our minds these dark and bloody times, and give thanks for the great redemption. Were Probus but with you, and to be with you, Piso, your cup were full. And he had been here, but for the voice of one, who just as the third lion had been uncaged, fixed again the wavering mind of Aurelian, who then, madman-like, set on him that forest-full of beasts. At that moment, I found it, Piso, discreetest to depart.'

'And was your hand in that too, Isaac? Were those lions of your training? and that knave's lies of your telling?'

'Verily thou mayest say so.'

'But was that the part of a Jew?'

'No,' said Julia, 'it was only the part of Isaac.'

'Probus,' said Isaac, 'was the friend of Piso and Julia, and therefore he was mine. If now you ask how I love you so, I can only say, I do not know. We are riddles to ourselves. When I first saw thee, Piso, I fancied thee, and the fancy hath held till now. Now, where love is, there is power--high as heaven, deep as hell. Where there is the will, the arm is strong and the wits clear. Mountains of difficulty and seas of danger sink into mole-hills and shallow pools. Besides, Piso, there is no virtue in Rome but gold will buy it, and, as thou knowest, in that I am not wanting. Any slave like Curio, or he of the

Flavian, may be had for a basket-full of oboli. With these two clues, thou canst thread the labyrinth.'

Though our affairs, Fausta, now put on so smiling a face, we do not relinquish the thought of visiting you; and with the earliest relenting of the winter, so that a Mediterranean voyage will be both safe and pleasant, shall we turn our steps toward Palmyra.

Demetrius greatly misses his brother, But what he has lost, you have gained.

What at this moment is the great wonder in Rome is this--a letter has come from the Legions in Thrace in terms most dutiful and respectful toward the Senate, deploring the death of Aurelian, and desiring that they will place him in the number of the gods, and appoint his successor. This is all that was wanted to confirm us in our peace. Now we may indeed hail Tacitus as Augustus and Emperor. Farewell.

* * * * *

Piso has mentioned with brevity the death of Aurelian, and the manner of it as first received at Rome. I will here add to it the account which soon became current in the capital, and which to this time remains without contradiction.

Already has the name of Menestheus occurred in these memoirs. He was one of the secretaries of the Emperor, always near him and much in his confidence. This seemed strange to those who knew both, for Menestheus did not possess those qualities which Aurelian esteemed. He was selfish, covetous, and fawning; his spirit and manner those of a slave to such as were above him--those of a tyrant to such as were below him. His affection for the Emperor, of which he made great display, was only for what it would bring to him; and his fidelity to his duties which was exemplary, grew out of no principle of integrity, but was merely a part of that self-seeking policy that was the rule of his life. His office put him in the way to amass riches, and for that reason there was not one perhaps of all the servants of the Emperor who performed with more exactness the affairs entrusted to him. He had many times incurred the displeasure of Aurelian, and his just rebuke for acts of rapacity and extortion, by which, never the empire, but his own fortune was profited; but, so deep and raging was his thirst of gold, that it had no other effect than to restrain for a season a passion which was destined, in its further indulgence, to destroy both master and servant.

Aurelian had scarcely arrived at the camp without the walls of Byzantium, and was engaged in the final arrangements of the army previous to the departure for Syria--oppressed and often irritated by the variety and weight of the duties which claimed his care--when, about the hour of noon, as he was sitting in his tent, he was informed, "that one from Rome with pressing business craved to be heard of the Emperor."

He was ordered to approach.

'And why,' said Aurelian, as the stranger entered, have you sped in such haste from Rome to seek me?'

'Great Caesar, I have come for justice!'

'Is not justice well administered in the courts of Rome, that thou must pursue me here, even to the gates of Byzantium?'

'None can complain,' replied the Roman, 'that justice hath been withheld from the humblest since the reign of Aurelian--'

'How then,' interrupted Aurelian, 'how is it that thou comest hither? Quick! let us know thy matter?'

'To have held back,' the man replied, 'till the return of the army from its present expedition, and the law could be enforced, were to me more than ruin.'

'What, knave, has the army to do with thee, or thou with it? Thy matter, quick, I say.'

'Great Caesar,' rejoined the other, 'I am the builder of this tent. And from my workshops came all these various furnishings, of the true and full value of all of which I have been defrauded--'

'By whom?'

'By one near the Emperor, Menestheus the noble secretary.'

'Menestheus! Make out the case, and, by the great god of Light, he shall answer it. Be it but a farthing he hath wronged thee of, and he shall answer it. Menestheus?'

'Yes, great Emperor, Menestheus. It was thus. When the work he spoke for was done and fairly delivered to his hands, agreeing to the value of an obolus and the measure of a hair, with the strict commands he gave, what does he when he sees it, but fall into a rage and swear that 'tis not so--that the stuff is poor, the fashion mean and beggarly, the art slight and imperfect, and that the half of what I charged, which was five hundred aurelians, was all that I should have, with which, if I were not content and lisped but a syllable of blame, a dungeon for my home were the least I might expect; and if my knavery reached the ear of Aurelian, from which, if I hearkened to him, it should be his care to keep it, my life were of less value than a fly's. Knowing well the power of the man, I took the sum he proffered, hoping to make such composition with my creditors, that I might still pursue my trade, for, O Emperor, this was my first work, and being young and just venturing forth, I was dependent upon others. But, with the half price I was allowed to charge, and was paid, I cannot reimburse them. My name is gone and I am ruined.'

'The half of five hundred--say you--was that the sum, and all the sum he paid you?'

'It was. And there are here with me those that will attest it.'

'It needs not; for I myself know that from the treasury five hundred aurelians were drawn, and said, by him, for this work--which well suits me--to have been duly paid. Let but this be proved, and his life is the least that it shall cost him. But it must be well proved. Let us now have thy witnesses.'

Menestheus at this point, ignorant of the charge then making against him, entered the tent. Appalled by the apparition of the injured man, and grasping at a glance the truth, all power of concealment was gone, conscious guilt was written in the color and in every line and feature of the face.

'Menestheus!' said Aurelian, 'knowest thou this man?'

'He is Virro, an artisan of Rome;' replied the trembling slave.

'And what think you makes him here?'

The Secretary was silent.

'He has come, Menestheus, well stored with proofs, beside those which I can furnish, of thy guilt. Shall the witnesses be heard? Here they stand.'

Menestheus replied not. The very faculty of speech had left the miserable man.

'How is it,' then said Aurelian in his fiercest tones, 'how is it that again, for these paltry gains, already rolling in wealth--thou wilt defile thy own soul, and bring public shame upon me too, and Rome! Away to thy tent! and put in order thine own affairs and mine. Thou hast lived too long. Soldiers, let him be strongly guarded.--Let Virro now receive his just dues. Men call me cruel, and well I fear they may; but unjust, rapacious, never, as I believe. Whom have I wronged, whom oppressed? The poor of Rome, at least, cannot complain of Aurelian. Is it not so, sirrah?'

'Rome,' he replied, 'rejoices in the reign of Aurelian. His love of justice and of the gods, give him a place in every heart.'

Whether Aurelian would have carried into execution the threat, which in a moment of passion he had passionately uttered, none can tell. All that can be said is this, that he rarely threatened but he kept his word. This the secretary knew, and knew therefore, that another day he might never see. His cunning and his wit now stood him in good stead. A doomed man--he was a desperate man, and no act then seemed to him a crime, by which his doom might be averted. Retiring to his tent to fulfil the commands of the Emperor, he was there left alone, the tent being guarded without; and then as his brain labored in the invention of some device, by which he might yet escape the impending death, and save a life which--his good name being utterly blasted and gone, could have been but a prolonged shame--he conceived and hatched a plan, in its ingenuity, its wickedness, and atrocious baseness, of a piece with his whole character and life. In the handwriting of the Emperor, which he could perfectly imitate, he drew up a list of some of the chief officers of the army--by him condemned to death on the following day. This paper, as he was at about the eleventh hour led guarded to his place of imprisonment, he dropt at the tent door of one whose name was on it.

It fell into the intended hands; and soon as the friendly night had come the bloody scroll was borne from tent to tent,stirring up to vengeance the designated victims. No suspicion of fraud ever crossed their minds; but amazed at a thirst of blood so insatiable, and which, without cause assigned, could deliver over to the axe his best and most trusted friends, Carus, Probus, Mucapor--they doubted whether in truth his reason were not gone, and deemed it no crime, but their highest duty, to save themselves by the sacrifice of one who was no longer to be held a man.

After the noon of this day the army had made a short but quick march to Heraclea. Aurelian--the tents being pitched--the watch set--the soldiers, weary with their march, asleep--himself tired with the day's duty--sat with folded arms, having just ungirded and thrown from him his sword. His last attendant was then dismissed, who, passing from the tent door, encountered the conspirators as they rushed in, and was by them hewn to the ground. Aurelian, at that sound, sprang to his feet. But alone, with the swords of twenty of his bravest generals at his breast--and what could he do? One fell at the first sweep of his arm; but, ere he could recover himself--the twenty seemed to have sheathed their weapons in his body. Still he fought, but not a word did he utter till the dagger of Mucapor, raised aloft, was plunged into his breast, with the words,

'This Aurelia sends!'

'Mucapor!' he then exclaimed as he sank to the ground, 'canst thou stab Aurelian?' Then turning toward the others, who stood looking upon their work, he said, 'Why, soldiers and friends, is this? Hold, Mucapor, leave in thy sword, lest life go too quick; I would speak a word--' and he seized the wrist of Mucapor and held it even then with an iron grasp. He then added, 'Romans! you have been deceived! You are all my friends, and have ever been. Never more than now--' His voice fell.

Probus then reaching forward, cried out, unfolding at the same moment the bloody list,

'See here, tyrant! are these thy friends?'

The eyes of Aurelian, waking up at those words with all the intentness of life, sought the fatal scroll and sharply scanned it--then closing again, he at the same moment drew out the sword of Mucapor, saying as he did so,

"Tis the hand of Menestheus--not mine. You have been deceived.' With that he fell backwards and expired.

Those miserable men then looking upon one another--the truth flashed upon them; and they knew that to save the life of that mean and abject spirit they there stood together murderers of the benefactor of many of them--the friend of all--of a General and Emperor whom, with all his faults, Rome would mourn as one who had crowned with a new glory her Seven Hills. How did they then accuse themselves for their unreasonable haste--their blind credulity! How did they bewail the cruel blows which had thus deprived them of one, whom they greatly feared indeed, but whom also they greatly loved! above all, one whom, as their master in that art which in every age has claimed the admiration of the world, they looked up to as a very god! Some reproached themselves; some, others; some threw themselves upon the body of Aurelian in the wildness of their remorse and grief; and all swore vengeance upon the miscreant who had betrayed them.

Thus perished the great Aurelian--for great he truly was, as the world has ever estimated greatness. When the news of his assassination reached Rome, the first sensation was that of escape, relief, deliverance; with the Christians, and all who favored them, though not of their faith, it was undissembled joy. The streets presented the appearances which accompany an occasion of general rejoicing. Life seemed all at once more secure. Another bloody tyrant was dead, by the violence which he had meted out to so many others, and they were glad. But with another part of the Roman people it was far otherwise. They lamented him as the greatest soldier Rome had known since Caesar; as the restorer of the empire; as the stern but needful reformer of a corrupt and degenerate age; as one who to the army had been more than another Vespasian; who, as a prince, if sometimes severe, was always just, generous, and magnanimous. These were they, who, caring more for the dead than for the living, will remember concerning them only that which is good. They recounted his virtues and his claims to admiration--which were unquestionable and great--and forgot, as if they had never been, his deeds of cruelty, and the wide and wanton slaughter of thousands and hundreds of thousands, which will ever stamp him as one destitute of humanity, and whose almost only title to the name of man was, that he was in the shape of one. For how can the possession of a few of those captivating qualities, which so commonly accompany the possession of great power, atone for the rivers of blood which flowed wherever he wound his way?

* * * * *

I have now ended what I proposed to myself. I have arranged and connected some of the letters of Lucius Manlius Piso, having selected chiefly those which related to the affairs of the Christians and their sufferings during the last days of Aurelian's reign. Those days were happily few. And when they were passed, I deemed that never again, so fast did the world appear to grow wiser and better could the same horrors be repeated. But it was not so; and under Diocletian I beheld that work in a manner perfected, which Aurelian did but begin. I have outlived the horrors of those times, and at length, under the powerful protection of the great Constantine, behold this much-persecuted faith secure. In this I sincerely rejoice, for it is Christianity alone, of all the religions of the world, to which may be safely intrusted the destinies of mankind.

END

Printed in Poland
by Amazon Fulfillment
Poland Sp. z o.o., Wrocław